SUZANNE JOHNSON

RIVER ROAD

headline

First published in 2012 by
HEADLINE PUBLISHING GROUP

1

Cataloguing in Publication Data is available from the British Library

ISBN 978 0 7553 9767 9

Typeset in Fournier by Palimpsest Book Production Ltd, Falkirk, Stirlingshire

Printed and bound in Great Britain by
Clays Ltd, St Ives plc

Headline's policy is to use papers that are natural, renewable and recyclable
products and made from wood grown in sustainable forests.
The logging and manufacturing processes are expected to conform
to the environmental regulations of the country of origin.

HEADLINE PUBLISHING GROUP
An Hachette UK Company
338 Euston Road
London NW1 3BH

www.headline.co.uk
www.hachette.co.uk

*To the people of Plaquemines Parish, Louisiana,
whose beautiful land and water provided
such a rich backdrop for River Road.
No lands at Pass a Loutre were burned by wizards
in the making of this book.*

River Road was completed shortly before the catastrophic Deepwater Horizon oil spill imperiled the fragile wildlife and way of life in not only Plaquemines Parish but all of coastal Louisiana, Mississippi, and Alabama. A percentage of all author royalties from this book will go to the Greater New Orleans Foundation for its Gulf Coast Oil Spill Fund, benefiting the communities of Plaquemines, St. Bernard, and lower Jefferson parishes.

I

The minute hand of the ornate grandfather clock crept like a gator stuck in swamp mud. I'd been watching it for half an hour, nursing a fizzy cocktail from my perch inside the Hotel Monteleone. The plaque on the enormous clock claimed it had been hand-carved of mahogany in 1909, about 130 years after the birth of the undead pirate waiting for me upstairs.

They were both quite handsome, but the clock was a lot safer.

The infamous Jean Lafitte had expected me at seven. He'd summoned me to his French Quarter hotel suite by courier like I was one of his early nineteenth-century wenches, and I hated to destroy his pirate-king delusions, but the historical undead don't summon wizards. We summon them.

I'd have blown him off if my boss on the Congress of Elders hadn't ordered me to comply and my co-sentinel, Alex, hadn't claimed a prior engagement.

At seven thirty, I abandoned my drink, took a deep breath, and marched through the lobby toward the bank of elevators. My heels clicked on the marble, their sharp *tap tap tap* contrasting with the squeaky shuffling of the tourists in their clean, white tennis shoes. I dodged a herd of them as they stopped to gape at the sparkle of crystal chandeliers and brass fittings. The old wives' tales about Jean Lafitte's hoard of gold and treasure must be true if he could afford a suite at the Monteleone.

On the long dead-man-walking stroll down the carpeted hallway, I imagined all the horrible requests Jean might make. He'd saved my life a few years ago, after Hurricane Katrina sent the city into freefall, and I hadn't seen him since. I'd been desperate at the time. I might have promised him unfettered access to modern New Orleans in exchange for his assistance. I might have promised him a place to live. I might have promised him things I don't even remember. In other words, I might be totally screwed.

I reached the door of the Eudora Welty Suite and knocked, reflecting that Jean Lafitte probably had no idea who Eudora Welty was, and wouldn't like her if he did. Ms. Welty had been a modern sort of woman who wouldn't hop to attention when summoned by a scoundrel.

He didn't answer immediately. I'd made him wait, after all, and Jean lived in a tit-for-tat world. I paused a few breaths and knocked harder. Finally, he flung open the door, waving me inside to a suite plush with tapestries of peach and royal blue, thick carpet that swallowed the narrow heels of my pumps, and a plasma TV he couldn't possibly know how to operate. What a waste.

"You have many assets, Drusilla, but apparently a respect for time is not among them." Deep, disapproving voice, French accent, broad shoulders encased in a red linen shirt, long dark hair pulled back into a tail, eyes such a cobalt blue they bordered on navy. And technically speaking, dead.

He was as sexy as ever.

"Sorry." I slipped my hand in my skirt pocket, fingering the small pouch of magic-infused herbs I carried at all times. My mojo bag wouldn't help with my own perverse attraction to the man, but it would keep my empathic abilities in check. If he still had a perverse attraction to me, I didn't want to feel it.

He eased his six-foot-two frame into a sturdy blue chair and slung one long leg over the arm as he gave me a thorough eye-raking, a ghost of a smile on his face.

I perched on the edge of the adjacent sofa, easing back against a pair of plump throw pillows, and looked at him expectantly. I hoped whatever he wanted wouldn't jeopardize my life, my job, or my meager bank account.

"You are as lovely as ever, *Jolie*," Jean said, trotting out his pet name for me that sounded deceptively intimate and brought back a lot of memories, most of them bad. "I will forgive your tardiness—perhaps you were late because you were selecting clothing that I would like." His gaze lingered on my legs. "You chose beautifully."

I'd picked a conservative black skirt and simple white blouse with the aim of looking professional for a business meeting, part of my ongoing attempt to prove to the Elders I was a mature wizard worthy of a pay raise. But this was Jean Lafitte, so I should have worn coveralls. I'd forgotten what a letch he could be.

"I have a date after our meeting," I lied. He didn't need to know said date involved a round carton with the words *Blue Bell Ice Cream* printed on front. "Why did you want to see me?"

There, that hadn't been so difficult—just a simple request. No drama. No threats. No double entendre. Straight to business.

"Does a man need a reason to see a beautiful woman? Especially one who is indebted to him, and who has made him many promises?" A slow smile spread across his face, drawing my eyes to his full lips and the ragged scar that trailed his jawline. I might be the empath in the room, but he knew very well that, in some undead kind of way, I thought he was hot.

My face warmed to the shade of a trailer-trash bridesmaid's dress, one whose color had a name like *raging rouge*. I'd had a similar reaction when I first met Jean in 2005, two days before a mean hurricane with a sissy name turned her malevolent eye toward the Gulf Coast. I blamed my whole predicament on Katrina, the witch.

Her winds had driven the waters of Lake Pontchartrain into the canals that crisscrossed the city, collapsing levees and filling the low, concave metro area like a gigantic soup bowl. But *NBC Nightly News* and Anderson Cooper had missed the biggest story of all: how, after the storm, a mob of old gods, historical undead, and other preternatural victims of the scientific age flooded New Orleans. As a wizard, I'd had a ringside seat. Now, three years later, the wizards had finally reached accords with the major preternatural ruling bodies, and the borders were down, as of two days ago. Jean hadn't wasted any time.

"So, Drusilla Jaco, I invited you here to discuss how you might repay me for being so grievously injured while protecting you after the hurricane. I also wish to appeal to you for help on behalf of a friend." Jean's accent wrapped around my old-fashioned name like a silk peignoir, all soft and slinky.

"What kind of appeal, for what friend?" I'd ignore debt repayment as long as I could and, besides, *grievous injury* was a relative term for the historical undead. They lived through the magic of human memory; the only way to kill Jean was to forget him. And he was quite unforgettable.

"*Un moment, Jolie.*" Jean rose from his chair and walked to the wet bar with a catlike grace honed by years—make that centuries—of walking the decks of sailing ships. He poured two fingers of brandy into crystal snifters and handed one to me. "Do you realize there are merpeople living near the mouth of the Mississippi River?"

The smooth burn of the brandy choked me, and I gave an unladylike hack.

"I thought not," he said, nodding. "The Delachaise clan has lived in this area for many years, back to my own time.

The Villere clan recently encroached upon their territory. There is a war brewing, Drusilla, which could affect the humans who ply the river. I thought you would wish to prevent such a thing."

Well, crap. The Port of New Orleans was not exactly a sleepy small-town enterprise, and the Mississippi River no isolated stretch of waterway. A Hatfield-McCoy feud among the merpeople could disrupt shipping and endanger the humans who made their living fishing the coastal waters.

I stared out a river-view window so big a pirate brigantine could sail through it. Cargo ships, barges, and cruise liners vied for docking space along the Mississippi's muddy banks. "And this involves you how?"

Jean took his seat again. "I wish to help my friend Rene Delachaise. He is young but intelligent, and has assumed leadership of his family members who live southeast of the city. Rene believes the Villeres have poisoned their hunting grounds and is determined to act. I have told him of my lovely friend Drusilla, the skilled wizardess, who would be most happy to assist him."

Uh-huh. Because Jean was helpful like that. He had an angle, and I'd get it out of him eventually.

"How does this Rene guy know the area is poisoned?" I tried to imagine what might constitute a hunting ground for a merman and mentally cursed the Elders for not letting me know there were freakin' merpeople in my territory. "And where is this hunting ground?"

Jean sipped his brandy and twirled the stem of the snifter.

"I do not know what the area is called in modern times, but it is near the mouth of the river, in the long slivers of land which"—he forked three fingers like a bird's claw—"reach into the Gulf."

"Plaquemines Parish?" Southeast of New Orleans. Not as populated as pre-Katrina but still a lot of people.

"*Oui*, just so. By trade, Rene and his family are fishermen and hunters. But the water has been fouled, and the Delachaises and Villeres blame each other. I convinced them to allow you to attempt a truce before they began *une mêlée grande*."

Jean Lafitte was no natural peacekeeper, and didn't have an altruistic bone in his body. I didn't want to even ponder the ironies of merpeople in the fishing industry. "Why didn't they come to me themselves? What's in this for you?"

Jean *tsk-tsked* me. "Such suspicion, Drusilla."

I crossed my arms. "I'm a sentinel, Jean. It's my job to be suspicious. Besides, I know you, remember?"

Tiny lines crinkled at the edges of his eyes as he grinned. "We do not know each other nearly so well as perhaps we might, *Jolie*."

Well, his come-on lines hadn't improved since our last meeting. I asked again: "Why didn't the mers just come to me in the first place?"

"They have no love for wizards." Jean shrugged as if that information should have been obvious, although it was news to me. "My considerable skills in persuasion were required to convince them the wizards should be consulted at all."

I took another sip of brandy and pondered my ability to settle a mer feud. I was a Green Congress wizard. I was hell on ritual magic but had no idea how to negotiate a truce with marauding bands of merpeople. My partner would be even worse. Alex's answer to anything he didn't understand was to shoot it with different ammo until something killed it. This could get ugly.

On the other hand, it could also be an opportunity to prove myself, depending on Jean's motives. "You have no love for the wizards either, unless we're useful to you. So unless you tell me why you're in the middle of this, our conversation is over."

"You have grown up, *Jolie*," he said with a small smile. "I hope you have not grown hard and calloused as so many of your fellow wizards are. I bring this to you because we are friends—perhaps more than friends. And friends help each other, do they not?"

We might be friends, in a loose manner of speaking. Didn't mean I believed him for a second. I continued to stare at him.

He set his brandy snifter on the coffee table with a thump. "Very well, then. I conduct business with Rene Delachaise and his brother on occasion. You do not need the details. If there is a war between the mers that makes passage through the waters treacherous and distracts Rene from our dealings, it will hurt my business."

He looked around at the well-appointed room, then back at me, his voice dropping to a seductive murmur. "If my business suffers, such fine accommodations might no longer be affordable to me, *Jolie*. In such an event, you might need to furnish me a home in the city, as you promised. Or allow me to share yours."

And there we had it, finally—the motive, followed by the not-so-subtle strong arm. The way housing prices in New Orleans had escalated since Katrina, I'd have to flip burgers at night if he insisted on collecting that debt. Taking on Jean Lafitte as a devious, oversexed roommate? I'd sooner move in with Hannibal Lecter and a pot of fava beans.

"I will talk to your friend Rene and the head of the Villere mers." I forced a decisive tone into my voice. I'd show him I wasn't the naive wizard he'd tangled with after the storm. "Also, I'll need to test the water. This might be a big misunderstanding."

"Perhaps." A small smile. "Or perhaps you do not want to discuss the debts you owe me, or what I might really want from you—or you from me."

My pulse sped up at Jean's appraising look, and I uncrossed my legs again, tugging on the hem of my skirt. "Stop gawking at me and tell me how to get in touch with the mers."

"Rene Delachaise and Denis Villere will not talk to you unless I am present." He smiled, his trump card played. No way I'd be able to cut him out of the negotiations. "They specifically said to tell you this. And they will speak only with you, not another wizard, nor your partner the murderous *petit chien*."

My little dog: Alexander Warin. And Jean wasn't just referring to the fact that my partner was a shapeshifter and an enforcer. They hated each other.

"Alex needs to be there," I said. However independent I wanted to prove myself, I wasn't stupid enough to meet Jean Lafitte and two angry mermen without backup.

"Very well." Jean crossed his arms and beamed at me. The man loved to negotiate, and had obviously foreseen he'd have to give in on the Alex issue. "Shall I show you where these hunting grounds lay?"

I hesitated. The Elders' intelligence was worse than mine these days. As much as I'd like to leave before Jean could make this personal again, I needed his input in order to plan a strategy. "Fine."

"I have a map here, which Rene provided me." He walked to a round table and a trio of chairs, all placed strategically in front of the large window. The evening view was breathtaking as the city lights outlined the broad, dark ribbon of the Mississippi. The sitting area had been perfectly set up so the well-to-do Monteleone guests could watch river traffic sail past as they noshed on room-service canapés.

I took a seat facing the window, and Jean slid his chair so close our arms touched. The historical undead weren't cold-skinned like vampires, and the heat radiated from his arm to mine. I didn't move away. If this was a battle of wills, I wasn't going on the defensive.

Instead, I focused on the map, a detailed, laminated representation of extreme Southeast Louisiana, centering on

Plaquemines Parish. Jean switched on the table lamp after a bit of fumbling. Guess that newfangled electricity would take some practice.

He traced the coastline with long fingers and swiveled the map to give us equal access. I caught myself admiring the strength of his hands as they splayed across the page and gave myself a mental kick in the head. I did not need to indulge an attraction to an undead pirate, however tempting.

He traced one scarred digit down the length of Plaquemines. In boot-shaped Louisiana, Lower Plaquemines is the bottom of the toe, a vulnerable peninsula of wetlands jutting into the Gulf of Mexico around the mouth of the Mississippi. About halfway down the peninsula, just south of Venice, Jean's index finger came to rest near the point at which the last real highway fizzled out.

"This is Orchard, where the Delachaise clan resides." Then, pointing an infinitesimal nudge west, "And this is *Mauree. Non.*" He squinted. "The English name is Tidewater. That is where the Villeres have recently made their home. And this"—he moved his finger southeast along the largely uninhabited wetlands around the mouth of the river and came to rest near the easternmost nub jutting into the Gulf—"is where the mers claim the water has been poisoned."

I frowned and looked at the spot he'd pointed to. The map legend read *Pass a Loutre.* "There's a town?"

"*Non,*" Jean said. "It is mostly *marécage.* Marsh."

Great. Isolated and hard to reach. "What has happened to make them think the water is bad?"

"There has been some illness, I believe, among both clans," Jean said, pushing the map closer to me and leaning back in his chair.

"That doesn't make sense." I studied the jagged edges of the coastal marsh. "Why would either clan poison the waters it wants as its territory?"

"Exactement," Jean said, nodding in approval like a teacher whose dunce pupil had finally come up with a rare bit of insight. "It might be that the mers simply want an excuse to fight over the marshland, as they tend to be a people of fierce temperament, or it might be that something else has fouled the water. Either way"—he reached out to brush a stray curl from my cheek—"it is a wizard matter, *non?"*

If the water was oil-slicked or polluted, it was not a wizard issue, but if there was even a chance it involved pretes . . . Damn it. He'd done the right thing by getting me involved.

His mouth curved into a smug smile. "From your expression, I know you realize my actions were correct. As you are an intelligent woman, I knew you would recognize this, so I have taken the liberty of arranging a meeting with both Rene Delachaise and Denis Villere tomorrow at the eleventh hour."

He was so damned pleased with himself, I couldn't help but return his smile. Big mistake. Give the pirate an inch and he'd take a fathom.

The strong fingers I'd been admiring slid around my wrist, and he traced small circles over my palm with his thumb.

"Now, *Jolie*, we should renegotiate the repayment of your debts." He stroked his hand slowly up my arm. I shivered as a tingle of warmth spread through me, and *raging rouge* danced a hot second-line across my face.

As much as some shameful part of me relished being the object of any handsome man's desire—even a technically dead man—I couldn't encourage him.

"Look, Jean. I like you. You're a very desirable man." The hand stroked a little higher and squeezed my shoulder. Oh, boy. I searched for the right turn of phrase, one that didn't include the word *dead*. "But we kind of have an age difference."

More than two centuries' worth.

Chuckling, he pulled his hand away, and I checked him out as he walked to the wet bar for another brandy, all powerful grace and lean muscle. The air practically moved out of the way to make room for him.

Stop looking.

He turned back to me. "You still cling to the old world, *Jolie*. Things have changed. I might be older than you, as you say, but you do not fit into the human world any better than I."

I stared at him, frowning, troubled that I couldn't think of a good comeback, troubled that he was right, in a warped kind of way. "Still—"

"Still, Drusilla, you owe me for saving your life. Why not repay me in a way that would be pleasing to both of us? You cannot afford to buy me a house, *non*?"

I had no answer for that and I felt my moral high ground turning to mud, so I stood up and gave him a little finger wave, grabbing my purse and striding toward the door. "Gotta be going. See you at the meeting tomorrow."

"*Jolie.*" His voice did that deep, sexy dive again. "What if one simple thing would erase all of your obligations to me?"

I stopped at the door with my back to the room, one hand on the knob, having an internal war. Jean was a devious pirate who always operated with an ulterior motive. On the other hand, he came from an era where favor begat favor. He wouldn't let this drop, no matter how much I wanted it to go away. One way or another, I'd pay.

"Okay, what?" I turned from the door and gasped. He'd followed me across the room on sneaky pirate feet and stood a scant few inches away. Heart thumping, I got a close-range view of his chin as he flattened his arms against the door on either side of my head, forming a big, warm cage.

"Just a simple meal with me—what your modern people call a dinner date," he whispered, leaning down to plant a light kiss on the side of my neck.

I closed my eyes and inhaled his scent of tobacco and cinnamon for a moment before pushing him away and pinning him with my best steely glare. "Just dinner?"

He raised an eyebrow. "You wish there to be more? Then, perhaps a stroll after dinner. Perhaps a kiss."

Except for the kiss part, this could work. Dinner would be public and painless, and how many people got to dine with a legend? Jean was handsome and could be entertaining when he wanted to be.

"So, just to clarify." I ticked off points on my fingers. "We have dinner. We talk. Maybe we stroll. We do not kiss. And then I owe you nothing." I couldn't see a loophole.

"*Mais oui*, I agree." He stepped closer and rested a hand on my waist. "Shall we seal our bargain with a kiss?"

"No, but we can shake on it."

He stared at my outstretched hand a moment, then took it in his own and lifted it to his lips. Just an old-fashioned kind of guy. Accent on *old*.

He reached around me and opened the door. "I will meet you at your office at nine tomorrow, Drusilla. We will talk to the mermen."

In my haste to escape before he thought of any other debts or requests, I reached the lobby before it occurred to me: How did he know where my office was? How did he plan to get there? And what did one wear on a dinner date with an undead pirate?

2

I cursed Jean Lafitte as I hoofed it toward my parking place in Outer Mongolia. A blister shot pain through my right foot from the accursed high heels, and my arch threatened total collapse. I rarely wore heels. In what part of my warped brain did Jean Lafitte rate heels?

"Hey, baby, trade ya some beads for a kiss." A short, stocky guy slung an arm around my shoulders and got his beer-breath way too close to my nose. Why did everybody want to kiss me tonight? Well, an undead pirate and a drunken fraternity boy. My man-magnets must be on high beam.

"In your dreams, junior." I punctured my words with a sharp elbow, which he didn't appreciate if the unsavory names he spewed my way were any indication. Lucky for him I didn't have my elven staff with me, or I could have fried him into next week. People from other places like to call New Orleans sin city, but it's been my experience that most of the sin is being committed by alcohol-soaked tourists.

It was only eight thirty, but crowds already swept along Bourbon Street in waves. Fratboy and his friends had been at it a while, judging by his *eau-de-brew*. By midnight, Bourbon would be wall-to-wall party hounds, which is why locals rarely ventured here—unless, of course, they had a business meeting with a pirate.

Fratboy and his pals dropped back to wield their charms on a group of drunken college girls who seemed more appreciative, so I shouldered my way a couple more blocks. Once I hit St. Louis Street, I'd ditch the crowds and cut over to my parking spot on a side street.

The familiar sign of a neon dancing alligator holding a cocktail caught my eye just before I turned off Bourbon—the Green Gator. A stab of sadness gutted any lingering annoyance with Fratboy, almost stealing my breath. I hadn't been to the Gator since the emotional days after Katrina, when everyone had been operating in a fog of post-traumatic stress and the preternaturals were making their power play to move into modern New Orleans.

Their scheme had worked. By the time the metaphysical dust settled, Alex had gone from rival to partner to best friend. His cousin Jake, who owned the Gator, had started out as a guy I thought might be Mr. Maybe and ended up a loup-garou, the werewolves' biggest badass—attacked by a werewolf simply because he had the misfortune of knowing me.

I hadn't seen Jake since a week after the attack. He blamed me, and I deserved it.

Still, Alex lived in one of the apartments over the Gator and I needed to tell him about the mer feud and our impending day-trip to Plaquemines Parish. I'd just have to pull up my big-girl pantyhose and go inside. Maybe it was time I saw Jake again.

A jazzy version of Louis Armstrong's "What a Wonderful World" enveloped me in sound as I entered. I squinted through the crowd at the small stage on the right side of the long, rectangular barroom to see if the singer was a good impersonator or the real undead king of jazz—one never knew when he might pop over for a tune or two.

Tonight's singer was merely a good impersonator, and the crowd swayed from a combination of alcohol and happy vibes. I screwed up my courage and scanned the area behind the polished wooden bar that stretched down the left side of the room. No sign of either Jake or Leyla, the tall, model-sexy assistant manager who'd always been in lust with Alex. Not that Alex's love life was any of my business, as he liked to remind me.

A couple of frazzled guys I'd never seen worked the bar, a sad reminder that even if the Katrina-era Gator stayed frozen in my mind, the real one had moved on.

I carved a path through the bar, making my way past the restrooms and kitchen and up a narrow stairwell near the back door. The sense of déjà vu hung heavy. My last visit here had been on one of the worst nights of my life, but it was long past time to put it aside.

I stopped halfway up the stairs and slid the ridiculous

heels off with a sigh of pleasure. I'd snag them on the way out.

After reaching the small landing, I knocked on the door to Apartment B and waited.

"He's not there, sunshine."

I whirled to see Jake standing in his own doorway across the hall.

Sometimes, after an absence, people look smaller or plainer than memory has built them up to be. Not Jake. His wiry frame had bulked up in a good way, and he still had the shaggy, sun-kissed blond hair and amber eyes that had made my heart speed up. I hadn't seen the killer dimples yet, but I knew they were under that stubble somewhere.

"Hi, Jake." That much was easy. What to say next wasn't. I'm sorry you got mixed up in my mess and became a loup-garou? I'm sorry you have to lie to all your friends because you're no longer human? Glad your combat injuries from Afghanistan healed themselves your first full moon?

I just stood there, guilty, mute, and tense, my muscles frozen.

"Alex had a date with Leyla," Jake said, leaning against the doorjamb and hooking his thumbs in the pockets of his jeans. "You want to leave him a note? Come on in—I'll get you a pen." Before I had a chance to answer, he turned and went into his apartment, leaving the door ajar.

My heart thumped in alarm as I remembered the blame and anger in his eyes during our last encounter. I wasn't sure I could handle a live replay. Still, I followed him inside. I could at least apologize, however useless it might be. I'd tried to apologize once before, when he was trying to figure out what I was and what had happened to him. He hadn't been ready to hear it.

I closed the door behind me. He'd gone into the small kitchen and was rummaging through a drawer, which gave me a chance to glance around at the shabby, not-quite-so-chic apartment. It still looked as if it had been filled with castoffs from an era when John Travolta wore platform shoes and danced beneath a mirror ball.

Jake handed me a small spiral-bound notebook and a pen. I looked at them a moment before laying them on the scarred wooden dining table.

"Jake, I don't . . ." I inhaled and started over. "I'm sorry. About everything. I know it's my fault that . . . It was all my fault." I trailed off, not sure how to continue.

He moved closer, reached out to put a hand on my shoulder, pulled back before touching me. "Let's not start throwing blame around again, sugar. We've already done it once. It's done."

He was going to be noble, damn it, which ripped the scab off my guilt and made me realize a part of me wanted him to yell and throw stones. Maybe even needed him to.

"There's plenty of blame for me, maybe even for Alex," I said softly. "But not for you."

He was the victim. A voodoo god had tried to take power in post-Katrina New Orleans, with more than a little help from my late father. Jake got caught in the middle, and ended up a loup-garou. His whole life had imploded while Alex and I walked out with no more than a few mental bruises. My father had died. The whole thing gnawed at me late at night—I tried to stay too busy to dwell on it the rest of the time.

"It's over, DJ," Jake repeated. "We shoulda let it go a long time ago."

The dimples made their first appearance as he stepped back and looked at my feet. "You know how glad I was to see you standing out there with no shoes tonight?" His teasing South Mississippi drawl carried the seeds of forgiveness, and with that realization an almost tangible weight lifted.

I lifted my eyes to meet his warm, honeyed gaze. "I didn't think you'd ever be glad to see me again."

He smiled—a little sadly, I thought. "That was true enough for a while. Then, after I'd waited so long . . ." He shrugged, and I nodded. After a while, it got easier to avoid each other than to have this awkward conversation.

I picked up the notebook and looked at it. I didn't want to write Alex a note. "I'll just leave a message on his phone—plus, it'll annoy him if I call him during his date."

Jake grinned at me, and that felt good. A mutual enjoyment of tormenting his cousin had always been a bond between us.

He grabbed his keys off the table and followed me into the hallway. "I need to get back downstairs anyway, make sure the new guys haven't given away all the beer." He locked the door behind him.

"Business must be doing well if you're hiring new people."

We had started down the stairs, but he stopped abruptly. "Alex didn't tell you?"

I slid my feet into the godforsaken shoes and turned to look at him. This didn't sound good. "Tell me what?"

"I'm gonna be backing up Alex as an enforcer, so I'll need more help around the Gator. Been training at Quantico the last six months."

I opened my mouth, then closed it, guppy-like. When we met, Alex had been a full-time enforcer, a member of the wizards' elite security force. When situations between sentinels and pretes got shot to hell, the enforcers came in and did cleanup. It usually involved killing something. Even now that he worked with me as a sentinel, Alex's idea of mediation was using smaller ammo in his specially modified guns.

"Uh, congratulations?" I'd never seen that killer instinct in Jake, but as a former Marine he had the military background. As a loup-garou, he'd definitely have the muscle. "You're happy about it?"

The dimples made another appearance. "Yeah, I am. For the first time since all this shit went down, I know where I belong. Maybe even for the first time since I left Afghanistan."

I hoped he was right. And I was going to have a little talk with good old cousin Alex to make sure he turned off the crazy rivalry he had with Jake and turned on his nurturing side. He had one; I'd seen it.

*

I celebrated my bravery in confronting both Jean and Jake in one evening by a stop at the Popeye's drive-through, where a box of spicy fried chicken and a container of red beans awaited, guaranteed to soothe any residual nerves.

Traffic crawled along St. Charles Avenue, so I wound my way to my house by back streets, pinching off bits of chicken to eat along the way. The pizza place across from me on Magazine had an overflow crowd, and my friend Eugenie Dupre's house across Nashville was dark, as was the sign for the Shear Luck hair and nail salon she ran from her first floor. Maybe she'd lucked out and had a date with someone who wasn't technically dead.

I juggled my food and purse—and the heels, which I'd taken off again—trying to unlock my back door. I'd forgotten to leave the kitchen light on, and something tangled in my feet just inside. My knees and shoulder hit the wooden floor hard, along with the shoes, the chicken, and the red beans. Somebody was going to pay.

"Sebastian—you just used up your eighth life!" I never shrieked until I became a reluctant cat owner. Now it happened frequently. A thunder of paws tore across the living room as I staggered to my feet and fumbled for the light switch. Toilet paper wound around both my ankles, trailed through the kitchen and living room, and curled out of sight into the downstairs bathroom.

I'd inherited Sebastian, a cranky, cross-eyed chocolate Siamese, when my father and mentor, Gerry, died in the Katrina aftermath. He'd bequeathed me a flooded, moldy house near a levee breach, an extensive library of obscure grimoires, a set of elven skills I hadn't figured out how to use, a lot of memories. And the world's most vindictive feline.

After gathering an armload of toilet paper and throwing it in the trash, I tracked down my dinner. The chicken box lay upended in front of the fridge and the red beans had rolled under the kitchen table. The lid had stayed on the beans, but I plucked the biscuit off the floor and looked stupidly inside the box at a single scrawny chicken wing. Suspicious, I stuck my head in the living room. Sebastian sprawled on an upholstered armchair, his black nose buried in a greasy fried chicken breast bigger than his head.

I hissed at him to get his attention. "Feline. Spawn. Of. Satan."

Not that the grease could do much more damage to the chair since he'd already used its back as a scratching post.

He raised disdainful crossed blue eyes in my direction, then slinked off in a huff when I snatched away the chicken breast and took it to the fridge. Eventually, I'd let him have it, but one should not reward feline insolence.

I took what was left of my dinner, grabbed my purse off the floor, and called Alex to give him a heads-up before I talked to the Elders and began what threatened to be an all-night merpeople cram session. I hadn't asked Jake where the happy couple had gone on their date, or if it was their first, or whether they'd been doing the nasty for months, although I doubted it. Alex would have bragged.

After five rings, he answered in his surliest voice. "DJ, something better be burning or dying."

Heh. "Having fun? Didn't disturb anything, did I?" Music and voices tangled in the background, so he and Leyla weren't engaged in anything too private. That relieved me, for some reason. Probably because Leyla never liked me much. I refused to entertain the idea of jealousy.

"Can this wait till tomorrow? The next band's about to start." His voice rose to match the background din.

Guilt replaced relief. After a few flirtations in the early days of our partnership, we'd agreed to keep things at the friends-with-no-benefits level. The man had every right to go on a date.

"Yeah, sorry," I said, meaning it. "Just don't make plans for tomorrow." I gave him the short version of the mer feud/water testing. "And why didn't you tell me Jake was in enforcer training?"

Long pause. The sound of a guitar being tuned and the trill of a horn filled the space vacated by conversation. "You saw him?"

"No, I learned of his enforcerhood by osmosis. Of course I saw him. Went by the Gator to fill you in on my meeting with Jean Lafitte and he told me all about it. Would've been nice if I'd heard it from you."

"You saw him at the bar? I mean downstairs, in the barroom?"

"No, up in his apartment." Nosy, much?

"You were alone with him?"

What was the problem? Had Leyla's flawless café-au-lait skin and big, adoring doe eyes zapped some of his brain cells? I tried not to sound testy. "Well, of course we were alone. What's the big deal?"

"I'll talk to you tomorrow." Another pause, then the call ended.

He'd hung up on me.

3

People jog at dawn for a reason. If they wait, their brains will wake up and convince them there are things they'd rather do. Like have oral surgery.

Which is why I was standing in the Fly at five a.m., half asleep.

A butterfly-shaped section of Audubon Park alongside the Mississippi River, the Fly was one of the few spots in metro New Orleans where one had easy access to the Big Muddy. The majority of riverfront property had long ago been consumed by the stuff of commerce: warehouses, wharves, cruise terminals, port offices. The rest butted against high earthen levees.

I groaned and propped my right foot on the bench beside a concrete picnic table, trying to stretch out a hamstring still sore from last night's pinwheeling kitchen disaster. Weak sunlight filtered through the massive live oaks hiding the park from the back of the zoo. On the other side, the river flowed wide and gray and choppy. At least the air was cool and the humidity hadn't yet reached ninety percent. Give it an hour.

Usually, Alex and I ran on the other side of the zoo, in Audubon Park proper. I had an ulterior motive for changing the route—the three empty glass vials in my pocket. I wanted some samples of river water that hadn't allegedly been poisoned by territorial mermen.

Alex hadn't arrived yet, but a half-dozen joggers already made their way along the riverfront. By six it would be downright crowded. *Crowded* had been the way of things in the Uptown neighborhoods unflooded by Katrina. Rebuilding hadn't made New Orleans a modern, efficient city like we'd hoped. Instead, recovery had been a stumbling, lurching journey filled with setbacks, scandal, and drama that somehow fit the city's dysfunctional charm. Lots of neighborhoods remained sparsely populated, and as every school year ended, a batch of weary storm survivors got discouraged and moved away. Optimistic new folks bent on saving New Orleans from itself replaced them.

That was just the human population. I didn't want to ponder the number of pretes coming into town now that the restrictions had been lifted, or how long before some powerful species decided it wanted to wrest political control from the wizards.

Gravel crunched to my left, and I turned as a shiny black Mercedes convertible pulled into the parking lot next to my dusty red SUV. Alexander Warin unfolded all

six-foot-three-inches of chiseled hotness out of the seat
and shot a killer smile at a couple of scantily clad redheads
ogling him and his car as they ran past. They might run
faster if they realized Alex was a rare true shapeshifter
who could turn at will into a chow-pony mix the size of
a small European nation, and that he rarely went anywhere
without at least one firearm.

I shook my head. He looked edible without trying. His
dark hair perpetually needed cutting, which made women want
to mother him, while that sculpted body he worked so hard
to maintain made them want to smother him. He wore shapeless black track pants that still managed to show off slim hips
and a red T-shirt that emphasized broad shoulders. My partner
had only to raise one dark eyebrow and women flocked to
him like drunken parade-goers begging for beads off a Mardi
Gras float. He didn't do a thing to discourage them.

"If you'd rather run with the redheads, you'd probably
get lucky before you got halfway down the riverfront path,"
I said as he walked up. "Bet they'd both do you."

He stared after them as if considering it, then grunted
something unintelligible. Full of his usual early-morning
charm. His voice was still rough from sleep. "Ready to hit
it?"

I set off at a lope. Alex had a tendency to be monosyllabic
until he warmed up. I'd give him time before I asked where
all the crap about Jake had come from last night—and broke
the news that Jean Lafitte would be joining our merman
confab. Nothing he could do about it. I'd already gotten the

go-ahead from the Elders, along with some ideas on a possible territory settlement.

He caught up with me and eased into his own steady pace, which meant I had to speed up. There's a big stride difference between five-four and six-three, so I figured I worked harder than him and therefore could stop sooner. He only ran with me because he thought I wouldn't do it otherwise. He knew if a beignet called my name, I'd leave the jogging trail in a dusting of powdered sugar and never look back.

Neither of us spoke till we reached the point of the path that edged closest to the river. "I have to stop." My breath rasped in and out like a bellows.

Alex ran a few strides ahead, then circled back. "This is pathetic, even for you."

"Ha, ha." I pulled the vials from my pocket and held them up. "I wanted to take some water samples here to compare with what we get at Pass a Loutre today. Baseline pollution. In fact, the water near the mouth of the river should be a lot cleaner than here."

"Good idea." Alex knelt to retie his shoe. "Figured out how you're going to test it?"

I carefully walked downhill to the river's edge, looking for a place where the bank looked solid and not slippery. "Not yet. I'll run tests for standard pollutants before I start looking for anything that might be caused by a merman." Whatever that might be.

I paced back and forth. Had to find the right spot. A spot where there was no chance of me reaching over too far and falling in. A spot where I wouldn't have to lie on my stomach in the mud and reach down the bank.

"Oh, for God's sake. Give me the vials." Alex held out his hand and I forked them over. So I'm a little afraid of water. I'm a wizard. We don't do water.

He squatted and stretched a long arm over the bank's edge, filling the vials and handing them back to me for stoppering. I held one up and looked through it at the sun rising over the river. It looked like a roux gone awry. "This is nasty stuff."

"Tell me about it." Alex grabbed the hem of my T-shirt and dried his hands, getting a kick in the shins for his effort. He grinned. "See why I tell you not to drink the tap water?"

"I never drink tap water." I drank soda and juice and wine and, on really bad days, bourbon. I had nothing to fear from the river.

I put the vials in the glove box of my Pathfinder and rejoined Alex at the nearest table. He'd stretched out on the concrete top, doing crunches. I peeled the wrapper off a chocolate bar and sat on the bench, enjoying the view—and I wasn't looking at the river. Just because Alex and I had agreed to be friends without benefits didn't mean I'd been stricken blind.

He finished some ridiculous number of reps and moved to the bench next to me. "So we have mer troubles in Plaquemines Parish? Give me the details, or should I say the details according to Jean Lafitte." He raked his hands through his thick hair and trained dark brown eyes on my face. His eyes were the same color as my Hershey bar, and equally melt-worthy. "He didn't try anything with you, did he?"

If Alex was jealous, I couldn't tell it, even with my empathic abilities, and it wasn't fair that part of me wanted him to be. Besides, his and the pirate's hatred was mutual. Alex didn't despise Jean because he might sully my honor or even because the man was a thieving pirate. Alex despised Jean because, as one of the historical undead, he was virtually immortal. My partner couldn't kill him. Such indestructibleness placed Jean in a gray area, and Alex liked things sharp and structured and straightforward.

Jean hated Alex for essentially the same reason. The short-term pleasure he'd enjoy from killing Alex wouldn't be worth the problems it would cause with the Elders. My partner and the pirate were at a homicidal stalemate.

I gave Alex an account of my conversation with Jean, omitting the little detail about the dinner date.

He watched a couple walking hand-in-hand near the river, his brows tightened in thought. "I knew there were some merclans in Southeast Louisiana, but I thought most of them were in St. Bernard Parish and the Atchafalaya Basin. How long have these two clans been there?"

How'd he know there were merclans outside the Beyond? I handed him the last third of my chocolate. "Jean made it sound like the Villeres just moved in but the Delachaise family had been there since his time. Well, his first time."

Speaking of which, I said a quick prayer. "By the way,

Jean will be at the meeting today—the mers insisted on it. He's going to ride with us."

I waited for the rant to begin, or at least a smartass comment. Alex pursed his lips, staring at the water. "You ran that past the Elders?"

"I did." He seemed to be taking the news remarkably well.

He finally slid his gaze to me. "You could have told me last night. Don't try to manage me. You're not that good at it."

I thought my Alex-management skills were excellent. "And you weren't managing me by hiding that little bit about Jake becoming an enforcer? We'll end up working together. I'd have found out eventually."

A mix of emotions played across his face before he clamped down on them, and for the first time this morning I was tempted to try my empathic skills on him. *Try* being the operative word. As a shapeshifter his emotional patterns took wonky twists, and as an enforcer he'd been trained to shield himself from mental invasion.

"Is this some kind of competition thing?" I kept my tone light. Alex and Jake were more like brothers than cousins, and had the near-sibling rivalry to prove it. "Why did you want to know if I'd been alone with Jake last night?"

He rubbed the back of his neck, and I was struck by how tired he looked. Not stayed-out-late-with-Leyla tired, but worried-as-hell tired. "I'm not convinced he has his wolf under good-enough control to be here, especially working for the wizards. The Elders want another enforcer in Louisiana now that the Beyond's opened up. Jake looks perfect on paper, but . . ." He trailed off, eyes following a cruise ship as it made its way upriver.

"He seemed fine last night." Jake thought this job gave his life meaning again, and I wanted him to have the chance to prove himself. I knew how that felt. "This is really important to him, Alex. He needs it."

"I know." Alex swung his legs over the bench and started back toward his car. "But I still don't want you alone with him."

4

After a quick shower, I threw on jeans and a tank with a denim shirt on top, scarfed down some toast, pulled my hair into a ponytail, and still made it to my Tchoupitoulas Street office with twenty minutes to spare before the nine a.m. rendezvous. A bracing cup of strong coffee in the peace and quiet of my office would help me prepare for what I expected to be a trying day. Angry mermen plus Jean Lafitte plus Alex equaled a tense DJ.

I unlocked the office and flipped on the fluorescent lights of my generic, rectangular home away from home. A tasteful sign, CRESCENT CITY RISK MANAGEMENT, had been painted on the door, which was protected by a magical security system that would cause discomfort in any human who felt an urge to drop in for a chat about insurance risks.

I hadn't felt the need for an office until recently, when the dissolution of the borders with the Beyond had become imminent. Before that, the only thing I'd needed for work was my upstairs library-cum-laboratory, where all the makings of a good potion were catalogued, sorted, and stored. I'd been a deputy sentinel mainstreamed as a risk-management consultant for nearby Tulane University. The perfect geek job.

No more. Now that the preternatural floodgates had opened and I was a full sentinel, tasked with wrangling misbehaving pretes and keeping the humans clueless, I figured it was only a matter of time before I came home from grocery shopping to find a fairy on my front porch or a vampire in my vestibule. I needed a neutral space to do business, thus my little strip-mall office halfway between Winn-Dixie and the Heavenly Ham store. At least lunch was handy.

At a yard sale, Alex had found a round table and some chairs to use for clients, and I'd set up Gerry's antique desk with a phone and laptop. There was room for Alex to put a desk of his own, but so far he'd declined. My partner's more of a fieldwork kind of guy. Unlike most sentinels, I wasn't an almighty Red Congress wizard who could summon vast amounts of physical magic at will, plus—God forbid—I was a woman. So the Elders had decided I needed a partner who knew his way around a weapon.

As much as Alex meant to me, it still stung.

I filled the coffeemaker with water, measured a hefty scoop of Colombian dark roast, and checked email. I got a good snort from the Elders' latest memo. The brass seemed to march a step behind when it came to developments with Southeast Louisiana's newest citizens. This morning they announced the presence of merpeople in the region. I didn't consider myself particularly well-connected in the prete community, so the fact I'd been the one to tell them about the Villeres' move and the simmering mer feud didn't bode well for their ability to manage this ridiculous post-Katrina world of ours.

Maybe we should hire Jean Lafitte as an informant so we'd know what was going on—unless the Elders knew more than they were telling.

I shut down the computer and opened *The Wizard's Field Guide to Water Species*. In reading last night, I'd been surprised to learn that mers were aquatic werecreatures who could half-shift into a classic mermaid/merman body, or shift fully into a fish. Different clans turned into different types of fish. I'd also discovered mers were born, not made, so I didn't have to worry about being bitten by an angry merman and turning into a big fish who was afraid of water.

I flipped through the book, studying the images of mermaids as depicted in folklore and literature. Not a single merman to be found, and all the mermaids lacked upper-body attire.

Alex opened the door, waiting half a heartbeat for the security wards to drop before entering. "I wish you'd fix those things so they wouldn't make my ears pop." He poured a cup of coffee, peered over my shoulder, and growled in appreciation. "That is one sexy pair of fins. I always wanted to meet a mermaid."

He'd changed into jeans, a muscle shirt, and boots—all black. The man considered gray a carnival color, but got huffy when I pointed out that he was a walking enforcer cliché. He stood still while I studied him, head to toe, trying to figure out where he'd stashed his gun. It was our version of a party game.

"Ankle," I finally said. Those jeans were eye-catchingly tight, and no way he'd even fit a flat holster under that shirt.

He grinned. "Search me and find out."

"One of these days I will, and it will scare the hell out of you." I thrust the book at him. "Here, entertain yourself. I'm only expecting merguys to be at the meeting today, and there are no pictures of them." Either the male mers didn't get out much or, more likely, men had written all the history books.

"How is Lafitte getting here?" Alex looked at his watch. "He's already late."

It was two minutes after nine, for crying out loud. "No clue. Maybe he's getting a taxi." I paused. "Think he knows what a taxi is?"

"He'll probably steal one of the French Quarter mules." Alex stuck one arm of his sunglasses into the neck of his shirt. "We're taking your SUV. I don't want to get mud and shit all over my car."

God forbid. "Fine, although the roads in Plaquemines

Parish *are* paved, you know." Well, mostly, until the roads ran out and one had to travel by boat.

We went outside, and I reset the wards on the office, wondering if the manager of the pet supply store next door thought it odd that Crescent City Risk Management stayed locked and dark half the time.

After putting a pair of rubber shrimp boots (black) in my Pathfinder, Alex leaned against his car, studying a map of Plaquemines Parish. I dug in my backpack to make sure all the day's necessities were covered. I didn't own shrimp boots, so my running shoes would have to suffice. I'd brought a bunch of vials to test the river water at different spots, a Saints cap in case the sun got too hot, some mosquito repellent, my wallet, my portable kit with the most commonly used potion and charm ingredients, and my elven staff for an extra dose of protection in case anyone on my little scouting team misbehaved.

My money was on the pirate.

The staff poked out the top of the backpack, and I grasped the end to jam it farther in. As usual, it vibrated at my touch and the carved sigils on its polished wooden surface glowed like a banked fire.

I'd found it in the attic of Gerry's flooded-out house after Katrina, but in my hands it was still like a live grenade in the grip of a toddler. I was never quite sure when it would go *boom* and leave me floating to earth in a million grisly pieces, but I loved the strong magic it let me channel.

As a Green Congress wizard my specialty was ritual magic, and I'd grown up forever trying to do what Red Congress wizards could accomplish with the flick of a finger. With the staff, I'd match my skills against any Red Congress wizard out there. The Elders thought I could use the staff because I had elven ancestors on both sides of my family tree—a rare thing, and something of which they were highly suspicious. I just thought it was cool to have a magical toy that wouldn't work for anyone else.

A squeal of tires echoed through the neighborhood as a cherry-red Corvette convertible screeched down Tchoupitoulas Street, sideswiped a stop sign on its way into the parking lot, and lurched to a halt inches from Alex's pristine paint job.

My mouth fell open. Where the hell had Jean Lafitte gotten a Corvette? And what moron had taught him to drive? Thank God it was still early enough on a Saturday morning that he hadn't run over anyone or crashed through a line of parked cars.

Jean killed the engine and climbed out, examining the remote-control lock with interest. His wavy dark hair was pulled back as it had been last night, but he'd traded his red linen shirt for a simple white tunic. He'd wedged a long-barreled pistol under his wide black belt, and I was sure a few well-placed knives had been tucked somewhere I couldn't see.

He needed to be more discreet with his weaponry. The pistol might look like a movie prop but it had a kick. I knew, because he'd once tried to shoot me with it. I wasn't sure what our relationship was, but it had at least advanced beyond attempted murder.

Jean and Alex greeted each other like old enemies under a temporary truce—with a raised eyebrow and slight nod.

Jean planted a chivalrous kiss on my cheek and gave me a frowning appraisal. "You look as lovely as ever this morning, *Jolie*. Although I hope for our dinner date you will wear a fetching gown rather than the clothing of a peasant farm worker."

I closed my eyes. Old Loose Lips *would* have to mention the dinner date. Alex's glare hit my back like a physical blow.

"Let's get started," I said, filled with sudden, brisk efficiency. "Where are we meeting the mers? I've written down the name of several boat-rental places in Venice since the road ends just south of there." I turned to Jean. "Can you navigate us to Pass a Loutre? We don't want to attract attention by hiring a guide."

The last thing we needed was a nosy guy from the river authority snooping around, or a friendly angler seeing a much bigger fish than he'd ever dreamed of, possibly a female variety with bared breasts.

Jean pulled a folded sheet of paper from inside his shirt. "I wrote down the name of the establishment where my friend Rene and the blackguard Denis Villere have agreed to meet. Then Rene says he will take us to Pass a Loutre on his fishing vessel."

I unfolded the sheet of Hotel Monteleone stationery and struggled to untangle the swooping loops and flourishes of Jean's handwriting: *The Black Velvet. Buras. 11 a.m.*

"What's the Black Velvet?" I asked, suspicious. Sounded like a naughty nightclub.

"It is a dining establishment," Jean said, watching with interest as Alex spread his parish map over the hood of my SUV. The pirate did seem to love maps. Maybe I'd buy him an atlas for his 250th birthday.

Alex stared at Jean a moment before finally jerking his head from side to side with audible pops. "What's the best way to get to Pass a Loutre?" he asked, sliding the map toward the pirate. They leaned over the hood and began debating directions and strategies.

Aw, the boys were playing nice. Maybe it wouldn't be such a bad day after all.

I stuck my backpack in the rear hatch of the Pathfinder and pondered the Corvette. I could not in good conscience let a member of the historical undead drive through metro New Orleans in a car he'd gotten . . . How *had* he gotten the car?

I slammed the hatch and joined them. "We can all ride in my truck but, Jean, where'd you get the Corvette?"

He looked blank for a few moments before my meaning sunk in. "Ah, the automobile." He said the word *automobile* slowly, tasted it, rolled it around on his tongue like a sip of new wine. "Is it not beautiful? You must accompany me to our rendezvous, and *Monsieur Chien* may follow us."

Alex didn't speak, but the map rattled as *Mr. Dog* refolded it with exaggerated care.

I shook my head. "No, everyone will ride with me."

The Corvette was gorgeous, except for the little crack in its fiberglass body and the missing paint where Jean had virtually mown over the stop sign to enter the parking lot. But I valued my life too much to ride in a sports car driven by a 230-year-old pirate even if it was a glossy cherry red with black leather seats.

"*Non.*" Jean frowned. "This is not acceptable. I wish to deliver the automobile to my friend Rene today. You must ride with me. My apologies, of course, *Monsieur.*" He looked at Alex without a hint of apology.

Alex crossed his arms over his chest, a bad sign. "Do you have a driver's license, Captain Lafitte?"

Jean smiled. "I do not, sir, but perhaps Drusilla will drive and give me automobile lessons, after which I might obtain such a document." Right, and I wanted to be a fly on the wall of the Louisiana Office of Motor Vehicles when he went in for his driving test.

The blanket of dread I'd been ignoring all morning settled over my head like a shroud. We weren't going to be in Buras in time to forestall a merman war if the shapeshifter and the undead pirate didn't stop posturing. If I were the most mature person here, life had reached a new depth of pathetic.

I tossed my keys to Alex. "Follow us in the Pathfinder. I'll drive the 'vette. Jean, hand over the keys. You're riding with me."

It was the only solution. Jean couldn't drive, he wouldn't leave the car, and if the two of them rode all the way to Buras together, someone would end up bloody.

5

We maneuvered slowly through the suburbs on the western side of the river, me driving the Corvette, Jean riding shotgun, Alex following behind. The 'vette was a beauty, from its shiny exterior to its velvety leather seats to a set of dashboard controls that would give Captain Kirk an orgasm. Alex loved cars, and I thought it ironic that I drove the luxurymobile while he puttered ahead in my seven-year-old SUV.

"Is this still New Orleans?" Jean asked, frowning out the window.

I laughed. "Sort of. New Orleanians who don't like New Orleans live on the Westbank and pretend they're somewhere else." Somewhere covered in concrete and strip malls, chain restaurants and the luxury of all-American convenience, just over the river and a world away from the historic city that birthed it—or the rat-infested, crime-riddled city that spawned it, depending on which side of the river one lived on.

We didn't have to worry about traffic since it was Saturday, and before long we passed Belle Chasse, the last sizable outpost of Greater New Orleans suburbia.

"I'm almost afraid to bring it up again, but how *did* you get this car?" Jean was an opportunist. I figured he'd won it in a card game and planned to sell it to the merman, or Rene Delachaise had bought it and was paying Jean to deliver it. Although I had to question the judgment of anyone who'd entrust delivery of an expensive sports car to a guy who first died before the Pony Express had been conceived.

"There is an interesting story of how I procured this automobile, *Jolie*. In taking a morning stroll near my hotel, I took a short route to the square of Andrew Jackson and there I discovered it, behind a building. An individual had left it for the taking."

Uh-oh. My blood pressure began a steady climb toward stroke level. "What building?"

"My apologies, but I do not remember precisely." He smiled, closed his eyes, and leaned back as the wind whipped across his face. My own enjoyment of the convertible dived into free-fall.

I groaned. "Some idiot left his keys in the car and you stole it. Oh my God, you're a freaking pirate. Of *course* you stole it." My gullibility sometimes amazed even me. I'd try to think the best of a person and—*boom*—some reality obvious to everyone else knocked the bejesus out of me. I'd never hear the end of this from Alex.

"I am not a pirate, but a privateer, a simple businessman. How could you think me capable of thievery, Drusilla?" Jean sounded indignant. This from a guy with more than two hundred years' experience in creative procurement. "*Voilà!* There it sat, just asking to be taken. Surely no person would leave a key in an automobile if he did not wish it to have a new owner, *oui?*"

Good Lord. What had I been thinking? What if we were stopped by the parish police? How could I explain driving downriver in a hot convertible with a big, armed Frenchman claiming to be the long-dead Jean Lafitte? I could be a little entrepreneurial in my problem-solving, but my willingness to act outside the rulebook didn't quite extend to grand theft auto.

Thankfully, no law enforcement showed itself as we headed down Highway 23 in silence. Traffic dropped off, and the air stung my nose with the salty tang of the wetlands that grew ever closer on the right while the river levee loomed on the left. Nature wasn't theoretical here; it was tied to the lifeblood of the place. We wound along a long stretch of blacktop that followed the path of the river. Occasionally, a ship passed and we had to look up to see it—another unsettling reminder of why this fragile land so far below sea level had gone completely underwater after Katrina.

I couldn't appreciate the exotic beauty while worried about potential incarceration. I phoned Alex. "Stop somewhere and let us ride the rest of the way with you. We need to ditch this *stolen* Corvette."

"Goddamn it." Alex let loose a string of expletives that would make a pirate blush—most of them directed at Jean.

I handed him the phone. "Here, this is your mess. You talk to Alex."

Jean examined the phone as if it were a new species of toad, and inched it toward his ear. "*Oui?*"

A grin spread across his face, and he gave a low chuckle. "*Non, Monsieur Chien*, I do not wish to do that to myself. I prefer a lady's company for such an activity." He waited a few seconds in silence before handing the phone back to me with a shrug. "I believe he is no longer there."

I believed Mr. Dog would not be speaking to either of us for a while.

We passed the town of Point a la Hache and arrived, if signs could be believed, at the community of Happy Jack, Louisiana. I pulled off the road at an abandoned gas station and drove behind what was left of the half-demolished building. Everything in Plaquemines Parish was either rotted, in the process of rotting, or new. Katrina had left no other options.

"I must deliver this automobile to Rene," Jean protested when Alex pulled the Pathfinder next to us and stopped.

Not my problem. "You can tell him it's behind the old Murphy Oil station in Happy Jack and he can come and get it, unless the sheriff gets to it first—because I guarantee Alex has already reported the theft." I left the keys in the ignition and walked to the Pathfinder, leaving Jean to follow me.

Alex stayed behind the wheel, but gave me a squinty-eyed glare as I climbed in the passenger seat and Jean slid into the back. "You got any wipes? Something to clean off that steering wheel and anything else you touched?"

Crap on a stick. Fingerprints. I dug through my backpack to find the towelettes I carried in case of spilled potions and went back to destroy evidence.

"Did you call it in?" I asked a few minutes later, crawling back into the passenger seat. I'd barely gotten the door closed before Alex slung gravel and U-turned toward the highway.

"No." His voice was hard and had dropped about an octave, so I knew he was mad. "I've never seen that stolen car. I don't know shit about that stolen car. If you get arrested, I don't know shit about you, either. And you owe me."

Great. Another debt to repay. The rest of the drive to Buras passed in silence. Even Jean kept his mouth shut. I knew Alex had cooled off when he started drumming his fingers on my steering wheel in time to the songs on the radio. He liked to snarl and growl and posture with his weapons, but beneath the Man in Black guise was one of the few genuinely nice guys I'd ever met. I just had to let him keep his delusions of badassitude.

Finally, we reached Buras and hooked a left toward the river, where we found the unassuming new building that housed the Black Velvet Oyster Bar and Grill. On the far left side of the otherwise empty lot sat a pair of suped-up

extended-cab pickups, one black and one white, with
MERTWIN1 and MERTWIN2 license plates.

"That is my friend Rene and his brother, Robert," Jean
said as we climbed out of the truck.

I'd been excited about meeting my first mermen, but Rene
and Robert Delachaise weren't what I expected. Without the
visual mythology of mermaids to sway me, I'd been free to
imagine my own kind of merman. Tall, I'd thought. Rugged.
Fierce. Trident in one hand, spear in the other. Kind of like
a werefish Poseidon.

The mers did look fierce, but it was more in an urban
street gang kind of way, like someone who might follow a
lone pedestrian down a dark alley with ill intent. Plus there
were two of them. Twins.

They both got out of the black truck, but the one Jean
identified as Robert waved at us and held back, finishing a
cell phone conversation. The other, Rene, stretched, making
fascinating shapes of the tattoos that spanned from shoulder
to wrist. They also danced on the back of his neck, beneath
his white mesh tank, and out of sight. I was thankful for the
tattoos—Robert didn't appear to have any, and it's the only
way I'd ever tell them apart in their identical jeans and tanks.

Rene pulled off an LSU cap and threw it in the truck
before slamming the door, then ran a tanned, wiry hand
through his close-cropped black hair. He nodded at Jean and
looked at Alex, nostrils flaring in surprise. "You a shifter?
Good. I like shifters."

He turned dark, liquid eyes to mine—such a dark brown

they were almost as black as his neatly trimmed Vandyke beard, with long lashes that would be beautiful if he weren't oozing hostility. "I don't like wizards."

Since the mers were in the werecreature family, I assumed I'd be able to pull some kind of energy off him even if I couldn't fully read his emotions, and I was right. Rene's aura was cool and smooth, rippled with restrained aggression, and the temperature seemed to drop several degrees as it skimmed across my skin.

Fingering the mojo bag in my pocket, I introduced myself, ever the professional in the face of extreme weirdness. It's a gift.

Rene Delachaise had a husky voice and a South Louisiana accent thicker than bayou mud. Alex had told me many of the Cajuns—descendants of the Acadians driven from Canada by the English in the 1700s—were mers working in the fishing industry. Rene shook my hand, then gave me a brazen head-to-toe appraisal that set off the alarm on my internal sexist-pig detector.

"Where's the head of the Villere clan?" I asked.

"Ain't here yet," Rene said. "Disrespectin' you already, wizard. You remember that."

"Aw, he'll be here, bro. Chill out." Robert joined us and introduced himself to everyone. Rene might be the head of the family, but he should hire his twin brother to handle public relations. Robert was more laid-back, friendlier. If he hated wizards, and his energy blast said he did, at least he had the decency not to say it to my face.

Once introductions had been made, we decided to wait for Denis in the Black Velvet. A motorcycle turned in the lot as I trailed the others inside. The restaurant had just opened and it was early for a lunch crowd to start arriving, so I figured our other mer had arrived.

"You guys go in. I want to meet him alone," I said over my shoulder, ignoring Alex's frown as the door closed behind him. The prickling of energy as I approached the biker was very similar to Robert's and Rene's. I waited for Denis Villere to turn off his bike and remove his helmet, and tried not to indulge the temptation to make a "fish on a bicycle" joke.

He was thinner, tanner, and considerably older than Rene, with a rough scar down one cheek, hard brown eyes, and silvering hair pulled tight in back and braided into a long plait that almost reached his waist. Several earrings curved along the cartilage of one ear. I wondered what happened to those when he shifted into a fish—fin piercings?

"Wizards be getting prettier." His sandpaper voice had an even heavier accent than Rene's—part French, part Southern, part swamp. "At least you got dat that goin' for you."

"Why don't you give me your side of the story before we go in," I said. Denis Villere seemed more neutral than his rival clan leader and, besides, much of the burden for making my treaty proposal work was going to fall on him.

Denis nodded. "Moved my family from over round Bayou Teche," he said. "Now da borders opened up, too many weregators settlin' there. Dey up around St. Bernard too, so we come here."

I swallowed hard, wondering if the Elders knew weregators were taking over the Atchafalaya Basin and St. Bernard Parish. I didn't blame the Villeres. I'd move away too.

"You settled in Tidewater?"

He gave a slow nod, and his long, snakelike braid slid around his shoulder. "We been usin' da eastern mouth of the river as our huntin' and swimmin' areas. The Delachaises got no claim to run us out, and dey poisoned the water. Even took a couple of shots at us when we was hunting at night. Next time, we gonna shoot back."

Curiosity burned to find out what mers hunted for, and whether it fell within the human hunting guidelines of Louisiana Fisheries & Wildlife. But first I had to set him straight—and hoped he wasn't armed.

"Look, I understand you wanting to get away from the weregators." I made a mental note to look weregators up in the Elders' online database. "But here's the deal. By the terms of the Accords following the Wizards' War of 1976, at least part of that land *has* been granted to the Delachaise clan, including Pass a Loutre."

Denis cursed in a French patois even Jean Lafitte wouldn't understand, but the word *sorciere*—wizard—popped up several times. "Rene and his people don't need so much space and dey made my son T-Jacques sick as a damn dog. He ain't been able to keep up wit' da fishin'. If that don't get cleared up right now"—he paused for a breath, then kept going—"and I mean *right now,* you hear? Then somebody's gonna pay. They gonna find out they messin' with the wrong clan."

What an ornery species mers were turning out to be. I stared past him at the high earthen levee that separated the highway from the river. I wanted to see what the water problem was, but I didn't buy the idea that the Delachaises would poison their own territory. That would be foolish, and whatever else he might be, I didn't think Rene Delachaise was a fool.

"Here is what the Congress of Elders is willing to do." I prayed he'd accept the idea I'd hammered out last night with my boss, Willem Zrakovi, head of the Elders for North America. "There have been no promises made concerning the marshland around the South Pass, near Burrwood. The wizards will add a section to the treaty assigning that territory to the Villere family. But there has to be a signed peace agreement between you and Rene. No poisoning. No shooting—by either of you."

Denis narrowed his eyes and I fingered the mojo bag again, almost sighing in relief as the magic-infused herbs blocked out his anger. I knew the fishing and gator hunting wouldn't be as plentiful in the southern end of the territory, away from the federally protected delta, and so did he. But the Delachaise claim was valid. They'd been here first. It was my best offer.

He jerked his head toward the Black Velvet. "Rene, he agree to dis?"

"You gonna have to talk to him to find that out—she ain't qualified to speak for Rene." Robert Delachaise had slipped up on both of us, and I wondered how long he'd been listening.

"You checkin' up on us, tadpole?" Denis bristled toward Robert, and Robert stepped forward till they were practically doing a chest-bump.

"You wanna fight, old man? I'll fight." Robert wrapped Denis's long braid around his hand and pulled hard enough to make the older man's head jerk, which got him a hefty shove in return.

Holy crap. We couldn't have a fish-fight in the middle of the Black Velvet parking lot. Heart pounding, I reached out with both hands and released a sharp burst of magical energy into each man's arm. Just enough to get their attention, and about all I could muster without the staff. Hopefully, they didn't know that.

They both fixed dark, angry eyes on me.

These oversized fish were pissing me off. "Do you really want me to have to settle this?" I pulled the elven staff from my backpack. As if on cue, it began to glow from within, a warm, golden light that practically dared them to mess with it.

The mers' disgruntled looks bled into uncertainty, and they each took a step backward.

Robert broke first. "I'm outta here—I got to pick up a car in Happy Jack." He wheeled and stomped toward his truck. "Old man there needs to talk to Rene. Decision's up to him. Tell Rene I'll see him later."

I nodded. "Denis and I are going inside to talk now." I looked at Denis. "Aren't we." It really wasn't a question.

He shot Robert another killer look and stalked toward the door of the Black Velvet. I lowered the staff and sighed. This was going well.

6

It took almost two hours of name-calling to negotiate exactly where each clan's territory would start and end. Alex and Jean had to separate the mers when Denis threw a fried frog leg in Rene's face—after dousing it in ranch dressing.

In the end, Rene and Denis reached an agreement contingent on the water problem, whatever it was, being solved to their mutual satisfaction. Rene insisted the contamination was Villere-induced, and vice-versa. It would be my job to either find the problem or convince them there was no problem. Something made T-Jacques and one of Rene's cousins sick. God forbid I should suggest they ate bad oysters.

The Black Velvet staff had been round-eyed and jittery around the volatile tableful of alpha males and one lone, frustrated woman clutching a two-foot-long stick of wood in her left hand while she ate with her right. They trotted out plates of seafood kickers and crawfish pies, catfish and oysters and shrimp, and stayed out of our vicinity except to refill tea and water glasses.

Mers, I learned, didn't eat red meat but they could pack away prodigious amounts of seafood, especially when the wizards were picking up the tab. That had been my idea and I hadn't gotten prior approval from the Elders. If I didn't get reimbursed, I'd be eating ramen noodles until payday. But I wanted to try to negate some of this hatred of wizard-kind, whatever had caused it, and if the price was a few platters of food, so be it.

Finally, everyone left except Alex and me. In an hour, Rene would meet us at the Venice Marina for the trip to Pass a Loutre on his boat. He and Jean had tossed me aside like an empty oyster shell and gone off in search of Robert after carefully writing down the location of the Corvette.

I was already exhausted from the stress of being polite and patient for so long—neither of which I'm very skilled at—and keeping everyone's overwrought emotions out of my head. My muscles ached and my head pounded and I wanted a nap. Instead, I propped my elbows on the table, watching Alex scrape the remaining mountain of grilled stuffed crab claws onto his plate. The man ate like a plow horse but he managed to turn it all to those pretty muscles bunching and flexing beneath his shirt.

Hey. If it's in front of me, I'm going to look.

"How'd you think it went?" I asked, watching as he squeezed lemon on his crab.

"I don't trust either of those guys to hold to his

word—especially if you can't figure out the water problem. If there is a water problem." He guzzled the rest of his iced tea and handed me the check with an evil smile before he resumed eating. "Hope your credit card's got a big limit on it."

That made two of us. If one man is sitting at a restaurant table with a hundred women, the waiter will always give the bill to the guy. It's a proven fact. Wouldn't have killed Alex to pay it—he made more money than me, a situation the Elders were soon going to be addressing, although they didn't know it.

Alex handed me the keys and I drove the rest of the way down Highway 23 into Venice. We parked near the marina just before two p.m., and spotted Jean leaning against the wall of the main building, smoking a slender cigar. Surrounded by boats and guys in shrimp boots, he didn't look nearly as out of place as Alex and I.

"Robert had automobile business to attend to, but Rene waits for us onboard the vessel," he said, tossing the cigar aside and rummaging in my backseat for his pistol. I hadn't let him take it into the restaurant. The Black Velvet staff really would have been alarmed had the muzzle-loader made an appearance. And I'd wager a case of ramen noodles that Robert's automobile business involved filing off VIN numbers and removing license plates.

To me, the *Dieu de la Mer* looked little different from the other fishing boats docked at the marina. Its hull was black, its name painted in white. All of the boats looked relatively new—probably because Katrina had swept their predecessors into a Mount Everest of nautical rubble. A windowed wheelhouse separated the short, raised foredeck from the long aft deck, and a complex arrangement of white rigging and netting stretched skyward.

Rene watched us from the aft deck. "You ready? Gettin' dark earlier now—we need to go."

Jean leapt aboard like Sebastian going after his favorite perch atop the fridge—all sleek and graceful. Alex was right behind him, throwing his shrimp boots onboard first. He and Jean headed immediately to the wheelhouse to look at their new toy. Guys. Didn't matter if they were alive or undead; show them something with an engine and they turned into ten-year-olds.

I stood on the pier, forlorn and abandoned, measuring the distance between me and the deck. I was five-four on a good day. I would not be graceful or sleek. There was a good chance I would end up in the water.

Rene stood with a wide stance and his fists propped on his hips like some sort of Cajun pirate, smirking. "Thought witches could fly, babe."

I gritted my teeth. "I am not a witch." Witches were to wizards as a common black bass was to a merman. It was an insult, and he knew it.

Chuckling, he leaned over the side with his arm outstretched. I grasped his tattooed forearm and he jerked me aboard with no obvious effort, if you didn't count my near-dislocated shoulder. Note to remember: mers might not be the biggest fish in the wetlands, but they were werecreature-strong.

I'd been on a boat only twice. My grandfather had tucked me into a bright orange life jacket and took me fishing one time on Smith Lake in north Alabama. I'd kept my eyes closed the whole time. Later, Gerry, who'd raised me since school age, had let me ride the swan boats at New Orleans' City Park. Of course, both of those boat rides took place before I was ten. I was a true wizard, meaning my swimming skills were theoretical. I understood the principle, but the execution left something to be desired.

As we set out hugging the western shore, I joined Rene, Alex, and Jean in the boat's small, windowed wheelhouse. I was clearly the fourth wheel—the fifth, if you counted the boat's navigational system. The guys hunkered over maps and asked Rene questions about the river, the bayous, the boat, the normal size of a redfish haul, the best time of night to shrimp, and the tricks of navigating the wetland marshes that had begun to spread around us as we left the world of automotive travel behind. I had nothing to contribute.

I spotted a single life jacket dangling from a hook over a long bench in back of the wheelhouse. If we went down, it was mine. Jean couldn't die, at least not permanently. He might drown, but he'd show up again in the Beyond, regain his strength, and eventually come back good as new. Rene could shapeshift into a fish, so death by drowning wasn't likely. Alex liked the water, so he had to be a better swimmer than me.

When Alex asked Rene how the hunting season for wild boar was going this year, I decided I'd find more scintillating conversation talking to myself. I walked to the side of the aft deck nearest the bank and watched the vegetation change from trees to tall reeds to flat marsh grass.

"It is beautiful, is it not, *Jolie?*" Jean joined me at the portside rail, watching as the tree line rose and fell, occasionally allowing a glimpse of the patchwork of land and serpentine canals and bayous around us.

"You spent a lot of time in these waters, didn't you?" I tried to imagine Jean in a small pirogue, smuggling contraband to and from New Orleans in this maze of waterways that made up just a small part of his empire. How strange it must be to view the world over more than two centuries, seeing what people had done right and what we'd screwed up.

He leaned on the rail, uncharacteristically silent.

Curious, I lowered my empathic barricades enough to take his emotional temperature. As a former human, he broadcast his feelings like a megawatt radio station. He didn't know about that particular skill of mine, and that's the way I wanted to keep it.

A whisper of melancholy seeped into me. Jean was lonely, and spending time on his old stomping grounds made him feel it more acutely.

I fingered the mojo bag in my jeans pocket and let the magic smooth his emotional fingerprint from my mind, but a residue of my own sadness remained. I didn't know how it felt to live well past all of the people I cared about, but I knew too much about loss and loneliness. Jean suddenly seemed a lot more human.

"Where do you live in the Beyond?" I knew he spent time in Old Orleans, that preternatural free zone between the modern city and the Beyond proper. It was like a New Orleans theme park with all the city's historical time periods represented in one finite area, on warp-drive. I'd been there once and didn't want to go back.

"I live in Old Barataria," he said, his voice soft. "It looks much as it did when I commanded my men there. I have a fine house on the beach. There are no—" He waved his hand in the air. "Bah. I do not know the word for the towers men use to find oil."

"Derricks," I said. The Louisiana waters were rife with them. Huey Long sold our coastline to Big Oil long before I was born.

I watched him lean over the rail, so natural and at ease on the deck of even a small boat such as this. Where I had to concentrate to steady my balance as the *Dieu de la Mer* cut through the waterways, his stance was effortless and natural as we passed the outpost of Pilottown and approached the choppy east pass connecting the Mississippi to the Gulf.

"What happened to your house in Barataria when you left?" I asked.

His jaw tightened. "The Americans burned it, even after I helped them win their little war." That would be the little War of 1812.

Jean was different from most of the historical undead, who were uncomfortable in the modern world. Even when summoned by a wizard or a magically adept human, they'd go back to their corner of the the Beyond without a fight. Not Jean. He liked keeping a foot in both worlds.

"Would you really want to live in modern New Orleans, where so many things have changed and you have to hide who you are?"

He glanced at me over his shoulder, then stood and slid an arm around my waist, tugging me against him. "Is that an invitation, Drusilla? I believe there would be many advantages to living in your modern world."

Fine. We'd had a nice conversation. I'd started to genuinely like him, even to glimpse what a burden he might carry. Now we were back to smarmy innuendo.

"No, it is not an invitation," I snapped, slapping his arm. "And everybody calls me DJ. Only you and my grandmother call me Drusilla." Which should tell both of us something.

"Bah." He looked as if he'd smelled a rotten fish. "That is not a proper name for a beautiful woman."

"I think it suits her just fine." Strong hands slipped over my shoulders as Alex joined us, standing so close I could feel his body heat radiating into my back. Had nothing to do with the weather; shapeshifters ran hot. Had nothing to do with affection, either. He squeezed my shoulders a little too hard for it to be a show of solidarity. I'd probably have bruises. He was marking his territory.

We rounded a curve, crossing the easternmost branch of

the river's mouth, and wound our way to Pass a Loutre, a wildlife management area that wasn't so much a place as a series of waterways providing entrance into the vast Birdfoot Delta. Other boats would pass occasionally, it being hunting season for various swamp critters, including, apparently, wild boar.

Finally, Rene navigated the *Dieu de la Mer* across a secluded bayou and through a twisting, turning set of channels. I understood the old stories now, about fishermen unfamiliar with the area who'd sailed into these marshlands and never found their way out.

The water was dark and murky, and the vegetation ranged from thick stands of trees overhanging the banks to, more often, wide swaths of marsh grass with vistas so broad I swore I could see the Earth's curvature. Birds squawked and cawed overhead, and the air smelled of saltwater and algae.

Alex had been silent after succeeding in his mission to drive Jean to the other side of the deck. We leaned on the rail, side by side. He spoke softly. "Are you really going to dinner with that clown?"

The clown in question cleared his throat from his spot a few feet behind us, just in case Alex didn't mean for him to overhear.

"It'll be fine," I whispered. "We'll have dinner, and then he swore he'd forget all the crap I promised him after Katrina."

Alex shook his head. "Just watch your back. And take the staff with you."

"Rene! Le bateau—arrêtez!" Jean bellowed suddenly, pounding on the side of the wheelhouse.

What the hell? Alex and I ran to Jean's side of the deck, and I caught my breath. Denis Villere sat on the bank holding a shotgun. A few feet away from him lay a man.

A man who was way too bloody to still be breathing.

7

After tethering the *Dieu de la Mer* a few yards down the bank, Rene joined us on the aft deck. Already in FBI mode, Alex was pulling on his shrimp boots. Denis hadn't moved.

"You"—Alex pointed at Jean and Rene—"stay onboard." He frowned at my bootless feet. "DJ, you stay too, at least for now."

"I got extra boots probably fit you if you need 'em, babe." Rene headed back into the wheelhouse and began digging through a bin. He emerged a few seconds later holding a pair of white rubber boots with big, glittery silver fish on the sides. Their sheer outrageousness was cool. I wanted them.

"Thanks." I sat down and pulled them on in place of my running shoes. I was going to have to buy my own shrimp boots when I got a chance. The last couple of years, there always seemed to be a swamp or a flooded house I needed to wade through.

By the time I stood up, Alex had splashed ashore. He squatted next to the body as he talked to Denis in a low voice. Surely it had to be a body. The man's lower legs were the only parts of him not covered in blood. Alex looked up at me and shook his head, and I shivered despite the sun.

Alex and Denis exchanged sharp words I couldn't make out. Finally, the mer thrust the shotgun at Alex, butt first. He looked mad as hell, which seemed to amuse Rene. What a jackass. Nothing about this was funny.

Giving a wide berth to the area immediately surrounding the body, Alex waded back to the boat, cracked open the shotgun, unloaded it, and handed it to me. Smart man. I wouldn't hand me a loaded gun, either. He stuck the shot in his pocket and climbed onboard, Denis's stony stare drilling holes in his back.

"Is there any way you can tell if our dead guy is human?" Alex asked. "If he is, I need to call the Plaquemines sheriff. If not, we need to call the Elders."

"I might be able to tell." I lowered my voice. "You think Denis did it?"

"He says no, that he was just coming to watch the water sampling to make sure Rene didn't pull any funny shit, but who knows. Guy looks like he's been dead a while, and he wasn't killed with a shotgun."

"He ain't one of my people, or a Villere either," Rene called from the foredeck, in case we didn't know he was listening. "Man's too tall to be a mer."

If the guy had been dead several hours, anybody could've

done it, including Rene or even Jean. "How about an animal attack?" I asked Alex. "One of those wild boars you guys were talking about?"

"No, he was definitely carved up with a knife. Something sharp that could cut through muscle and bone, like a filet knife." Alex shifted his eyes to where Rene and Jean sat in the shade on the foredeck, looking daggers at Denis. "You know, like a hunter or fisherman might use. It would take somebody strong."

Well, hell. Could be Denis. Could be Rene or Robert or T-Jacques or just about anybody else in Southeast Louisiana. "Leave me alone a minute and see if I can feel anything."

Back in the old days, before Katrina, the sentinels had sophisticated equipment to tell us when a preternatural came across the border from the Beyond. Now, there were so many pretes strolling in and out of the region we'd quit using the trackers. I'd have to do it the hard way. Or, more accurately, the elven way.

Alex joined Rene and Jean on the shaded foredeck and motioned for Denis to climb up. With the back of the boat to myself, I walked to the rail nearest the body and closed my eyes. My daily grounding rituals to control my empathy involved focused meditation, and I used those skills to shut out the extraneous sensations, including the weight of four pairs of eyes watching me.

First, I honed in on the sounds. The caws and croaks of the swamp birds, an occasional splash, water lapping in soft swells against the side of the boat, buzzing flies in a frantic aerial dance around the body.

Shutting those out, I took note of the smells. Fish. Muddy water. Grass. The iron-rich tang of blood.

I let it all go, except what I could feel on my skin. The warmth of the soft October sunlight, an occasional pale wisp of breeze that was gone so quickly I wondered if I'd imagined it—and overlapping washes of energy.

Every living thing has an aura, and my empathy—an elven skill—lets me feel it. I recognized Alex's and Jean's distinctive signatures, and the overwhelming sensation, fluid and cold, that came from a double dose of merman. But beneath it all, as faint as that gentle puff of wind, lay another spike of power, familiar but just beyond my grasp. I couldn't pin it down long enough to identify it.

I took a deep breath and opened my eyes, the sunlight bringing tears as it seared into my retinas. The exertion to isolate so many sensations had ratcheted my headache from woodpecker to jackhammer.

"Something's there, but I can't be sure what," I said, joining the others. "I might be able to tell more if . . ." I swallowed a rising swell of nausea. "It might help if I touched him." Touching amped up the elven magic.

Alex snorted. "Forget it. I won't have you barfing on my crime scene."

Oh, *his* crime scene, was it? Nothing raises a girl's hackles like being treated like a girl, even if she's acting like a girl. Besides, if I wanted the Elders to treat me like an equal partner in this job, I couldn't wimp out. "If you can look at it, I can look at it."

"Okay, but I'm warning you. It's one of the ugliest I've seen, and there'll be no yarking on the body." He had obviously mistaken me for some delicate flower from his past. Alex eased over the side of the boat into the shallows. I sat gingerly on the rail and swung my legs to the outside, said a quick prayer to whatever saint kept wizards from crime-scene yarking, and jumped. I splashed like a whale but managed to land on the big white shrimp boots and remain upright.

"Try to walk in the footprints I've already made," Alex said. "If we need to call the sheriff we'll catch hell for mucking up the scene."

My feet slid around inside Rene's boots and my soaked jeans weighed me down as I clomped along the muddy bank like Bigfoot. I kept my eyes off the body as long as possible, but eventually it was in front of me and there was nowhere else to look. My crab cakes threatened a second appearance.

"You okay? You're turning green." Alex rubbed my back like a mother soothing a fractious baby but I had no doubt he'd use that same hand to jerk me away from the dead man if I even hinted at a gagging noise.

"I'm okay." I finally looked at the body. Really looked, trying to understand it. "What happened to him?" My voice came out in a strangled whisper.

Alex squatted beside the gruesome wreckage that a few hours ago had been a man. "Has ritual killing written all over it. My guess is what actually killed him was a slashed throat." He made a horizontal motion across the guy's bloody neck. "And parts of him have been cut off."

He pointed at the groin, a ragged, bloody hole where the guy's genitals had once been, and at the face. I tried not to think of hamburger, but couldn't help it. The tip of the man's nose and one eyeball had taken a vacation. His remaining brown eye stared at the sky, registering shock at the indignity of his final moments.

"The tips of his fingers have been cut off, and the entire ring finger of his left hand," Alex said.

"Think he had an angry wife?" I looked away, gazed over the grassy marshland, and tried to settle my churning guts. "You sure an animal didn't do it? You know, bite the . . . stuff off?"

"Nope, it was human—or prete. Look to your left."

The missing parts were lined up in a neat row on the bank a few feet from the body, and were already covered in ants and flies. The finger still had a wedding ring on it. My head swam at the horror, and I couldn't imagine the fury or madness that would spur someone to do such things. I hoped the poor guy was dead before the chopping started.

I'd never been squeamish before, but it seemed like a good time to start. I turned my back and took a deep breath to stop the horizon from spinning. A deep breath turned out to be a bad idea. I couldn't wimp out now. This was some-thing only I could do, and I needed to do it.

I knelt near the man's feet with my back to him,

swallowed hard, and forced a hand down to rest fingertips on his ankle. The skin felt cold and immobile. Somehow, it helped that it didn't feel like flesh. I cleared my thoughts, letting my mind process the sensations as sunlight and shadow played across my eyelids. A faint trace of familiar magic pulsed in the air, and it wasn't coming from me.

I opened my eyes and swiveled to stare at what was left of the man's bloody face.

"What is it?" Alex put a steadying hand on my shoulder as if he expected me to collapse in a mewling heap. I might when I got home, alone, but not now.

"He's a wizard," I said. "Or either he's human and another wizard was here recently—I mean a wizard other than me. The sensation is fading, but I'm sure of it."

Alex and I both turned to study the pair of mermen on the boat, who'd stopped glaring at each other so they could watch us. Jean sat behind them, making a big show of polishing a dagger on the hem of his shirt. I suspected he was keeping it close at hand in case the mers started fighting.

"I can't speak for the other two but I'm sure it wasn't Jean," I whispered, hoping they couldn't hear me. "Ritual murder's not his style. He's more direct." There was a famous story of another pirate, only one, who dared question Jean's authority, calling him out while Jean was having his dinner. The pirate Lafitte walked outside his house, shot the guy in the heart with barely a blink, then went back inside and resumed his dinner. No added drama. No wasted effort.

Alex looked at Jean. "I agree. He'd have slit the guy's throat and let him bleed out. This kind of slaughter takes rage, and our mers have plenty of rage. Be nice if we knew whether our vic was a wizard or if we should add a wizard to our suspect list."

We needed to search the area—with at least one fewer witness. Jean and Rene couldn't leave because we needed them to get home, but Denis's continued presence only increased the likelihood of a fight.

"I'm going to put a tracking charm on Denis so he can't disappear back into the Beyond or the swamps, unless you need him to stay here," I said, standing. "It'll make keeping the peace a lot easier."

"Yeah, long as you're sure we'll be able to find him when we need him. He better not make me chase him down." Alex jingled the shotgun shells in his pocket. "Tell him I'm keeping the gun till he's cleared. And tell Rene we're going to be here a while."

I'd be really popular with the mers once I delivered all those messages. "I think I'll see if Rene will still get the water samples for us since he has to hang around anyway." I could fill a couple of vials in the shallows, but I wanted water from the deep areas where the mers got sick.

I made my way back into the water, and although Denis reached over the side to help me aboard, he didn't look happy about it. I shivered at the cold energy from his hand—a much stronger signal than when we'd met back at the Black Velvet. Maybe he was nervous, or maybe he was turning on some merman mojo to intimidate me. If he thought that would work, he had the wrong wizard.

"You don't have to stay," I said. "I just need you to accept a tracking charm so we can find you. We'll want to talk to you again."

"You won't blame dis on me." The anger shimmered around Denis like a cloak. "Wizards ain't gonna mark me like a criminal. Screw dat, screw your goddamn treaty, and screw you and every other wizard."

He turned and stalked toward the far edge of the deck, jerking his shirt over his head. That freaking merman thought he was going to jump overboard and swim out of here? Over my dead elven staff.

I raced to retrieve it from my backpack, which I'd left in the wheelhouse. By the time I ran back, the urgency had passed. Jean held the mer in a tight armlock, dagger point resting above the jugular. He was spitting a torrent of French in the shorter man's ear, and from the glower on Denis's face, he understood every word of it. I really needed to take French lessons.

"Let him go, Jean," I said. "I'm sure Denis wants us to find the real killer." I was getting really tired of the angry-merman crap too, but Jean didn't need to accelerate it. Besides, he was clearly on Team Delachaise in this brewing war, and everybody knew it.

Denis's eyes flashed defiance. I'd never been face-to-face with such open hatred, and it shook me. Why did the mers hate wizards so badly?

"I'm sorry," I said. "I'm sure you're telling the truth about not killing this guy, but we need to be able to find you later so we can officially rule you out."

He slipped his gaze from me to Rene, who'd been lounging against the side of the wheelhouse, watching the show. He'd stripped off his own shirt, probably ready to shift and chase down Denis as soon as he hit the water.

"You mark me, you gotta mark him too, bitch," Denis said.

I flinched, but let it pass and looked at Rene.

He gave a slight nod. "Sure thing, babe. I got nothin' to hide. Wasn't me sittin' on the bank with a dead guy."

"Terrific," I said. "Tracking marks for everyone." Except Jean, who'd gone back in the wheelhouse and was reading a book. I squinted through the windows and blinked at the sight of his face scrunched into a frown over *The Collected Stories of Eudora Welty*. Just in case this day hadn't been surreal enough.

"Do this thing, and let me go." Denis's hiss brought my attention back to the mers at hand.

I knelt and pulled my portable magic case from the backpack. Tracking charms were one of the common recipes I kept mixed in advance, and I pulled out a vial of ground pine bark mixed with corroded bronze and iron sulphate, plus a couple of squares of parchment.

"I need a drop of your blood to activate this." I looked up at Denis, who crossed his arms, his mouth a taut line across his face.

"I ain't gonna bleed for a wizard."

"Stupid sonofabitch fish-for-brains." Muttering, Rene dropped to his knees beside me, pulled a penknife from his pocket, and jabbed the sharp tip into the pad of his index finger.

"Thank you." I tapped a small amount of the metallic powder on the parchment and held it out. He squeezed a couple of drops of blood atop the powder, and I stirred it with my finger, sending a miniscule jolt of energy into the mixture to activate it.

"Where you want it?" I stared at Rene's chest and arms, where elaborate tattoos of animals and fish frolicked. I could study him for days and not see it all. The body wasn't bad, either.

"Don't matter—ain't gonna hurt my ink, right?"

I shook my head. "It isn't permanent."

He held out his arm, and I pushed it down to rest on my knee. Swiping my finger through the blood-fueled ink I carefully drew an eye inside a triangle inside a circle, using his forearm as my canvas. As soon as the circle was complete, the ink glowed silver and seeped into his skin, clearly visible over his own tats.

"Won't wash off?"

"Nope." I hoped Denis was paying attention. "It won't come off until I take it off, even when you shift." I held Rene's arm a moment longer, tracing my non-bloodied finger along an eel that curled its way between wrist and elbow. The skin was slightly ridged along the lines of ink.

"How did you get these to stay?" Weres and shifters heal just about anything. I wouldn't have thought he'd be able to have tattoos.

"Put salt and vinegar with the ink and it holds okay. Or use acid. Fades a little so you have to add extra color."

I shuddered. Rene Delachaise had an extremely high pain tolerance. Good thing to know.

"Do this if you're gonna do it, wizard." Denis knelt beside me with his own knife, and I readied the mixture. Once the blood was added, he turned his back. "Put it where I don't have to see it and think of you."

I had a feeling I wasn't going to be on the Villere Christmas card list.

As soon as the tracking charm was applied, Denis stood, strode to the far side of the deck, and leapt into the water without a word. By the time I got to the rail, he'd disappeared.

"How long does it take you guys to shift?" I folded the parchment squares and sealed them inside envelopes in my pack. I could use the leftover ink to track them down later, if needed. "That seemed really fast."

Shifting was easy and almost instantaneous for Alex as a true shapeshifter. Weres usually had a harder time.

"Bout thirty, forty seconds for me, prob'ly faster for someone old as Denis," Rene said. "We shift underwater."

"Thanks, by the way. You made that a lot easier."

"Wizard owes me a favor, that's a good thing, babe." He poked at the tracking mark on his arm. "What's next?"

I turned to see where Alex had gone. He moved slowly amid the vegetation inland from the body. Seeing photos of the marsh, I'd always assumed the grass was the height of, well, lawn grass, but some of this had grown so high I could see only part of Alex's head.

"Are you still willing to get the water samples?" I asked Rene.

"Might as well. Gotta stay here anyway." He pointed down the bank. "Around that bend is where one of my people got sick. Also where T-Jacques Villere was supposed to have been, so I figure he was the one poisoned the water."

"Is it going to make you sick to swim in there?" All the Elders needed was a litigious bunch of mers claiming we'd forced them to swim in contaminated water. The inter-species governing council hadn't even been set up yet. Every group, including the wizards, thought they should be in charge of it.

"Don't plan on staying down there that long." As he talked, Rene had been ridding himself of clothes and I took a deep breath as he shucked the jeans. I hated working with weres and shifters. They'd get naked at the mere mention of changing form. I'd seen way more of Alex Warin than I should have, not that the view was bad. And not that he didn't like being admired, the dog.

Still, I studiously dug in my backpack for the empty vials and tried to hand them up to Rene without getting an eyeful of merman.

"You a little shy, babe?" Rene took the vials and, damn it, I had to see what he was going to do with them. It wasn't like he had pockets. He'd hung a pouch around his neck, and placed the small tubes inside it.

"Of course I'm not shy but—" I gawked, not at Rene's hard, tanned body per se but at a particular bottle-nosed dolphin tat where I didn't know tats could go. I felt myself turn the color of a ripe tomato.

"Oh, I wish you wasn't a wizard." Rene laughed as he walked to the opposite side of the deck, where the water was deepest. "I'd take you home with me, *chère*."

The weirdness factor in my life had shot into the ozone. As soon as the splash sounded from Rene's departure, I checked on Alex again. He'd need me to help him search, but I knew he wanted to look alone first. He was the investigator here, even if I hadn't yarked on his crime scene.

I walked back to the wheelhouse, half wishing Jean had dog-paddled off with Rene so I could stretch out on the bench for a nap. I hadn't burned much magic to zap the mers or to fuel the tracking charms, but the more of my limited physical magic I used, the less juice I had until I could sleep and replenish my metaphysical batteries.

"How do you like Eudora Welty?" I asked.

Jean looked up at me, brows knit. "Among your modern women, to what does the word *brassière* refer?"

I tried to gauge whether he was serious or starting another round of inappropriate banter. "What did it mean in your time?"

He mumbled in French a moment, trying to translate. "One used it on the arm if it had been broken, as a brace."

"And why are you asking about brassieres?" I hadn't read any Eudora Welty in a while, but didn't recall her writing about underwear.

He brandished the book. "To her friend, a woman is offering"—he began reading—"a 'pink brassiere with adjustable shoulder straps', as if this were a desirable thing to have. This woman, however, did not break her arm. So it is perhaps an article of clothing?"

I bit my lip. He would take offense if I laughed at him, and then I'd owe him even more favors. "It's a woman's undergarment, sort of like a corset, only smaller." Surely even pirate women wore corsets.

"Ah." His gaze settled on my chest, and a smile ticked up the corners of his mouth. "You will show me this article of clothing?"

Uh-huh. When Britney Spears became president. "We have a murder victim on our hands. No time. Sorry."

"That is unfortunate," Jean said, returning his attention to the book. I didn't think he was referring to the dead man.

8

A splash and thump near the front of the boat diverted my attention from Jean and his preoccupation with Eudora Welty's underwear. Alex had levered himself aboard and was rooting through boxes and other paraphernalia on the aft deck.

"What are you looking for?" I shucked my denim shirt and draped it across the top of my backpack. Only the fear of an inter-preternatural incident kept me from peeling off the jeans still heavy and wet from my earlier splashtastic landing in the water.

"You got any Ziploc bags or anything we could use for evidence?"

"What did you find?"

"I think it's our guy's clothes, back in the grass." Alex picked up a covered bucket and looked inside, wrinkling his nose as he clamped the lid back on and set it aside. "Bait."

His focus settled on my backpack.

"Oh, no. You aren't using my pack for murder evidence," I said. "Don't make me sic Charlie on you." Yeah, I had named the elven staff. It was as much a pet as Sebastian and treated me with more respect.

Behind me, Jean leaned over the side of the boat and pulled up Rene, back in human form and shaking off water like a dog. He gave me four stoppered vials of water and a glowering scowl before going into the wheelhouse to get dressed. I held the vials up to the light; it was a lot cleaner-looking than what I'd collected in New Orleans early this morning. I unstoppered it and sniffed, but it smelled like brackish water, nothing else.

Yet when Rene returned and leaned against the side rail, he looked a little green around the gills—which had probably been literally true a few moments earlier.

"That water is some nasty shit, wizard," he said. "First time I been that deep since the problems started. You lock Denis Villere up, and his boy. Otherwise, me and Robert, we'll take care of it ourselves."

I was beginning to think the mers just wanted to fight, period. The water gave them a convenient excuse. "You have to give me time to test it," I said. "Two days, three tops."

"Maximum," Rene said. "And only if the Villeres stay away from us."

Like I had any control over where Denis and T-Jacques and all the other little Villeres dipped their fins.

Alex joined us. "You got any plastic bags we can use for evidence?" he asked Rene.

The mer's expression shifted from irate to neutral for Alex, who as a non-wizard was automatically more popular than me. Rene retrieved a roll of heavy-duty plastic trash bags from a wooden trunk under the bench in the wheelhouse. "These work?"

"Thanks." Alex pulled a couple of bags off the roll. "This'll go faster if you help search," he told me. "If it turns out to be a sheriff issue, we'll just have to get the Elders to send in one of their cleanup teams to reconstruct the scene unless . . ." He handed me a bag. "Can you do that kind of thing?"

"No, the cleanup teams are all Blue Congress." It took specialized skills to do cleanup tasks like tamper with medical records and re-create crime scenes.

Alex stuffed half the trash bag into his pocket. "Then since we're fairly sure there's a wizard involved, let's see what else we can find and not worry about where we walk or what we touch. If the guy's clothes are out there, we might find something else."

I hadn't seen Alex this pumped in a while. There hadn't been a lot to shoot or investigate since Katrina, when he'd still been in serious enforcer mode. I had a feeling that with the borders down now officially, that was about to change. I wondered how happy he would be with sentinel work. As an enforcer, he'd been on the extreme end of the Elders' security teams, and he'd been good at it. How long could an adrenaline junkie keep the peace and smooth out problems before getting bored out of his skull? Something to ponder.

I tied the big plastic bag around my waist and followed him to the rail, sliding back into Rene's shrimp boots and splashing into the water with a lot more ease than the first time. I looped in a wide circle to avoid getting near the body and trailed Alex into the high reeds, stopping next to a dense bush a foot taller than me.

"I'll look this way, you take that way," he said, pointing me to his left. "Easiest method is to pick a couple of landmarks and cross back and forth between them systematically to make sure you don't miss anything."

Right. Landmarks. The bush would be a good one. I turned to my left and picked another—a tree about thirty yards away, the only thing sticking up high enough for me to see above the grass line.

I walked slowly, scouring the ground in front of each step and pushing aside vegetation taller than me to clear a path. The towering reeds pressed in on all sides, with nothing but green stalks visible around me and a patch of blue, cloudless sky above. I held my breath as something rustled on my right, followed by a deep-throated groan and a snort. My pulse began to pound hard enough to feel throughout my body.

"Alex, is that you?" I whispered. The rustling stopped, and everything fell silent. Alligators lived out here. Nutria, the monster-sized rodents with long orange teeth. Wild boar. I didn't want to meet any of them.

I took a deep breath, determined not to scream like a pansy so one of the men would feel obligated to come and rescue me. Rising on tiptoes, I scanned the top of the grass for my tree and continued toward it. One quiet step in front of the other, stopping to listen in between.

I don't know how far I'd gone before I spotted something dark a few feet ahead. Focused on it, I quit watching the ground and *eeped* as the next step sunk my left leg knee-deep in swamp mud. My other foot landed on the edge of my garbage bag and slid, pitching me shoulder-first into the muddy grass. So the land wasn't quite solid. Good to know.

After heaving my buried leg free from the goop, I sat there a moment, using a muddy hand to scoop mud off my arm and neck, listening for movement. More rustling reeds, then nothing. My breath sounded loud enough to echo.

I rose to my knees and crawled. Standing seemed like too much effort since I'd probably just fall again, plus I'd make a bigger target for the herd of wild boar skulking nearby and making dinner plans with me as the entrée. I dodged the big hole I'd made and advanced at the pace of a snail's grandmother, trying to be quiet. A few feet ahead, I finally found it—the small leather square wedged in a dense thatch of grass. A wallet.

Sitting on a clump of brush, I wiped my hands on my tank and lifted the wallet by the edges, touching as little surface as possible. A distinguished face looked back at me from a Louisiana driver's license. Jeffrey Klein. I did some quick subtraction and figured his age at thirty-five. An address in New Orleans' Mid-City neighborhood. A Visa and MasterCard peeked from the card slots, and more than fifty dollars in cash was arranged neatly in the center partition. I felt in the enclosed section behind the driver's license window and extracted two additional cards. A Tulane University faculty I.D. identified Jeffrey Klein as a member of the biology faculty. The other was a certification card from the Congress of Elders. Professor Klein was not only a wizard, but a member of the Green Congress. My congress.

Goose bumps spread over my arms as I sat surrounded by the tall reeds, and I froze as the rustling resumed, a dry, crackling noise like wind passing through a field of corn. Except there was no field. No corn. No wind. Even Rene had remarked about it being an unusually still day in Pass a Loutre.

Something touched my shoulder from behind, and I screeched.

"Why are you sitting on the ground, *Jolie*?"

Crap on a freakin' stick. I'd have killed Jean if he hadn't already been technically dead. "It's easier to go into cardiac arrest down here," I snapped, waiting for my heartbeat to return to normal. I had a serious case of the creeps. "What the hell are you doing out here?"

Not covering up evidence that would implicate his buddy Rene, I hoped.

Jean grabbed an arm and hauled me to my feet, raising his eyebrows as I turned to face him. He held his bulky pistol in his right hand. "I was searching for you after hearing the call of a *cocodrie*."

"Holy shit." That grunting noise was an alligator? I needed to go home and have a drink.

Jean frowned. "You should not use such language, *Jolie*. It is not befitting a young woman. And why are you coated with mud? You must avail yourself of a . . ." he frowned as he sought the word he wanted ". . . shower. There is a room in my hotel suite in which water comes from the wall and one may bathe standing up."

Imagine that.

"I fell down," I said. "And I need to get out of this grass. Let's go back to the boat." We'd discuss my foul mouth at a later date, preferably somewhere an alligator wasn't stalking me.

After dropping the wallet into the mud-coated trash bag, I followed Jean back to the water's edge, where I splashed my face and stomped around in the shallows, trying to get the worst of the mud off Rene's boots. My jeans and tank were hopeless. I looked like I'd been mud-wrestling in a WWE title bout, and lost.

Alex emerged from the marsh behind me, carrying his own garbage bag. "Found something else," he said. "Did you scream? What did you—" He stopped when he saw me, then treated me to a slow, thorough appraisal before biting his lower lip.

"I was practically devoured by an alligator," I said. "And if you laugh, I swear I'll turn you into a toad and leave you in the swamp. Don't think I can't do it."

He might suspect I was lying, but he wouldn't risk being wrong.

He cleared his throat. "I didn't say a word."

"Anyway, I found our dead guy's wallet," I said, holding up my bag.

Alex frowned and held up his own bag. "So did I."

9

One pair of pants, a single shirt, one pair of shoes, one dead guy—and two wallets belonging to Green Congress wizards who both taught biology at Tulane. Add them all up, and my headache got a whole lot worse.

Alex and I compared driver's licenses and tried to match one of them to the body. "The face is too messed up to be sure, but the hair looks like Doug Hebert's," Alex said, raising his driver's license higher and studying what was left of the face.

"Yeah, and Jeffrey Klein is only five-nine and a little heavy-set, and this guy looks thinner and taller—how tall was Doug Hebert?"

"Six-even." Alex squinted at the laminated card and growled, sounding a lot like Gandalf, as I'd named his canine alter ego. "You're Green Congress. You don't know either one of these guys?"

I shook my head. "There are at least fifty of us in New

Orleans because of the river and the universities." Greens tended to mainstream as professors or researchers since our strengths were in potions and ritual magic, which had a lot of ties to biology and mathematics and engineering and chemistry. Our abilities made us good environmental researchers and scientists—or risk-management consultants. We're the wizard version of Geeks-R-Us.

"I thought I'd met most of the wizards in town, but I don't know these guys," I said, thinking that if the killer wanted to make the body hard to identify he'd done a good job. "And if this is Doug Hebert, where is Jeffrey Klein?"

"Maybe Jeffrey Klein is the killer," Alex said. "I still don't know for sure if this is a case for the sheriff or the Elders."

"We start with the Elders," I said. "If this is Doug Hebert, any kind of blood or genetic testing in a medical examiner's lab would have scientists lining up to write papers on the freak show, at least if he's a wizard by blood, and I assume he is." Humans with magical abilities—sixth-sensers—could work their way up to witch or minor mage but rarely had the chops to make it into one of the four congresses.

Jean's assertion that I didn't fit into the human world any better than he did popped into my head, and I quickly brushed it aside. So I have a few unusual blood components and an odd DNA strand or two. Big freaking deal. Still didn't put me on the pirate's undead playing field.

"I'm going to call them," I said. "They earn the big bucks."

We rejoined Jean and Rene on the boat. The mer still looked a little peaked. And—what a surprise—he was still pissed off.

"There's somethin' awful down there in that water, wizard," he said before I'd even gotten both feet back on deck. "If you gonna take three days to figure it out, you got to pay me for lost income I'm missin' by not bein' able to hunt while you screw around with your magic spells. And if the wizards want me to play taxi, bringin' you out here again by boat, I want to get paid for that, too."

I was hot. I was dirty. My head ached. Another aquatic bully was not on my wish list.

"Look, Rene, here's the deal." I advanced on him, ready to fight. "We'll solve the water problem as soon as we can. If Denis or one of his clan poisoned it, we'll take care of them. See that dead guy out there? He comes first. If you and your brother try to go around me, you'll be the ones I arrest."

By the time I finished, the mer and I stood nose to nose— well, nose to Adam's apple—and I reached in my pocket for my mojo bag so I could keep his cold, hard anger at bay. The bag was soggy from my adventures in the swamp, but its protective magic still wrapped around me like a soothing blanket.

I edged around him without breaking eye contact. "I have to make a phone call."

Turning my back on him, I walked to the rail and pulled off the shrimp boots. The left one came off with a squishing sound, and I upended it, dumping an inch of water and a golfball-sized clump of mud over the side. Pulling my phone from my backpack, I limped into the wheelhouse in muddy sock feet. We'd probably have to pay to have the deck hosed down as well.

Cell service was spotty out here, but I had no doubt I could press speed dial for the Elders and be talking to someone in authority in a matter of seconds. The big guys could do crap like that.

I was right.

The Speaker of the Elders, Adrian Hoffman, answered with a rich, resonant voice that would have been pleasant if I hadn't known the sharp tongue attached to it. He was fortyish, with skin the color of toffee, a taste for expensive-looking ear jewelry, and a sawed-off shotgun of an attitude. I'd never figured out if he was a real Elder or just a PR flack, but he always answered the Elders' hotline.

I gave Hoffman the highlights on the trip to Pass a Loutre. "Is there any way for you to know if the body we found was Doug Hebert?" I asked. "Or to know where Jeffrey Klein is? Also, we've decided to let the mers go with a tracking charm but I can't promise they won't kill each other before we get the water tests back."

I'd had plenty of sarcastic exchanges with Adrian Hoffman over the last three years, and he'd always made me feel one tiny step short of total idiothood. Which was okay because I thought he was a pompous ass. I tapped my foot and waited for him to verbally abuse the way we'd handled the situation.

Instead, he sighed and uttered a few vague curses. The click of a keyboard echoed from his end of the connection. "Doug Hebert's life force disappeared from our tracking database this morning, so I assume that is whose body you found," he said. "We were in the process of contacting his wife to find out what happened."

More clicking, and another put-upon exhale. "Jeffrey Klein, it would appear, died a half-hour ago."

Crap. "Do you have any way of knowing where he is?" I looked out the front window of the wheelhouse, where Rene and Jean stood talking. Alex had returned to shore and was scouring the area around the body again.

"Unfortunately, no," Hoffman said. "But we'll need to examine Doug Hebert's body. Create a transport and send him to us. 4B, Edinburgh."

Elder Central, in other words.

"What about the mers?"

He muttered something about frying a fileted mer for dinner and eating it with chips. "Question all of them, and make sure Mr. Delachaise and Mr. Villere understand their entire clans will be held accountable for any violence. We'll send the whole bloody lot back to the Beyond if need be."

Yeah, I'd be delivering that message. When I got around to it.

"In the meantime," Hoffman concluded, "we'll have our local enforcer start a search in the area for Jeffrey Klein's body."

"You mean leave Alex out here?" That was a bad idea. I

was about tapped out for the day, magically and physically. Plus, Rene's patience was gone.

"Not the *sentinel* Warin," Hoffman said, assuming his *you're a blithering idiot* tone for the first time. "Jacob Warin, the new enforcer. Chances are the body is in the same vicinity you are in now. And tomorrow, not today. It will soon be getting too dark there to search, will it not?"

"It will." I wished Jake didn't have to come out here and deal with pissed-off mermen and dead wizards. Was he ready for it? I looked over the marsh, the water feeling eerie and malevolent around the dots of land despite the bright sunshine. Somewhere, maybe nearby, Jeffrey Klein had died only thirty minutes ago.

I thought about the fading sense of magical energy I'd felt when we arrived—an energy now gone. We'd been here almost three hours. Had his killer been watching us? Had Jeffrey Klein already been left for dead by the time we arrived? Could we have saved him if we'd thought to look for someone else?

Now I was totally spooked. "What about the dead wizards' families?"

More keyboard clicks. "Douglas Hebert has a wife, but no children," Hoffman said. "She is a mundane, but knew her husband was a wizard. The Elders will notify her, then you and Mr. Alex Warin can talk to her. Dr. Klein was not married and lived alone. Neither wizard was active in the magical community, and had not been for many years. That's about all I can tell you."

While I had Hoffman in a relatively jovial mood, I also filled him in on the tentative territory agreement Rene and Denis had made, contingent on the water problems being resolved.

"What has that mercenary Jean Lafitte's role been? What is he after?" Hoffman asked.

I looked out at Jean, still deep in conversation with Rene. "I think he and Rene Delachaise have some business dealings he doesn't want to see disrupted by a mer war." I decided not to mention the hot Corvette. "If he has another agenda, I haven't figured it out. Well, except he's a nosy SOB. What about paying Rene for the use of his boat and for lost wages? We could rent a boat in Venice if you don't want to pay him."

Hoffman paused; his breath echoed through the phone in huffy snorts. "Bloody extortionist—he knows the investigation will go faster if we use him, plus we can keep an eye on him. Agree to pay him the going day rate for a boat in that area, and not a farthing more."

Yeah, I'd be mentioning the farthing to Rene, too, right after the part where I threatened to exile him to the Beyond.

I ended the call and sat in the wheelhouse, procrastinating. I was exhausted. I knew it was a combination of physical magic and stress, but I'd also seen too much death the last few years. Gerry's death and the revelation that he was my father weighed heavily on me when I didn't lock it away. Sometimes, the sadness leaked out anyway.

My phone chirped to let me know the battery was low, startling me so that I dropped it on the console. My nerves were shot, too.

But I still had a body to dispatch. I left the wheelhouse and pulled my backpack off the winch platform, digging inside for a small jar of unrefined sea salt and retrieving the elven staff. I stared at the salt for a moment, then swapped it for a jar of iron filings. There were a bazillion insects out here, and my transport needed to be super-strong to avoid being broken by a horsefly or a swamp rat. A boar or a gator, I could do nothing about.

Returning to the bank, I filled Alex in on my conversation with Hoffman while trickling a stream of iron from my fingers. The standard symbols for transport consisted of an interlocking circle and triangle, and I created one around Douglas Hebert's body. Making solid lines on the uneven soil proved tricky, so I worked slowly.

I studied the insect-covered treasures off to the side, namely Doug Hebert's excised body parts laid out like gory souvenirs. I would bite off my own nose before I'd pick them up and move them.

Instead, I extended the circle around them, shooing flies away and trying not to breathe too deeply or look too closely.

Touching the elven staff to the transport for an extra kick of energy to complement my own waning powers, I willed magic into the invisible field that arose and quietly spoke the words to send the body to the Elders, along with a mass of teleporting insects. A quick shimmering of air and a few sparks from the end of the staff, and Doug Hebert's body vanished.

Even using the staff for the ritual, my head swam and my arms and legs felt cast in iron. A transport was one of the most energy-draining actions a wizard could take, which is why we didn't do it more often and magically fling ourselves willy-nilly around the globe.

I sloshed back to the boat and didn't protest when Jean leaned over the edge to help me in, still singing the praises of that newfangled shower contraption. Couldn't argue with him. This wizard needed a bath and a nap.

Alex followed me, even letting Jean help him aboard. In today's sea of bad behavior, they'd both remained cool and professional. I hadn't given either of them enough credit.

"You left the transport open?" Alex asked.

I nodded. "If Jake finds Jeffrey Klein's body tomorrow, he can send it back to the Elders without me having to do it. It'll hold for about twenty-four hours unless something big like a gator slides through and breaks the energy field. Worth a try."

If I never visited Pass a Loutre again, it would be okay with me.

10

Jean took the helm on the return trip, delighting in the novelty of a motorized vessel. He looked at home in the wheelhouse, his sharp blue eyes scanning the coast to our right and the open water ahead. I wondered how he must have looked commanding his heavily armed schooners as they crisscrossed the Gulf, looking for Spanish ships to pillage.

Alex had his cell phone plastered to his ear, putting in the formal request to the head of the enforcers for Jake's assistance, so I went to talk to Rene, who was leaning against the rail on the portside aft deck. Maybe I could do a little merman fence-mending.

"I've been thinking about the water problem." I stopped beside him, watching the shoreline slide past. He no longer projected hostility, a positive sign. "It doesn't make sense that either your family or the Villeres would poison the water you want as your hunting grounds."

He turned dark, long-lashed eyes to study me. "We didn't do it, so who else could it be? Somethin' is definitely wrong with that water, babe."

I stared at the changing vegetation—more trees, fewer reeds—as we got closer to civilization. "I don't know. But I promise I'll find out. Just don't do anything crazy till I've had time to find an answer, okay?"

He grunted, probably as close to an agreement as I'd get.

I had a sudden thought. "You say the water contamination seemed stronger today when you swam deeper, right?"

"Yeah, so?"

"That means the contamination is probably coming from the riverbed. Maybe it's something buried in the bottom that keeps sending out poison. It has to be some ongoing thing; otherwise, the poison would already have spread out and be too weak to make anybody sick."

Rene turned and propped against the rail with his back to shore, frowning. "Makes sense, but that don't mean the Villeres didn't do it."

He wasn't going to let go of that idea until I could prove him wrong. "I'll test the water as soon as I get home—it's the only way we'll know." I wondered if the water problem had any connection to the dead wizards or if the deaths, the water contamination, and the mer feud were three separate issues. All it did was make my headache worse.

If mers had populated South Louisiana for centuries, long before the Wizards' War of 1976, how many more were there now? Were there clans we didn't know about, scattered all along the coastal areas? Were all merpeople mainstreamed, or did some still live in the Beyond?

"Were you around during the war?" I asked Rene. Like wizards, mers were long-lived, and I had no idea how old he was. He looked about thirty, but looks meant nothing. Jean Lafitte didn't look much older, and I knew better.

"I was just a kid, but my papa, he had a bad time of it." He paused a long time, eyes seeming to reflect faraway thoughts. "The wizards weren't no friends of ours, of any of the water people."

"Is that why you hate wizards?" Could it be something that old and deep-seated?

His jaw tightened. "I shouldn't have said that. But yeah, that's where most of it started."

"What happened?"

"We ain't talking 'bout this, babe. You want a history lesson, ask your Elders."

We lapsed into silence. The wizards required training in magic via a mentoring system, but Gerry hadn't dwelt much on magical history. I knew the war had begun when a small group of rogue wizards joined forces with Vampyre, Faerie, and a couple of lesser territories in the Beyond and tried to overthrow the wizard gatekeepers. They wanted to pull down the borders between the Now and the Beyond, and they'd almost succeeded. I didn't even realize the water species had been involved.

We finally got back to Venice. While Alex and Rene made plans for a return trip, I called Letitia Newman, a Green

Congress wizard and an old friend I'd seen way too little of the last couple of years. She'd been Gerry's significant other as long as I could remember, even though they'd never married, and I wondered how she'd coped with his loss. I'd avoided her because it just hurt too much. But Tish worked as a water engineer for the port authority. If anyone could help me figure out what was wrong with the water, it would be her.

By the time I left a message on her voice mail, Rene had gone home and Jean and Alex stood beside the passenger door to my Pathfinder, having a metaphorical pissing match to see who'd be riding in front.

Yawning, I threw my keys at Alex. He caught them in mid-air. Good reflexes. "You drive. I'm going to nap. Play nice."

After spreading out a newspaper to keep from leaving a pound of bayou mud all over my backseat, I climbed in and quickly locked the door behind me, just in time to keep Jean from following. I would not be napping with the undead.

Fats Domino began singing from my backpack about the time we reached Belle Chasse. "Walking to New Orleans" had been my ringtone since before Katrina. It seemed especially appropriate today since walking to New Orleans was what Jean would be doing if he didn't stop watching me over the back of the passenger seat. He'd ruined a perfectly good napping opportunity because I was afraid I'd drool or snore, and they'd make fun of me.

I dug the phone out of my pocket and looked at the caller ID. Jake Warin's name brought a smile to the end of a long, stressful day.

The strains of an old BeauSoleil song filled in the background when I answered the phone, which told me he was calling from the Gator.

"Hey there, darlin'. Is this a bad time?"

That soft Mississippi drawl could make sparks fly out my ears. Our conversation Friday night had reminded me of all the things I liked about him. Not that Alex didn't have the same deep drawl, but he never used it to flirt, or at least not with me.

Jean whispered something to Alex and I knew from their stillness they were both eavesdropping.

"Your timing's fine, but my phone's almost out of juice," I said, looking daggers at Jean. "I'm on my way back from Plaquemines Parish with Alex and Jean Lafitte."

"Has Samantha been a busy girl today, twitching her nose and doing magic tricks?"

If only. "Today's show was more like *Bewitched* meets *The Texas Chainsaw Massacre*. And don't call me Samantha—she was a witch, not a wizard."

Jake laughed, and I heard a snort from Alex's side of the front seat. Jean likely had no idea what we were talking about, not having yet discovered late-night sitcom reruns.

"Yeah, I just got my orders to look for a body out there tomorrow so I'll need to get the details."

My heart sank more than it had any right to. He hadn't called for me. He'd called for Alex. "I'm water problem; Alex is murder problem. Hold on, I'll put him on."

"No, wait."

I put the phone back to my ear. "What?"

"If I wanted to talk to my cousin, I would have called him, wouldn't I?" The background music changed to a slow Cajun ballad, a sexy swirl of fiddle and accordion.

I smiled again, and saw Alex raise an eyebrow as he watched me in the rearview mirror. "Yeah, I guess you would have."

"What you doing Wednesday night?"

I had a standing date with a grouchy cat and a DVD, but he didn't need to know that. "You tell me."

He chuckled. "Since we're speaking again, why don't we do something outrageous. Maybe dinner. Some music—Zachary Richard's gonna play a set at the Gator. My first marriage didn't last as long as it's taken us to go on a real date. Talk about foreplay."

"I can do outrageous, and I can definitely do Zachary Richard—well, you know what I mean." I wanted to say I could do foreplay, but knew Alex's head would explode and Jean would want foreplay defined. "What time?"

Jake and I finished making plans. If he was cracking jokes about his failed marriage that began just before his Marine deployment and ended just after his discharge, he must be handling life okay. Alex shouldn't worry about him being an enforcer. He was a Marine. Weren't they always prepared? Or was that the Boy Scouts?

As I ended the call, I glanced at the rearview mirror again and locked gazes with Alex briefly before he turned his attention back to the road. He'd just have to get over it. Jake and I were going to eat dinner at a restaurant and listen to one of my favorite musicians. No big deal.

Around us, ancient live oaks draped with Spanish moss gave way to more suburban clutter, and a burnt-orange sunset eased us toward nightfall. It was only five thirty, but already the shortening days felt like a clock running down and drifting toward winter.

"Your rogue wolf might not have adjusted as well as you hope, *Jolie*," Jean said in a soft voice. "The loup-garou will find it difficult to live here, where his heart is."

"Exactly what I've been telling her," Alex said, flicking his glance to my mirror image again.

What strange bedfellows those two annoying busy-bodies made. I watched the traffic flow around us and ignored them.

"Most of the loup-garou live in the Beyond, right?" Alex asked Jean.

"*Oui*. The legends say the Acadian settlers brought a demon with them, one who appeared as a man unless the full moon shone overhead or he became angered. The loup-garou are larger than your werewolves and do not join packs. Even other werewolves fear them."

I got sucked in despite my determination to pretend I wasn't listening. "Since so many weres are mainstreamed, why do most of the loup-garou live in the Beyond?"

Jean and Alex exchanged a look. "Because their self-control is so bad," Alex said in a flat voice. "They can change in an instant, putting everyone around them in danger."

"Not Jake." He might break my heart but he'd never hurt me physically. I hadn't known him that long or that well, but I was a decent judge of character. "The enforcers wouldn't have let him come back here unless he could handle himself."

"I hope you're right," Alex said, his grim focus on the road ahead. "For all our sakes."

I I

When my front doorbell rang after dinner, I figured it was Alex, ready to do his alpha dog routine and give me hell about embroiling him in the hot Corvette fiasco.

Instead, I opened the door to a pretty brunette in her early fifties, with soft brown eyes, a clear olive complexion, and an ability to strip a person's heart bare with a single look. Tish Newman had been a fixture in my life since childhood, present for all the highs and lows as I grew up with the love of her life. Gerry's death had opened a crevice of pain between us. My fault, not hers.

"I got your message and thought I'd drop by instead of calling," Tish said, hugging me hard.

Unexpected, unshed tears pressed behind my eyes and I pulled away. I didn't want a trip down memory lane right now. Stress and magic had worn me down today, and seeing her ripped the scab off a wound that had festered instead of healed.

"I just closed on a modified shotgun house up on Carondelet." She threw her purse on the coffee table and shrugged off her light jacket. "I can't decide whether to rent it out for the extra income or move into it myself because it's closer to work—and closer to you." She looked around at the double parlors. "You've done some redecorating since I was here last."

I looked around, doing a quick tally. "Yeah, Jean Lafitte shot a hole in that armchair with the fleur-de-lis upholstery and I couldn't replace the fabric. I burned up the ceiling fan and coffee table with the elven staff. I bled all over the old sofa."

Since Alex had lived here briefly after the storm, trying to accordion his bulky frame onto a frilly daybed, I'd also turned the downstairs office into a proper guestroom.

Tish didn't respond, and I turned, expecting to see pity. Instead, she had her teeth firmly clamped together, fighting laughter. She lost the battle, breaking into a bray that made me laugh too. "That's pathetic, DJ."

"Yeah." I smiled at her, unable to shelter my heart by keeping her at a distance. I shouldn't have tried. "I've missed you."

"How are you, really?" Tish asked. "Are you happy about all the changes, or wish things were back like they were before the storm? The relaxed borders will affect the sentinels and enforcers more than anyone else."

I had to think about my answer. I missed the innocence of life before the storm, not just my own innocence but the city's. Before Katrina we all had a deep-seated naïveté that we might have our problems but somehow our foibles would never escalate into a full-out catastrophe. Katrina had been a big eye-opener.

I shrugged. "It is what it is. There's good and bad. Not like we can do anything about it."

She smiled. "Very practical. Very Gerry. You're a lot like him."

I laughed. "So people keep telling me." A comparison to Gerry wasn't necessarily a compliment, although I knew Tish meant it that way. The Elders had viewed him as impulsive and unpredictable, and he'd died in the act of betraying them. I suspected "sins of the father", as much as my gender and non-warrior status, kept them from giving me the job as sole sentinel. Although after today, I had to admit Alex's steady nerves and investigative skills had been impressive.

I pulled out the vials containing the water samples and spread another set of testing jars along my worktable. I conducted meetings at my office, but the real business of magic took place here, on this long mahogany table surrounded by shelves of books and the building blocks of spells and potions.

While Tish unpacked her water-testing supplies, I filled her in on the day's events in Pass a Loutre. "Any ideas on how to do this?"

She picked up one of the vials and poured a few drops into each of three culture dishes. "I'm just going to use a commercial kit for lead and other pollutants, so we can rule them out. There will be some—there always is—but if levels are high enough to make people sick we should be able to tell. The first thing to check for is E. coli. That'll take a while to test—we'll have to put the water samples in a growth culture, see if we can grow a colony."

Ick. "How long will it take?"

"About twenty-four hours, and it has to incubate in the fridge. Forty-eight hours otherwise."

I'd told Rene three days, which was cutting it close. Moldy leftovers were one thing, but I really, really didn't want to incubate an E. coli colony in my refrigerator. "The mers can wait," I said.

She finished setting up her dishes, covered them so Sebastian wouldn't wander into the E. coli forest, and set them on a shelf. "That should do it for normal pollutants— we'll know in a couple of days. I don't have a clue how to detect magical contamination in water, though. We're going to have to figure out how to do that."

We left the worktable and eased into the armchairs near the windows. My house had weathered Katrina well. The high ceilings and soft lamps, the tall windows with their old Victorian crown molding, and the slate hearth in front of the coal-burning fireplace gave the room a solid, secure feeling. Nothing says permanence like an old house that has weathered hurricanes, high tides, and a few wars.

"I'll have to do some research," I said, thinking about how spending another night pawing through magical texts was the last thing I wanted to do. Would I ever get skilled to the point where I'd just know stuff, and not have to pull all-nighters figuring out obscure things like merman lore and magical water contamination? Would Gerry have known what to do?

"You look exhausted," Tish said. "You don't have to do this tonight, do you?"

"I have some mermen ready to kill each other over this, which will bring the Elders in to do damage control, which will piss off the mers in other areas, and then we'll have a big mess on our hands," I said. Plus, it would make me look like a doofus. "So, no, it can't wait. If there really is a problem with the water, there are lots of humans who hunt and fish in that area. What if the food fish are being poisoned?"

She nodded. "Not to mention a couple of dead guys that this Denis Villere or Rene Delachaise might or might not have killed."

"Not to mention them," I said. "I can see Rene and Denis killing each other with the flick of a fin. But why would either one go after a college professor? And Doug Hebert wasn't just killed. He was mutilated, so it was personal. Maybe it was just a coincidence that Denis showed up when he did."

"Doug Hebert was the one killed?" Tish frowned. "I know him. Well, I know who he is. We worked together for a few months when we were young, but I haven't seen him in years." She shook her head. "I didn't realize he was the victim. Who was the other one?"

I grabbed my notebook off the table and flipped through it. "Jeffrey Klein. Also a Tulane prof."

Tish paled. "I knew him too, or I did a long time ago. We all worked for the Elders after the war in '76 but lost touch after that. They were both really mainstreamed. Last I heard they were doing wetlands research, working on some big federal project to try and stop the land loss. They'd had nothing to do with the active wizarding community for years, as far as I know."

So our professors were doing wetlands research and had been murdered in the wetlands, or at least one of them had. Where Jeff Klein died was still a question mark. Had they stumbled across something they shouldn't have?

"What did Green Congress wizards do in the war?" I asked. "I thought Red Congress saw all the action—they're the fighters."

"We were all young and wanted to be involved, so the Elders gave us odd jobs that didn't require a lot of physical magic," Tish said. "Nothing serious or dangerous. I had to check the trackers every day and keep a list of what wizards were in town and where they were going. New Orleans wasn't very involved—most of the power struggles happened in Europe."

The feeling of Rene's anger and Denis's outright hatred came back to me. "Changing the subject, do you know anything that happened during the war to make the mers hate wizards so much?"

Tish laughed. "DJ, every prete group hates wizards. We're the biggest group, we have more powers, and we can mainstream easily. The mers aren't alone, although . . ." Her brow furrowed in thought. "You know, a lot of the water species were put in kind of detention camps while the postwar treaties were being sorted out. Stripped of their territory, forced to live in a defined space. The mers were probably part of that."

Maybe Rene and Robert's father had been one of the mers locked up and stripped of his land. That would certainly be enough to make them hate wizards, especially for Cajun mers who'd already been through it when they'd been forced to leave Acadia.

I filed it away to research later, when I didn't have more urgent things to figure out. "Okay, back to testing water for magical contamination." I returned to the worktable and picked up one of the Pass a Loutre samples we hadn't yet used for testing. "If I can detect magical energy on the surface of things, I wonder if I could detect it in water?"

Tish joined me at the table. "It's worth a try—that's one of those stray elven skills your gene pool handed you. I can't think of a potion or charm that would work in water."

I looked around the room and, sure enough, Charlie sat propped against the doorjamb. I went over and grabbed it, bringing it back to the table.

"I swear that thing was downstairs when I got here," Tish said, reaching out to touch it. The staff, under her hand, was an inert stick of wood. "Is it still following you around?"

"I usually have to think about it for it to show up now." I brushed my fingers along the raised sigils, and it glowed slightly. When I first found it, the thing followed me indiscriminately. Maybe my charm was wearing off.

"Sorry, DJ, but that's just creepy."

I smiled. I used to think so. Now, Charlie was sort of like the affectionate pet Sebastian would never be. I'd had a great dog for a while, but it turned out to be Alex. So I was reduced to having a stick of elven wood for a pet. Talk about pathetic.

I took a soft cloth from a drawer beneath the table and polished the wood to a warm sheen. "I'm going to try it using the staff. If I waste all the water, our diving merman's going to get some more samples tomorrow anyway."

Tish settled back in her chair to watch as I poured a palmful of the water from Pass a Loutre into my left hand and grasped the elven staff in my right. I closed my eyes and went through the process I'd used earlier in the day, sorting through sounds and senses.

I should have tried meditation using the staff earlier. It amplified everything, clarified the sensory inputs, and helped me release them so I could focus on the energy in the room. Riding above the warm buzz of Tish's wizard energy were the faint traces of two other powers coming off the water in my hand. The first one, which didn't surprise me, was the cold, hard buzz of a mer; the other, once I isolated it, clogged my lungs and sped my heart rate, a dense and pulsating sensation I'd never encountered. I dropped the staff, wanting to be rid of its power before the sensations suffocated me.

"What happened?" Tish had stood up and crossed the room without my realizing it. For a few seconds, I'd been lost in the sensations.

Holy crap. Rene was right. Something awful was in that water.

Tish and I batted theories around for an hour but still had no idea what my great discovery meant. Only that whatever was contaminating the water, it wasn't E. coli.

About eight, Tish left with tentative plans to join tomorrow's scouting party to Pass a Loutre. I also called Alex and asked him to go so I could stay home and wrestle with the water problem. I didn't know if Jake was ready to deal with the weirdness we'd encountered today without help and, judging by how quickly Alex agreed to go, I suspected he thought the same thing. Jake would hate it if he knew we were trying to protect him, so he'd just have to never know.

I collapsed on the sofa in my upstairs sitting room, trying to unwind. On TV, chef Bobby Flay was in Kitchen Stadium concocting five courses from a rare species of fish. I felt like I'd had five courses of merman today, and it was a serious overdose. Sebastian sat next to me, giving me the Siamese cross-eyed stare of death until I put a nibble or two of my ice cream on the carton lid for him.

My thoughts raced around the water problem. The fact that I felt mer energy in the sample didn't really implicate any of them. It could have been residual aura from Rene diving for the water samples. I needed to find out what that other energy was.

Maybe it would help to have someone from another species collect the samples tomorrow. Then if the mer energy was still present, it would move them higher on the suspect list.

I set the ice cream on the coffee table and went to my library for my laptop. I called up the rudimentary database the Elders had sent, giving contact information for the heads of prete groups that had formally settled into the area—or at least the ones they knew about. It was a short list. The Realm of Vampyre had a Regent who'd set up shop in the Quarter, running a tour business. The weregators had a representative in Iberia Parish, the area from which the Villere clan had moved. Neither the fae nor the elves—the other major prete groups—appeared to have moved outside the Beyond.

I paused over the next-to-last name on the list. Interesting. The official representative for the merpeople was Toussaint Delachaise, with an address in Chenoire, St. Bernard Parish, just northeast of New Orleans. Delachaise wasn't that common a name, even in these parts, so it looked like Rene and Robert were well connected. Was it their father?

The final name on the list was the one I was looking for, but I winced when I saw it. The Greater Mississippi River Nymphs was headed by someone named Blueberry Muffin. Really? A prete who doesn't understand humans enough to pick an unsuspicious name is probably going to fail at mainstreaming. I didn't hold out much hope for the nymphs.

I got my cell and punched in the number. Did I call her Blue? Berry? Muffin?

Turned out to be a non-issue. The woman who answered the phone identified herself as Libby. "Muffi isn't here right now," she said, her voice husky and sultry and designed to make a guy roll over and beg. Then again, she was a nymph. How else should she sound?

"I need to hire a diver." I introduced myself and launched into what I hoped was a not-too-revealing but still coherent explanation of the river problem—excluding anything to do with dead wizards or merman suspects. "I know it's short notice, but we really need someone to go with us to Plaquemines Parish tomorrow. Do you think Muffi will be back by then?"

"Who else will be going?" Libby asked. "I'm sure Muffi will want to know."

I wondered how nymphs got along with other species. "Uh, we'll have a wizard, a werewolf, a shapeshifter, and a merman," I said. Come to think of it, that assortment would scare me away. At least the undead pirate wouldn't be along this time.

"I'll handle it, sweetie. Just tell me where and when, and we'll have someone there," Libby purred. "Because we just *love* fur and fins."

12

I returned from my jog a little before six a.m., craving coffee and a shower, maybe at the same time. Alex had begged off running this morning since he'd stayed up late getting Jake prepped for his first official enforcer assignment, so I was surprised to walk in my back door and find him sitting at my kitchen table in his jeans and a black T-shirt. He was drinking the coffee I'd put on before I left and doing what looked suspiciously like paperwork for the Elders. The work had him so engrossed he didn't look up.

I poured myself a cup of Kahlua-flavored roast and settled into the seat opposite him. "Is that what I think it is?" The Elders loved reports. Early in our partnership, I'd tried to out-report Alex, but it didn't last long: He was all about following the rules and I was all about procrastination.

"Yeah, figured I might as well do it while—" He blinked at me. "Have you been running? I thought you were still asleep." The fact I'd just come from outside at the ass-crack of dawn wearing shorts, Nikes, and a T-shirt finally made it past his obsessive alpha brain waves. "I figured you'd back out when I said I wasn't going."

"Don't flatter yourself." I liked running now that I was used to it, but I'd never admit it. "I just woke up early."

He smiled at me. Alex was a serious guy, but when he smiled he looked like a kid. A really big, sexy kid. "I knew it. You like it. You should alternate it with weights. I can pick out some starter hand-weights for you."

Yeah, that was happening. I closed my eyes as the hot, sweet coffee spread healing caffeine through my system. "I will never lift weights. I don't need to lift weights."

Alex scanned my body with a clinical detachment I found alarming. "It'll be great for your upper body strength. Let me see your biceps. I bet you have no muscle tone."

I reached in the corner behind me, picked up the elven staff, and pointed it at him. "I have enough to lift this, hound."

I settled back in my chair, laying the staff on the table. "Oh, by the way, a representative from the Greater Mississippi River Nymphs, possibly someone named either Libby or Blueberry Muffin, will meet you at the office at noon to dive for water samples. Tish Newman is going too."

After Alex and I talked to Doug Hebert's widow, I planned to lock myself in my library and figure out what was wrong with the water. Somehow.

Alex sipped his coffee and tried to keep a serious look on his face, but lost. "A nymph named Blueberry Muffin is going? Makes me *hungry*." He put a little growl in his voice for emphasis.

I laughed. "Stop being such a guy. Just make sure she dives for some water samples without the mers being in the water. After that, I don't want to know what you do with her." Well, actually, I could get every sordid detail from Tish, although the idea Alex might engage in any nymph-scapades made me extremely grumpy.

"Jean Lafitte's not going, is he?" Alex sifted through papers as though the answer didn't matter, but I hadn't done my grounding ritual this morning and got a sense of uneasiness wafting from him. Normally, Alex was unreadable.

"No, Jean's out of the picture unless we have problems with the mers. Why?" I couldn't interpret Alex's expression, but thought it looked kind of nervous. He and Jean had coexisted well yesterday once we were past the Corvette issue, but nothing about Jean had ever made Alex nervous. Homicidal, maybe.

"I just asked because I didn't want to be party to another felony. I do have friends on the NOPD." Alex got up and poured the rest of his coffee into the sink, but stayed at the kitchen window, his back to me. "Remember I said you owed me for not turning him in for auto theft?"

Uh-oh. "I thought you were being hypothetical."

"Hypothetically, then, I'll consider us even after next Saturday." He still had his back to me.

I felt my own nerves skittering. That was a week from

yesterday. "Hypothetically, what might be happening then?"

"My mom's birthday dinner. She's expecting my girlfriend to come with me."

Alex didn't have a girlfriend unless Leyla had been promoted. Oh, God. I knew where this was going. "And who might that imaginary girlfriend be?"

He cleared his throat. "You know, the one I've been seeing since Katrina. The one who works for the FBI, that I met on a case. The one named DJ."

I banged my head on the table. Alex and I had posed as a couple after Katrina. It had been easier to explain than the whole *Tracking-Down-a-Rogue-Voodoo-God* thing. Word had eventually filtered back to Mama. But that was three freakin' years ago.

It took all my resolve to keep my voice calm and not lob my coffee cup at his head. "Why is she expecting your girl-friend DJ to come to her birthday dinner?"

Alex sighed and flopped back into the kitchen chair. "Because I never told her we weren't really a couple?"

I stared at him, trying to understand how this big hulk of a man who collected weaponry with such relish was afraid of his mother. The woman had to be a class A harpy. A harpy who thought I'd been dating her baby boy for a long, long time. Just kill me now.

"We will not be even after this," I told him. "You'll owe me. This is much bigger than covering up a felony." Plus, I could always come down with a last-minute illness. Come to think of it, I felt feverish already.

Relief washed over Alex's face. "You're right. I'll owe you big-time."

For someone who hadn't had a date since the Stone Age, my dance card was looking full between my evening with Jake, Norma Warin's birthday party, and my dinner date with Jean Lafitte. I couldn't help but reflect on the fact that none of the three guys was human, or even a wizard. Maybe I'd make like a nymph and start collecting species. Rene and Robert were handsome in a volatile, semi-hostile kind of way.

Of course they could also be wizard killers.

I left Alex to finish his paperwork and went upstairs to shower and dress for my new job. What does an investigator wear? As a deputy sentinel, my usual uniform had been jeans and a sweater or T-shirt. But it seemed that if I were going to interview witnesses and such, my look should say "professional" and not "Café du Monde".

I stared into my closet. Nothing says serious like a suit, and I had one. Only one. I needed to go shopping for a more professional wardrobe.

I took a shower, tugged a fitted gray jacket over a black tank, and shimmied into the black pencil skirt I'd worn to meet Jean Lafitte. Low black pumps raised me all the way up to five-six. I dabbed on a little makeup, wrangled my unruly hair into a loose twist, and I was set.

Since a wizard murderer was on the loose, I stuck the elven staff in my oversized bag, along with more vials for the nymph to collect water samples.

Alex, who'd added a sports coat to his enforcer ensemble in a nod toward dressing up, gave me a crash course in inter-rogation on the way to the Heberts' house in Metairie. I'd never admit it, but ever since I'd learned our job as sentinels was expanding to involve prete investigations, I'd been obses-sively watching old reruns of *Law & Order*.

"I'll do most of the talking," Alex said. "But don't be afraid to ask Melinda Hebert questions—trust your instincts."

My instincts told me to stay home and let him handle it. "So, will we play good cop/bad cop? I want to be the bad cop. I'm not the warm, nurturing type."

He cocked an eyebrow at me. "Really?"

Jerk. "So, what should I do?"

"Stop watching cop shows, for one thing. Look, Melinda Hebert's going to be raw—her husband just died and all she knows is what Elder Zrakovi told her when he transported over to give her the news last night."

At least Zrakovi told her and not Adrian Hoffman, who I suspected had the compassion of a fruit fly. Why that man had the job of being the public face of the Elders, I'd never understand.

Doug's file had held very little information about his wife. "She's a human, so I should be able to read her emotions," I said. "But Doug wasn't a practicing wizard. He never formally gave his magic up, but he wasn't active. I don't know how much she'll know about anything wizard-related."

Alex nodded. "Except we don't know for sure his death is wizard-related. Maybe he had enemies at Tulane."

I huffed. "Get real. College professors make formal complaints to the faculty ombudsman, and bitch and moan to their department chairs. They don't slit their colleagues' throats and carve off body parts." University politics were brutal, but leaned more toward psychological mutilation and career sabotage.

"All I'm saying is to keep an open mind," he said. "Listen to anything she says that doesn't ring true, even things she doesn't think are important. People usually know more than they think, even if it's a new habit or quirk. Just make conversation."

"I can do that." I stared out the window at the glut of traffic as we left Uptown and eased into Mid-City. "Think Jake's ready to take on some merman and nymph weirdness today?"

Alex paused before answering. "We'll see. I just hope he can hold it together. Your buddy Jean was right about the loup-garou. I've never seen one that could maintain control under stress. Four out of every five weres I've had to put down as an enforcer have been loup-garou."

Put down. Alex had killed loup-garou. No wonder he was freaked. "Jake's a Marine. They do all that mental toughness training, right? It should give him an advantage."

Alex took his eyes off the road long enough to give me a measured look. "I wasn't kidding about you not being alone with him, DJ. Whatever you guys do Wednesday night, keep it public."

I bit back a smartass comment. Jake was a subject best

left alone, at least until after Wednesday night. If whatever spark we'd had before the loup-garou attack was gone, the need to argue about it evaporated. We might have dinner, make small talk, listen to music, and decide that's all there was. Besides, I wasn't talking to Alex about anything Jake and I might or might not do in private.

I stared out at the buildings of Mid-City as we headed toward the I-10. The devastation to this part of town had been one of the biggest shocks to me when I'd come back to New Orleans after Katrina. The news had somewhat prepared me for the Lower Ninth Ward and even Lakeview. But not Mid-City. It's the place I still have nightmares about, all the houses leaning from the winds and marked by ugly brown bathtub rings that recorded the flood levels. Now, the water marks were gone, and so were a lot of the old buildings. Some new ones had sprung up in their places, others had been raised on high piers, and still others had been replaced by weed-infested vacant lots.

We drove into the suburb-on-steroids that was Metairie, turning in to a neighborhood of small, neat wood-framed houses. At the corner of Iris and Tomkins, we parked and got out at a tidy white house with a screened-in porch. It had the solid, square look of the 1930s, before brick took over and ranch-style houses sprouted on every street.

Alex stopped the car in front, and I opened the Mercedes door. I sat there, frozen, trying to decide how to get out. My narrow skirt hemmed in my legs like I'd been mummified. I'd managed to get in the car with some measure of dignity, but exiting was a different matter. My friend Eugenie had talked me into buying this skirt, but she hadn't given me lessons on getting in and out of cars in mixed company.

Finally, I grabbed the hem of the skirt, hiked it to mid-thigh, and swung my legs out. Once I was on my feet, I tugged it back down and turned to catch up with Alex. I'd assumed he was already at the Heberts' front door, but he was sitting in the car, watching me.

I leaned down and looked in at him. "What's the problem?" If he was laughing at me, I'd kick him with one of my pointy heels.

His expression was unreadable. "You should wear that skirt more often. It's hot."

A couple of seconds ticked by as I waited for the punch-line, but he just pulled his keys from the ignition and got out. I tried to dip a finger into his emotional pool; his mind was locked tight. We kept our relationship on the level of fourth-grade banter. That hadn't felt like banter.

Alex and I had admitted to a mutual attraction early in our partnership, but I wasn't sure how to feel about him actually verbalizing it. I followed him silently to the entrance of the Hebert home.

The door, painted dark blue to match the house's shutters, opened before we got there. Melinda Hebert met us with red-rimmed, puffy eyes. Under different circumstances she'd have been extraordinary—tall, with dark copper hair and a complexion perfect enough to advertise skin-care products.

Today, though, her hair hung lank, and a shapeless Tulane sweatshirt and jeans enveloped her. A pretty, marquis-cut green stone that looked like peridot hung on a silver chain around her neck, her only adornment.

Alex introduced himself and flashed his FBI badge. I had my Green Congress sentinel and FBI consultant badges with me but both of us flashing badges seemed overkill. This was his gig. I stayed behind him and kept my mouth shut.

Melinda Hebert frowned. "FBI?" She stared at Alex and gave me a questioning look, then shook her head. "I expected the NOPD."

Alex nodded. "We help them out on cases when there's an overload, and they're shorthanded right now," he said. Smooth. The man could lie like a politician the week before election day.

Melinda Hebert stared at the floor, her expression vacant.

Alex cleared his throat. "Mrs. Hebert, could we come in for a few minutes?"

She looked startled at her breach of Southern etiquette and alarmed when Alex introduced me as the region's sentinel. "One of the wizards was here last night," she said, wide eyes scouring my face, looking for . . . what? "Doug wasn't involved with the wizards anymore, but he said that was okay. Is"—she swallowed hard—"*was* he in trouble?"

"No, ma'am, it's just a formality," I said. The cops on *L&O* always said *ma'am* and *sir* to the people they interrogated. I smiled, trying to put her at ease, but I had to wonder why she'd think her husband could be in trouble with the wizards. Was he up to something he didn't think they'd approve of?

Maybe she was almost in shock. Wives of college professors, even non-practicing wizard professors, didn't expect this kind of violence to impact their lives. I hoped to God Elder Zrakovi hadn't told her too many details about her husband's death, especially about the mutilation, and wondered how they'd manage the burial. Glad funeral arrangements weren't on my list of duties. At least not yet.

Melinda led us into the family living room. Magazines lay in an orderly stack on the coffee table, and the furniture smelled of wood cleaner and wax. Shiny hardwood floors reflected the sunlight filtering in through open windows adorned with white plantation shutters. The room was magazine-picture-perfect, and just as sterile. I liked my drafty old Victorian with its uneven floors and patina of age.

The faint buzz of Green Congress magic permeated the room, even came off Melinda when I shook her hand. Residual magic from a non-practitioner who'd been gone at least twenty-four hours shouldn't have been this strong, but maybe after a person had spent a lot of time with a person or place it lingered.

"How long have you and Doug lived here?" I asked Melinda. Alex sat on the white leather sofa, notebook in hand, and Melinda perched as far from him as she could get and still be in the same zip code. I took an adjacent armchair covered in a soft aquatic pattern of blues and greens—ironic, given her husband's wetlands research.

She twisted her hands in her lap. "We've lived here almost ten years," she said, darting her eyes from coffee table to desk to potted plant. "Is something wrong?"

She was seriously paranoid. "Nothing wrong," I assured her. "I can sense magic here, which is odd since Doug wasn't practicing." I looked around the room. "Did he do any spells or work a charm on anything in the house recently?"

After a pause, Melinda pointed toward the back of the house, to a room through whose door I glimpsed a refrigerator. "He fixed half the appliances in there using charms," she said with a wan smile. "He always said there was no point paying repairmen when he could do it." She sniffled. "He liked to tinker with things."

Alex lifted his eyebrows in question. I shook my head. I'd never known magical energy to hang around a place long, but then again, I didn't use magic for home repair. Physical magic took a huge energy toll, especially on wizards outside the Red Congress, so to me it wasn't worth the trouble. Not implausible, though.

"When will I be able to see Doug's . . ." Melinda choked on her words, her breath coming in short, shallow bursts. "When will I be able to see him? It won't seem real until I see him."

Alex and I exchanged glances again. I'm sure I looked like a deer facing an oncoming eighteen-wheeler. He looked like the big rig had already run him down. Melinda really didn't need to see what was left of her husband. Besides, I'd zapped his body to Edinburgh.

"He's still in the medical examiner's hands, Mrs. Hebert," Alex said in a practiced, reassuring tone. "We'll let you know."

Again, very smooth. I needed to practice lying. I wasn't good at it.

Alex moved ahead before she could ask more questions. "Do you know what your husband was doing early yesterday? Did he get any phone calls? Talk to anyone?"

"He and another professor, Jeff Klein, had an early-morning meeting with someone yesterday but I don't know who," she said.

The Elders said Doug died several hours before we found him in Pass a Loutre, and the mutilations had taken place before the mortal knife wound. The thought of it made me want to lock my doors and vow hermit-hood. Doug had to know his killer, or at least be connected. That kind of torture was personal.

Melinda rubbed her eyes and got up, retrieving an appointment book from the desk. "When the wizards called me, I was already worried because Doug hadn't come home." Her voice trailed off and she began to cry. I automatically fingered the mojo bag in my pocket. I'd done a good grounding ritual before we left so I hadn't picked up any emotion from her so far. I didn't want to start.

"The wizards told me Jeff was missing, too?" She looked at Alex for confirmation.

"Yes, ma'am." Obviously, Zrakovi hadn't told her Jeff was dead, so Alex didn't either.

She flipped the appointment book open and a photograph fell out, landing on the floor near my foot. A happy couple looked up at me. Doug and Melinda wore hiking boots and shorts, and stood in front of a fall view of mountains covered with orange- and gold-leafed trees. Doug was handsome and smiling, a far cry from the ruined man I'd seen on the bank of the bayou at Pass a Loutre.

I wished I hadn't seen the photo, hadn't been forced to put a whole face with that mutilation. It made him more real.

Melinda took the photo from me with shaking hands, and I lowered my empathic shields a bit to see if she was going into shock and needed medical help.

I waited for the onslaught of her emotions—and waited, and waited. Nothing. I couldn't pick up any feelings at all. I tried to puzzle it out as Alex continued to talk.

"What do you know about this meeting Doug was supposed to have?" he asked, reaching for the appointment book and bringing Melinda's attention back to him. "Did he set it up, or did Dr. Klein?"

She shook her head. "Doug got a call from someone night before last on his cell phone. He was all pumped about it and called Jeff. He said they were going to meet with one of the new species that had come in after Katrina. I didn't think it was that important."

Tears slid down her cheeks. "He was so excited, but I was tired. I wanted him to help me do some stuff around the house but all he cared about was work, especially since the hurricane changed so many things. Maybe if I'd taken a bigger interest . . ."

Alex handed her a box of tissues from the corner of the end table, and I dropped my emotional barricade altogether, flummoxed. From Alex, I got flashes of tension; he hated doing this. From Melinda, nothing. She was crying, so I should be pulling in all kinds of grief and sadness.

I needed an excuse to touch her, but feared if I grabbed her arm the poor woman would collapse.

Alex continued with his questions, unaware of my empathic dilemma. "What type of research did your husband do?"

"Water quality, and he was working on a couple of National Science Foundation projects on wetlands preservation with Jeff," she said, dabbing at her eyes. She tightened her jaw, swallowing down the hurt.

I recognized the gesture. I'd done it a lot myself the last few years, especially right after Gerry died. I could also have told her swallowing pain doesn't make the loss hurt any less or go away any faster. Nothing did.

"He was excited about all the new preternatural species being allowed in." Melinda dismantled the tissue into tiny shreds. "I wanted him to leave it alone."

The Heberts' marriage sounded less than perfect. "Do you remember him mentioning any particular species?" I asked. "Merpeople, for example? Nymphs or nixes or naiads?" I touched her arm as I spoke, a soft gesture, non-threatening.

Absolutely nothing hit my emotional radar. I'd never had a human read blank before when I was actively trying to read her.

She stared at me as if I had materialized from an alien planet and begun speaking Martian. "I don't know about any of those things," she said slowly, looking down at my hand on her arm. I pulled it away. "Magic just . . . didn't factor into our lives much. He'd talked more about it the last few weeks, because of all the changes."

We stayed a while longer, but other than Doug Hebert's planned meeting with Jeff Klein and an unidentified prete, there wasn't much to go on.

"Do you have some family we could call, someone who could stay with you?" I asked. Despite her emotional void, she seemed too fragile to leave alone, her movements jerky, skin paled almost to translucence.

"I . . . I don't know how to reach my family anymore." Her voice trailed off, disconnected. "I'll be okay."

I looked at Alex, and he shrugged. What else could we do?

Back in the car, Alex called his and Jake's friend Ken Hachette. Ken was a former Marine from Jake's unit, former co-owner of the Green Gator, and, more relevant to our current problems, an NOPD homicide detective who might be willing to do a favor for Jake's cousin, no questions asked.

Alex had gotten Doug Hebert's cell number from Melinda, and Ken agreed to run a check on his incoming and outgoing calls. The phone itself had probably sunk into the marshes of Pass a Loutre.

I fixated on Melinda's emotional readings—or lack thereof. Her grief seemed genuine, but why couldn't I read her? It bothered me but I didn't have anyone to ask about it. Empathy was nonexistent among wizards, and I couldn't exactly call up an elf. If she weren't human, the Elders should have known. And human or not, I should get some kind of energy from her. The whole conundrum gave me a headache.

"Isn't the significant other usually the prime suspect in a murder?" I asked Alex, who was muttering curses at the glut of traffic on Veterans Boulevard. After all, Doug Hebert's ring finger had been hacked off.

"You watch too much TV," he said, then looked at me with a whisper of a smile. "Usually, though, yeah. We weren't going to get anything out of her today. I didn't pick up any clues that their marital problems went that deep. Sounded like the usual tension between a stay-at-home wife and a husband married to his job."

Massaging my achy temples, I longed for the days before Katrina, when I could have just sent all the mers back into the Beyond and any murders would automatically be the purview of the Elders or local law enforcement.

Alex and I stewed in our respective thoughts until we got on the route through Mid-City. He stopped at Liuzza's to pick up po'boys, which gave me a chance to make a phone call. The connection with Adrian Hoffman, everybody's favorite wizard mouthpiece, was instantaneous.

"Yes, Ms. Jaco?" His voice bristled with annoyance. What else was new?

"Is there any way Doug Hebert's widow isn't human?" I explained about the emotions, or my inability to read them.

He might be in Edinburgh and I in New Orleans, but his sarcasm traveled through the ether just fine. "Did it ever occur to you that perhaps your all-powerful empathic abilities just didn't work?"

"No, it didn't." Asshat. "My empathic abilities always work on humans, and I can usually read at least some kind of energy off non-humans."

Since empathy was an elven trait, the Elders, in their infinite arrogance, thought it irrelevant.

I finally got Hoffman to say he'd look into Melinda Hebert's background more closely, and snapped the phone shut. The bureaucratic tangles of the Washington, D.C., political machine had nothing on the Elders. *Obfuscate and Intimidate*: that should be their motto. It should be printed on our badges.

We ate in the car, then met Tish and Jake in the parking lot on Tchoupitoulas at noon. Jake and Alex huddled next to the Pathfinder, talking strategy—namely, how to find Doug Hebert's cell phone, look for Jeff Klein's body, keep the nymph on task, and not piss off the mermen.

I'd exchanged keys with Alex so he could drive to Plaquemines in my SUV again. He didn't want people tracking swamp mud into his Mercedes, and Jake's pickup didn't have room for Alex, Tish, and the nymph.

Even at noon on a Sunday, the strip mall parking lot was full, and Tish and I studied every woman who strolled past, looking for signs of nymphomania.

"Uh-oh," she said. "Tramp alert, due north."

I followed her gaze to the end of the parking lot, where a tall woman in a short white skirt walked toward us. Not walked. *Walked* was like calling the Pope *some religious dude*. She swayed, swerved, virtually glided. If her hips twisted any more she'd be moving backward. Wavy dark red hair, almost burgundy, cascaded over her shoulders, her white tube top, and halfway down her back. She was barefoot, curvaceous, impervious to the midday sun, and oozing slutty sex appeal. She smiled and waved to the guys, who'd fallen silent to watch her approach.

"Nymph," I hissed. I already felt inadequate. Make that short, dumpy, and inadequate.

"Look at them." Tish nodded toward Alex and Jake. It would take a spatula to scrape their wagging tongues off the pavement.

The nymph stopped next to the guys. She was at least five-eleven and could look Jake square in his glazed-over amber eyes. Alex watched her too, but he wasn't giving her a goofy guy-face like Jake, which was odd. Maybe she wasn't his type.

"Good luck," I told Tish. "They may need a chaperone. Make sure she actually gets the water samples we need."

The nymph ran a set of red manicured nails down Alex's arm, leaving him frowning after her as she turned and headed toward Tish and me.

"Which of you is the wizard I spoke to on the phone?" Her voice was low and husky, laced with an exotic accent and guaranteed to make a guy think about doing bad things in the dark. I'd recognize it anywhere.

I looked up into her green eyes. She had at least five inches on me, even taking my heels into account. "That's me—you're Libby, right?"

"That's right." She smiled, and her aura wrapped around me like a warm blanket. Probably a nymph thing. "I see the fur is here." She looked back, caught Jake's gaze, and licked her lips. "I've always wanted to taste loup-garou. What fun."

I poked Tish as soon as Libby swiveled off to ogle Jake up close. "Make sure she sits in the backseat and keeps her claws to herself. Alex doesn't seem interested, but Jake's out of his league."

13

Two vials sat undisturbed on my worktable, one full of river water, the other empty. I sat in the armchair in the corner, surrounded by discarded grimoires and common spellbooks. Sebastian reclined on the mantel, licking sugar off his paws after upending a kitchen canister. He'd left a trail of white granules through every room of the house.

I was stumped. I'd tried a regression charm on the water to see if I could track where its components had come from, and it hadn't worked.

I'd tried hydromancy, and got a crystal-clear image of Pass a Loutre, complete with the *Dieu de la Mer* and a topless Libby sunbathing on the aft deck with both Rene and Robert at her side. Who the hell was collecting water samples—Jake and Alex?

I'd tried a dissolution charm to break down the water samples, hoping one element would be unusual enough to give me a clue. No dice.

Sebastian leapt from the mantel to the worktable, missing the vials but knocking the elven staff off with a heavy thud. Yowling, he followed the staff to the floor and tried to bat it around. It rolled toward me, and I snatched it up before he tried to use it as a scratching post and zapped himself into Elfheim. Honestly, why people kept feline pets was beyond me. They won't fetch. They won't do tricks. They are only good company when they want something and feel the need to suck up.

I held up the staff, studying it and pondering the elven abilities I'd inherited from my nebulous double line of genetic material. Gerry had given me the ability to communicate through dreams on occasion, although I rarely had reason to use it. The empathy, and the ability to feel and identify magical energy, must have come from my mother's side of the elven gene pool, but she'd given up her magic about the time I was born and had died when I was six. So I'd never know.

None of those skills seemed to have any use in identifying the water contamination, but what if there were other elven things I could do—things I didn't know about? Maybe I was approaching the problem from the wrong direction.

Gerry had been fascinated by his elven heritage, and he'd collected not only the staff but all kinds of books on elven magic. I scanned the titles on the shelves, pulling out a worn, leatherbound volume with no title. It was in a mismatched cluster of books Gerry had called black grimoires. He'd picked most of them up in back-alley shops in Europe before he'd been assigned to New Orleans. Some black grimoires contained spells of black magic, but others simply contained unapproved magic. Magic, in other words, the Elders didn't understand and therefore didn't sanction. I remembered this one as being elven in origin.

It was almost three p.m., and illegal elven magic goes down better with chocolate, so I went downstairs and settled in on the sofa with a candy bar, a soda, and my book of illegal spells.

I read a lot about nasty-sounding mental magic that elves could do to others, and ways for them to keep wizards' magic from working on them. There were truth enchantments and allures that would obliterate someone's force of will. No wonder the elves scared the hell out of everybody.

The only consolation was that they thought themselves entirely too lofty to fool with other pretes so they kept to themselves in Elfheim. Or so I'd heard. Other than Elder Zrakovi, I'd never even met anyone who'd seen an elf.

I finally came across something that might work: an origination allure. I had the basic ingredients—it was assembled like a wizard's potion but could only be enacted with elven power. Maybe the staff would give my magic enough of an elven spin to work. It was worth a try. Time could be short before someone got seriously ill or the Delachaise-Villere war broke out.

I went upstairs and made sure Sebastian was out of the room before I closed the door—I'd learned the hard way, after he took a sip of the bespelled holy water I used for scrying and had gone on a hallucinogenic kitty trip, that it was best he stay away from magic.

Propping the grimoire on a bookstand, I began assembling ingredients. It was a complex spell, with pinches of botanicals added at different temperatures as the solution heated. I pulled my portable induction range from the storage area beneath the table and plugged it in. Most wizards' potions that had to be cooked could be done in a microwave, but I was afraid to try it with the elven magic. If the staff was any indication, it was too powerful. Blowing up my house would be counterproductive.

I collected more than two dozen ingredients and began assembling them in a heavy cast-iron pan over the burner, using the remaining Pass a Loutre water samples as my base. By the time I'd raised and lowered the temperature and added pinches of this and bits of that for what seemed like an hour, I thought it was ready.

Retrieving Charlie from the sofa, I returned to the worktable. Should I point the staff at the solution and will a bit of energy into it, or stick the end of the staff in the solution? Would a vision appear above the bowl, or inside the liquid mixture?

"Okay, Charlie," I said. "Do your thing." I stuck the end of the staff into the solution and waited. It vibrated, then stilled. My excitement plummeted. Damn, it wasn't going to work.

Frustrated, I shot a bit of my own energy into the staff, and got an electric zing up my arm in return. As my vision blurred, I pulled the staff away from the solution but couldn't let go of it.

Searing pain shot through my skull, knocking me to my knees. I rolled to my side, still clutching the staff. My heart raced in panic as the room darkened, and the dustballs on the floor in front of me gave way to a muddy stretch of ground in a swamp. It looked like Pass a Loutre. Had I just fried the inside of my brain to learn the water came from exactly where I knew it came from?

Another thrust of pain pulled me into a fetal position, and I screwed my eyes tightly against it, tears escaping my closed lids. I heard a splash, and cracked them open. Pass a Loutre was gone, and I lay on a rock ledge overlooking a dark body of water under a blackened sky with a mist-shrouded full moon.

What the hell had happened? I tried to sit up, but was paralyzed, my chest heavy, breathing labored. The water in front of me swept past, swift and thunderous, before it narrowed through a chasm between two tall stones. Through the chasm appeared a boat, a small wooden craft carrying a hooded figure who controlled its progress against the churning current using a pole. Yellow reptilian eyes shone from inside the hood, and black wings curled behind its back.

I held my breath, somehow knowing it to be a demon and sure that if it saw me, it would take me to a place from which I'd never return. It would take me to Hades.

As suddenly as it appeared, the image faded, replaced with a floral area rug and dust bunnies. I shuddered and realized

I could move again. Cautiously, I opened my grip and let the staff roll free. As soon as I released it, the heavy weight lifted off my chest and I could breathe. A drop of blood dripped onto the floor by my nose. Every time I drew too hard on elven magic, I got a nosebleed and a killer headache.

That was the least of my worries, though. If the vision were true, the contaminated water in the Mississippi River didn't come from the hands of a territorial merman. It came from the underworld. It came from the River Styx.

14

My hands shook as I slid the grimoire back into the book-case and cleaned off my worktable. I grabbed a half-dozen tissues and plastered them to my nose on my way down-stairs, tripping over Sebastian. He bounded to the kitchen counter, wanting his dinner. God forbid the River Styx leaking into the Mississippi should interrupt his culinary routine.

The cat food sounded ridiculously loud as it hit the metal bowl. I absentmindedly broke up bits of Friday night's stolen chicken breast over the food and plopped it on the floor. What would cause water from the Styx to contaminate the river at Pass a Loutre? Did it have anything to do with the mers, or were they victims? And what about the dead wizards?

The clock read six p.m. The soft October sun had already crept below the treetops, so Alex and the gang should be headed back. I dug in my pocket for my cell phone and couldn't find it, so I went to the guest room for the land-line phone. Most people didn't have them anymore but I got Internet and cable cheaper by buying the package deal.

I punched in Alex's cell number and cursed when the sound of some deep-voiced country singer blasted out of my backpack in the living room. Alex had been on a country music kick for a while now, but I couldn't tell any of those singers apart. I think they were all named Tracy or Trace or Trisha.

If Alex's cell phone was in my backpack, that meant he probably had my phone. I called my own number, got voice mail, and left him a message he wouldn't have the password to retrieve. Since I figured I'd hear from him eventually, I heated up a microwave pizza and sat at the kitchen table to eat and wait. A trickle of blood still dripped from my nose, so I added a splash of medicinal bourbon to my soda.

It was almost seven by the time Alex used his key to come in the back door. He set the water vials on the counter, unstrapped his shoulder holster and hung it on the hook beside the cabinets, gun and all, then tossed my cell phone on the table in front of me.

"Your undead boyfriend called and wants you to call him back"—he slipped into a bad Jean Lafitte impression— "to arrange the details for our dinner date, *Jolie*." He sounded more like Pepé Le Pew, the romantic French skunk from the cartoons.

I flipped to the list of calls received, saw a number for the Monteleone, and shook my head. "Jean Lafitte can use a telephone now. God help us." The man was learning his way around the modern world entirely too well. Driving, taking showers, and now making phone calls. He'd probably even learned to turn on his lamp.

Alex opened a beer and got halfway into the seat opposite me before he really looked at me. "What the hell happened? You look like Mike Tyson took a punch at you." His gaze fell to the pile of bloody tissues. "Ah. The staff. What'd you do?"

He moved to the chair nearest me and lifted my chin with one finger so he could get a better look. I let him. Slapping him away would have taken too much energy.

"Doesn't look too bad. What happened?"

I filled him in on the elven origination allurement and the Styx.

Alex took a sip of his beer, looked at the bottle a moment, then finished draining it in one long guzzle, followed by a belch. Nice. "That was a smart move. But the Styx? This whole thing just gets more and more screwed."

Tell me about it. He hadn't just had a close encounter with the ferry into hell.

He got up and plucked another beer from the fridge. "Want one?"

"No, I'm wiped. Too much magic today—mine and the elven stuff both." Not to mention a little blood loss.

"Come on." He slid my chair out with me in it and tugged

me to my feet, shuffling me toward the living room. "Sofa. Head elevated."

I collapsed on the sofa and settled on my back with my head on the padded arm. He sat on the other end with my feet in his lap. Touching him made me feel better, safer. I finally relaxed and the pressure in my head eased. This was why Alex and I could never be lovers. We worked too well as friends to jeopardize it, and I didn't have so many friends that I'd risk losing him.

"Tell me about today," I said, smiling as he gave me a foot massage. "Except if you keep doing that, I'm going to fall asleep and we have murders to solve, Stygian leaks to plug, mermen to pacify."

"And nymphs to avoid," he said. "Did you know they could enthrall people like vampires?"

I sat up, forgetting about my feet. "What? Libby?"

He slouched down on the sofa. "Tish is the one who finally figured it out. I knew Jake was staggering around stupid, but it didn't seem to work on me. Libby didn't try to enthrall Tish, so once she figured it out, I got Jake to stop making eye contact with her. Guess it works on weres but not true shapeshifters."

I didn't know whether to be horrified or snicker. "What about the mertwins?"

Alex shrugged. "Who knows. They liked her anyway, especially Robert, so it's hard to tell. Libby ended up staying behind when I left with Jake and Tish. I think she was going back to Orchard with them."

Great. Now I could add prete matchmaker to my list of skills. "Did she at least get the water samples before she seduced everybody on board—well, except you and Tish?"

"Yeah. She claimed she didn't feel anything wrong with the water, but she brought the samples back anyway."

Well, crap. I just realized the only way to test these new samples against the old was to do the origination allurement again. Maybe if I did my grounding ritual first, it wouldn't affect me so badly. Also, it wouldn't surprise me this time. Now that I'd had time to think about it, I was pretty sure the demonic ferryman couldn't see me. It had simply been a vision.

"Since you haven't mentioned it, I gather you and Jake found no sign of Jeff Klein's body or the missing cell phone?"

"Nope. I'll call Ken at NOPD tomorrow and see if he had any luck with the phone logs." Alex leaned back and closed his eyes. He had impossibly long eyelashes. Why did guys get the good eyelashes? Not that I should be looking at his eyes, or the strong jawline, or the way his thick hair curled around the collar of his shirt. *Friends.*

I settled back on the sofa. "We have two dead wizards, contaminated water from the River Styx, and two merclans with a territory dispute." What a freakin' mess. "Do you think they're related?"

Alex lifted his shoulders in a tired approximation of a shrug. "I think it's too much of a coincidence. I mean, the area around Pass a Loutre's not exactly a main waterway."

"Yeah."

We sat in silence for a while, until I finally said the words I'd been uttering way too often lately. "I guess it's time to call the Elders."

"Why don't you call Zrakovi directly instead of going through Hoffman? His number's on my cell—I assume you have my phone since I had yours."

"I do." I rolled over and pulled my backpack toward me, digging out Alex's phone and tossing it to him. "You call him. I've already made my Elder call today, trying to get Hoffman to dig up info on Melinda Hebert."

Add the oddly emotionless grieving widow to our gumbo of weirdness.

Willem Zrakovi was the head wizard for North America— each continent had one grand poobah that served on the Council of Elders and above them all was a single First Elder. Below them were the heads of the four congresses, then the sentinels, then the licensed wizards. The enforcers were a group unto themselves, part FBI prete team and part assassins. How Alex managed to be such a nice guy, however much he tried to hide it, I could only credit with his upbringing. But I didn't want to think about Mama Warin right now.

Alex's version of the day's events for Zrakovi was succinct yet thorough. Probably why he was so good at reports. Once he got to the elven stuff, he threw the phone at me.

I set it to speaker. "Doing a little elven magic, are we, Drusilla?" Zrakovi's voice was a lot calmer than the last time I talked to him, when he'd been yelling at me for, I think, doing a little elven magic. Alex leaned back on the sofa with his eyes closed again, but a smile threatened to break through.

"Uh, yes, sir." I launched into a patchy, un-succinct, slightly defensive account of the origination allurement. "But in the end it was worth it," I said. "I found the source of the contamination was the River Styx."

Long silence. Really long silence. "Are you sure?" Zrakovi's voice deepened a register.

I described the boat, the demon, the river. "I don't know how I knew where I was," I concluded, realizing how lame it sounded. "I just knew, and I'm absolutely sure."

Zrakovi said a few curse words that had Alex and me both looking at the phone with raised eyebrows. Somehow, an Elder dropping an F-bomb was just . . . wrong. "Make a transport and send me the remaining water samples here in Boston," he said. "The head of the Yellow Congress is in town and I'll have him look at them tonight. He might be able to verify it without you repeating the elven ritual."

Fine with me. I had enough hellish things in my life without actually visiting the place twice. "One more question," I said. "If there was some sort of rift between the Mississippi River and the Styx, wouldn't it show up on the Elders' tracking devices?"

Zrakovi sounded as weary as I felt. "Now that the borders

are down, we have no way to tell. We're working on a new tracking system but it's going to take a while."

I didn't share this with Zrakovi but, in the words of my grandmother, who lived in a small town in Alabama, it sounded like the Elders were trying to close the barn door after the horse had run off.

15

By the time Alex showed up with bagels on Monday morning at seven, I'd finished a marathon series of phone calls. I'd missed our run because I was already on the phone with Willem Zrakovi—again—before six.

The head of the Yellow Congress had verified the water's origin as being the Styx, although Zrakovi admitted they wouldn't have known what to test for if I hadn't done the elven ritual first. The good news for me: no more nosebleed-inducing visits to Hades. Bad news: I needed to come up with at least a stop-gap fix, and fast. The Elders would do what they could to help, but they were shorthanded and it was my job and blah blah blah.

Next, I'd gotten a call from Jean Lafitte to verify a time for our dinner date on Sunday night. He was definitely getting way too comfortable with the telephone, and someone needed to explain to him that just because he, in his undead state, no longer needed to sleep, that did not apply to the rest of us.

Jake needed the don't-call-before-breakfast memo, too. He wanted to verify a time for our dinner-and-a-concert date on Wednesday night. My sudden popularity was epic.

Tish had a few ideas to try on the Styx problem, which I would certainly do if I could get off the phone.

I had only a scowl for Alex when he blasted in the back door, shouting greetings at my neighbor Eugenie over his shoulder—I was meeting her for dinner tonight to catch up on girl talk unless more crises intervened. He wore a caramel-colored short-sleeved shirt and khakis. Big-boy clothes without a trace of black. It looked good on him.

The bagels cheered me up. I pulled one in front of me, slathering on the softened cream cheese.

He poured coffee, got a plate, and pulled out a bagel for himself. "You're quiet. Convo with Zrakovi went that bad?" He carefully spread a thick layer of cream cheese on each side of the bagel and took a monstrous bite that gave him chipmunk cheeks.

I told him about the Styx confirmation. "I'm going to have to assume there's a physical rift that we can plug up, and see if one of the mers will risk diving again to check it out," I said. "I guess that means going back to Pass a Loutre this afternoon."

"I can't." He dabbed a few crumbs from his shirt into a napkin, folded it, and put it on his saucer. "I was up late fabricating documents to show the NOPD why the feds are taking over the missing-persons case they didn't know about."

That was too complex a thought after my marathon of phone calls. "What are you talking about?"

"I talked to Zrakovi again last night." He took a sip of coffee and grimaced. "What is this—chicory and chocolate?"

I nodded. "Put some cream in it if you want to be a wuss, cuts the bitterness. What about Zrakovi?"

"We decided the only way to explain Doug Hebert's and Jeff Klein's absence was to not try to explain it—make it a missing-persons case," he said. "By weaving in some phony evidence from Mississippi, it threw the case across state lines and into federal jurisdiction."

"So you can legitimately question people and get warrants without worrying about the NOPD. Makes sense." I pushed the rest of my bagel away. "But you realize it's going to be all over the *Times-Pic*, even the local TV stations. Two missing college professors is big news. And then some reporter is going to call Melinda Hebert, which will be a disaster." I didn't know if the woman was stable enough to refrain from babbling about wizards and preternatural species.

"I'd hoped you could go and talk to her again today, convince her to keep her mouth shut. Maybe get her to go out of town for a few days till we figure this out."

My cell phone rang before I could answer him. I looked at the caller ID and groaned. "Hotel Monteleone—has to be Jean. What does he want now?" Would the hotel disconnect his room's phone service if I bespelled the manager? Or maybe I could get into his suite and put a mild electrical-shocking charm on the phone itself.

Pepé Le Pew appeared at my kitchen table again, disguised as Alex. "When shall we meet for our dinner date, *Jolie*?" he mocked.

I flipped him a one-fingered salute with one hand and flipped the phone open with the other. "Jean, didn't we just talk a half-hour ago? Seven o'clock Sunday night. I haven't forgotten."

Jean's voice was uncharacteristically grim. "Drusilla, I have spoken with Rene. One of his family members has fallen ill, and he is threatening to kill that blackguard Denis Villere. On this occasion, I believe he might be serious."

Great. "Was his family member swimming at Pass a Loutre?"

"*Non,* that is the difficulty," he said. "She was near the head of passes, at the convergence of the river mouths, where the river pilots gather. It is a popular spot with the mermaids."

Yeah, I just bet it was. "Pilottown?"

"*Oui.*"

I closed my eyes and beat the phone against my head before putting it back to my ear. "Give me Rene's phone number."

For the second time in three days, I wound my way through the concrete jungle of the Westbank and left New Orleans for the wilds of Plaquemines Parish. This time, I was alone and headed to Orchard, where I'd try to work out a deal with Rene Delachaise to do the underwater work to unravel the Styx question. He didn't answer his phone, but I'd activated his tracking charm so I knew he was there.

Rene or one of his kinfolk weren't off the hook as suspects for the wizard murders, but we were going to have to work together. I made jokes about not being able to swim, but it wasn't just me. Wizards and water are a bad mix, especially saltwater or brackish water like that in the South Louisiana marshes—it made our magic hard to channel, probably because we were too freaked out to concentrate. If we needed work done in water, we had to hire it out.

Alex and I had decided to treat the water problem and the murders as separate cases until we found something to link them. Alex and Jake had headed off for a day at Tulane, interviewing the associates of the professors. Then they'd tackle the NOPD, smoothing out red tape, getting a warrant for the professors' homes and offices, and soliciting detective Ken Hachette's help in finding Doug Hebert's missing car. The cell phone records had shown nothing but a call from a pay phone outside a convenience store in Marrero, a Westbank suburb.

Meanwhile, I had a Styx problem to fix, and didn't have a clue how big it was or what would work—only that if the contamination had reached Pilottown, it was getting way too close to endangering humans.

I'd done some quick homework. A triangle of land near the point where the Mississippi river mouth branched apart at the gulf, Pilottown was home base for not only a number of oil outposts but one of the river pilots' associations.

Before going to Orchard, I decided to pay a surprise visit to the Villere family in Tidewater. I'd also checked to make sure Denis was at home. Now, as I reached the end of Highway 23 and wound my way along the narrow Tidewater Road, with water encroaching on both sides and no other traffic, I questioned my sanity. The few narrow side trails had names like Chevron and Halliburton, and the skeletons of Katrina-slain warehouses and boats peppered the landscape.

I finally came to a small path that branched into a marshy area and turned in according to the directions I'd gotten from an online map. I switched into four-wheel drive as the Pathfinder bounced over ruts and ridges, sending clumps of mud skyward. I eased my way toward a house set deep into the tall reeds.

The scents of new wood, saltwater, and fish surrounded me when I climbed out and looked around. I reached into the front seat and pulled out the elven staff. My backup. As my senses sharpened, what had seemed like silence gradually filled with the calls, clicks, clacks, and occasional splashes of the nearby marsh.

"*Vous n'avez aucune raison de venir ici!*"

An undignified squeak escaped me before I could squelch it, but I thought I'd just been ordered to leave. I swirled to stare into a pair of bright eyes buried in a face of tanned wrinkles. An old woman, wispy white hair escaping from a faded blue do-rag, hissed up at me. Worn steel-toed boots peeked from the hem of her old cotton dress.

"Uh." I tried to collect my wits and calm my thumping heart. "Do you speak English? I'm looking for Denis Villere."

"La sorciere," she said, poking me in the ribcage with a surprisingly strong finger, a much better option than the wicked kitchen knife she held in her other hand.

I took a step backward. I sure didn't want to use Charlie to zap an old lady.

"La sorciere. Va-t'en, ou je vais vous faire bouillir pour le dîner!"

"Denis Villere?" I said again, backpeddling. I had no clue what she was saying, except the serrated blade of her knife was waving awfully close to my nose.

"You ain't gonna boil da wizard for dinner, *Grandmère.*" A young man approached us from the back side of the house. Yegods. I'd never been so happy to hear English, especially since Grandma had apparently been threatening to serve me at the family dining table.

"Hold on a minute," the guy told me. He wrapped a muscular arm around his vicious little grandmother and escorted her back to the wide porch that stretched along the front width of the house. Once she was settled back into the rocking chair from whence she must have sprung like an aged, lethal mousetrap, he trotted back to me. He was in his late teens or early twenties, with long black hair, warm brown eyes, and a compact, muscular build.

"Sorry 'bout dat—*Grandmère* don't like wizards. You the one my pop talkin' 'bout?"

He was smiling, and no further mention of boiling had been made, so I began to relax.

"Drusilla Jaco," I said. "DJ."

"TJ Villere, or T-Jacques or Tit-Jacques to the old-timers," he said, shaking my hand. "My pop's awful pissed at you for puttin' dat tracking tattoo on him. I thought it was kinda cool, me."

"Where is your dad? I wanted to talk to him about the water contamination." I looked around at the small house, which looked to be a mix of old and new construction. They must have taken a Katrina-damaged place and patched it up.

"Just missed him, you. Went out lookin' at the property you givin' us now. He ain't happy 'bout dat, neither."

No kidding. "It's the best I could do. The Delachaise clan has been on the Birdfoot Delta a long time so it was the best compromise we could come up with. But I wanted to tell you guys to stay away from the area around Pilottown, at least for the next few days. There's more contamination."

"Yeah, I'll tell him," TJ said, cocking his head at the staff in my right hand. "Dat the stick you threaten my pop with?"

Pop sure didn't keep anything from his son, who looked healthy enough—he had the build of someone who either worked hard or worked out. If he'd been sick, his recovery had been complete. I threw the staff back in the front seat, lest TJ or his granny thought I was threatening them.

"Just tell your dad about the new water problem, and call me if you have any questions." I dug a card out of my pocket and handed it to him.

He frowned. "Risk analysis? What kinda wizard stuff is that?"

"Just a cover. But the phone numbers are good. Call me if you run into any problems."

I started to climb back into the Pathfinder. "And I'm glad you're feeling better—sorry the water made you sick."

His eyebrows bunched, and he looked puzzled. "I ain't been sick."

16

I stared at T-Jacques. "You didn't get sick from swimming in the water around Pass a Loutre? I thought—"

"Oh, yeah. Forgot about dat. I'm okay now, me." He grinned at me.

I grinned back. He was lying through his teeth. I could feel the uneasiness wafting off him along with his cold, slippery mer energy. Why had Denis lied about T-Jacques getting sick from the water? An excuse to start a fight with Rene? To cover up the fact he'd poisoned it himself? But how had a mer gotten access to the Styx?

I wanted to pull my hair out. But first I wanted to leave before *Grandmère* came after me with a pot of boiling water and a big serrated knife. I wasn't going to get answers from TJ.

"Glad you're okay," I repeated, climbing into the SUV.

"*Bon chance,* sentinel."

Good luck? I couldn't get out of here fast enough. These people gave me the creeping willies.

The drive from Tidewater to Orchard was short—just a mile of dirt road surrounded by a lot of water. The Delachaise land sat inside a wide path that looped out next to the marsh, encircling what looked like three or four acres of wilderness. Different types of boats sat tethered to a dock, and several small houses perched on high piers around the land, some with vehicles parked underneath. I recognized the twins' pickups. This wasn't a homestead. It was a compound, and the Delachaises were clearly more prosperous than their angry Tidewater rivals.

I parked behind Rene's truck and got out, reaching across the front seat to retrieve my backpack. The elven staff lay on the passenger seat. I needed the twins' help, and Robert, because of his little tiff with Denis in the parking lot a couple of days ago, knew I wielded the staff as a weapon. I closed the Pathfinder's door with Charlie inside.

I didn't want to go in armed. Not the signal I wanted to send.

"Hey, darlin'."

I squeaked again as Robert put a hand on my shoulder from behind. I was either going to have to become more aware of my surroundings or take a sedative.

"Kinda jumpy there, wizard."

Yeah, that's me. Jumpy. With good reason. Robert wrapped one arm around my waist and the other jammed in the pocket of his shorts as he propelled me toward the house.

"You should try a massage. Robert has very talented hands." I peered around Robert's shoulder, looking for the source of the deep, sultry voice. Libby the nymph stretched artfully across a lawn chair at the side of the house, soaking up rays. Technically, she was wearing a swimsuit, although I'd seen dental floss more substantial.

"Hi, Libby. Didn't expect to see you here."

Robert left me and slid onto the lawn chair next to Libby, reaching over with his talented hands to smooth a swath of tanning oil across her thigh. I'd seen about all the hand-talent I needed for the day. "Is Rene around?"

Robert pointed to the small building nearest the water, a blocky, concrete structure and the only one not raised for flood protection. "Out in the fish house. Our cousin Amanda, the one that's sick—she's up in the main house."

I started toward the concrete building, but stopped and looked back. "Is Amanda going to be okay? Do you want me to see if I can help her?"

Robert raised an eyebrow. "Don't think so, wizard. You just fix the water problem and get rid of the Villeres."

I'd already decided to tell them about the Styx. I didn't want word spreading too far, but I also didn't want more of the mers getting sick. "About the water. Somehow, the River Styx is leaking into the Mississippi," I said, wondering if he was so mainstreamed he'd even grasp the danger of it.

Robert's talented hand stopped mid-stroke and he sat up. "Shit. You sure 'bout that?"

Guess he did grasp the danger.

"That's awful," Libby said. She stood up and tugged a migrating string of dental floss back in place. "Has anyone else gotten sick?"

"What you plannin' to do about it?"

I blinked at them. Neither had shown much interest in the contamination till now. "I tested the water using"—a mindblowing elven trip to hell—"a magical procedure, then we confirmed it with a second test," I said. "I'm hoping all of you can help with repairs."

"Of course we'll help," Libby said, flipping a strand of red hair over her shoulder. "We don't want any more of the mers to get sick."

Robert jerked his head toward the fish house. "Go on and talk to Rene. He's pretty pissed off, but tell him what you told us and he'll help. Then we gotta figure out how them Villeres got water from the Styx."

I left them murmuring behind me and headed to the fish house. Was it a place they kept fish? Was it a ceremonial name since they could *become* fish? The door stood open, and a blast of cold air hit me as I knocked on the doorjamb and stuck my head inside. "Rene?"

"Hold on, babe." A disembodied voice came from inside what looked like a walk-in commercial refrigerator or freezer. I waited at the door to the building, the cold air sending goose bumps to pimple my arms below the sleeves of my light cotton shirt. Had nothing to do with the alien ambience I'd enjoyed all afternoon.

The room was windowless, with unadorned concrete-block walls and industrial tile floors that had drains set into them. Metal shelves and cabinets lined two walls, and there were several home-sized freezers in addition to the big walk-in cooler. A stainless-steel worktable the dimensions of a queen-size bed took up the middle of the floor.

"Had a feeling you'd show up. Woulda answered my phone if I'd wanted to talk to you." Rene came out of the cooler with a dead alligator slung around his shoulders, head hanging off one side, tail off the other. "How 'bout you close the cooler door behind me."

I edged along the wall, giving him and his gator plenty of space, and pushed the heavy door shut. He shifted the reptile off his shoulders, lifted it over his head, and slapped it onto the worktable. The gator looked to be about six feet long—small, as gators go. But it probably weighed a couple hundred pounds and he'd just hefted it as if it weighed no more than a puppy.

"What are you going to do with it?" Gator-hunting season had just ended. Guess that was one of the things mers hunted, but I couldn't see the attraction. Gators had claws like Freddy Krueger and a temperament to match. Their meat did make a nice sausage, though.

"Gonna eat this one," Rene said. "Hide's too little to be worth much. You ever skin a gator?"

Uh-huh. "Sure, that was a required class in wizarding school." He raised his gaze to meet mine, and I could've sworn he almost laughed. Maybe I was growing on him.

"Grab a stool and learn from a master." He pulled out a drawer underneath the worktable and retrieved a black leather case filled with shiny steel knives. The kind of knife that killed Doug Hebert?

I looked around and found a stool. "Can you talk while you work?" I could always wait outside. In fact, that might be a good idea. I'd hate to barf all over his meat.

"Sure thing. Sit down." He slid the strap of a white apron over his head and fastened the ties behind him, then pulled a short-bladed knife from the case and skated it back and forth across a black-handled sharpening steel.

I focused on an area behind his head and tried to close my ears to the sound of leathery skin being cut. "We did some tests with the water samples and we know what the problem is. The contamination is caused by water leaking in from the River Styx."

"Shit! Motherf . . ." Rene's knife slipped, slicing deeply into his left hand. He grabbed a handful of towels and started applying pressure to stanch the bleeding.

"Hang on." I retrieved my backpack from where I'd dropped it next to the door, and pulled out my portable magic case. "I have a healing charm that should take care of that." I guessed it would work on mermen. We'd see.

Rene looked dubious. "Won't do anything else, will it? I mean, I don't want no horns or wings, nothing like that. I'm a were—it'll heal in a half hour anyway."

I laughed. "No horns or wings, I promise. Give me your hand."

He'd cut a two-inch gash through the tender web of skin between the thumb and forefinger. Using my teeth to pry the lid off the potions vial, I tapped a little of the clear liquid on top of the wound and used my finger to spread it.

Rene snatched his hand back. "That hurts."

"Big baby. Wipe it off again and look at it."

He took another wad of paper towels and wiped the blood off gingerly. The skin beneath it was unmarked. "Well, damn. Guess wizards are good for something."

I'd take that as a thank-you. "Yeah, what we're not good for is diving, and I want to see if you or Robert or one of your family members would help us try to figure out how the Styx is leaking into the water around Pass a Loutre. And now Pilottown, sounds like. Don't even start about the Villeres. We've got to fix the leaks first, then worry about how they're getting there. Otherwise, somebody's going to die."

He flipped the gator on its back and went back to slicing while I returned to my stool.

"What you got in mind?"

"We'd gear you up with a wetsuit if you want to dive without shifting, or at least a mask and oxygen tank if you want to partially shift, so you won't get sick." I'd been up half the night devising this scheme. "See if you can find a rift of some kind. If so, I'll make up some charms so you can patch it at least temporarily while I look for a long-term solution."

Most simple charms only held for a finite period. I'd have to come up with something more complex for the magic to hold permanently underwater.

"You gonna pay us? Cause if we take another day off work you need to pay us. We ain't doing wizard charity."

"Sure, we'll pay—" I stopped, aghast, as Rene deftly flipped the gator on its belly again and used a longer knife to split its tail near the body and slice off the bony ridge along the animal's back. He tossed that aside and continued cutting a couple of minutes more. Then he lifted the intact hide off the gator and spread it out.

"Cocodrie jolie," he said. Great, me and the gator were pretty. I'd have to tell Jean Lafitte.

"What will you do with the hide?" I asked in horror as he took a large tablespoon and scraped stray bits of meat off the inside of the skin before salting down the hide and rolling it up. I wished I'd skipped the bagels.

"Sell it," he said. "Sell the skull too, and the feet." He chopped off the massive, clawed feet and tossed them aside, then took a serrated knife toward the head.

Oh. My. God. That was my cue to leave. "What time can you go tomorrow?"

He paused and looked up, breaking into a smile. "You in a hurry, babe?"

"I don't want to watch you cut off its head." Okay, so I'm squeamish when it comes to decapitation.

"I ain't cuttin' off the head. I'm slicin' out the jaw meat."

I looked at him, traumatized.

He chuckled. "Meet you at the marina at nine. Make sure your boss is gonna pay us, or it's no deal. And we want the masks and tanks. Ain't gettin' sick doin' wizards' work."

I escaped into the warmth, rubbing my arms, and walked back to the Pathfinder. Finally, it felt like we were doing something, or at least had a plan to do something.

Robert was chasing Libby around my SUV with a stick, all playful again. Damn it. Not a stick. Charlie.

"Hey!" I shouted. "Hands off the staff."

They came to a stop and watched me approach. "No harm done, *chère*," Robert said, handing me the staff. "We didn't hurt your little wand. Just wanted to see what it would do."

I wondered what he'd planned to do with it. "My guess is that it did nothing. It only works for me."

He jerked his head toward it. "That don't feel like a wizard thing."

"It's very lovely," Libby said. "Did you make it yourself?"

"No, I'm not much of a wood-carver." The staff looked okay—as Robert said, no harm done. But I wouldn't be leaving it in the car anymore.

17

I'd just finished dog-earing some charm recipes I thought might temporarily seal a possible rift between the Mississippi and the Styx when Eugenie bopped in the back door. I'd almost talked myself out of going to dinner—as boring as a sandwich with Sebastian sounded, it fit my energy level. Mer negotiations had proven tiring.

A distant rumble of thunder promised rain and cooler temperatures, so it seemed like a good night to stay in. I'd dressed appropriately—jeans and an old JazzFest sweatshirt.

A cloud of guilt settled over me every time Eugenie came around these days. Before Katrina, we'd spent part of every weekend together, doing girl stuff. Shopping, movies, moaning over the lack of available men, and whining about trying to run a business in America's most dysfunctional city. Well, mostly she whined and I pretended, since my fake risk-analysis business was a front for my fake FBI career. Or that's the story I was currently telling.

"Guess what's calling my name?" she asked, closing the door behind her. A loud clap of thunder rattled the windows, signaling a storm's imminent arrival. She wore her usual low-slung jeans with a midriff top of a brilliant purple. It matched the lavender tips in her hair and showed off her belly ring and the assortment of celestial tattoos on her back. I wanted a tattoo but hadn't summoned the nerve, couldn't decide what I wanted, and didn't know where to put it. A mistake seemed so . . . permanent.

What might be calling her name? "Cool Beans?"

We had a running joke about the coffee shop across the street that closed for Katrina and never reopened despite not flooding or having any wind damage. The empty building still had plywood over its windows, and gang tags covered it from top to bottom. Sad thing was, I'd gotten so used to seeing it that way it had begun looking normal.

"No way. I do have some news about that place, but what's calling my name is Franky & Johnny's. Wanna go?"

I weighed the value of a good dinner against the angst of making up phony FBI cases now that I was supposedly an out-of-the-closet consultant for the feds. Eugenie had never taken much interest when she thought I was in risk management. Now she thought the Tulane job was a cover while Alex and I did secret, nebulous work for the FBI, so she was persistent in her pursuit of details about our glamorous adventures as federal agents. I'd share a few lies and plead confidentiality on the rest.

A break from anything reeking of prete politics sounded good. The only water species we would see at F&J's would be deep fried and served with a side of green pepper rings.

A light drizzle had started by the time we pulled into the gravel parking lot and entered the cavernous darkness. Tucked in the first floor of a yellow-brick building with a residential area upstairs, not only had Franky & Johnny's not changed its décor in decades, but the same grease had probably coated the wooden bar since the 1960s and the same Miller High Life sign hung outside the front door. Katrina flooding had done nothing to change it, thank God.

Blinking to adjust to the dimness, we made our way across linoleum floors through the bar area, past pinball machines and old framed sports memorabilia, following our noses toward the smell of fried food.

Red and white checked oilcloth covered the tables, and we pulled back vintage red-cushioned chrome chairs to sit near the middle of the restaurant.

"Girl, we haven't had a chance to catch up lately," Eugenie said. "You and Alex figured out you're the perfect match yet?"

I laughed. Eugenie was convinced Alex and I would end up being more than just business partners. "How many times do I have to tell you? Just friends. Besides, the man's such a straight arrow, if he accidentally mixed business and pleasure his head would explode."

We waited while the waitress informed us the meatloaf was sold out, and placed our orders for po'boys and beer.

"But I do have a date with Jake tomorrow night." And Norma Warin's birthday dinner on Saturday and dinner with Jean Lafitte on Sunday night, but I didn't volunteer those. Eugenie didn't know about the historical undead, and she'd read way too much into my upcoming meeting of The Mama.

She took a sip of Abita Amber and processed that information. "I thought you and Jake had a falling-out after the storm, about your uncle Gerry's place. So you've made up?"

That had been the cover story—I was just full of cover stories. I practically needed a database to keep all my lies straight.

"Yeah, I ran into him in the Quarter the other night and we decided to try again."

"You're deluded." She waited till the server put our order of bell pepper rings and ranch dressing on the table. "Don't get me wrong—Jake's hot. But you and Alex are going to end up together. It's inevitable."

"Yeah, yeah." I was tired of that conversation. Besides, she was biased. If Alexander Warin had a fan club, Eugenie would be president for life. He could turn on the charm like a spigot of cream, and she lapped it up. She hadn't seen his monosyllabic, neanderthal side, and she hadn't seen him play with a live grenade. I had.

"How's business at Shear Luck?"

"I'm busy—the college girls from Tulane and Loyola all want highlights for Halloween. Wish you'd let me give you some. Some light and dark strands would look great in that honey color of yours."

"Maybe." A change might be nice. Things had been so crazy since Gerry died and I'd partnered with Alex, I hadn't done much with it except braid it or tie it up. It was too long. Eugenie had been wanting to give me a makeover since I'd met her five years ago. Maybe it was time for me to put the stress and sadness of the last few years away, at least symbolically, and get a fresh start. Or at least a fresh look.

"Oh!" Our po'boys arrived and Eugenie had to try a shrimp before she could continue. "Cool Beans has been sold. A new nursery and landscaping business is opening up. Plantasy Island."

We both groaned at the name but, really, it was kind of cute and I was glad the Cool Beans eyesore was going away. "Who bought it?"

The Mona Lisa had nothing on Eugenie's wicked little smile. "My date Friday night."

I almost choked on my oyster. "Fast work, woman. Who's the guy?"

"His name's Quince Randolph and boy, is he not my type. He's a serious tree hugger. Wants to save the wetlands and the pelicans and the French Quarter rodents. You name it, he wants to save it." She swigged her Abita. "The man doesn't even drink."

"So, what, you're joining him on a nighttime wharf-rat rescue or something? Why are you going out with him?"

She laughed. "I have no idea what we'll do on our date, but I know what I'd like to do." She waggled her eyebrows.

"Quince Randolph is smokin'. Tall, blond, big hands, good teeth."

"You make him sound like a horse."

"Yeah, a stud."

We giggled and ordered more beer. Why not? It had been a weird, stressful day, and tomorrow promised more of the same. I deserved to unwind.

"Is this a new business for Quince, or is he moving it from somewhere else? He didn't buy the house next door to mine too, did he?"

The young couple who owned the green shotgun house to the left of mine had put it on the market a few months ago. They'd come back to New Orleans after Katrina, but Eileen got pregnant and they were still paranoid about the ugly local politics and fast-rebounding crime rate. There had been an "offer pending" sign in front for about a week.

Eugenie shook her head. "No, I don't know who's buying that one. Quince just moved here from California. He'll be living on the second floor over his business, like I do."

"Did you warn him that running a business here could be, uh . . ." I looked for the right word. "Challenging?"

She laughed. "I don't want to scare him off. He'll find out soon enough."

It helped to think of New Orleans as a picturesque Caribbean outpost rather than a modern American city so the laid-back inefficiency seemed quaint instead of making us want to slit our wrists with dull knives.

The city got under a person's skin, though. Just when we'd think it wasn't worth the aggravation, NOLA would seduce us anew with trills of jazz floating through the heavy night air, the aromas of pralines and crawfish boil assaulting our senses, the clang of old streetcars rumbling beneath a canopy of live oaks, or the peal of ships' horns echoing off the river far into the uptown neighborhoods.

A river, I remembered, that could be in peril from the underworld sector of the Beyond and its poisonous waters. My beer suddenly tasted bitter, and I motioned for the waitress to bring our check. I had work to do.

Two hours later, a little before ten thirty, I'd made up every temporary charm I could think of that might help. I had to be physically present to do a ritual spell since words of power must be evoked, and a potion would become too diluted to work in water. Whatever temporary measures we used had to be solid, potent, and portable. Which left charms that could be placed inside amulets or weighted containers for the mers to carry. The Elders had already arranged for diving masks and oxygen tanks to be delivered to Venice.

I made cleansing charms from black cohosh and holy water that were supposed to purify anything within a three-yard radius. Sealant charms using magic-infused ground acacia twigs should spread a layer of protection across a span of several feet. And since the Styx was the river of the dead, I threw in a few different death charms—not to cause death, but to protect the living from the effects of the dead.

The death charms were complicated and required all the physical magic I could summon after such an exhausting day. Eventually, they were encased in weighted amulets the mers—and Libby if she wanted to help—could loop around their necks when they dove. My muscles ached from magical exertion, but my brain spun like a fastball at a Zephyrs game. No way I'd be able to sleep yet.

An hour later, I'd put on my Harry Potter pajamas to celebrate the first cool night of the year and settled in with a mug of cocoa and a DVD of *To Catch a Thief*. All I needed to complete the picture was a dog and an undead Cary Grant. The cat who'd just sauntered past me with a rubber rat dangling from his lips was not a relaxing-on-the-sofa kind of pet. That rat would be buried in my bed within the hour. Even knowing it was there, I would scream. It had become a nightly event.

I took a sip of cocoa and rested my head against the back of the sofa, watching the movie. My half-closed lids sprang open at the sound of footsteps on my stairs from the first floor. Leaning forward quietly, I eased Charlie off the coffee table and breathed deeply to slow my galloping heart rate. My protective wards were in place, so how had anyone gotten in?

Setting the mug on the table, I stood and pointed the staff at the stairwell opening. One of the disadvantages of having most of my living space upstairs is the potential for being trapped. I'd learned that the hard way during one of my early run-ins with Jean Lafitte, back before he'd decided I was a better ally than enemy. Short of selling my house or learning how to land a jump from the second floor, I wasn't sure what to do about it.

My emotional radar told me the intruder was a disgruntled shapeshifter and I relaxed. Only one grumpy shifter could get past my wards and he had a key to my house, which he'd been using far too liberally.

Alex's voice beat his body up the stairs by a couple of heartbeats. "Put down the staff. If you zap me with it I'm going to have to hurt you."

"How'd you know I had the staff?"

He rounded the top of the stairs and gave me a heated look. I still held the two-foot carved piece of wood in front of me, aimed at his head. "You might be able to tell how I feel, but I know how you think. Either use it or put it down. I'm tired."

I propped the staff in the corner, reclaiming my cocoa and my spot on the sofa. "You're tired? I spent the day with creepy mermen and Libby the airhead and watched an alligator get his feet cut off." Although, to be fair, I kind of liked the Delachaise mers and Libby had been decent enough and almost clothed.

Alex stopped, sweeping his eyes from my face to where my feet balanced on the coffee table in their fuzzy blue socks. "What the hell are you wearing?"

I looked down at my black sleepshirt featuring the movie cast on the front and the pants emblazoned with Gryffindor logos. "Well, crap. Now the matching Harry Potter PJs I bought you for Christmas won't be a surprise."

Chuckling, he flopped on the sofa next to me. "I thought you hated Harry Potter."

"I don't hate Harry Potter. I am jealous of Harry Potter," I said. "He can do too many cool things I can't."

Alex yawned and reached a long arm out to snag my cocoa. He took a sip and grimaced. "Is this that crappy microwave shit?"

I took the mug away from him. "You don't like it, make your own."

"I'm too tired." He slouched on the sofa and watched a black-clad Cary Grant prowl over the rooftops. "We talked to everybody in the Tulane biology department today, along with a couple of administrators and their public relations VP," he said. "Took half the day and I'm still waiting on a warrant to search Doug Hebert's and Jeff Klein's offices. And the NOPD brass are being assholes."

"I thought Ken would be able to help you on that end." I'd met the detective a few times after Katrina and he struck me as being Mr. Dependable.

"His hands are tied. He can't use department resources until we have the chain of command established. They're balking at turning this case over to the feds because it's going to be high-profile."

"Told you. Has the *Times-Pic* already got the story?"

He nodded. "Yeah, front page tomorrow, I'm sure. The Tulane VP said reporters have already tried to get to the president and the department chair. Tomorrow, we've got to ride herd on the media, get the NOPD in line, and talk to the Elders about whether to plant Doug Hebert's body back in the swamp somewhere or let him stay missing forever."

"Not 'we.' I've gotta go back to Plaquemines tomorrow."

He cracked his neck from side to side, popping out the tension. "Sorry. I've been on a rant. What happened today?"

The rundown on the visits to Tidewater and Orchard didn't take long, and the weirdness didn't translate well. Saying Robert picked up the elven staff without permission and T-Jacques lied about his illness didn't sound as menacing as living it.

"The upshot is, I have to go out tomorrow and let Rene and Robert try to place these charms at Pass a Loutre and Pilottown," I concluded. "Not to sound like a wimp, but they creeped me out today. I want backup that knows how to shoot." I could slip a potion to a misbehaving mer but it took too long and didn't make the same impression as a bullet. And I didn't know how to use the staff to subdue anyone. I could only start fires or fry someone like a Cajun Thanksgiving turkey, which usually proved fatal. Alex kept trying to talk me into shooting lessons. If I'd listened, I wouldn't be in the annoying position of having to ask for help.

Alex shifted sideways on the sofa to face me. "I need to run interference with the NOPD tomorrow, but maybe I can shuffle things around enough to take at least the morning off."

Easy enough solution. "Jake can go with me."

Alex propped an arm on the back of the sofa and studied me. I could practically see the wheels spinning. He didn't want me heading into wizard-hating mer territory alone, but he didn't want Jake going with me for fear his cousin would lose control and shift into a gullet-ripping monster. I didn't even have to dip into his emotions to read him.

"Call Jean Lafitte," he said.

I looked around the room for another person, because no way that idea came from Alex. I couldn't even form words to list all the ways that was a bad idea.

"He can shoot, he's a sneaky sonofabitch, and he and Rene are friends," he said.

"But . . ." I was speechless. Alex hadn't surprised me this much since he broke the news that he and my goofy adopted Katrina dog were one and the same.

"Look, I don't trust the guy. Hate that you seem to like him. Really hate that he wants you. But he's smart. He'll help you because he knows the wizards would come down on him like a brick shithouse if he didn't."

Oh, good grief. "He doesn't want me. He wants to figure out a way he can use me to his own advantage."

Alex's eyes were dark and unfathomable. "Oh, he wants you."

He moved slowly, inching toward me till we were nose-to-nose, giving me a close-range view of velvet brown eyes and dark evening stubble. I wanted to back away but refused to let him see he made me feel unsettled. "Just remember this when he makes his move."

His lips met mine. He tasted of cocoa and mint, and the hand that slid to the back of my neck felt like fire. He pulled away with a hard nip at my lower lip.

"Ouch!" I beat him over the head with the nearest weapon I could find. Unfortunately, it was only a throw pillow. "What the hell is wrong with you?"

He grinned and ruffled my hair like I was a precocious five-year-old. "Just sayin'."

Alex rolled to his feet and headed for the stairway. "I'll talk to you when you get back tomorrow."

I stared after him. "Just sayin' what?"

18

Jean was sitting outside the Riverside Market Walgreens when I arrived at my office at eight thirty. I parked the Pathfinder and watched him a few moments, sprawled across the bench like a ruler surveying his kingdom, long legs splayed, arms stretched along the wooden seatback. He watched people coming and going from the drugstore, his glance occasionally lingering on certain customers. It wasn't attractive women he was ogling, I finally realized. It was customers leaving the store with large bags.

Probably thinking of ways to rob them and resell the merchandise.

As I got out of the SUV, he spotted me and rose, catlike, to prowl my way. His blue tunic, with black pants tucked into the black boots, made him look even taller and more broad-shouldered than usual, but at least he didn't have his gun visible. It was there somewhere, though.

"I was most pleased that you called for my assistance last

evening, *Jolie*. However, I am disappointed you chose to once again dress as a field worker."

I looked down at my jeans and lightweight sweater. "They're blue jeans, and I'll have you know they cost a small fortune." Plus they had boot-cut legs that made me look taller.

He followed me in the office door, trailing too close, resting a hand on my shoulder. I thought about Alex and what he'd said, and the kiss. I'd already thought about that kiss too much. It kept me awake half the night, wondering what it meant and wondering what I wanted it to mean. Which was just, no doubt, what Alex had intended. Manipulative alpha shapeshifter.

I shrugged from beneath Jean's hand and pointed him to a chair. "We're supposed to meet the twins and Libby at ten, so we've got a few minutes." I made coffee and began a quick check of my e-mail. The Elders had sent a new memo letting all the regional wizards know the nymphs had formed a coalition called the Greater Mississippi River Nymphs. Glad to know the big guys were on top of things.

Jean sipped some Amaretto Mocha dark roast and looked at his coffee cup in disgust. "Who is this Libby?"

I gave him the scoop on the nymph. "She's kind of an airhead, but Rene and Robert like her, so mostly we want to keep her from distracting them from their dive," I said. Maybe Libby would dive herself—I'd brought an extra mask. "Have you had experience with nymphs?"

I expected a ribald comeback or at least a good leer, but

Jean answered seriously. "I have long heard stories of how they lure sailors to their death but I have never met one. This Libby does not interest me. I will ensure she does not interrupt your business."

That sounded ominous.

"You can't kill her," I said. Such a fiasco would generate enough paperwork to keep me filing reports for months. I finished my e-mail, shut the computer down, and grabbed my backpack, making sure the elven staff was seated firmly inside. "Let's do it."

"Do it?" Jean followed me outside with a put-upon sigh. I turned to lock the door behind us. "People have lost the proper art of language. It is a great pity."

Yeah, yeah. Whatever. I wasn't going to take diction lessons from the Miss Manners of the historical undead. "You ever been to a drive-through?"

Louisiana Highway 23 was becoming overly familiar, but we were too busy slurping chocolate milkshakes to banter. Jean was content to sip quietly after he got the hang of using a straw.

Four hours later, as the *Dieu de la Mer* bounced over the choppy water outside Pilottown, the milkshake was a distant memory. I was hot, hungry, and annoyed.

We'd gone to the small settlement at the head of passes first. The mouth of the river spreads out like tree roots into the Gulf of Mexico. The point at which the roots all joined the trunk, or the river proper, was the head of passes.

Like the rest of Plaquemines, Pilottown was a blend of new construction and Katrina debris. A new plantation-style raised house shone white in the soft sunlight, linked to smaller buildings by sidewalks built on posts above the swampy, unreliable land. Piers stretched into the water, several with boats docked at them that had PILOT printed on the sides of their wheelhouses. Oil derricks dotted the water in the distance.

"River pilots can stay here overnight when they waitin' for a ship to come in real late or real early," Rene explained, easing the boat beside a pier. Seagoing vessels navigating the Mississippi were required to have a licensed river pilot aboard.

Jean and I had spent most of the trip in the wheelhouse with Rene, trying to avoid the antics of Robert and Libby. They'd turned the aft deck into a combination tanning salon and boudoir. To my surprise, Jean had proven old-fashioned when it came to PDA. Apparently, he liked his affection more private.

Rene did the first dive just outside the Pilottown marina and confirmed a rift in the riverbed big enough to swim through. Robert and Libby dove with the amulets. All they had to do was open them and lodge them into the mud near the rift. Rene waited an hour after their return, then dove again to make sure the charms were still in place and the water clean.

So far, so good.

Now we were headed back to Pass a Loutre. Once we

got out of the main current of the river and the water was smoother, I climbed onto the railed area above the wheel-house to enjoy the mild October sun and think. Rene and Jean began talking softly as soon as I was gone, and while I couldn't hear them I had no doubt they were cooking up some new business scheme. I wanted no part of it.

The good thing about charms is they're quick to make and can be invoked easily by a second party. They also work fast. The bad thing? None of today's charms would last more than seventy-two hours. I had another three days to come up with something permanent.

And I had to figure out how the rifts were happening. Had something come in from the Underworld, creating its own improvised transport? Were the rifts spontaneously appearing because of some weakness in the fabric of reality between the modern Mississippi and the Styx?

The boat slowed as we made the turn toward Pass a Loutre, and I climbed back down and joined the happy couple on the aft deck. Rene guided the *Dieu de la Mer* into an area of dense growth about fifty yards past the place we'd found Doug Hebert's body.

The breeze had died down, and the call of birds and buzz of insects were the only sounds other than the soft slap of water against the hull.

Jean and Rene joined us on the aft deck. "Same routine here as before?" Rene asked.

I knelt to the deck and pulled the remaining charm amulets out of the front pocket of my backpack. "Whoever dives might as well take these on the first trip. Since there was a rift at Pilottown, we can assume there's one here as well."

"Makes sense, babe. Robert, you wanna take this one?"

"Sure thing." He looped the amulets around his neck, slid the tank on his back, pulled on the mask, and dove.

Rene joined Jean in the wheelhouse to continue their conversation. That left me on the aft deck with Libby.

So she made me feel short and dumpy; I'd have to live with it. I flopped to the deck next to where she lay sunning in her barely there swimsuit. What did one talk about with a nymph?

"You seem to like the twins," I said. "Do you know a lot of mermen?" I almost bit off my own tongue, for fear she'd think I meant "know" in a biblical sense.

"They are my first." She sat up and offered me some sunblock. I took a dab and spread it on my face and hands—the only part of this sunbather that was exposed. "I find them interesting. They are like most men, however. They see what they want to see and believe whatever I tell them."

I lowered my sunglasses and looked at her. "You mean they make assumptions about you, and you take advantage of it?"

"Of course. Don't men make assumptions about you? That you are not as smart as they? Or that they know what you need more than you yourself?"

I pushed my sunglasses back up and reclined on the deck. Damned if Libby and I didn't have something in common.

How had that happened? "Yes, I know exactly what you mean. But, no offense, you do kind of encourage them to not take you seriously, you know."

She stretched out beside me and closed her eyes. "Well, of course. I am a nymph. It is my nature."

Glad we got that straight. I lay in the sun and thought instead about the Stygian rifts. I had been pondering a permanent solution short of donning a wetsuit and diving myself. Because even if the Underworld opened up and Hades himself came swimming through, I wasn't going in the water. Yet any long-term fix would require direct use of magic.

Early this morning, I'd come up with a crazy plan involving a sealing ritual that would permanently adhere a blanket of magic over even a large rift, but Tish and I needed to talk about it, and I needed to gauge how far I could trust the Delachaise twins.

I sat up when I heard a splash from the foredeck and saw Jean at the rail. I joined him, looking around for Rene. "Did he go in too?"

"*Oui*, since Robert was taking longer than usual and Rene sensed one of the Villeres in the area, he wanted to ensure no harm had come to his brother."

I hoped Robert was okay, but the absence of both Delachaises gave me time to play *Grill the Pirate*. "How long have you known the twins?"

He eyed me a moment before answering. "Rene, I have known for several years, perhaps ten. Robert I met only one or two years ago. They are good men."

"Which one of them is the most reliable?"

He frowned at me. "That you like my friends is pleasing to me, *Jolie*. As long as you do not like them too much."

I turned with my side to the rail and looked up at him. Jean was completely misconstruing my interest, but I pushed ahead. "I don't like them too much. I just want to know which you feel is most trustworthy."

"Bah." Jean shrugged. "How does one measure the honesty of a man's heart?"

Great. He'd be spouting poetry next.

"However, I will only say this: of the two, Rene is the more serious of purpose. Robert is a fine man, but he can be easily distracted from the task at hand. Does this answer your question, Drusilla?"

"Yes it does. Thank you." Although it occurred to me that asking Jean Lafitte for a character reference was akin to getting relationship advice from Hugh Hefner.

"But I must say this in my own defense, *Jolie*. That I made your acquaintance before my friend Rene."

I hadn't felt the need of my mojo bag today since I'd done a heavy grounding ritual this morning before leaving, but I felt possessiveness wafting off Jean as he leaned closer to me.

"Jean—" I'd been about to repeat my whole "you're sexy as sin but this isn't going anywhere" spiel when shouts from the front of the boat drew both our attention. A rolling tangle of arms and legs and fists ping-ponged from one side of the deck to the other, while Libby leaned over the rails on top of the wheelhouse, watching.

Holy crap. A merfight had broken out right under our noses. I grabbed my staff as Jean barreled past me, leaping nimbly around the narrow edge of the wheelhouse and onto the foredeck. I carefully sidled behind him, fearful I'd fall in the water. A dark braid flew above the fray before a hand grabbed it and used it for leverage to throw a punch. Denis Villere had indeed appeared from somewhere, and he and one of the twins—Rene, I thought—were beating the crap out of each other. Libby played the role of wanton cheerleader.

Jean struggled to separate them, and ended up with a fist to his nose. Instead of stopping the fight, he shouted French epithets I couldn't understand, and decked Denis with a powerful roundhouse punch. Great. The three men separated briefly before Denis took another lunge at Jean, Rene tried to get between them, and all three toppled over the side of the boat with a leviathan splash.

I briefly considered letting them kill each other. It would solve all kinds of problems—Rene and Denis would be out of my hair, and Jean would go back to the Beyond to lick his wounds a couple of weeks before coming back good as new. But then the war would just mutate to Robert and T-Jacques.

I ran to the rail and looked down. The three men, looking like mud-covered swamp monsters, had moved their brawl onto the bank. Jean was making no attempt to stop it. In fact, he and Rene were exchanging punches as well.

"Better stop 'em, wizard." Robert had reappeared during the excitement, and was slipping back into his clothes.

"Why don't *you* stop them?" It was his brother, after all.

"No way, darlin'. Rene and Jean get rid of Denis, that's a good thing."

Idiots. I raised the staff and pointed it at a tree a few feet beyond where the men fought. I prayed my aim would be true, although it usually wasn't. I really needed to take Charlie out somewhere and practice.

I released a bit of my own energy into the staff. Red ropes of flame shot out, hit the bank, and glanced off the shoving, punching tangle of bodies before ricocheting into a stand of reeds behind them. Reeds that promptly burst into flames.

"Merde!" Jean propelled himself into the shallow water, followed by Rene and Denis. Their smoldering clothes doused, they sat side by side with water lapping at their bodies, staring at me in a combination of shock, horror, and outrage. They looked like prete versions of the See No Evil monkeys.

On the positive side, I'd stopped the fight and no one was dead.

"Sorry," I said. "But I—" My self-defense was interrupted by a loud *whoosh* as the fire moved beyond the grass to engulf the low-hanging limbs of the small tree that had been my original target.

Holy crap. I was burning down the Louisiana wetlands.

I grabbed a couple of tarps and eased over the side of the rail, dropping like a boulder into the water. By the time I clambered to my feet, soaked and dripping, Denis had shifted into his full fish form and used his big caudal fin to splash me in the face before swimming away. Rene climbed back onto the boat, cursing.

Jean held out a hand for a tarp. "We should put out the fire, Drusilla. Your ability to aim your magic stick has not improved."

"You think?" I handed him one of the bundles of heavy, wet plastic and I took the other. He tackled the tree; I beat down the fire in the reeds. After several minutes and a lot of smoke, the fire had been reduced to a black patch that reeked of wet ash and singed moss.

Jean looked around him. "Something smells amiss, Drusilla, and it is not your poor aim. It carries the scent of death."

My heart sank. Had I killed someone after all? What if T-Jacques had been hiding in the tall grass and I set him on fire? "Help me look," I said.

We began searching farther off the bank. About ten yards on the other side of my burned tree, I tripped again. This time, what caught my foot was a decomposing body, and when I fell I got a close-up view of the remains of Jeffrey Klein.

Four hours, three calls to the Elders, and one transport to Edinburgh later, I straggled in my back door looking like something even Sebastian wouldn't drag in. My muddy clothes had dried into stiff brown sheets, my hair sported highlights of mud and ashes, and I didn't want to even know what my face looked like. I was not only exhausted, but depressed. On some level, I had hoped the Elders had been wrong and we'd find Jeff Klein alive somewhere.

I was not happy to see Alex and Jake at my kitchen table, two pizza boxes open between them. Why weren't they at the Gator, tending to business and eating at their own apartments?

I slammed the door behind me. "Have fun on your rough day talking to cops and college professors?" If this was how the division of labor was going to break down, I was getting that raise.

"Zrakovi said you could give us the report on Jeff Klein," Alex said, coughing in an ill-disguised attempt to keep from laughing.

Jake tried to take a sip of beer but collapsed into a laughing fit. I made a fool of myself in front of Alex often enough that I'd come to accept it as a fact of life, but I really, really hated that Jake was here to complete my embarrassment. Besides, two wizards were dead and I'd just been up-close-and-personal with a decomposing body.

Jake managed to get himself under control. "Sorry." He squinted in the vicinity of my stomach. "That hole in your sweater looks like it's been burned."

"I forgot to tell you. She set the Birdfoot Delta on fire." Alex picked a mushroom off the pizza and popped it in his mouth.

"I'm taking a shower." I slipped my muddy shoes off by the back door and left a trail of dried mud as I passed them. "Save me some pizza."

"DJ, wait." I turned at the foot of the stairwell to find Jake standing in the guest room door. "I've gotta head back to the Gator—I'm short-staffed, so Alex can bring me up to speed later. Just wanted to say I'd pick you up at seven tomorrow night. Sound okay?"

I smiled, and felt mud crack on my cheeks. Terrific. "Sounds good. I'll try to be clean by then."

His soft laugh washed over me like a sweet breeze. "See you then, hotshot."

19

I expected to spend all Wednesday researching the Styx, trying to find a connection between the water rifts and the professors, and angsting over my date with Jake. What to wear. How much he'd changed since turning loup-garou. Whether we'd have anything to say to each other.

Alex got the rest of his debriefing on the riverbed rifts during our morning run. Last night, he'd been too busy laughing and I'd been too tired to hear more than a cursory report. Jake had been assigned to work with his former Marine buddy Ken as the NOPD/FBI go-between, and Alex's boss, the head of the secret Elder/FBI enforcer division, had smoothed over the paperwork and jurisdictional issues. Alex finally had his search warrant for both Doug Hebert's and Jeff Klein's homes and offices.

Instead, while Alex rifled through the dead men's desks and Jake went to see if Melinda Hebert knew of a next of kin for Jeff Klein, I filed an emergency slew of reports. Use of unauthorized magic. Using an unauthorized incendiary device, although I thought calling Charlie an incendiary device was a stretch. Arson on federally protected property. Explanations to counter accidental injury claims being made by both Denis Villere and Rene Delachaise.

Jean hadn't filed a complaint, and Rene shouldn't have since I used a healing potion on him as soon as the fire was out. I'd have healed Denis, too, if he hadn't fled the scene. A scene that was his fault, I added to my report.

I won't say Elder Willem Zrakovi was the last person I expected to see walking in my office at eleven a.m. I'd have been more shocked to see Brad Pitt, for example, or Hugh Jackman, though I'd have welcomed either with open arms.

Elder Zrakovi had to make do with a startled blink and a handshake.

He looked around the office before settling into the chair facing my desk. "You need some decoration." He cast a disapproving eye at the bare walls and drab institutional carpet.

Surely the biggest cheese in my corner of the wizarding world hadn't come all the way to Louisiana to discuss office décor. "Yes, I thought I'd put up some JazzFest posters. But things have been a little busy lately."

Zrakovi smiled. "Perhaps we can find you an assistant. We've recruited a few young sixth-sensers who have good computer skills. With all the new species coming in, you and Mr. Warin will need help."

He could skip the assistant and give me a raise, but I didn't say so—yet. I'd started a report on that. Instead, I fixed a pleasant expression on my face and waited for Zrakovi to get to the point. He seemed to be stalling and fidgety, which made me nervous.

Zrakovi was on the short side, about five-seven or eight, with close-cropped gray hair, a prominent nose, and a penchant for expensive tailored suits. His restless hands fiddled with his emerald signet ring, which reminded me that he was originally a wizard of the Green Congress himself. Like most wizards, age was impossible to tell. He could be fifty; he could be a hundred.

"I have a couple of issues to discuss with you," he finally said. "First, do you need help in finding a solution to the problem with the Styx? I could have the head of the Green Congress to come in and direct the operations, or bring in the sentinel from Las Cruces."

I'd never get any respect from the Elders if I let someone bail me out, especially a former fling (Dante of the Green Congress) or a pompous Elder wannabe (Las Cruces).

"I have it under control," I said. "We put in temporary repairs yesterday, and I have an idea on how to make them permanent." Technically, I had one idea, it was borderline insane, and I had no intention of sharing it with him until I'd tried it and it had either worked or failed disastrously. There wasn't much in between. "Any word on Jeff Klein?"

"His throat was cut, similar to that of Doug Hebert," Zrakovi said. His face sagged, the stress of the post-Katrina years showing in a patchwork of wrinkles. "He was not mutilated, however, so we believe Doug was the target and Dr. Klein was just in the wrong place."

A blanket of sadness settled over me. I wasn't sure how long it would be before I could close my eyes without seeing that ruined body. Still, it was better I found him than a mundane.

My cell phone pumped out my familiar Fats Domino tune. I glanced at the screen, saw Jake's name, and set it back on the desk.

"Go ahead, I don't mind waiting," Zrakovi said.

Whatever else he wanted to talk about, he seemed in no hurry. Troubling.

I grabbed the phone. "Hey, what's up? Did you talk to Mrs. Hebert?"

"Negative," Jake said. "Melinda Hebert's gone—and I mean gone as in missing."

"What happened?" I penned MELINDA HEBERT MISSING on a sheet of paper and held it up for Zrakovi.

"Newspaper's still in the yard, mail from yesterday still in the box, no car at home. Front door was unlocked, so I let myself in and looked around. None of her stuff seems to be missing, so it doesn't look like she went on a trip. But here's something interesting. There was a photo album layin' out on the bed with about a half-dozen photos either missing or torn in half."

That would be more interesting if we knew what it meant. Had Melinda killed her husband and left with a few photo mementos? Had the killer taken Melinda and removed incriminating photos?

After ending the call, I turned back to Zrakovi. "I asked Adrian Hoffman to check her out. I thought she was behaving strangely when we were there." I told him about my inability to read her emotions. "I know you guys don't put much stock in my empathic abilities, but I've never been unable to read a human before."

He frowned. "Adrian is looking into her background, as you asked. I'll talk to him later today and see if he's learned anything. Actually, your empathic skills are part of the other thing I want to talk to you about."

Damn, it was about the unauthorized magic. I knew using that staff would catch up with me eventually but it was stupid to have a tool and not be able to use it. "I would like to be able to use the staff without it being considered"—I thumped the stack of reports in front of me—"unauthorized magic or an incendiary device." I sighed. "Although I am sorry about the fire."

He studied me a moment, his expression unreadable and his mental shielding too strong for me to burrow into his brain. "Agreed. You should be able to use the powers you've been given, although you need to learn to control the elven magic better. But your continued use of that staff has drawn the attention of the Elven Synod. They began researching some of their ancestral weaponry to see if it was significant."

I didn't know what an Elven Synod was but it didn't sound like anything I'd want attention from. "What did they learn?"

Zrakovi leaned back, relaxing now that he'd let the lion out of its cage. "Do I smell coffee?"

While I found a clean cup and poured, he talked. "The Synod is the elven version of the Congress of Elders. There are four members, one representing each of the tribes." He took the cup. "Their leader, Mace Banyan, knows you found the staff in Gerry's attic after the storm and doesn't like the fact that a wizard can call on elven magic. He wants to meet with you."

Well, crap. I'd really gotten attached to Charlie. I thought of the staff as a wooden security blanket. "Why now?" I asked. "Why didn't they show up the first time I used it?"

"I think they only recently figured out which staff you had and how powerful it is. It's very old, made by members of the original Synod, and there were only four made. Two are still in elven hands; the other two got lost over the years. Mace Banyan says yours is the staff known as Mahout and belongs to the clan of the Fire Elves. It is an important part of their history and they aren't happy Gerry had it all those years without them knowing it."

That was because it didn't work for Gerry. "What does Mahout mean?"

"Don't know." Zrakovi sipped his coffee and made a face. "What is this?"

"Kahlua medium roast." If people didn't like my coffee they should go to Starbucks.

"I don't know what the name means, but I explained to Mace that you are in the middle of an investigation so they'd have to wait. At some point, however, you'll have to meet with him if for no other reason than to satisfy his curiosity. I asked if the Synod wanted the staff back, but he said now that it had claimed you, no one else can wield it as long as you are alive."

As long as I was *alive?* I slumped back in my chair. Freakin' elves. I should never have picked up that staff in the first place. I should have figured using anything that threw off sparks and gave me a nosebleed when I touched it could only lead to grief.

"How does the Synod know I've been using it?" Did metaphysical alarms ring in the high halls of Elfheim whenever I picked the thing up?

Zrakovi shrugged. "News travels. You can't imagine how creatures in the Beyond like to gossip."

Pot. Kettle. Black. Wizards would gossip about drying paint.

"Anyway," he said briskly, all business now that he'd unloaded his little burden, "we're negotiating the time and place, and who will be allowed to accompany you to meet with them. At the very least, I will be there. And it probably won't be for another month or so. I just wanted to let you know so you could do some research in your spare time."

Right. Because I had so much of that these days.

"So they want a get-to-know-me meeting?"

"More like a how-can-they-use-you meeting, I suspect," Zrakovi said drily.

I caught a vague stirring of doubt from him, which ratcheted my own anxiety up a few hundred notches. He must be
really unsure about this meeting if he was broadcasting
feelings so clearly.

"In other words," I said slowly. "You don't know why
they want to see me?"

He took a deep breath and nodded. "Precisely."

20

I stood in the middle of my bedroom, surrounded by towers of girly stuff. Skirts, dresses, heels, boots, camisoles. Half of the clothes still had price tags dangling from them. I felt like a fifteen-year-old wallflower faced with the prospect of a date with the high school quarterback. Totally out of my comfort zone and with a serious case of nerves.

Jake was a jeans kind of guy, so if I trotted out my little black dress, it might be too much. What if he thought I looked slutty? If I wore a skirt and jacket I'd look like I was headed to a business meeting, ready for more of a hostile takeover than a successful merger. Not that I was planning on a merger, but it never hurts to be prepared.

Jeans and a sweater might imply I didn't care if I impressed him or not, which wasn't the case. But we were going to listen to music, so I didn't need to overdress.

Maybe I was overthinking it. I'd have to give that some more thought.

I sighed and looked around at the mess, searching out something that was sexy but not trampy, casual but not sloppy, flattering but not too dressed-to-impress. I was down to two hours and counting. I felt hopeless. My stomach ached and I kept wandering in circles, looking at the same piles of clothes and coming up with the same lack of ideas.

Tish would have laughed at me, so I would never call her for help. Eugenie would laugh at me too, but then she'd dress me like a Barbie doll, which is the level of intervention I needed.

I snatched my cell phone off the nightstand and called her. "Help me," I whined. "Date in two hours. Nothing to wear. Freaking out here."

Sure enough, she cawed into the phone—sort of half laugh, half snort—then hung up. Less than two minutes later, I met her at the back door. She marched in with a bright blue makeup case and an air of purpose. Dressed for a last-minute date with new neighbor Quince Randolph, she wore a purple tunic with black embroidery and a pair of dark jeans and boots.

Maybe I should go out with the new neighbor. Hippie plant guy seemed easier to prepare for than loup-garou guy.

I pulled a soda out of the fridge for her, and she stared at me in horror.

"You don't want the soda?"

"The soda's fine. It's you. How long do we have?"

Well, *that* made me feel better. I looked at my watch. "One hour, forty minutes."

"Oh my God." Eugenie grabbed my arm and pulled me up the stairs.

I had a moment of panic as she rounded the stairwell entrance and went into the den. What if I'd forgotten to lock my library? I'd been in such a sartorial panic I hadn't noticed. Eugenie did not need a tour of all my magical paraphernalia.

I gave an inward sigh of relief at the sight of the closed door. As far as Eugenie was concerned, I kept that room closed off to save on energy bills unless guests were expected. I thought maybe I'd talk to her soon, test her out with a little magical show-and-tell, but not tonight. I hated having to lie to her so often, and selfishly wanted a friend to really confide in.

She marched into my bedroom, cursed at the heaps of clothes on the bed and chairs, and began digging and sorting.

"I don't really know where we're going to dinner, but then we're going back to the Gator to listen to Zachary Richard, and Jake's a really casual guy." I felt the need to speak up when she hauled out the short black mankiller dress I'd bought on a whim and never worn. I'd wear jeans and my Tipitina's nightshirt before I wore that dress. It would scare Jake to death. Well, okay, it would scare *me* to death.

"We've gotta make you look taller and play up your eyes,"

she mumbled, jerking out a few sweaters and turning around to study me. I felt like a teal-eyed dwarf.

She settled on a dark purple cashmere sweater. "You can't lose with cashmere and it's kinda cool tonight. Looks good, and soft to the touch." She looked at me and squinted. "Remember, DJ. Touching is good."

I thought touching Jake Warin would be very good, but however long I'd known him, it was still our first real date. I'm not exactly one of the vestal virgins, but I'm not the Happy Hooker, either.

I nodded. "Yeah, that's a good choice. And jeans." I picked up my favorite pair.

She jerked the stonewashed denim out of my hands. "Not happening." Digging around on the bed with the skirts, she came up with a black flirty number short enough to make my legs look longer but not short enough to risk arrest. Ironically, the only time I'd worn it was the first time I'd met Jean Lafitte, right before Katrina. As I recall, he'd been fond of it. Maybe I'd wear it Sunday night on my date with him as well.

With Eugenie's help, I finally managed to get dressed, including my simple black heels and gold earrings. After much discussion about the pros and cons of up-do's and whether or not they were conducive to making out (Eugenie, who'd put in a lot more make-out time than me, said no), I wore my hair down.

She finished my makeup and stepped back to survey her handiwork, smiling. "That should earn you a wolf whistle or two."

I laughed, a tinge of hysteria in my voice. Wolf whistle. She had no idea.

Jake Warin was two years older than Alex, four or five inches shorter, and the polar opposite in personality. He was laid-back where Alex was intense, better at improvising when the rulebook didn't work, and had a better grip on his temper—at least before the loup-garou attack. And dimples.

They were the first thing I saw when I answered the back door just before seven. The last three years evaporated for a few seconds, and he was a normal human guy with no idea the prete world existed, and I was just a girl he was attracted to. Except I'd never been "just a girl," and now he knew it.

He didn't say a word, but smiled, stepped into the kitchen, and pulled me into a hug. He smelled like sunshine and aftershave through a silk shirt the color of copper pennies, but I noticed a tired, worried edge to his eyes. It disappeared when he smiled again. "I missed you, cupcake. It took a long road for us to get here."

"I'm glad we did." I led him into the double front parlors. "What's the plan tonight?"

"I made reservations at Commander's. That okay?" He grinned, knowing what my answer would be. I loved Commander's.

Ask a baker's dozen people their favorite New Orleans restaurant and you'll get a baker's dozen answers.

Jacques-Imo's had moved into my number-two spot, but give me any excuse for a splurge and I head straight for Commander's.

"What time does Zachary Richard start his first set?"

"Just doing one and it starts at ten. We don't have to be there early." He laughed. "I know the owner."

We made small talk on the short drive to Washington Avenue, traded stories about Ken and Alex and the extended Warin family over turtle soup and sugarcane-grilled pork and bread pudding soufflé, heavy on the whiskey sauce. An intricate tapestry of soft jazz wove through the tables, blending with the rise and fall of conversations, clinking silverware, and laughter.

"What do you think about the enforcer work so far?" I said, waiting for the coffee to arrive.

He leaned back and took a deep breath. "I think I'm gonna like it. I wish I'd finished the training right after the change, but I had to get my head around it first. I started it, then quit and came back here. It hasn't been easy."

I nodded. I'd grown up knowing I was different, that the world wasn't like most people thought. Having that truth thrust on you, suddenly and violently? "I think it says a lot about how strong you are that you've been able to make something positive out of it."

He reached across the table and laid his hand over mine. "I'm sorry I stayed mad at you so long." He paused, looking at the table then back up at me. "I have to ask. You and Alex. Are you . . . ?"

"Friends," I said, firmly pushing The Kiss out of my mind. He'd bitten my lip, for one thing, and for another, he'd only kissed me to mess with my head. "He's going out with Leyla Friday night. So don't be thrown if I show up as his 'date' "—I crooked my fingers into quotation marks— "at his mom's birthday dinner Saturday. It's just because he's a chicken and doesn't want to admit he's been lying to her all this time."

Jake grinned. "You're gonna meet Norma and pretend to be Alex's girlfriend?"

I shrugged. "We've been dating since Katrina, didn't you know?"

"I hadn't planned to go, but now I have to. You and Norma." He shook his head, laughing. He didn't seem jealous, and I hoped that was a sign the cousins were outgrowing their fierce rivalry.

We fought over the check, but Jake insisted on paying so I let him. I was still out for the big seafood fest all the mers had enjoyed in Buras. The Elders were waiting on a detailed expense breakdown and a report on why they should pay for it.

We stood out front while the valet went for Jake's truck, and I closed my eyes, feeling content. The night air was crisp and cool, and being here with Jake felt right. It was nice to step away from mermen and dead wizards and the River Styx for one night.

"You ready for some music?" Jake stood behind me and slipped an arm around my shoulders. "I have it on good authority he's going to play a couple of your favorites."

"I do love to hear that man sing, even though it's in French and I can't understand most of it." I leaned against him and smiled. The real world would come barging back in soon enough. Tonight, I was content just to be.

The Gator was already packed when we arrived, but Jake shepherded me to the front, where a small table sat before the stage with two chairs, two glasses, a bottle of wine, and a RESERVED sign in the middle.

Jake pulled out a chair for me and grinned. Here was a man who knew what a girl wanted.

For ninety minutes, we sat side by side, Jake occasionally leaning over to whisper something about a song and, once, to plant a soft kiss on my jaw. When Zachary finished with an unplugged version of "Lumière Dans le Noir," one of my favorites, I almost purred like Sebastian.

I met Zachary without making too big an ass of myself, and finished my wine while Jake made sure the man got safely out of the bar without being hassled.

Business at the Gator continued without missing a beat. The jukebox grooved out BeauSoleil, and the crowds settled in for the night. The last I'd spent any real time here, National Guardsmen and emergency workers assigned to New Orleans for post-hurricane security comprised most of the crowd. Now, college kids and tourists slammed down hurricanes and Abitas and a bouncer stood at the door.

"Want to go upstairs for a while?" Jake held up the bottle of Riesling.

I thought of Alex's warnings about not being alone with Jake, and realized he was just trying to manage me by planting doubts in my mind. Big jerk. Same as making me think of his talented lips when I was with Jean Lafitte.

"I'd love to."

Jake leaned over and said something to Leyla that sent her big doe eyes narrowing in my direction, and we headed for the back.

He went into his small kitchen to get fresh glasses, and my gaze was drawn to the table. It was covered with guns, boxes of ammunition, and things I couldn't identify but looked big and nasty and lethal.

"What's the arsenal for?" I frowned at the biggest piece of equipment. Rocket launcher? Flamethrower? Whatever, it looked like it could kill something big.

He flicked his eyes over the collection. "Welcome to my new life, sunshine. Every monster needs its own flavor of weapon. I'm still trying to learn what all of them do, and which ones are needed for which pretes."

He picked up a box and held it open for me to see.

"Bullets?"

"Silver," he said. "To kill werewolves and loup-garou."

Yikes. "You're helping Alex with the investigation, not so much with prete calls. How much of this stuff do you really think you'll use?"

His voice was soft. "I'm going to be killing things, DJ.

Alex is doing sentinel work, not me. Enforcers don't just investigate."

He handed me a glass of wine and walked back into the living room, setting the bottle on the coffee table in front of the sofa. "That's what I'm suited for now anyway. I like it, even though I think I shouldn't. It bothers me that I want to kill things." His grip on his wineglass tightened.

"Sometimes you don't have a choice." That sounded lame, but I wasn't sure how to handle the direction this conversation was taking.

Alex had been trained as a killer, but he didn't talk much about his enforcer runs. He liked his weapons, but seemed to have a clear vision of what was good and what was bad—and no qualms about killing what was bad. Sometimes Alex's life outlook was too black-and-white for my taste, but Jake seemed to be wandering lost. Maybe Alex had been right to worry about him, and I had been arrogant to think he was okay.

I followed Jake into the living room, sparsely furnished with an old bookshelf full of video and stereo equipment, a couple of chairs and lamps, a beat-up coffee table, and the same old worn brown sofa that had probably been here when he and Ken first bought the bar.

I noticed an empty square on the wall that was a lighter shade of beige, where the shadowbox with his Marine Corps medals had hung. He'd taken it down. Just how much emotional trouble was he in?

Even though I'd promised myself to stay out of his head tonight, I tried to get a read on Jake's emotions. Nothing came through but a fuzzy were signature. Loup-garou didn't broadcast well.

I took a sip of wine, sat beside him on the sofa, and tried for an easy subject. "Tell me about your leg. Is it healed?"

He flexed his right knee and looked down at it. "Yeah, before I shifted the first time, the surgeons took out all the rods and pins and put it in a cast. I split the cast during the change and when I shifted back, it was healed. Just like I'd never been hurt except I'll always have the scars."

Jake had been backed off a cliff in an attack on his Marine unit in the mountains of Afghanistan in 2003. The fall saved his life, but the damage to his leg had been permanent. Or so they thought.

"Alex says you're running again."

His smile had an edge to it. "Yeah, like it never happened. It makes me wonder what the hell we were even doing over there."

I frowned. "You mean in Afghanistan?"

He stared somewhere past my shoulder. "The world we were fighting to protect? Doesn't exist, never did." He shook his head, jaw tight. "Sorry. Didn't mean to go there tonight."

"But—"

"Hush." He leaned over and put his wineglass on the coffee table and moved closer to me, taking my glass and setting it beside his. "Been thinking about you a long time, and we're not gonna talk about anything except what's right in this room, right now. You and me."

A stupid smile plastered itself on my face before I could stop it. Not that I tried very hard. "Yeah? What are we going to talk about?" I'm so sophisticated it's scary sometimes.

He slid his right arm around my waist and angled in for a kiss. It was sweet and soft, and I ran my hand down his cheek.

"We've kissed before," I reminded him.

"Yeah, but you weren't sober so it gets thrown out on a technicality." I caught a flash of the killer dimples and started to laugh before he moved in for round two and put a little more heat into it, winding his fingers through my hair and tracing his other hand in slow circles on my back. I quit laughing.

Jake groaned when Fats Domino began singing out of my purse on the coffee table. I was starting to dislike Mr. Domino. "Ignore it," I said, grabbing Jake's collar and returning his attention to the matter at hand, namely me. I couldn't remember the last time I'd made out on a sofa, but it was all coming back to me.

"I didn't hear a thing." He slid a hand under my sweater and began kissing his way toward my collarbone.

He eased me to my back and shifted his body alongside mine, nuzzling my neck and breathing in deeply before tilting his head up to kiss my ear. I brushed my hand through his hair and tried to pull him to my lips, but he growled and continued moving along my neck, nipping at my earlobe. My head tipped in an effort to catch his mouth for another kiss, but strong, rough hands—too rough—clutched my hips and held fast, one muscular leg slipping between mine.

Laughing, I slapped at his shoulder. "Do you always go this fast on a first date? I can't move."

He stilled, his breath heavy and hot against my neck, and I realized something had changed. I was still at playful, but he'd moved into possession. He held me too tightly, his mouth had grown too still over the artery thudding against his lips. If he broke skin, I'd be furry by Thanksgiving. The thought sent my heart rate into hyperdrive, and I felt him inhale deeply, taking in my fear.

Scent could send a wolf over the edge before he could think better of it.

"Jake?"

My voice sounded too uncertain. *Calm it down, DJ.*

"Hey, Marine. Let me up."

He made an unintelligible sound, and I struggled against his grasp. He shifted more weight onto me.

"DJ . . ." The low growl of my own name rumbled through me. It wasn't a sign of consciousness, but a warning.

I froze as the long, deep kiss he'd planted on my neck turned into a bite. My skin was between his teeth. I didn't even want to breathe.

I eased a hand to his shoulder and did the only thing I thought might bring him around. I shot a jolt of magical energy at him—just a mild electrical shock, not enough to hurt him and not even a heavy tap on the scant physical energy I possessed as a Green Congress wizard.

He jerked his head away and looked at me with eyes that had turned a flat, reflective golden-yellow. His wolf.

"Jake? Stop. Listen to me."

"Shit." He pushed himself off me and stood up, looking down with eyes that were slowly darkening back to amber.

I took a deep breath and blinked, trying to force my muscles from shaking with the drain of adrenaline. *Calm, DJ. Don't upset him.* I sat up and forced a smile. "It's okay. No big deal. We just moved too fast."

I stood and reached for his hand, but he jerked it away.

He started pacing, and I didn't need to read his emotions to see he was scared. "No, it's not okay. I thought I could control . . . I can't . . ." He slammed his fist into the wall, smashing through the plaster and sending out a cloud of white, chalky debris. The electrical wiring inside the broken lathing lay exposed.

"Jake—stop!" I reached for him as he thrust his fist toward me, stopping about two inches from my nose. It took every-thing I had not to flinch, but instinctively I knew if I showed fear now, we'd never come back from it. *He* might never come back from it.

"Watch," he said. His knuckles were bloody and raw from impact with the wall, but as I took his hand the skin reknitted itself. Within thirty seconds, he was unmarked but for a fine coating of plaster dust and an earthquake crevice in his psyche. I'd never known a were could heal that fast.

But as people kept telling me, loup-garou were not ordinary weres.

"I'm a long way from human, DJ," he said, then laughed. It sounded as bitter as chicory coffee the morning after. "I thought I had the damned wolf under control, but he's still controlling me."

I held his fist in my hand and forced his fingers to uncurl. "I've never been purely human, Jake. We'll just take it slow. I know you won't hurt me."

But even as I said the words, I wasn't sure I meant them. Moments ago, I hadn't known it at all. I'd been scared.

His voice grew hard and he still wouldn't look at me. "I wouldn't hurt you but *he* might."

With horror, I realized he hadn't accepted his situation at all. He'd just become a better actor. Until he came to terms with what happened, he would never be able to control himself. "You *are* him. The wolf is not separate."

He pulled his hand away and clenched his fist again, holding it at his side. "I am *not* him. I won't *be* him."

God, what could I say? He had to calm down before he shifted spontaneously, and as brave as I tried to sound, I wasn't sure how either one of us would react if that happened.

I practiced breathing and kept my voice low and level. "You have to accept what you are. You have to make peace with it."

He avoided my eyes as he walked past me to the kitchen counter and grabbed his keys. "I better take you home. It's getting late."

"Don't push me out, Jake. Let me help."

He looked at me finally, and the pain in his eyes made me want to cry. "I don't know how to let you help me. I don't know how to help myself, or even what *would* help."

He chuckled and shook his head, looking at the floor. "I think you pushed a whole set of buttons the folks at Quantico didn't anticipate."

I smiled a little at that. I knew one of the things his sponsor had done was bait him to lose his temper, to see how far they could push him before he lost control and shifted involuntarily. He must have achieved a good mastery of the wolf or the enforcers wouldn't have let him come back to New Orleans. But anger wasn't the only strong emotion, was it?

"We'll call it a night, but I'm not willing to give up on us." I grabbed my purse and headed for the door. "Let's slow it down and start over."

He nodded, but wouldn't look me in the eye.

The drive home was silent and tense. Finally, he asked, "Who called? It might be about the case."

If I'd answered my phone, could we have avoided that catastrophe? I pulled it out of my purse to check the call log. "Alex."

Jake grunted. "That figures. I'm not sure my cousin's too happy to have me working with you guys."

"He's just worried about you." I unbuckled my seat belt and shifted around to face him. "Look, I know it's different for him as a shifter than it is for you, but he can help you. Let him."

He didn't answer, just kept his eyes on the road, so I punched the buttons to retrieve the phone message. It was brusque.

"DJ, call me when you get home. A fisherman just found Melinda Hebert's body on the riverbank in Plaquemines, near another breach."

21

Tish sounded half asleep when she answered the phone at six a.m. "DJ, do you know what time it is? What's wrong?"

I gave her the text-message version on the latest Styx rift and Melinda Hebert, then asked her to stop by. "I have an idea on how to permanently seal these rifts, but I want somebody to know what I'm doing."

In case it goes badly, I didn't add.

"I don't like the sound of that," Tish said quietly. "What are you planning?"

"Stop by and I'll tell you."

I didn't want to explain over the phone. I could plead for her silence better in person.

I'd been up late last night, making sure all the pieces were in place. Alex had told me Melinda Hebert's body had been carefully laid out on the bank of the river near Duvic, fully dressed. A fisherman checking his traps had found her. The cause of death wasn't known, but the body had been snapped up by the Plaquemines Parish authorities and Alex couldn't get anywhere near it.

He also had run into Denis Villere, who was angry that we were using the Delachaise twins for all of our work. To appease him, Alex hired him to dive in the area where Melinda's body had been found—thus the discovery of the new rift near Duvic, which was upriver and alongside human populations. I didn't know what would happen if someone drank water contaminated with cooties from the Styx but it couldn't be good.

Thankfully, Alex had been so preoccupied he hadn't asked about the date with Jake, so I didn't have to decide if I'd be helping or hurting Jake by keeping my mouth shut.

I thought everything was ready. Alex would be tied up most of the day trying to get access both to Melinda's body and the police reports, and Jake would be digging through the contents of Doug Hebert's filing cabinets. Their investigation hadn't yielded any results so far, but at least my window of opportunity had opened.

My last call of the night, after much soul-searching, had been to Rene Delachaise. He'd been suspicious but agreed to be at my house by two, as long as I paid him for another day's lost wages. If this didn't go well, an overdrawn bank account and some pissed-off Elders would be the least of my worries.

I was sitting in the living room reading the paper when Tish arrived at seven, looking rumpled and frantic.

"What have you done?" She barged in the back door before I had it fully open, and tossed her purse on the table.

Settling her hands on her hips, she looked me up and down. "Nothing looks out of place, just dark circles under your eyes. Are you getting enough sleep?"

Great. Add concealer to the shopping list. "Stop playing mama and pour yourself some coffee," I said. "I haven't done anything yet."

"I don't want coffee." She sat in the chair facing mine and gave me a she-bear scowl. "What are you up to?"

"Have you come up with any ideas on how to permanently seal the rifts between the Mississippi and the Styx?" I laid the paper aside and crossed my arms, knowing she hadn't.

She slumped. "No, it's complicated, isn't it? I mean, wizards aren't built to do work underwater, yet unless some kind of direct magic is used, the repairs won't be permanent. I've wracked my brain to think of another species that could do it, and I come up blank."

Exactly. "Do you know anyone who's ever done a power-transfer?"

"Oh my God." Her voice cracked, and she went to pour herself a cup of coffee after all. "You are not going to transfer your power to anyone," she said, panic taking her voice into the ozone. "Are you insane? What if it doesn't work and you end up losing your magic altogether or, worse, draining so much you kill yourself?"

Her eyes grew narrower with every word. "And what if it does work and whoever you give your power to figures out how to keep it? Honestly, DJ. This is a million times worse than dilly-dallying with Jean Lafitte. Tell me you're kidding."

I just looked at her.

She set the coffee mug on the table and rubbed her eyes. "You aren't kidding."

She wasn't taking it well, but at least she hadn't threatened to tattle.

"I swear to God if you tell me you're serious about this, I'm calling the Elders. You need to be saved from yourself. You're just like Gerry."

"Ouch." Gerry had died in the process of going rogue. If his prete partner hadn't killed him in a double-cross, the Elders would have given him the death penalty. This time, she hadn't meant it as a compliment. "Look, Tish. I know it's risky, but I think it can work. I've found a ritual for a short-term sharing of power, not an outright transference. Twenty-four hours, max. And we have to do something—the contamination is too close to where people live now. The Elders will drag their feet until it's too late."

"You don't even know what's causing the rifts."

"No, but how many people do we let get sick—or worse— while we're figuring that out?"

The rise and fall of her shoulders told me I'd won. She couldn't think of a better idea, either. "Who are you going to do it with? Alex?"

I took a deep breath. "No. Alex is not to know about any of this till it's over. I mean it. Not. A. Word."

Her lips tightened into a narrow ridge. "Jake? I don't think he's stable enough."

She had no idea how unstable Jake was. "One of the

Delachaise twins. I considered each of them and finally decided on Rene."

Tish didn't answer for a long time. A really long time. Enough time for me to rinse out both of our coffee mugs and put them in the dishwasher.

"That's a really smart idea." I could tell she almost choked on those words as she watched me wipe down the counter. "Are you sure you can trust him?"

"Well, there's the million-dollar question." I returned to the kitchen table, where I'd piled a couple of Gerry's black grimoires—the kind that still had instructions on things like power transference rituals, before they'd been outlawed by the Elders. I felt a twinge of guilt that I'd made Tish complicit in this harebrained scheme. But if Rene and I accidentally killed each other or I'd misjudged him and he was going to add me to his list of murdered wizards, I wanted somebody to know how stupid I'd been in my final moments.

"I don't have much to go on except intuition, but my gut tells me Rene is a good guy." Of course I also liked his Corvette-stealing friend Jean Lafitte. There were those— Alex, for instance—who'd say my judgment had a few flaws.

Tish nodded. "Robert seems less antagonistic toward wizards, but I don't think he's serious enough. I agree Rene's the one to do it with. How can I help? Do you want me to be here?"

I thought about it. Knowing she was keeping an eye on things would make me feel better, but I thought my best chance of convincing Rene to do this was if no one else was involved.

Finally, I shook my head. "Just help pick up the pieces if it goes south."

About two p.m., Rene Delachaise stood in the middle of my library, looking down at the shards of glass that until a few minutes earlier had been an 1882 vase in a pattern called Fish and Seaweed. The irony was not lost on me.

"Can you wave your wand around and clean it up?" he asked.

"You've seen too many movies." I allowed myself a moment to mourn the vase as I pulled a broom and dustpan out of the upstairs storage closet. It had been one of my favorites. At least it hadn't been full of herbs or iron shavings.

"Did you cut yourself?" I asked. Rene hadn't thrown the vase when I'd proposed the power-share. He'd been holding it when I explained my idea and squeezed it so hard it imploded.

"No. Sorry about that, babe. What the hell you mean about sharing power?"

We sat in the armchairs, and I let him read the spellbook—in itself an act that would make the Elders hemorrhage—and explained how the ritual would work, at least theoretically. "I'll give you the words to say, and you should be able to channel enough of my magic to do the underwater spells that will permanently seal the rifts." *Should* being the scary-factor word. What abilities I'd get from him was a mystery. I just hoped I didn't sprout fins.

I sat quietly while he stared at the floor. He wore tattered jeans and his usual tank, which showed off hard, muscular arms underneath the tats. He was a sober, serious man, and I thought I'd made a good choice—if he went for it. His only flaws were a hair-trigger temper and an innate dislike of wizards. I couldn't read his emotions, but his energy felt less malicious around me than it had in the beginning. I was growing on him.

"You done this before? You know it'll work?" His dark eyes bore into mine.

I had to be honest. "I haven't done it before. I don't know anybody who has—in fact, it's illegal and I'll get in a shit-load of trouble if anybody finds out."

He grinned, his teeth even and white in his tanned face. "How you know I won't knock you off, keep your power, and become the Mer King of Louisiana, babe?"

Well, that was ambitious. I swallowed hard. "I don't. I'm trusting you as much as you're trusting me."

"Yeah, you right." He stared out the library window at Eugenie's salon across the street. An elderly woman with a head of powdery, white poofy hair tottered down the steps toward a waiting cab. "I want the water cleaned up 'fore anybody else gets sick, and if there's a rift at Duvic, there's gonna be humans gettin' sick too. And we don't know what it's doin' to the wildlife." He looked back at me and nodded. "I'll do it."

If we performed the ritual now—assuming I'd calculated the timing correctly—we'd both have several hours to get used to our new skill sets and go on the water at daylight to do the repairs. While Rene would pull power from me, I'd also pull from him. I had no idea how long it would take either of us to recuperate. But by the time my man Alex and I went to his mama's birthday dinner, I should be back to normal. If not, and I had to stay home, what a pity.

Ever the optimist, I'd gotten the space ready before Rene arrived. I dragged chairs against the wall, tugged aside the large area rug to clear an end of my library floor, and used first chalk, then salt, then iron shavings to literally make an ironclad circle to contain the magic. Despite my vow to avoid using Charlie—make that Mahout—I would need the staff's power to make sure I had enough amps to fuel the ritual.

I carried Rene's gaze like a tangible weight as I set candles on the four points of the circle, then placed a large Fuji apple and a silver knife in the center. The apple had soaked in a magic-laced belladonna tincture for twenty-four hours, and I hoped it wasn't too strong. Belladonna was powerful in transference up to a point; beyond a certain measure, it led to a swift, ugly death. This little experiment was fraught with peril.

I turned to Rene and took a deep breath. "You ready?"

"Hell no." He grinned.

We were both barking mad. "Me neither. Let's do it."

After I lit the candles and we entered the circle, I sliced into our left palms with the silver knife and we held our hands together, our mingled blood dripping into a small dish I held underneath. When I thought I had enough, I used the tip of the knife to mix the blood thoroughly and place a pea-sized drop on five points along the circle's edge. I bent down, touched the staff to the circle, and shivered as the power raced around its circumference and trapped us inside.

Rene hissed and closed his eyes. He'd felt it too. "Now what?"

"Now we sit." I was winging it at this point. The ritual instructions ended at *close the circle and share the apple*. I wasn't sure it mattered whether we stood or sat or held a Cajun *fais-do-do*, but my legs felt wobbly from nerves. We sat cross-legged, knees touching, and I picked up the apple.

"I don't eat fruit," Rene said.

"You only have to eat one bite and swallow a couple of seeds." I cut it in half horizontally. "The seeds form a pentacle design, representing the four elements plus spirit. Trust me."

Yeah, famous last words. We were trusting an ancient book of unknown origin that Gerry had probably found at a rummage sale.

I took one slice of apple and halved it, each portion containing two seeds. I handed Rene his slice and took my own. "Now we eat it."

"Should we hold hands or something?" Rene asked.

Hell if I knew. "Yes, my left hand and your right," I said somberly. We clasped our hands together and ate the apple. Rene reached over and grabbed my other hand as we chewed. We stared at each other and waited. I was almost afraid to breathe. My heart pounded, and he swallowed so hard his Adam's apple shifted.

"What's supposed to happen?" he asked.

"I don't—*whoa*." My head spun and I tilted to the right. Without the anchor of Rene's hands I would have fallen over.

"You're freakin' me out, babe. What's going on?" He barely had the words out before a visible shudder passed through his body and he closed his eyes and threw his head back, nostrils flaring.

I've never felt this strong. I should have found a wizard earlier. Wish I was swimming now. I'd take Libby down to that cave under—

"Hey!" What the hell . . . I could hear his thoughts, and they were grossing me out. I snatched my hands back. "Why do I know what you're thinking? I don't want to know what you do with Libby. Don't even think about Libby. She's an alleycat. You can do better."

This wasn't like my empathic insight. I was inside his flippin' brain.

"Shit." He leapt to his feet and looked around, frantic. I felt him slamming mental walls up, but not fast enough to block out his fear. "Is it gonna kill me to get out of this circle, wizard?"

He was imagining himself keeling over and thinking how humiliating it would be to fall into a dead faint in front of me. Idiot.

He glared at me. "Don't call me an idiot, witch."

Damn it. He could hear me too.

"Yeah, I can."

I reached out with my foot and broke the circle. The release of energy eased the pressure inside my head, and Rene sighed in relief as I clambered to my feet. "I can still feel you, babe, but it's not as bad."

"Me too." I stumbled to one of the armchairs in front of the window and flopped into it. Rene took the other.

Neither of us spoke for a while. It was four p.m., and I think we'd done it. If the power part of it worked, by this time tomorrow the rifts would be sealed and I'd be alone inside my head again. Of course, we had a good thirteen hours before we could go out on the water. Unless we could do it now.

"No, too dangerous after dark," Rene said. "We'll go at daylight."

I groaned. "I didn't say that out loud."

He closed his eyes. "Shit."

22

I heard my cell phone ring, persistent and annoying, but I was enjoying myself too much to answer. Or, rather, Rene was enjoying himself and part of my brain was doing a ride-along.

He'd hung around for a couple of hours while we tested the extent of our unexpected brain-meld—we could hear each other like background static on a radio, but had to concentrate to get thoughts or images. We also experimented to see how much of my magic he could channel. The elven staff wouldn't work for him, but his own mer energy seemed to give my magic an extra zap, and vice versa. He definitely had enough to enact the ritual I'd prepared for tomorrow morning. I'd written the ritual words down for him to take home and memorize.

An hour after he left, he'd shifted—akin to what I imagined it felt like to be pulverized in a food processor—and now he swam through cool, deep water. I gave myself over to his pleasure, felt the rush of the current on my skin, and, if I closed my eyes, the strange, dark beauty of the marsh bottom played like a movie across the back of my eyelids.

"I'm at Pass a Loutre, babe. You hear me?" I almost *eeked* myself off the sofa in fright.

Crap on a stick. He could talk to me. I concentrated and sent a thought back: *I hear you. This is seriously freaky.*

"Tell me about it—you been swimmin' with me. I felt you." He swam deeper into the dark water. "I'm going near the rift. Tell me if you feel anything."

I closed my eyes, and watched a turtle swim past as we swooped over and around a series of logs lying on the bottom of the pass. Small, colorful stones pebbled the marsh bed, with mossy growth on larger rocks and big chunks of wood probably left from Katrina.

Urg. I rolled to my side as a wave of nausea coursed through me, making my eyes water. No wonder the mers were getting sick. *I feel it; get out of there, Rene.*

Even after he swam near the water's surface and away from the contamination, my tongue felt too big for my mouth and I took deep breaths to quell the overwhelming urge to upchuck. Tomorrow morning couldn't come soon enough.

"Over and out, wizard. Be in Venice at five thirty. We gonna leave from there instead of my place—the fewer people know about what we done, the better."

Gotcha. I couldn't agree more. The pressure inside my head eased as we stopped trying to communicate, and I let him swim in peace. I forced my eyes open and *eeked* again. Alex stared at me from an armchair he'd pulled in front of the sofa. He did not look amused.

His voice was low and constrained. "Tish tried to call you twice. When you didn't answer, she called me in full-tilt meltdown. I've been sitting here trying to talk to you for five minutes, DJ. What the hell have you done?"

I eased to a seated position and waited to see if the nausea came back. It didn't. Instead, hunger gnawed at my stomach lining. Swimming built up an appetite. "I need shrimp," I said. "Let's go to Felix's."

Alex moved to sit beside me on the sofa. He slid an arm around my shoulders and tugged me against him. This was nice; I hadn't expected him to be understanding, much less supportive. He was big and snuggly and warm.

He lowered his mouth to my ear, and his whispered words puffed against me in soft minty bursts. "You have exactly one minute to convince me not to call Zrakovi. Tick. Tick. Tick."

Rene laughed in my head as I elbowed Alex. "I'll tell you over dinner. And if you call Zrakovi, I'll tell him you looked the other way when Jean Lafitte stole a car, then falsified your reports. He expects me to do things like that but not you. You'll be down in the Elder doghouse with me."

Rene and I laughed. "*Doghouse*, get it?"

Alex pulled away and looked at me. "Are you all right?"

"No," I said, getting to my feet. "I'm starving."

I explained the ritual over dinner. I ate a dozen fried

shrimp with fries and slaw and an extra side of onion rings. I'd ordered a dozen oysters on the half shell before it finally occurred to me I might be eating for two. I frowned and concentrated. *Rene, what are you doing?*

His voice came through like crystal. "Enjoyin' your dinner."

Get out of my head. I'm going to be sick if I eat any more.

"I want to keep you busy, babe. I don't want to be there while you and your shifter do it like doggies."

An oyster slid down the wrong way, and I collapsed in a fit of coughing. *Out!*

His laughter rattled my eyeballs. Who knew Rene could be so annoying?

"DJ." Alex's tone matched the one generally reserved for the extremely old or the mentally decrepit. "You're making weird faces again, and you're eating like a . . ." He clamped his lips shut, clearly realizing he was on shaky ground.

I shoved the oyster plate away. "Rene's inside my head. We're sharing a brain. He's talking to me and, let me tell you, that fish needs a life." Except if he had one, I'd have to live it with him, at least for another nine hours or so.

Alex laughed, and I relaxed a little. I'd rather he laugh at me than threaten to turn me in to Zrakovi. The Elders wouldn't give a fig that he'd known about that car theft, and he knew it. They *would* care that I'd done an illegal power-share with a merman who was technically still a murder suspect.

"So, what did Rene say that got you so choked up?"

I arched an eyebrow. "He wants me to eat enough to make myself sick so he won't have to ride along, so to speak, if we decide to have sex."

I expected Alex to laugh or use some of his favorite Mississippi cuss words. Instead, his mouth edged up in a smile—not a teasing smile. A serious smile with more than a touch of wicked. "We could do that."

Oh no we couldn't. Could we? A wave of warmth washed across my face.

His eyes crinkled at the corners. "That's cute. I made you blush."

"Did not," I said automatically, breaking the hold of his gaze and motioning to the waiter with a little more gusto than necessary. I couldn't handle my partner getting all weird on me. "Could we have the check?"

Alex leaned back in his chair with an infuriating chuckle.

Another laugh tickled my eardrums from the inside. "He's got your number, babe."

That's what I was afraid of.

Friday morning dawned warm and clear, with the blue skies and low humidity that marked late October in Louisiana. It was the perfect day for a swim.

Alex and I rode in uneasy silence as we left New Orleans heading southeast. He'd insisted on driving this time, probably out of fear that my merman mind-meld would send us into a watery grave.

Were things changing between us in some subtle way,

or was it my imagination? Of one thing I was sure: any relationship examinations would have to wait. We'd bought a *Times-Pic* on our way out of town, and the lead story was about an odd, nasty strain of stomach virus sweeping through several communities in South Plaquemines. Three people from Duvic had been hospitalized, and more than a dozen from the general area had sought medical attention. Which probably meant at least ten times that many were sick—most men had to think they were at death's door before they'd see a doctor. I didn't have proof the Styx contamination caused it, but I didn't need proof. I knew it.

Halfway there, Alex finally broke the silence. "What should I expect today?"

I had no clue. "What I hope is that Rene can dive to the rifts and seal them. They need to be set with magic to make them permanent. He's going to be drawing magical energy from me, but I don't know how it will affect me. He swam around all night practicing how to focus the magic to a single area." I knew, because I'd been there with him whether I wanted it or not. And the more magic he pulled, the more my muscles ached and head throbbed.

Alex cleared his throat and didn't answer for a while. When he did, his voice was soft. "Why couldn't you trust me with the truth? I wouldn't have tried to stop you." He smiled. "Well, yeah, I would have. But you'd have done what you wanted anyway. I could've been there if something went wrong."

It was a serious question and deserved a real answer, even if it made me sound like a sap.

"I didn't want you stuck in the middle if I screwed it up." One of the things I most respected about Alex was his strong sense of right and wrong. Not that I didn't want to do the right thing and follow the rules, but my world had more shades of gray in it and I was comfortable with that. "It isn't that I don't trust you—I trust you more than anybody. I just don't like what it costs you to support me sometimes."

I didn't have to explain what I meant. My insistence on trying to handle things in my own screwy way after Katrina had forced Alex to choose between me and his duty to the Elders. That, and Jake's attack by the loup-garou, had shaken the way he looked at the world. I wouldn't put him in that position again.

"We're not done," Alex said, turning into the parking lot of the small marina where Rene's truck was already waiting. "We'll finish this later."

My partner wasn't big on soul-searching talks, so maybe he'd forget about it. I had nothing else to add.

23

By the time we'd finished repairs at Duvic and Pilottown, I was drooping from Rene's drain on my energy. As soon as Pass a Loutre was out of the way, this little wizard planned to nap until the power-share wore off.

Rene, on the other hand, bounced around the *Dieu de la Mer* like a kid on a sugar high. I sat on the aft deck, leaning against the side of the boat, and listened to the stream of thoughts running nonstop through his head while Alex navigated.

How his gator season would have been even better if he'd had my power last month. How he wished Denis Villere would show up before the ritual wore off so he could buzz the hell out of him. How he could run the whole mer empire if he married me and had access to my power whenever he wanted it. All he needed was a night alone with me and he could do things that would knock my socks off, although he'd have to get rid of Alex first.

Then I was treated to a visual image of what might knock off my socks.

Good grief. I slumped over and curled into a ball, resting my head on a coiled pile of rope. I focused on details around the deck to try to shut out that steady stream of inner mer babble. Compared to this, my empathy was easy. He did have a big black hole at the back of his thoughts he was keeping on tight lockdown, though, and he'd snarled at me when I tried to pry my way in. So Rene had some secrets he didn't want me to know, and that made me uneasy.

I had learned a few useful things. He'd spent a lot of time wondering about the Styx rifts and how they might have been made. His theory was that the Villeres, who were part of the Houma tribe and had some native magic of their own, summoned the water to drive the Delachaises away, or even kill them. That theory had more holes than a box of doughnuts, and I had mentally told him so at about three a.m.

I'd also learned what kind of business he and Jean Lafitte engaged in, and it wasn't as bad as I'd feared. He bought things that had value in Old Orleans—alcohol, alligator skulls and claws for voodoo rituals, tobacco, even fresh foods—and Jean sold them in the Beyond at highly exaggerated prices. The currency of Old Orleans was gold, which Jean would then bring back to Rene to cash in at high twenty-first-century values. The Corvette had simply been a crime of opportunity.

What Rene *didn't* think about was the murder of the wizards. Not a wisp. Either it wasn't important enough for him to exert brain cells on, or it was locked away in that black hole.

"You okay there, babe?" I jolted awake from my doze. Rene sat behind me, massaging my shoulders. I relaxed into it, until I remembered his sock-knocking aspirations. "We are not making this permanent," I muttered, almost moaning as his fingers dug into my tight shoulder muscles. "I don't care how well you visualize that sock thing."

He jumped to his feet, pulling me with him. "We're almost there. I better steer us in before Alex runs us to ground."

Yeah, whatever. I propped on the rail as Rene returned to the wheelhouse and began winding us toward Pass a Loutre. I spotted an alligator sunning on the bank; as the boat passed, it raised its massive armored head and streaked into the water in a gray blur. Alex and I had been lucky not to stumble across one when we'd combed the bank for clues on the professors.

Rene killed the engine and tethered the boat to an over-hanging tree near the rift, then disappeared onto the foredeck beyond the wheelhouse. He'd gotten fast at donning the mask and strapping on the oxygen tanks. By the time he splashed into the water, I'd already slumped back onto the deck and lay curled up with my head on the ropes again.

I closed my eyes as I watched the repairs play out through Rene's eyes: the muddy bayou bottom, the hole in the mud where tainted water rushed through, the beauty of the ritual as Rene drew on my magic to embed charmed stones in a circle around the rift and then invoke the spell to reknit the solid bed beneath him. I was even able to mentally prompt him on a few words of the ritual.

He was heading back to the surface when I sensed Alex sitting beside me. "Rene's on his way back," I mumbled a few seconds before we heard the thump of the mer climbing onboard.

Alex pushed my hair away from my face and placed his hand on my forehead. "How you doing? You look pale."

"Just awesome." I sat up, and had to wait a heartbeat for the dizziness to pass. "Rene's wearing me out. For a guy who doesn't talk a lot, he keeps a constant chatter going in his head. And he's enjoying my magic way too much."

Alex sat next to me. "We should try it sometime. I always wondered what it would be like to channel energy that way."

Was he insane? "Do you really want me to know every thought that goes through your head? Because I would. I can tell you things about Rene Delachaise his twin brother doesn't even know."

Alex watched Rene climb back aboard, strip off the diving mask and tank, and shake off the water. "Like what?"

"Like what he and Libby did in the pirogue Robert uses for fishing." I shuddered. Food, sex, money. Rene's driving needs, or at least the ones he let me see. Was that a mer thing, or just a guy thing?

"Yeah," Alex said. "But I'd know every thought you had, too."

Exactly. Such a bad idea.

My response was cut off by the buzz of a boat engine as

a smaller, lighter craft rounded the bend in the bayou and pulled up alongside the *Dieu de la Mer*. Libby stretched the length of the boat like Cleopatra being sailed down the Nile by her faithful mer-servant, Robert.

He tied the smaller boat off and jumped aboard, joining Rene on the aft deck, where he was getting dressed. In under a minute, they'd raised their voices. I heard the word "wizard" more than once, usually with a four-letter word preceding it.

"Incoming," Alex warned, and I got to my feet just in time for Robert to stride around the side of the wheelhouse and get in my face. "What the hell you done to him? Your smell is all over him." He grabbed my shoulders and pulled me toward him. "And his is all over you."

I smelled like Rene? Robert was wrenched away from me by Alex, who had wrapped a big hand around the mer's upper arm. "Calm down, man. She hasn't done anything to him."

Alex was a full head taller and a lot broader than the pissed-off mer, so Robert finally stepped back and I released a breath I hadn't realized I was holding.

Libby climbed onboard and cozied up to Rene as he joined us. "You do smell like wizard," she said, wrinkling her nose. "Hope that washes off."

Great. I hated weres and shifters and that enhanced-sense-of-smell thing. I always felt the need to sniff myself.

Robert gave Alex a wide berth and circled back to his brother. "You only leading this clan 'cause Papa wanted to stay in Chenoire," he said. "Soon as he hears you screwin' a wizard, you're gonna be back shrimpin' in St. Bernard and livin' next door to him." He shoved Rene hard enough to crack his brother's head against the wheelhouse wall. "You know what wizards done to him after the war. He had to sell out his own people just to get his land back. You think about how you sellin' us out when you with her."

I hadn't brought Mahout with me. Now that I knew the elves could tell when I used it, I was trying to wean myself. But I wished I had it. My reflexes were slow, and Rene still had access to any physical magic I possessed.

He pushed Robert back. "Fuck you. I ain't sellin' out nobody." I watched, openmouthed and helpless, while he grabbed his twin around the neck with one arm and gave him a good zap in the chest with the other, using my freaking magic.

"Oof." Robert sank to his knees at the same time my legs gave way, my energy depleted. Only Alex's quick move to catch me prevented me from tumbling next to the mer. He dragged me out of Robert's reach and lowered me to the deck. "Don't move."

Like I could. "Stop them." Rene's rage filled my mind with red heat. He didn't know how to tamp my energy when it was fused with his. If he used more magic on Robert, he'd end up killing his brother and I wasn't sure what it would do to me.

As soon as Robert caught his breath, he launched himself at Rene, and the two traded punches while Libby sat on the rope coil and watched, smiling.

Alex tried to separate them, but couldn't. They'd tuned

out everything but their rage for each other. I closed my eyes and groaned, trying to send Rene calming thoughts. I couldn't penetrate his anger, which had started much earlier than today. Rene had been pissed at Robert a long time for not doing his share of the work, not sending money to the family in St. Bernard Parish, not taking his responsibilities in the clan seriously. At least I'd done my grounding ritual and had my mojo bag in my pocket, so I couldn't tell what Robert felt in return.

I felt a sizzle of power in the air and opened my eyes as the air around Alex blurred and crackled. Within seconds, a two-hundred-pound pony of a golden dog stood in his place, surrounded by discarded clothing. Gandalf.

Teeth bared, he plowed into Rene and Robert, knocking them off-balance and startling them so much they stopped fighting to stare at him.

"Ooh, I wondered what he could turn into—a big, warm, furry thing." Libby leaned forward to snag Alex's shirt, held it to her nose, and took a whiff. I wanted to rake her eyes out, just on principle.

Rene and Robert remained on their butts, staring stupidly at Gandalf as he bared his teeth and growled menacingly at first one, then the other. "Yeah, okay, shifter. You made your point," Rene said.

Robert wiped blood off his lip and felt inside his mouth for loose teeth. "Sorry, bro. But you gettin' too close to the wizards if they've given you powers and got you doing their dirty work."

"Ain't like that," Rene said, climbing to his feet. "We had to get the water cleaned up before somebody died. Didn't want it to be one of us."

His sharp teeth no longer needed, Alex walked to his clothes, snagged his pants leg in his teeth, and trotted toward the wheelhouse. He paused briefly next to Libby, who still held his shirt, and growled. I didn't think he was flirting.

The trip back to Venice was blissfully uneventful. I curled up on the bench in the wheelhouse while Alex steered and Rene navigated. The power-share was beginning to wear off; Rene's thoughts were just white noise in the back of my head, and he seemed almost as subdued and exhausted as I was.

On the drive home, we hit a drive-through in Belle Chasse and the food revived me.

"Think you can go through that again if more rifts show up?" Alex asked.

"Don't even say it." I was pleased with the way the actual repairs had gone, but round two? Uh-uh. "And after all that, I still don't know if Rene is off the suspect list for killing the wizards, although he didn't try to hurt me. He had a lockbox in his brain he was able to keep me out of."

"What about Robert?"

I sighed, wondering if this was a safe conversation to have. I wasn't hearing Rene's thoughts anymore, and my attempts at mental conversation were going unanswered. I assumed he couldn't hear me either. "Don't know about

Robert, either. Only that the twins are not getting along that well these days."

Alex grunted. "You think?"

"Smooth work back there, Gandalf." I looked at the muscled shoulders and arms that flexed as he turned the steering wheel and drove onto the Westbank Expressway. No tattoos, just smooth, tanned skin over muscle. I needed to write Libby a thank-you note for keeping Alex's shirt.

"I didn't want to shoot them, and you were out of commission. Why didn't you bring the staff?"

"Elves." I told him about my pending date with the Elven Synod. "They can tell whenever I use it, so I'm trying not to. They seem to make Zrakovi nervous, and that can't be good."

Alex nodded. "How are you feeling now?"

"I'm okay. Nothing a nap won't cure now that the power-share is wearing off. Where are we with the murder investigation?"

He thrummed his fingers on the steering wheel, which told me we were exactly nowhere. "We don't know anything about the professors—absolutely nothing turned up in their offices or homes, and the university's clueless. After I drop you off, I'm going to see Jake and find out what the status of Melinda Hebert's autopsy is. She's got to be connected."

We did know one thing. "The missing photos tell us whoever killed Melinda—and probably Doug—was someone they knew well enough to have in a photo album." I stuffed my empty soda cup into the bag. "But I still haven't figured out the Styx connection. We've been running so hard trying to plug up the rifts I haven't had a chance to do research on the Underworld and see if I can find anything from that direction. That's next."

Alex wound his way through Uptown and stopped to let me out at my house. "You think you'll feel like going to Picayune tomorrow?"

Picayune. Mama Warin's birthday party. I'd like nothing more than to say I was too tired, but a promise was a promise.

I slid out of the car, already envisioning the sensation of cranking the AC down low and sliding between cool sheets in my darkened bedroom.

"I'll be ready at noon."

24

Norma Warin's picture should be in the encyclopedia under the listing for Iron Maiden, or so I deduced. From Alex and Jake, I'd heard wild stories that I hoped had been exaggerated. Norma escorted by security from a Little League game for threatening to tell the umpire's wife where he'd been the previous Saturday night (it involved a poker game and a stripper). Norma frightening noisy neighborhood kids with a single well-placed look from her living room window. Norma reducing her husband and four grown sons to utter subjection with a steely glare and a compression of lips.

I pondered Norma as Alex drove the Mercedes onto the I-10 ramp, headed north. I'd been reduced to soliciting Eugenie's help again, and we'd settled on a simple pair of dressy black pants and a solid red cashmere sweater she'd loaned me to go with it. I argued against red—scarlet letters and brothels being red-related words I didn't want Norma

Warin thinking about—but Eugenie assured me once again that one could never go wrong with cashmere. It had been so *helpful* on my date with Jake.

Showing up on the arm of Norma's baby boy, even if he was six-three and usually well-armed, was guaranteed to put me under a microscope. I'd met Alex's older brother, Don, and I'm sure Alex-and-DJ sightings had been reported to Norma on multiple occasions since Katrina. Families never believe the *just friends* story, even when it's true, and I blamed my big, clucking partner for letting this farce drag on.

I rarely heard anything about Norma's other half, Thomas, so I had him pictured as a tall, thin rabbit of a man who did his best to stay out of his wife's way as she bulldozed through life.

I wondered if Jake still planned to be there. He hadn't called me; I hadn't called him. I wanted to tell him not to pull away from me out of fear, but I hadn't come to terms with my own reaction. Things were more awkward now than when he'd first been turned.

"Do you know if Jake's coming today?" I asked Alex.

"Probably." Alex turned down the volume on his satellite radio, pumping out contemporary country tunes that were about to put me to sleep. "Keep waiting for one of you to mention your date the other night. How was Zachary Richard?"

I smiled at the memory of the music, the crowd, Jake. If you sliced off the last hour of the date, it had been amazing.

"He was terrific. I still can't believe Jake got him to play the Gator." It helped that the proceeds had all gone to wetlands preservation.

"So you just went to dinner, then listened to music?"

He was fishing like a merman, his tone too detached and casual.

"Yep." I wasn't going to lie, but I also wasn't volunteering anything.

He glanced over at me. "What are you not telling me?"

I huffed. "I'm not giving you a minute-by-minute break-down of my date, Mr. Snoopy. I don't ask you what you're doing every minute you spend with Leyla." As badly as I wanted to, especially since I knew they had gone out last night while I was sleeping off my merman hangover.

"Leyla doesn't have Jake's issues," Alex said. "But I'll tell you anything about my date you want to know."

I wanted to know how he felt about Leyla. No, scratch that. I wanted to know how he felt about me. And I hated that I wanted to know.

I watched the urban sprawl of New Orleans East fly by as we sped toward the Mississippi state line. "I don't want to know anything about your date."

Of course I did, but the questions were all highly inap-propriate. It was none of my business if he bonked Leyla till dawn or if he wished she were in the car with him today instead of me. This was all Alex's fault. One kiss and a couple of innuendoes, and he had me wondering things I shouldn't.

I changed the subject. "What did Jake find out about Melinda Hebert and her autopsy?"

Alex cursed as an SUV whipped in our lane and cut us off. "Just more weirdness. We all assumed she drowned and somebody found her and laid her out there on the bank, but there was no water in her lungs. No signs of trauma to the body. They're waiting for tox reports to come in, but early assumptions are it was a suicide because she was distraught over Doug's disappearance."

"She took poison or overdosed on something, then went out and arranged herself on the riverbank in Duvic?" I didn't buy the suicide theory. It would work fine for the Plaquemines authorities but they were missing some key bits of information. Like the fact her husband had been mutilated, and that a breach with the river of the Underworld was found near her body.

"I've been doing research on the Styx, but things have been so busy I haven't gotten very far with it," I said. "That's what I'm doing tomorrow, though. I'm going to figure out what the connection between the Styx and the dead wizards is if it kills me."

Alex cleared his throat and assumed his sarcastic faux-French accent. "Would that be tomorrow before your dinner date with Jean Lafitte?"

"Did you know you sound like a cartoon skunk when you do that? And besides, I don't meet him till seven. I have all day."

He shook his head. "I have nothing else to say on that subject."

Good. Because now that it was getting closer, I was nervous about it. It had been quite a while since Jean had tried to kill me, but, as Alex pointed out, the man always had an agenda and I hadn't figured out how dinner with me was going to benefit him.

My partner reminded me I had more immediate worries. "We need to create some dating history before we get to Picayune."

I banged my head on the car window, and a sudden onset of nerves sent my heart skipping. "If we've been together since Katrina, we're probably at the stage in our relationship where we bicker and sit around watching reality shows and eating off TV trays."

Alex grinned. "That's what a long-term relationship looks like to you?"

I thought about it. "Well, yeah. What does it look like to you?"

He paused, then lifted his shoulders in a shrug. "No idea. Never had one. You just described my parents."

This would not be fun. Since being sent to live with Gerry as a kid, I hadn't been around a big group of extended family—or even a small group, for that matter. My own family had imploded after my mom's death. First my dad shunted me off, then my grandparents, and I'd ended up orphaned on the doorstep of the man I'd eventually learned was my father. And Gerry had no other family except Tish.

The Warins bred like bunnies. Alex was the youngest of four and Jake the oldest of three. Except for Alex and Jake, all the siblings were married and had kids of their own. I'd never keep them all straight.

A thrill of fear ran chittering across my nerve endings. What if Norma thought I was a potential grandchild producer? "Is it too late to back out? We could do something fun, like go to a shooting range. You could teach me all about the different kinds of guns."

Alex frowned until he looked over, saw my face, and recognized desperation setting in. "Mom has called three times this week to make sure you're coming," he said.

"Great. She'll be expecting someone taller." And prettier, with better social skills and a domestic bone or two.

"She probably thinks you're pregnant since I'm finally bringing you home to meet the family."

Oh my God. I closed my eyes and tried to regulate my breathing.

Alex laughed and turned the radio back up. The sound of banjos was not comforting.

I fidgeted the last five miles, until he finally steered the convertible off the interstate, through a twisting set of two-lane highways, and onto a loose gravel road into the woods.

He cursed as the car bounced over what wasn't much more than a rocky path. "They built this house as their retirement home right before Katrina, then spent three years repairing it. Still no driveway."

We reached a clearing where a redbrick split-level house nestled on a wide swath of autumn-browning grass. An arc of spindly pines surrounded the back and one side. On the other side, a herd of children rolled in a thick layer of straw, throwing prickly pinecones at each other and screeching in shrill pitches only the very young can achieve. Alex pulled behind one of several pickups littering the drive. I recognized Jake's shiny red Ford.

"Uncle Alex!" A sturdy boy of about four, dark curls bouncing in the chilly breeze, broke from the pack and came running, full-tilt. Alex caught him mid-air and roughhoused as the whole herd stampeded our way.

Where had my enforcer gone? The guy who once stood in my house and tossed a grenade up and down just to intimidate me? The man who tried to give me a gun as a token of his esteem? The fellow who threatened to kill tomorrow night's undead date? He'd obviously been abducted by body snatchers and replaced with this handsome, laughing alien. I smiled and stood back, letting the kids maul their uncle.

The front door opened, and Jake stepped onto the porch, descended the steps, and walked toward us across the yard. One of the kids, a blond boy of three or four, broke from the group and ran to him, and Jake bent and picked him up easily. He looked strong and sure. Only that tightness around his eyes gave away the stress he was under, and I wondered how he'd explained the disappearance of the pronounced limp he'd brought home from Afghanistan.

"Hey there, cousin." He and Alex shook hands, just a nice canine-shifter and loup-garou, meeting for a family outing. Jake turned to me, a trace of his teasing drawl and a flash of dimples reminding me what might have been.

"Norma's just dying to meet Alex's girlfriend after all these years. She's all a'twitter."

The front door opened again and my stomach lurched, but it was another child joining the fray. I couldn't do this. "Send me out a plate if you get a chance," I told Alex, and turned to flee back toward his car.

He extricated himself from the kids and grabbed my arm as I went by. "It won't be that bad." He jerked me closer to him and put an arm around my waist. From a distance it probably looked affectionate, but he held me in a vise grip. I wasn't going anywhere he didn't go, and he was heading toward the front door, from which a formidable woman with a helmet of dark hair had just emerged with a big smile on her face.

"Well, bless your heart, you must be Drusilla." I swear to God Norma Warin sounded just like Shirley MacLaine's character in *Steel Magnolias*. "We've just been dying to meet you, honey."

She gave Alex a quick kiss, then grabbed my arm and pulled me away from him and into the house. "Aren't you just the cutest thing? I didn't realize you were such a little bitty girl. Come on in the kitchen with the rest of the ladies."

I threw a helpless look over my shoulder at Alex and Jake, who stood side by side in the doorway, laughing. Maybe my misery could bring them closer.

*

The family gathering wasn't that bad, at least not until the fried chicken and mashed potato leftovers were all put away and everyone had finished a big hunk of the coconut cake Jake's mom, Liz, always made for family to-dos.

I'd been roasted and grilled by every female in the family and emerged battered but intact. My Alabama roots gave me some street cred in Picayune that helped make up for the deficiencies of growing up in New Orleans, which every upstanding citizen of the world knew was nothing but a hotbed of vice and corruption and licentious behavior.

During the process of dumping leftover peas and broccoli casserole into plastic containers and burping the lids, Jake's sister Juli informed me in no uncertain terms where I stood.

"You better not be stringing Alex along, and I see Jake watching you. Didn't think I saw that, did you? I swear, you better not hurt either one of them or you'll answer to me. I don't care if you are some hotshot FBI chick from New Orleans."

I nodded.

She dumped at least a pound of banana pudding into a container and shoved it at me. "Take that home—it's Alex's favorite. You probably don't even cook for him, do you? I wish he hadn't settled on a career woman. Are you even a Baptist? Because your kids can't be raised Catholic. We just can't have that. We eat meat on Fridays clear through from Mardi Gras to Easter."

I didn't know where wizards and shapeshifters would fit into the grand scheme of things or exactly when she expected said kids to be born, so I just nodded again. It would all be over soon.

Plus, I'd had a flash of insight into Alex and his family dynamic. The fried fowl wrapped in tinfoil wasn't the only chicken here today. *Cluck cluck cluck*. He wanted me here, pretending to be his girlfriend, so the women would quit asking him when he was settling down and spawning new Warin babies. Since Jake was divorced it freed him from the family's fear of his eternal bachelorhood, even though he had no kids to show for it.

Juli and I emerged from the kitchen and joined the rest of the adults in the big family room. Things were winding down, and the TV had been turned to the local news—or at least news from Hattiesburg, the nearest station that didn't have the taint of New Orleans on it.

A little girl with wispy-fine blond hair and honey-colored eyes, no more than six or seven, tugged on Juli's arm. It was Corey, her oldest. She looked like a short, female version of Jake, and I wanted to hug her.

I needed to get away from all this domesticity before it rubbed off on me in some permanent way.

"Mama." She got louder the more Juli tried to shush her. "Look."

Our eyes followed her finger toward the front window, from which we could see across the porch and into the yard. Backlit by the low-hanging sun of early dusk, Jake and Alex stood nose to nose, arguing intensely. I didn't think they were discussing Liz's coconut cake.

"I bet they're fighting over you," Juli said, loud enough for the mamas, Norma and Liz, to hear. I'd have given her a good, hard magical zap if I could've gotten away with it and wasn't still suffering from merman-lag. "You need to break it up before they start throwing punches."

I considered slipping a silencing potion in her glass of iced tea. I had all the basic ingredients in my purse and it didn't take any curing time. A quick trip to the bathroom and I could have it ready.

Tom Warin, every bit as tall and but not quite as browbeaten as I'd imagined, spoke up for the first time. "Those boys been fighting their whole lives. It ain't like this is the first time and it won't be the last. Just let 'em go at it. They never hurt each other too bad."

His pronouncement made, he turned the TV to the Weather Channel and ignored the storm brewing in his front yard.

His brother Ed, shorter and the source of his son's dimples, chuckled and leaned his own chair back to assess the situation. "Nothin' serious." He returned his attention to the TV. "They ain't even bleeding yet. Looks like a cold front's headin' in next week. Better check on that shipment of space heaters."

I sighed and walked onto the porch to get a better look. Jake's dad was wrong; it was serious, whether anyone was bleeding or not.

"Hey guys," I said softly, moving off the porch and stepping between them. Probably not the smartest move, but I didn't know what else to do. I turned my back to Alex and faced Jake. Alex had better control, and Jake was about to lose it.

I put my hands on his chest. "Look at me, Jake." I repeated it three times before he finally dropped his gaze from Alex and turned cold, calculating eyes to me. Fear shot through me, and I saw his nostrils flare. Jake was barely home, and the wolf smelled my adrenaline rush. Again.

He blinked hard a couple of times and backed up, shaking his head. "I. God. Shit." He stuffed his hands in his pockets and looked at the ground. "I should never have come back. I don't think I can do this."

"What happened?" I turned to Alex with raised eyebrows.

"We were just having a discussion." Alex looked mad enough to chew glass. He grabbed my wrist and pulled me toward the house. "Get your stuff. We need to head back."

We packed up the wrapped plates of food and the container of banana pudding, and got back on the road with a minimum of drama.

I waited till we hit the I-10 before I started. "Tell me."

Alex feigned ignorance. "About what?"

"You and Jake. What was that about? He was about a second away from going all loup-garou on you, and you weren't backing him down."

He chuffed, sounding more like Gandalf than Alex. "He told his enforcer sponsor he wants to take field assignments, not do investigative work. It's a bad idea."

I thought about Jake's admission that he wanted to kill things. Field assignments would let him do that and maybe burn off some of that feral energy. But what if the more he killed, the less picky he was about *what* he killed?

"What does his sponsor say?" I shifted in my seat. "I can see both sides of it. I mean, admit it, you miss the field work too, don't you?"

Alex clammed up. I had a quick ethical argument with myself over whether or not it was fair to try to read his emotions, then said to hell with it and did it anyway. I pretended to watch the shadows of the new Twin Span bridges rising along the edge of Lake Pontchartrain while I opened my mind to his.

Alex had always been hard to read, but he was upset enough that he was broadcasting more than usual. Frustration and anger didn't surprise me. Jealousy did. He was jealous of Jake?

Maybe it wasn't so surprising. Jake was treading on Alex's turf while Alex was stuck doing sentinel work. It put them in prime position to restart the macho rivalry that had died down the last few years as Alex maintained his FBI cover and Jake ran the Gator.

Lightbulb. "You don't want the competition." I turned as far sideways in my seat as the seat belt would allow. "You don't want Jake competing with you as an enforcer."

"That's ridiculous," Alex snapped.

Yep, that was it. I'd nailed it. "Is not."

No answer. Clenched jaw. Big frown. I could see them in the soft lights from the dash as darkness fell.

I turned back around in my seat and watched the ocean of dead trees that, this long after Katrina, still marked the entry to New Orleans East as they streamed through the car's high beams. Alex pulled to the side of the road and killed the engine. Backwash from passing eighteen-wheelers jostled the car.

"What are you doing?" I had a fleeting fear he was so mad he'd put me out on the shoulder of the highway and make me walk home.

"I'm going to talk and you're going to shut up and listen." His voice rasped with tension. "I don't give a shit about competition from Jake, at least not as an enforcer. We need the help. With investigations like we have going on now, I can't take off for a day to take an enforcer run. But he's not ready."

Alex was so damned rigid. "Let him take a run. See how he does." Why make everything so complicated, I wanted to add.

I flinched as Alex slammed his hand on the roof of the car, jarring the overhead light cover. "I'm worried about him, damn it. He's loup-garou. He's going to have to develop iron control over his wolf or the enforcers will kill him. Do you understand that? He's not a normal were. If he screws up, they won't move him somewhere else and give him a new assignment. They'll kill him. Put him down like a goddamn lame horse. He slips up one time and that's it."

I shivered, noticeably enough that Alex reached over and cranked the car so the heat would cut back on. My shivers had nothing to do with the temperature. "What if you could take some runs with him, till he's ready to do it by himself?" My voice shook. For the first time, I saw a hint of what Jake was up against and I was afraid for both of them. They might fight and argue with each other, but if Alex had to hurt Jake, he couldn't live with it.

Alex leaned his head against the headrest. "I'd like to do that. But we've got so much work of our own. I can't take the time off right now."

I wanted to tell him to take the time off, that I could handle things, but as much as I wanted to prove myself to the Elders, the thought of losing Alex made me want to cry.

"DJ, I need an honest answer about something."

I looked out the side window and wiped away a tear, hoping Alex didn't see me. "Okay."

"Did Jake lose control with you?"

The mental image of flat yellow eyes looking down at me flashed through my mind, the feel of his teeth on my neck, his arm pinning me so hard I couldn't move.

"You're not answering, so I take that as a yes. Shit." Alex rubbed the back of his neck. "What happened?"

I didn't know the right thing to do, except to be honest without being graphic. "He didn't lose it, not completely. The wolf started slipping in and I had to zap him to get his attention—Jake's attention." I had the wolf's full attention, which was the problem. "We were both a little shaken by it."

Alex took a deep breath. "What were you doing when this happened?"

Good question. And *making out on the sofa in his apartment* would not be my answer. "Nothing really, just fooling around."

Alex narrowed his eyes, and I could feel him studying my face in the semi-darkness. "Okay, I'll take *fooling around* to mean something a little more private than listening to Zachary Richard in a crowded room."

I blessed the dark as I felt my face heating up. It was probably the same shade of scarlet as my sweater. "Well, yeah, but it wasn't like we were—"

"Don't tell me." He held up his hand to cut me off. "I get the general idea. What was Jake's reaction?"

Haunted eyes, a fist jammed through a plaster wall, bloody knuckles. "It scared the crap out of him. He shut down and took me home."

Alex exhaled and leaned against the headrest again. "Good. That's what he's supposed to do, and he needs to be scared. Did you ever feel like you were in danger? And I want an honest answer. You won't help him by lying to protect him."

"It scared me when it happened." I'd had time to think about it, and realized that when Jake grew so still, he'd been warring with the wolf and, to some extent, holding it off. "But I don't think he would have hurt me." I hope to God I was right about that.

"Good."

I still didn't think we'd gotten to the heart of the problem. "You said you weren't jealous of Jake because he was an enforcer. Is there something else going on?"

"None of your business." He started to pull the car back on the interstate, then stopped again, shifting it back into park. "But we are going to talk about your merman stunt."

Good Lord. The man was a grunting caveman half the time. Now he was channeling Oprah on the side of the I-10. "Fine. Let me have it."

"We're partners. I have to know you're not keeping shit from me. What if I hadn't found out about the power-share with Rene, hadn't gone out with you yesterday? Robert could have killed you, or worse—and you didn't even have the staff. Or Rene could have gotten so out of control he drained everything you had."

Damn it. I knew he was right, but I had my reasons. "I just—"

"Don't protect me." Alex's voice was gruff. "Don't make decisions for me. Don't be afraid I'll take off if you do something I don't like. I'm not going anywhere. Even if I end up back on field duty at some point, I'm not leaving *you*."

My own tears caught me by surprise, and I turned away before he could see them. Everybody leaves. If I'd learned one thing in life it was that. They might die. They might betray your trust. They might stay until life got too hard or inconvenient. But in the end, the people you cared about always left.

His hand brushed my wet cheek. I'd planned to get in his head and somehow, instead, he'd gotten in mine. "I'm sorry," he said. "You just don't seem to understand that this isn't a one-sided thing with us. I don't want to lose you either. Not because you've put yourself in danger protecting me or because of the shitty baggage you drag around from your screwed-up family." He paused a heartbeat. "And not because of Jake."

He said that last part so softly I barely heard him. What did that mean exactly—he was afraid Jake would hurt me, or he didn't want to lose me to Jake? It was such a startling thought that I decided to keep it to myself to gnaw on a while.

We pulled back onto the road and drove into the city in silence. At the red light nearest my house, he finally said, "I'm the one who bought the house."

"What?" I'd stared out the passenger window so long I was almost in a trance. "What house?"

"Next door to you. The shotgun. I close on it next week."

I didn't know what to say. Was that good or bad? Did I want Alex for a neighbor? Was he buying that house out of feelings for me, or was I giving myself way too much credit?

But houses were major commitments. If he was buying a house, he wasn't going anywhere, at least not for a while. I smiled, not wanting to examine that warm, safe feeling too closely. "I'm glad."

25

Twenty-four hours later, I stood in the middle of my bedroom again, wrapped in a towel, surrounded by heaps of clothing and looking for something to wear on a date. Life had been much simpler when I had no social life, plus my dates weren't exactly dinner-and-a-movie guys. One had serious control issues, one seemed to be changing the rules of our relationship and was almost scaring the crap out of me more than his werewolf cousin, and the third wasn't even alive in any normal sense of the word.

I couldn't call Eugenie this time, not and lie my way through an explanation of a dinner date with an undead pirate who couldn't even come and pick me up because cars hadn't been invented during his lifetime. Of course, that hadn't stopped him from stealing one.

Whatever I wore, I had to make it snappy. I'd spent the whole day combing through everything I could find on the River Styx, looking for the elusive connection between the mers, the dead wizards, and the water breaches. The situation seemed to deteriorate hourly.

Denis Villere had called late last night with news that a member of his family found a new breach in Plaquemines, between Buras and Port Sulphur. A lot of people lived between Buras and Port Sulphur. The media was full of what some clever reporter had deemed the "Plaquemines Plague," the state water officials were squabbling with the Army Corps of Engineers over jurisdiction, and the Elders wanted it all to just go away before some smart water engineer figured out there were substances in the water that didn't conform to any known contaminant or life-form.

The fact that Denis had found the new rifts raised him on my suspect list, except for that little issue of motive. If the seafood in the area was impacted, it would hurt not only the Delachaise clan but the Villeres as well. So against my better judgment, I agreed to pay Denis to place the temporary charms over the new rifts until Rene and I could do a repeat of our ritual. I knew he'd be willing but I needed another day or two to recuperate. Plus, we needed to find out how the breaches were occurring and put a stop to it.

Alex's investigation into Doug Hebert's and Jeff Klein's deaths had stalled. We were still waiting on the toxicology report on Melinda Hebert, and Jake said the NOPD was bristling at FBI interference.

I pulled the slinky black dress from the pile for consideration. It was basic mankiller stuff: short, off the shoulder, curve-hugging. I set it aside. Not the message I wanted to give a man who thought "no" was a word used to begin negotiations.

What message *did* I want to give the pirate, exactly? I sighed and nudged a pile of clothes far enough to sit on the edge of the bed.

I had a little pixie angel DJ on one shoulder telling me how bad Jean was. *He's violent and unpredictable. He hit you once—hard. Oh, sure he saved your life later but it was in his own best interests. Plus, you have absolutely no common sense where he's concerned, and we won't even mention the dead thing.*

I hated pixie angel DJ.

On the other shoulder sat pixie devil DJ: *He's a preternatural being just like a werewolf and a shapeshifter, so you're splitting fine hairs by saying he isn't human. What's more, the pirate is practically immortal, which means he can't get killed on you, and he's sexy as hell. Plus, he accepts himself for who and what he is.*

Who was I to argue with the devil? I snatched up the little black dress and slid it on with a smooth rustle of silk, enjoying the irony of wearing a mankiller dress on a date with a man who, for all intents and purposes, had already been killed. Sapphire and silver jewelry set it off, and I left my hair long and loose. I picked up my sensible black pumps and threw them in the back of my closet, instead pulling out a pair of strappy (not to mention crazy-expensive) Manolo Blahniks Eugenie egged me into buying on clearance two years ago. I'd never worn them. New Orleans isn't a Manolo Blahnik kind of town, at least not in my social circles, where an unscuffed pair of Nikes was practically formalwear.

I picked up the elven staff that had bailed me out of trouble with Jean Lafitte in the past. The thigh holster Alex helped me rig for it would look ridiculous with my dress. Note to self: get Alex to pick out a nice all-purpose handgun that would fit in an evening bag. If I was going to date outside my species, I needed to be armed. The fact I even considered the need for a gun on a date should have rung a few alarm bells, but tonight I'd be going weapon-less.

On the drive to the French Quarter, I rethought the whole outfit. What if Jean wore his customary black pants and linen shirt? I'd be grossly overdressed. What if he thought my dress was too short? The guy probably liked powdered wigs and petticoats.

Still, I was excited by the promise of an interesting evening. Whatever else Jean Lafitte might be, he was not dull, nor was he likely to dredge up emotional crap that would leave me in tears.

I tapped on the door of the Monteleone's Eudora Welty Suite, and when Jean answered I got an eyeful of early nineteenth-century gentleman that made me forget about being overdressed. He'd tucked fawn-colored trousers into matching soft leather boots, and a fawn vest topped a formal white shirt. A blue scarf around his neck added a dash of color, and I saw a blue waistcoat draped over a chair.

We stared at each other. I recovered first, and laughed. "May I come in?"

He stepped back and smiled. "You look magnificent, *Jolie*. More beautiful than even I realized."

God help me, I blushed. Again. "You look kinda hot yourself."

He frowned and looked down at his clothing. "But I am quite comfortable. Why would you believe I was hot?"

I bit my lip. "Sorry, it's just a modern term to mean that you look very handsome."

"Ah, *trés bien*." He smiled, handed me a brandy, and pointed me toward one of the suite's facing sofas. I sat close to the arm of the nearest one and was pleased to see he sat a respectful distance away. Good pirate. There would be no making out on this sofa.

"Drusilla, I have chosen a special place for us to dine tonight. I reserved a table, but you must decide if you are willing to go."

I took a sip of brandy, which sent a sweet burn all the way to my toes, and tried to keep a pleasant expression on my face despite being able to tell he was uncertain. I'd done my emotional grounding ritual before leaving the house, but the dress was too clingy for my mojo bag to be hidden anywhere. I'd left it at home, accepting that I'd be pulling in some unwanted emotion tonight.

Jean didn't think I was going to like whatever he was about to tell me. "What did you have in mind?"

"I would like to take you to Antoine's."

I blinked at him. Antoine's was culinary royalty in New Orleans. I had only eaten there once. My salary was more in the cheap corner dive range, and Antoine's was even more expensive than Commander's.

"Well, of course. I'd love to go to Antoine's." I hoped he didn't try to pay for dinner with gold doubloons. If he did, I could always slip the waiter some plastic and pray my credit limit held.

"Do not answer in haste, *Jolie*. I do not refer to the modern restaurant, but the original. Antoine Alciatore himself will be preparing our meal." Jean looked pleased with himself. "Of course, you must accompany me into the Beyond for the evening."

I set my brandy snifter calmly on the coffee table but gave away my alarm by crossing my arms tightly. I wasn't sure if it was to keep from wringing my hands or throttling him. "I don't think that's such a good . . . No freaking way. Not just no, but *hell* no." The only time I'd gone over the border into the Beyond, I'd barely made it back alive.

Jean *tsk-tsk*ed me. "Such language you modern women use."

Yeah, like pirate wenches didn't curse. I've read those novels.

"I know your only other venture into the Beyond did not go very well," he said in the world's biggest understatement. "But we are not going to Old Orleans, where things are so treacherous, but back in time itself."

I tried to be calm and practical. "Jean, my magic doesn't work in the Beyond, or at least not very well." The elven staff worked just fine but it was lying on my bed at home.

"You are not going to fight tonight, Drusilla. We are going to have a fine meal prepared by Antoine himself, and then we will come back here and take a walk beside the river. You have seen only the bad side of the Beyond. All is not evil there as long as one knows where to go."

I felt my resolve weaken. I hadn't known you could do things like have dinner at the original Antoine's in a past version of New Orleans, but I suppose the legendary restauranteur, much like Jean himself, was immortalized by memory.

And why not go? If nymphs and mers could live in the modern era, why shouldn't a wizard be able to cross the other way for dinner?

Jean watched my thought processes with a bemused expression. "I can tell you are beginning to think this is a good idea, *oui*?"

I looked down at my mankiller dress and Manolo Blahniks and shook my head. "I left my bustle and corset at home. I think if I walked into a nineteenth-century restaurant like this I'd be arrested for indecent exposure."

"Exposed, but not so indecent, *non*," Jean said in a soft voice, giving me a look that made me blush again.

What had I been thinking, wearing my mankiller dress? I needed a therapist, and wondered if the Elders had a wizard Dr. Phil who could cure me of my pirate obsession and impulsive decision-making.

Jean interrupted my moment of horrified clarity. "There are others from elsewhere in the Beyond who go there to dine. You will not feel out of place."

I knew there were a baker's-dozen good reasons not to go, but I found myself smiling back at the blue-eyed black-guard, and he knew he'd won. He might as well have rolled a ride in a stolen cherry-red Corvette into the deal just to make my stupidity complete.

We strolled from the hotel to Jackson Square, then crossed over to the small gardens behind St. Louis Cathedral. With his custom-fitted suit and confident stride, Jean attracted double-takes from quite a few of the tourists strolling through the Quarter. The locals are far too jaded to find anything worthy of a second look.

St. Anthony's Garden, behind the cathedral, was one of several permanent transports the Elders had established between modern New Orleans and the Beyond. Last time I'd been here, the transport had still been temporary. I'd been half-battered and on the arm of Jean's pirate half-brother, Dominique You. He was remembered enough by pirate fans and scholars to have a life in the Beyond, but not enough to sustain him in the modern world for very long at a time.

"Uh, we won't be running into Dom tonight by any chance, will we?" The pirate disliked me because he thought I was a bad influence on Jean. Imagine.

Jean shook his head. "I do not believe so. He spends most of his time in Old Barataria."

No tourists were in sight, so we stepped into the inter-locking circle and triangle that had been formed to look like a rock garden and permanently inlaid with magic for transport into the Beyond. Tiny green crystals glittered throughout the rocks, dancing under the streetlights like twinkling stars underfoot. The magic-infused crystals would temporarily seal the transport closed if a human accidentally wandered onto the rocks. Couldn't have the mayor of New Orleans falling into Old Storyville. He had enough problems with his constantly squabbling city and his scandal-riddled administration.

As soon as we settled into the transport, Jean mumbled something in French and the air around us shimmered. I closed my eyes to fight the feeling of being compressed into an impossibly small space. Finally, the pressure lessened, and I opened my eyes to the Beyond.

26

Jean radiated excitement. I could tell he was pleased to bring me here, and not only because his eyes glittered and he smiled a lot. Unlike my magic, my elven empathic abilities worked fine in the Beyond. I'd be hauling in emotions from everyone.

I looked around with curiosity. When I'd gone into Old Orleans, it was always nighttime, and the city was a mishmash of different eras. This was quiet, a level much deeper into the Beyond, and sat in deep twilight. We picked our way carefully around St. Louis Cathedral toward Jackson Square.

"So, we are in 1850 New Orleans?" I looked up at the back of the cathedral, which didn't look very different in the dim light.

"*Oui.*"

I frowned. The Elders always lectured wizards about the dangers of going into the Beyond. There was no way to control where one landed, they told us. You might want to go to 1850 New Orleans, but could just as easily end up as an unwilling blood donor in the Realm of Vampyre.

So unless the Elders had suddenly discovered new ways to transport, which I doubted, they'd been lying to keep wayward wizards under control. It bore more thought later on. For now, I planned to enjoy my adventure.

We rounded the corner of the cathedral and made our way through the dim murk of Pirate's Alley and into the broad expanse of Jackson Square. Except it hadn't yet been renamed for Andrew Jackson.

"It's the Place D'Armes!" I realized for the first time the amazing thing I was doing. People in nineteenth-century clothing strolled through the softly lit, wide expanse, absent its modern landscaping and statues. Meetings and public hangings took place here, militias drilled, and people walked to see and be seen. The Louisiana Purchase had been signed here only a few decades earlier.

With no cars or electric lights, the stars lay heavy overhead and looked close enough to touch. A damp breeze blew unobstructed from the river.

By 1850, Jean had been gone from New Orleans about thirty years. "How is this time period different from your day?"

He smiled. "It does not smell so bad as in my day, for one thing. The streets are covered with paving stones and not mud. There are more people, more types of people. Still many Frenchmen, but also others."

I took his arm to keep from tripping on uneven flagstones

in four-inch heels and tried to ignore the scandalized looks from the bustled-up women we passed. Their male companions smiled a lot, teeth gleaming between muttonchop sideburns and heavy moustaches.

It came as no surprise that Jean had grossly exaggerated the number of modern people strolling around 1850 New Orleans. So far, the grand total was one blond wizardess in a mankiller dress and five-hundred-dollar shoes, hanging on to the arm of a famous pirate.

We turned up Royal Street, headed toward St. Louis. Gaslights flickered atop ornate iron posts, and horse-drawn wagons and carriages clattered through what in modern times would become a pedestrian area. Several men and couples we met along the way greeted Jean by name, confirming yet again my suspicion that he did a lot of traveling around the Beyond in addition to his forays to the modern world.

"How difficult is it to travel here?" I asked.

"One would simply hire a carriage, *Jolie*."

"No, I mean, to other parts of the Beyond. If I wanted to travel from here to Vampyre, for example, how would I do it?"

He raised an eyebrow. "You do not wish to go to Vampyre, Drusilla. They would eat you."

I laughed. "I don't want to *go* there. I just wondered how hard it is to travel between different parts of the Beyond. I mean, you seem to have traveled to a great many places."

He grimaced. "I have been here many long years to do so. But, to answer your question, there are track lines through the Beyond that lead from one place to another. One finds the correct path and follows it. Occasionally, the lines move and one has to be wary until the new track has settled."

He looked down at me and frowned. "I have mapped out these lines because I have an interest in navigation, *Jolie*, but do not ever try to travel within the Beyond yourself. It is *trés perfide*, treacherous and difficult. Traveling in your transport is safer, as long as you are precise in stating where you wish to go."

We reached the corner of St. Louis and Royal and I looked in confusion for Antoine's.

Jean herded me toward the river. "The original location was this way." We clattered over the wooden banquette to the restaurant, marked by a small, simple sign: ANTOINE'S. Next to the restaurant was a rooming house also operated by the Alciatore family.

Couples from a variety of eras walked along the banquettes, but I saw only one other woman in modern clothing. I wondered at her species, but some experiences cross all barriers and we exchanged woeful looks at each other's short dresses and modern shoes. We also seemed to be attracting a lot of stares from well-heeled nineteenth-century gentlemen who probably thought we were brazen ladies of ill-repute. The emotions I pulled in from passersby were mostly calm and domestic. Jean had been right—it was much more pleasant than my disastrous visit to Old Orleans.

We stepped from the cool evening air into the warmth of the restaurant, and were met by a young, dark-haired man with a heavy beard. He greeted Jean in French, and I could feel his goodwill and pleasure at seeing Jean again. I smiled and looked polite.

"Drusilla, this is Antoine Alciatore," Jean said. I was surprised to see how young the famous restauranteur was. He looked about my age. Of course, at this point in time he wasn't yet so famous.

"Welcome, mademoiselle," he said in heavily accented English. "It is a pleasure to welcome a friend of Monsieur Lafitte's."

I assured him the honor was mine, and it was with a sense of the surreal that we were seated at a white-clothed table beneath a gas wall sconce. Jean drew as many stares as I did, not because of his clothing but because he was a celebrity from a time not so far past, and apparently a frequent visitor to this time-warp version of New Orleans. Forget the Elders—I wanted Jean to draw *me* a map of the Beyond.

We feasted on rich Canape Balthazar, a succulent blend of cheeses on crusty bread, followed by Dinde Tallyrand, a creation of turkey and fresh mushrooms, and Antoine's already much-talked-about Pommes de Terre Soufflé.

"Tell me about your life here," I said, spooning a mouthful of the potato soufflé and closing my eyes in appreciation. "How much time did you spend in the city, and how much on Grand Terre?"

Grand Terre, a small barrier island off the coast of Jefferson Parish, had been the center of Jean's empire.

"It changed with time," he said. "We took orders here in the city, and filled them with goods stored at *Le Temple Grand*."

Uh-huh. I'd heard of the Great Temple, a massive warehouse full of stolen goods shipped to New Orleans and up into central Louisiana plantation country. The man was a pirate, after all, not the founder of Neiman Marcus. "That would be goods looted from other people's ships?"

"Bah. Only those belonging to the dogs of Spain. Do not ever trust a Spaniard, Drusilla. Or an Englishman."

Spoken like a true Frenchman. "I'll remember that."

Jean finished his meal with a small glass of brandy and enjoyed a cigar while regaling me with stories from his early days in New Orleans. I suspected they were highly embellished, but it really didn't matter. My favorite was when Governor Claiborne, tired of the pirates eating into his rich cronies' legitimate commerce, posted a $500 reward for Jean's arrest.

"Such behavior could not be tolerated." Jean shook his head with a mischievous smile. "So in response I offered a fifteen-hundred-dollar reward to anyone who would deliver Governor Claiborne to me at Barataria. I had signs posted throughout the city. Everyone was *trés amusé*."

You had to admire the guy's sense of style, if not always his methods.

We'd been finished with dinner for a while and were getting ready to leave when a middle-aged man of slender build approached the table. I looked up, interested in meeting another of Jean's acquaintances—or maybe someone who'd had unhappy business dealings with him, judging by Jean's tense posture and sudden intake of breath.

The man wasn't looking at Jean, but at me. Great. He was probably going to give me a morality lecture about flashing too much leg in public. Except his shirt and slacks looked like those of a modern man in his forties, and his salt-and-pepper hair was stylish and layered to offset a short dark beard. Deep brown eyes glittered with amusement above high cheekbones, his face lean and tanned. He looked like he'd walked out of the pages of *GQ* rather than a history book.

"Are you by chance Drusilla Jaco?" His voice was pleasant, cultured, with no trace of accent.

"Yes, and you are?" I glanced at Jean, then did a double-take. The pirate looked like he'd seen a ghost, which was saying something considering his undead status.

"We must leave, Drusilla," Jean hissed. *"Tout de suite."*

"I'm Mace Banyan," the man said, and held his hand out to shake.

I reached for his hand, trying to remember where I'd heard that name and ignoring Jean's attempt to stop me.

As soon as my palm touched Mace Banyan's, my mind exploded in a kaleidoscope of colors and images. Faces and events from the past came unbidden, and I felt as if I were being sucked into a vacuum of memories. I was vaguely aware of being pulled to my feet, of falling, of men shouting in the distance.

My back hit the wall with a jarring thud, and my head bounced hard against the plaster. It jolted me back to awareness. Finally, I could see again, breathe again. But I was held against the wall by a big, solid body that smelled of cinnamon and tobacco, Jean's scent. My nose was pressed into the back of his dark blue jacket.

Squirming, I tried to move from behind him, but he pressed me against the wall more firmly. Craning my head around his broad shoulders, I caught a glimpse of the man Mace Banyan. What the hell happened?

"We will not forget this, Mr. Lafitte," Mace said, and from the small corner of his face I could see by ducking my head under Jean's arm, he looked angry. "We will have access to her eventually."

"It will not be today, nor while she is with me." Jean's voice, usually a playful baritone, was rough with anger. It was a tone that had commanded a thousand outlaws through cunning and violence.

I rested my forehead against his back, no longer struggling. What had that man done to me? My head felt as if my brains had been taken out, scrambled in an omelette, and stuck back inside. When Jean stepped forward, I almost fell, and saw a dark stain on the back of his jacket.

He shoved me into a chair a little more forcefully than was necessary, pulled a handkerchief from his vest pocket, and stuck it in my face. "You are bleeding, *Jolie*. Use this."

Freaking nosebleed. I never got them until I used the elven

staff and . . . Holy crap. "He's an elf." I looked up at Jean. "Mace Banyan's an elf."

"*Oui*, and a very powerful one," Jean said. "Are you able to walk? We must leave, and as quickly as possible."

"Fill me in on Buras. I have to think about something besides elves." I sat in the kitchen about nine, eyeing the muffalettas Alex had picked up as soon as Elder Zrakovi had ordered him to babysit me. I'd already eaten a quarter of the crusty round Italian loaf, and was eyeing my second quarter. Either the stress of meeting my first elf had burned up everything I ate at Antoine's or I still had the residual effects of Rene's prodigious appetite. If we had to share power many more times, I'd have to buy a new wardrobe in a larger size.

"Go ahead. Quit staring at it and eat it." Alex shoved the plate toward me. "Are you sure you don't want me to stay tonight?"

He'd offered to spend the night on the sofa, but I'd called Tish instead, just to appease him. She wouldn't hover as much as Alex.

Zrakovi thought Mace Banyan knew what I looked like (creepy), had spotted me in Antoine's (coincidental), and took advantage of a chance opportunity (a load of crap), as I explained to Alex for the third time. But I still didn't want him to stay—he was too tightly wound and I wanted to do some work.

"The elves are not going to come storming into New Orleans to . . ." I had no idea what they wanted to do, or what had happened when the elf touched me—except I didn't want it to happen again. "To do whatever it is they do," I finished. "When I meet with them again, Zrakovi will go with me."

"Fine." He gathered up the wrapping from his muffaletta half and put it in the trash. "But I'm not leaving until Tish gets here."

Like either one of them could help if a horde of elves descended on Magazine Street, although I guess Alex could shoot them. But Tish's visit had a dual purpose. She knew more about the water species than I did, and I wanted to pick her brain. I'd gone through every text I could find about the Styx except a couple of Gerry's old books that were written in Greek, and I'd need a charm to read those—they'd have to wait until tomorrow.

The elven staff stood in the corner of my kitchen, looking like a perfectly harmless old piece of wood. Since Katrina, I had been hauling it around like a useful toy, even when I said I wouldn't use it anymore. After meeting Mace Banyan, I didn't want to ever touch the thing again.

Alex turned to see what I was looking at. "I'm sorry this happened, but you shouldn't have gone into the Beyond with—"

"Don't," I said, sounding harsher than I'd intended. The last thing I needed was an *I told you so*. Besides, this hadn't been Jean's fault any more than it had been mine. "Jean couldn't have known anything was going to happen. We have bigger issues—Buras breach? Murders? It's been over a week since the problems started."

He rubbed the back of his neck. "Hell if I know. All we have are questions."

Which wasn't good enough. "If we don't find some answers, the human population of Plaquemines Parish is going to start dying."

27

By the time I woke up with an elven afterburn, Tish already sat at the kitchen table, guzzling her first cup of coffee. She'd shown up late last night, relieving Alex from babysitting duty.

"Thanks for staying the night, although I think it was silly." I poured a cup of coffee and threw some frozen biscuits on a cookie sheet, then slid them in the oven. It's my version of baking.

"No problem. It's nice to have an excuse to spend some time with you." Tish shook her head, and a shadow of sadness crossed her face, almost too quickly to see. Almost. "We shouldn't need an excuse. Just because we lost Gerry doesn't mean we should lose each other. I still think of you as family."

"Me too." I grinned. "Wonder what he would have said about my dinner date with Jean Lafitte."

We both laughed. "Personally, I think you need a shrink,

but Gerry? He'd have told you to go for it, and then want all the details." She examined me over the rim of her coffee cup. "Are there any details to share? I mean, you know, *details?*"

"No, we kind of had an elven intervention. Although he was really protective, anxious to get me home and away from the Beyond. It was kinda sweet." Although now that I thought about it, it had been sweeter for Jean than for me. He'd managed to maneuver me into calling Zrakovi, then parlayed his ability to navigate the Beyond into a potential business deal with the Elders.

Fifteen minutes later, I pulled the biscuits out of the oven and set them on the table. I hadn't planned to eat anything since I was meeting Eugenie and her new romantic interest for lunch, but I swear Rene had spent too long in my skin. I pulled a biscuit onto my plate and slathered it with butter.

"Since you're off today, can you help me do some research into the Styx? We've got to figure out how those rifts are being made, and how it ties into the murders of Doug Hebert and Jeff Klein. Well, Doug Hebert, at least. He seems to have been the target. It can't be a coincidence."

Tish looked thoughtful. "It's so weird about those two guys. Thinking about them has brought up a lot of memories about the war. I finally remembered what their job was."

I perked up. "Did they fight?"

She snorted. "Have you ever seen a Green Congress wizard who could fight? It would be like sending Mister Rogers into combat against Godzilla."

I nodded. Sadly, that was true.

"Plus we were really young then," she said. "Got any jam?"

I moved some jars and bottles around in the cabinet and found a few packets of jelly I'd saved from the military rations we'd lived on in the early days after Katrina. I looked for an expiration date but didn't find one. "So what did they do after the war, our murdered Green Congress wizards?"

She took one of the packets, ripped off the end, and sniffed before shrugging and squirting the strawberry preserves onto her plate. "I'm almost certain they were part of a team sent to keep an eye on the water species after the fighting was done and the Elders were back in charge. They were minimum-security prison guards, basically. Until the skirmishes died out and the treaties were agreed to, the Elders moved a lot of the water species to these containment camps. It was easy duty since the water folk are all peaceful except for squabbles with each other."

My pulse zipped up a notch. Maybe we finally had a connection. "What species did they work with?"

"All of them—selkies, kelpies, miengu. The most plentiful were the nymphs and naiads and . . ." Tish paused, staring at me. "And mers."

I wanted to beat my head against the table. We should have made this connection earlier. The Elders should have made it for us, useless old gits with their treaties and intrigue. "Who had the biggest grudge after it was all over?"

She sat back in her chair, brows furrowed. "Well, all the pretes hate the wizards just on principle because there are more of us and we've historically been the ones manning the barriers between this world and the Beyond. They've always thought we were oppressive bullies."

Imagine that. The more I thought about angry pretes with wartime grudges, the worse my feeling about the Delachaises. Robert seemed too laid-back to undertake some nefarious scheme although he'd brought up their father's experience, and Rene could have taken me out easily during our power-share. Although he did have that part of his mind he'd been able to block from me. Denis Villere also had an ugly temper and a chip that went all the way from his shoulder to the tip of his odd little braid. Had he been in the watery prison camps in 1976? He was old enough. His murderous, knife-wielding mother certainly was old enough.

"Think about it—it could be important," I urged Tish. "Which water species hated wizards the most back then?"

She shook her head. "I know what you're thinking—one of the merpeople. But did the mers hate us more than the nymphs or the others? I honestly don't know. It was so long ago and the water species aren't usually violent. You know, they'll try to seduce you but they won't slit your throat. Look at Libby."

"No thanks. I've seen enough of Libby. Although she's a lot brighter than she acts."

"So where does that leave us?" Tish asked.

"Exactly where we started."

After a couple of hours at the office, I headed to La Boulangerie for lunch with Eugenie before digging into my afternoon of research. I was anxious to see her out of sheer prurient curiosity. She was bringing our new neighbor, Quince Randolph. I'd never seen her fall for anybody so fast.

I'd been busy the last week, what with the Styx contamination, the murder investigation, my close encounter with an elf, and my disastrous date with Jake, so I hadn't found time to meet the new guy. His Plantasy Island sign had gone up over the weekend, and Eugenie said his landscaping business was almost stocked and ready to open. The neighborhood already looked better since he'd stripped the windows of their graffiti-covered plywood.

The god of parking spaces found me an opening a block from the restaurant, and from the door I spotted Eugenie waving from a small table in back. Since I'd had a late breakfast, I just picked up a coffee on my way through the shop, although I looked longingly at the array of croissants and breads and inhaled the feel-good aromas of fresh-baked cookies as I passed the counters. I wondered if Rene was enjoying any of my quirks. Would serve him right if he'd developed a taste for Cheetos.

Eugenie looked great, her short spiky auburn hair edged with conservative blond tips and her face wearing a minimum of makeup. Must be Mr. Natural's influence. I gave her a hug and turned to meet Quince, who was sitting across from her.

Okay, I could see the attraction. He had thick, honey-blond hair pulled back in a ponytail not unlike my own, and a green gemstone stud in one ear. Mr. Green Jeans. He reached out and grasped my hand, shaking it firmly. "It's great to meet you. Eugenie talks about you all the time."

"She talks a lot about you too, Quince." The man had no idea.

He smiled, and his blue-green eyes were almost enthralling. "Most people call me Rand, but Eugenie likes my real name better than my nickname."

After a half hour of small talk, I wasn't sure I liked Quince Randolph. He was drop-dead gorgeous, no question about that. But there was something off about him I couldn't quite pinpoint. He stared too hard when he talked to you, made more eye contact than a normal person. I tried to dig into his head a little but came up blank, which was weird, except I'd done a heavy grounding ritual this morning.

"You know, I just noticed something." Eugenie had a funny look on her face. "You guys have the same hair and eye color. I'd never realized it till I saw you sitting there across from each other."

"Maybe we're very distantly related." Rand smiled.

"I doubt it," I said, frowning. "I don't have much family. And if we were related, I'd be pissed off that you have better cheekbones."

Eugenie giggled like a thirteen-year-old at a Justin Bieber concert. She never giggled. Quince or Rand or whatever the hell his name was laughed with her, all pleasant and soothing. Too bad I wasn't joking. He did have better cheekbones.

"So DJ, I'm sure Quince won't mind hearing a little girl talk. How did your date with Jake go? I need details."

He turned to me with a slight smile and a tilt of the head.

"It was fine." My voice brimmed with ill temper. "We're going to take it slow and see what happens."

"What would you like to happen?" Quince looked at me so steadily I worried Eugenie would notice. What kind of busybody question was that?

"Lord, she's the last one you should ask," said my blind and lovestruck friend. "DJ is hopeless when it comes to men. The one she really likes is his cousin, her FBI partner—she just doesn't know it yet. That one's a keeper if she can hold her temper and smartass tongue in check."

I thumped a sugar packet at her. *"Moi?"* She needed to let this Alex thing go. I was beginning to get fixated on it myself.

"You have a temper?" Rand's eyes never left my face.

What was *with* this guy? I was going to have a serious talk with Eugenie to see how much she knew about him. What was that man's name back in the 1980s who was such a charming, handsome guy that he was the darling of single women everywhere—right until they found the three dozen mutilated bodies in his basement? I got that vibe off Quince Randolph.

I started to pull her aside while Rand went to get the car but she was happy and, really, what was I going to tell her? That I didn't like the way he looked me in the eye when he talked to me? That he was too charming?

Maybe I was spending way too much time with grumpy men.

Instead, I went home and spent the afternoon with Tish, lounging around my library and reading up on the Wizards' War of 1976 and pondering theories about how it could be related to the mutilation of Doug Hebert and contamination from the River Styx.

I found a description of a generic sacrificial ritual where the pertinent body parts were cut off to appease a god for a wrong done. But it wasn't specific to any species.

We stopped long enough to order Chinese, and I got an update from Alex—the full autopsy report on Melinda Hebert, complete with toxicology report, should be in his hands by tomorrow noon. Maybe it would have some answers.

About eleven, I closed my book with a thump. "I'm not finding anything. I'm going to make up a translation charm to use on those books of Greek mythology tomorrow morning."

Tish laughed. "Leave it to Gerry for his most thorough Greek mythology books to be written in Greek."

Tish decided to sleep over again since it was late, so I left her to make her way to the guest room downstairs and I went into my bedroom. Mahout was lying across my bed.

"I don't think so, elf stick." I stuck it in the back of my closet, then magically sealed the door shut using a premade charm and a little physical magic. Since the power-share, I'd been holding back my magic, letting it regenerate. When we had to do it again, I needed enough juice built up for Rene to borrow.

The room was quiet, the ceiling fan turned off, and the outside air left the house in that rare late-October state requiring neither heating nor air-conditioning. Big bad wizard that I am, I left my bedside lamp on. If elves broke in, I wanted to see them.

Shadows stretched across the deep green walls I'd painted last summer, and I drifted into pre-sleep, wondering how Jake was doing and if we'd ever be able to even be friends again. Whether Alex really was changing the rules of our relationship, and how I wasn't sure what to think about that. How mermen and nymphs and poisoned water and dead wizards might possibly be connected.

I awoke with a jolt. I thought I'd just drifted off to sleep, but the bedside clock read 3:00 a.m. I started thinking again, and I came up with an idea. Jean Lafitte had been around a long time, and had a lot of experience with all kinds of pretes from his years in the Beyond. He was also extremely smart in his own self-serving kind of way. I should ask his opinion. I could even offer him a consulting fee. If he helped us solve the case, I'd owe him another debt. He'd like that.

I thought about calling him, because I was pretty sure the

historical undead didn't have to sleep. Probably should wait until morning, though.

I sighed and crawled out of bed, wide awake. I was a borderline insomniac. If I woke up during the night, it was hard for me to go back to sleep. Maybe cocoa would help.

Walking out of the bedroom into the den, I heard the radio downstairs playing soft bluesy tunes. If Tish was up, it meant I could go to the kitchen and make cocoa without bothering her. Maybe run my Jean Lafitte brainstorm past her.

I padded down the steps in the T-shirt and jogging pants that made up my non-Harry Potter winter lingerie. "Tish! You are not going to believe this."

She wasn't in the office/guest room, but the radio next to the daybed played on the bedside table. The kitchen lights were on, but no sign of Tish. I threw some instant cocoa in a cup and set it in the microwave, then stuck my head into the front double parlor. No sign of her there, either, but the front door was ajar. She was probably having a smoke.

I retrieved the hot cocoa from the microwave and headed to the front porch. One of the benefits of being a wizard, I guess—we seemed immune to diseases like lung cancer and emphysema. I just didn't like the smell of cigarette smoke, although tobacco was nice. Now, I would forever associate it with the pirate.

I felt my protective wards pressing against me lightly as I crossed the threshold. Just outside the door, my foot hit something slippery and shot from beneath me, and I cursed as I crashed at an awkward angle on my butt. The mug of cocoa went flying.

"Damn. Tish? Where are you?" I got to my feet, my hands wet. I looked out on the darkened street, wondering if it had rained, then reached inside the door and turned on the porch light.

Nothing registered at first. Blood covered my palms, but I was still frowning at it dumbly when I looked down and saw it pooled around my feet. Tish lay facedown and still.

Oh my God. I couldn't move for a few seconds, couldn't breathe. I dropped to my knees, my hands hovering over her, unsure whether I should touch her. Finally, I stretched shaking fingers to press the side of her neck, underneath her curly brown hair. I couldn't feel a pulse, and her body had already begun to cool.

"Tish?" My voice sounded like someone else—someone shrill—as I reached out and turned her over. My eyes riveted onto her throat. A horizontal slash, a harsh red cut in the shape of a smile on her pale neck, had bathed her body in dark crimson. I couldn't look away from it.

"Let me call someone for you, DJ. Does she need an ambulance? Do you want the police?"

I screamed and started, staring into the shadows at the bottom of the porch steps. Quince Randolph stood there in a dark brown sweater and jeans, his hair falling loose around his shoulders.

"What have you done? Why her? I will kill you." I knew something was off with him. I ran down the stairs, hoping

I had enough physical energy to do him damage and wishing I hadn't sealed the staff in my closet.

Rand met me halfway and dragged me back to the porch, avoiding the bloody heap that had been my friend and my last link to Gerry.

"You son of a bitch." I raged at him and gouged at his eyes with my fingers as he reached toward me, and then zapped him with a ragged burst of magic. He hissed and stepped out of touching range, but when I didn't move to follow, he reached for me again. I slapped at him, getting blood on his face.

"DJ, I didn't do this." His voice was calm, steady. "I was on my way home from Eugenie's and saw your porch light. Who do you want me to call?"

"Call Gerry."

"Who is Gerry?"

I quit fighting and stared at him, feeling the emptiness where Gerry had been, glad my mentor—my father—wasn't alive to see what had happened to the woman he loved.

Rand tried to pull me against him, and I tried to zap him again but I didn't have enough physical magic to do anything more than make him flinch a little.

"I don't know how you're doing that, but I just want your cell phone," he said, dodging my hands.

I jerked it from my pocket and threw it at him.

He kept talking at me until I finally gave him Alex's name and collapsed to the porch, leaning against the wooden spindle railings, looking away from Tish.

Rand walked back to the yard with my phone, and I heard him talking in a low voice, too softly for me to hear.

I jumped when he returned a couple of minutes later, then settled back in my stupor, shivering. It was so cold out here.

"Your partner is on his way." Rand slid down and sat next to me, but didn't try to touch me again. I tried to get in his head, to read his emotions, but I couldn't focus enough to get anything.

My eyes landed on Tish again, and tears threatened. Had she made a sound or did someone take her by surprise? Was the reason I woke up the sound of her falling? Dying?

I closed my eyes and shivered in the night air. "Cold, she's got to be cold. I need to get something to cover her up." I tried to get up, but Rand slid an arm around my shoulders and held me still.

A car door slammed, and I heard Alex running through the house from the back door. He still has my house key, I thought idly. Probably a good idea to let him keep it. I wondered vaguely what time it was, and leaned back against the porch rails as Rand pulled his arm away and stood up. He was talking to Alex. Did he know Alex? Had I told Alex about Eugenie's new boyfriend?

Alex knelt beside me and I slapped at him as he reached for me. "Stop it, DJ. You're going into shock." He picked me up and hauled me through the front door, careful to step over the blood I'd already fallen in, and carried me into the front parlor.

"Get a blanket out of the guest room," he told Rand, and

next thing I knew Alex was wrapping it around me after setting me down like a fragile china cup.

"DJ, talk to me." Alex pushed my hair out of my eyes, knelt next to the chair, and turned my face to look at him.

I squinted. When had Alex gotten here? Frantic, I pointed toward the door, and tried to get up. I needed to show him what happened. Alex could help Tish.

"Shhh." He pulled me into a hug. "It's okay. Jake's with her. Are you hurt?"

I buried my face in his chest, feeling his strong arms around me and smelling the soft scent I recognized as Alex. Once the tears started, I couldn't stop them. He just held on and let me cry.

"Here, drink this." In my peripheral vision, I saw Rand's hand extended, holding a mug, and Alex pulled away to let me take it. I couldn't hold it still enough to drink, and Alex wrapped a big hand around mine and guided it toward my mouth.

The tea smelled like apples and cinnamon, and I inhaled deeply before drinking. The effect was immediate. Warmth washed through my body, and my mind cleared. It cleared so quickly, in fact, that I sat up straight, scraped my sleeve across my eyes, and frowned at the mug.

"What is this?" Either I'd just experienced the quickest recovery in history or Rand had slipped me an endorphin cocktail.

"It's just herbal tea," he said. "I found apple juice in your fridge and added it."

I was too glad to have my brain working again to argue about it. "Does Rand need to stay?" I asked Alex. I'd have to thank Rand later for helping, and apologize for lashing out at him, but I didn't have it in me to do it yet.

"Yes, sorry. The police are on their way." He turned to Rand and began firing questions at him.

Good, let him deal with things. And of course the NOPD had to get involved. We were in the middle of the city, and Rand had seen the body. There would be no whisking this off to the Elders.

The tears started again as I thought of Tish's family. Her parents and brother had all lost their homes in Katrina, and her folks weren't in good health. Who would tell them? It would have to be me.

I used the edge of the blanket to dry my face. "Alex," I interrupted him mid-question.

He turned back to me. "You okay?"

"I need to call Tish's family and her boss—there's no one else to do it." I didn't know how I would say the words, but it had to come from someone who cared about her. Loved her.

A clatter of feet near the front door and the reflection of flashing blue lights from out front signaled the arrival of the NOPD. The siren of an EMT van echoed down Magazine Street—they were all on their way.

"You'll have to wait till we finish here before you call—and we can notify the family unless you know them." Ken Hachette wasn't a large man but he had a presence about him that filled the room with a crackling energy. About five-ten and lean, his skin was the color of milk chocolate, his eyes a greenish-brown, his demeanor exactly what one would expect from a homicide detective. I'd never seen him crack a smile, but then again, the only time I'd met him was outside murder scenes. And here we were again.

Ken shook hands with Alex, ordered him and Rand into the kitchen, then pulled the other armchair next to mine. "Let's talk about what happened."

28

I closed my eyes and leaned my head back, relaxing against the soft leather seats of Alex's car as we sped across the long Causeway Bridge over the middle of Lake Pontchartrain. Neither of us was in the mood to talk. We both wore basic black, appropriate for the first part of our day. We were headed to the tiny town of Bogalusa, to Tish's funeral.

It had been a long three days since Tish died. The Elders had questioned me repeatedly, but I didn't have any answers. It was three a.m., so the normally busy restaurant across the street was closed, as was the coffee shop down the block. No one had seen anything—except Alex, who found traces of brackish water on the steps before the EMTs arrived and was able to get a miniscule sample.

No headway had been made on the case. My only foray had been to go back to Melinda Hebert's house and snoop around. In the bottom of a fly-covered can of outdoor trash, I'd found the missing photographs—or at least pieces of photographs that had been ripped apart. I'd shoved all the tiny pieces into an envelope, which still sat on my kitchen table.

Alex and Jake were convinced Tish died at the hands of the same person, or creature, that had killed the two professors, though they were waiting on the medical report. They also thought I was the target, not Tish, an announcement that had sent me into another day of weeping. How many people had to die or have their lives ripped apart because of me?

Alex fiddled with the radio, finally settling on a classical station. "I think I need to move back in with you till this case is solved." He didn't look at me, but I could see the tension in his posture.

I didn't want him moving into my house, where he'd automatically become a target. I wanted to lock myself in, put up my strongest wards, and sleep for a month. "I can protect myself—I pulled the elven staff out of the closet." If the elves had a problem with it, too bad.

"No arguing, DJ. The only reason the killer didn't come after you was because you were smart enough to put up your wards."

"Then the wards work," I said. "I don't understand why I'd be a target anyway. I didn't know either of the professors. If it is some revenge thing related to the war, I wasn't involved—I hadn't even been born. Tish was more involved than me." None of it made sense.

Alex thrummed his fingers on the steering wheel—a sure sign he was thinking hard. "But you're involved in the investigation, and Tish wasn't, at least not directly. I think you're getting too close to figuring it out."

Glad the killer thought I was close. I sure didn't. And I didn't care what the elves thought; Mahout was going everywhere with me from now on.

"What have you done on the investigation the last few days?" Alex asked.

I frowned, thinking. "I've been researching the water species and looking through the Elders' records for anything specific on the Delachaise and Villere clans. I've also been leaving messages with the new office of the Greater Mississippi River Nymphs to check out Libby's background, but I swear those women are so unorganized I doubt they could find their keys on a keyring." I tried to remember the week—the last three days had all been a long, sad blur. "I've asked Adrian Hoffman to send me background files on Melinda Hebert to see if I can find something he missed. Oh, and I have the torn-up photos." I also needed to use the translation charm to read Gerry's remaining Greek texts on the Styx.

The first person had died from the "Plaquemines Plague," an elderly woman who lived south of Buras. More than fifty people had sought medical help, and the Army Corps of Engineers was testing the river for contamination. My test for standard pollutants had come up negative, but they had more sophisticated equipment. Would they find something they couldn't explain? This had disaster written all over it, but at least officials had told people to use bottled water until the tests were complete.

"Have you met any of Tish's family?" Alex's voice broke my reverie.

"No. She and Gerry had been an item for years so she didn't have a spouse or kids. She has a brother and sister, and nieces and nephews. Only her parents knew she was a wizard—it came from her dad's side of the family, and they didn't realize she was practicing." I stared at the sprawl of commerce that had exploded north of the lake after Katrina. "I wondered if I should even go. As soon as they hear my name, they'll know I was the one who . . ." Found her. Got her killed.

"Jake wanted to come, but he was going down to Port Sulphur with Rene and Robert to replace the temporary charms," Alex said. "You know Jake thinks one of the twins might be our murderer—he wanted to keep an eye on them today."

I nodded. "I don't know much about Robert, but I just don't think it's Rene." I hadn't told anyone because I was afraid to, but Rene and I still could communicate a little bit mentally. It took a lot of concentration but I'd get occasional words or images, and so did he. At least he couldn't still pull power from me. We'd agreed not to do another ritual until all the other loose ends were tied up. I was afraid of being linked to him forever. Neither of us liked that idea.

"What about Libby?" Alex said. "You said yourself she's a lot smarter than any of us gave her credit for. Think she could have done it?"

I shrugged. "What's her motive? What's any of their motives? A grudge after the war—that's all we have. It could be any of them or none of them. It could be some species that's come in since the borders dropped that we don't even know about."

Alex shook his head. "Rule of thumb is, if you hear hooves, look first for a horse. Don't run off looking for a zebra. Chances are good that our murderer is not some mystery species we don't know about."

Alex slowed as he reached a crossroads and the car's GPS voice told us to turn. "The thing about the mers, though— they've been mainstreamed for years. If they'd wanted to go after wizards, they've had plenty of time to do it unless they were waiting for other species to blame it on."

"Except Denis has anger issues, and his mama is insane." And has a nice, sharp knife.

"The Villeres are crazy, but they don't strike me as dangerous," Alex countered. "I like the mertwins, but I'm not willing to give either one of them a pass yet. And Libby has been watching the repairs more closely than she wants us to think. She only pretends her goal in life is screwing Rene's and Robert's brains out. And Jake's and mine, if we'd give her a chance."

"Ick."

He gave me a dirty look. "Until you stop dating the undead Pirate of the Caribbean, you have no room to judge."

My smile faded as he turned into the parking lot of a small funeral home located in a dark-shuttered colonial-style building. A few cars peppered the pavement, and I wondered how many from the river authority would drive up from New Orleans.

It struck me again how lonely and isolated most wizards were. Tish was kind and good, and she should have been mourned and celebrated by a parking lot full of people who loved her and really knew her, people who understood who and what she was. All of us spent too much time hiding our real selves from the people who were supposed to care about us.

Alex parked the car and we got out in silence. I took his hand, and he squeezed mine back as we got ready to say good-bye to our friend.

I sucked the salty orange remains of a bag of Cheetos off my fingers and checked my watch. I'd made up a translation potion, thinking if I read the text aloud in some approximation of Greek, the potion would translate my words as I spoke them. No such luck.

We'd gotten back from the funeral a couple of hours ago, and I'd finally convinced Alex to leave. He was going to Orchard to talk to the twins, then to Tidewater to see Denis and T-Jacques Villere. I hoped he listened to my warning about the murderous granny.

I rubbed my eyes, and tried to think. I didn't know any potion or spell that would automatically translate printed Greek into English, but I could bespell a pair of glasses.

Upstairs in my library, I pulled out my backpack and retrieved my portable magic kit. I kept a translation potion ready for encounters with multilingual members of the historical undead such as Jean Lafitte. He was fluent in Italian and Spanish, as well as French and English, so when I pissed him off he was prone to rant in a language I couldn't understand. It worked well on most prete languages as well.

I found a dusty pair of reading glasses on a shelf and poured the potion over them in a bowl—a simple mixture of ground sage, sunflower, hawthorn, and purified water, infused with a little magical energy. I added pomegranate essence, a bit of olive oil, and coated the lens of the glasses. Sounded more like a salad, except for the magic part.

I let them cure for a half hour, then wiped them off and took them downstairs to where I had the old texts spread out on the kitchen table.

I pulled a book from the stack and was relieved to find the charmed glasses worked perfectly. The Greek characters swirled and reformed themselves into English.

Looking up the lengthy entry for the River Styx, I began to read. *The River Styx was one of the five rivers of the Underworld,* blah blah blah. *The goddess Thetis dipped the infant Achilles into the river to make him invulnerable, holding him by his heel,* blah blah blah. *Oaths sworn by the waters of the Styx could not be broken,* blah blah blah. *The water was so poisonous it corroded clay containers,* blah blah blah. *The river was named after a nymph . . .*

A chill ran through me. How closely were nymphs affiliated with the River Styx? I rifled through the piles of books and found a yellow-paged, dog-eared book on nymphs that had been in Gerry's collection.

I began scanning. *Styx was the eldest daughter of the god Okeanos.*

There was a Mardi Gras krewe of Okeanos—could they be involved? No, too far-fetched.

Lived in Hades. Had a slew of daughters. Can't resist honey. Sexually aggressive and promiscuous.

No kidding.

Can cause nympholepsy, described classically as "divine madness" or mental rapture.

That could be what Alex was calling enthrallment.

I frowned and took off the glasses. Marking the page, I shoved the book and glasses aside. I needed to talk to some nymphs.

Digging out my contact sheet again, I called the Greater Mississippi River Nymphs office, but got a machine message: *Hi, this is Blueberry Muffin—call me Muffi. We're ready to escort you to your next event, or make all your wildest dreams come true. Leave a message, and we'd loooove to call you back.*

Escorts. Talk about a thinly disguised service industry.

I set the phone aside and picked up the Melinda Hebert photo pieces. I'd always been good at jigsaw puzzles, and that's essentially what this was. You do the outside edges first, then fill in the middle.

I worked a half hour and had three photos outlined. Still no answer at the nymph office, so I kept working. Finally, one was almost finished. I could see a happier, prettier

Melinda Hebert standing alongside another woman. I looked for eyes among the remaining unused pieces, and slipped one into place, then stopped breathing. I had about eighty percent of a beautiful likeness of Melinda Hebert and a woman who looked a lot like her, only trampier: Libby.

29

The Nymph line was busy now, so I ran to the Pathfinder and drove like a lunatic to the Faubourg Marigny, a neighborhood just east of the French Quarter.

A small sign on the door of the renovated double said, complete with exclamation points: GREATER MISSISSIPPI RIVER NYMPHS! ESCORTS AND MORE!!! It looked like every other house-turned-business in this gentrified neighborhood: cute and Victorian, with lots of gingerbread.

The large front window had been covered with a mural. At first glance, the brown river winding through the center of the painting appeared to be surrounded by banks covered in thick trees and brush. Closer inspection showed that among the vegetation cavorted dozens of nubile young things in various stages of, uh, activity. I was tilting my head and trying to unravel a confusing tangle of limbs underneath a nicely painted live oak when the door opened.

"Oh my Zeus, you scared me!" A little blond bombshell with painted-on leggings and a sports bra squealed as she ran into me.

"Are you Muffi?"

The bombshell giggled. "Oh no, Muffi's inside at the front desk." She looked at me with vacant blue eyes and a tiny frown creased her perfect brows. "We don't get many women customers, but that's okay. Muffi can talk to you about our new male escorts."

Yeah, I'd be talking to Muffi about a lot of things once this case was done. I had a feeling the nymphs were not going to mainstream well.

I stepped inside the cool, dark entry filled with old wood and the cloying smell of incense and flowers. A small fountain to the left of the door, behind the mural, added a tinkle of water to the air-conditioned quiet, and a staircase rose behind the single desk in the room. A parlor to the right was filled with heavy sofas, oversized chairs, and a few contraptions with handcuffs. I *so* didn't want to know.

Another petite blonde sat at the desk, smiling.

I smiled back. "Are you Muffi?"

"Yes, and we have just the thing you need—I don't know how you found out about it so quickly but it's going to be great," she said with a chirp. Before I could interrupt her, she picked up the phone.

"No—wait. I don't want an escort."

She frowned. "Are you sure? They're satyrs!"

Good Lord. I was so going to shut them down when I had time.

I took a deep breath. "Let's start over here. I'm Drusilla Jaco, the wizards' sentinel for the region, and I came here to talk to you about some murders in Plaquemines Parish, and in particular a nymph named Libby."

"Libby?" Muffi pointed me to a seat while she pulled out a file folder. "I don't remember a Libb—oh, wait. Here we go."

She pulled out a sheet of paper and studied it. "We keep records on all our people coming in from the Beyond. No one works in New Orleans without checking in with us." She looked up at me anxiously.

"That's good," I said. "You need to keep up with them. What about Libby?"

She shrugged and handed me the paper. It contained exactly four words: LIBBY. OCTOBER 13. VISITOR.

"So, Libby isn't a member of your organization?"

Muffi beamed, pleased at my insight. "Nope. I remember her, though. Tall woman. All the Mississippi girls are blond and petite. You could pass for one of us!"

Yeah, next time I needed to go undercover. "So you didn't send Libby to help the wizards with a diving project?"

She looked at me blankly. "We didn't send anyone."

A chill raced through me. Libby had been hanging around whenever we did repairs, and she egged on the fights between the mers. If she was coming in from the Underworld via the Styx, she'd have to create new rifts in the riverbed every time we plugged the old one up. I didn't have a clue what her motive might be, but in that photo she and Melinda Hebert looked enough alike to be sisters.

30

Jake called my cell as I drove home, looking for Alex.

"I haven't seen him since we got back from the funeral," I said. "He's supposed to be in Plaquemines, talking to the mers." What was I, the Warin social secretary? "Did you get Melinda's autopsy report?"

"Yeah, he dropped by here but it came in after he left, and he's not picking up his cell. Anyway, here's the reason it's taken so long." Papers rattled in the background. "The coroner for Plaquemines Parish sent his reports to the state, and they sent it on to the CDC—they're all in a pig-swivet. Her blood doesn't type—they've never seen anything like it." He paused and let that sink in. "She ain't human, I'm thinkin'."

Holy crap.

Damn it, I'd known there was something off with her. I've always been able to read the emotions of humans, and the Elders wouldn't take me seriously. I thought about

Melinda as she'd been that day Alex and I interviewed her. The disheveled appearance, the sweatshirt, the necklace. The freakin' necklace.

"Shit." I pulled my car against a curb before I wrecked it.

"What's wrong?" Jake's voice rose, tinged with anxiety. "Where are you?"

"I'm okay—I just need to talk to the Elders. I'll call you back."

I speed-dialed Adrian Hoffman.

He sounded resigned as he answered the phone. "Yes, Ms. Jaco? What do the mermen want now?"

"What happens if a nymph marries a wizard?" I asked.

Long silence as he shifted mental gears. "Well, there's no law against it. You'd just have to put in a request to the Elders and the head of the Water Species Convention and get it approved. I'd advise against it. The nymphs tend to be emotionally unstable. What wizard are you talking about?"

"Doug Hebert. Actually, I'm talking about Melinda Hebert," I said impatiently. "Is there a chance she is a nymph? Wouldn't you guys have a record of that somewhere?"

And if I'm right, you idiots should have figured this out before Tish got killed. I fought to keep the anger out of my voice.

"There's nothing in his file," the Speaker said, and I heard the sound of a keyboard. "It clearly states on their marriage record that she is human."

I thought furiously. "I think the nymph who's been supposedly helping us, Libby, could be our murderer, and has a connection to Melinda Hebert. I found a picture of them together." I took a deep breath and kept going. "Do you verify that a spouse is human? I mean like require blood tests or something?"

Hoffman snorted into the phone. "Why in Merlin's name would we do that? And you have absolutely no proof that the nymph is the murderer. Nymphs are very simple, peaceful creatures."

I thought about Libby cheering as Jean, Robert, and Denis tried to tear each other to shreds, and our talk about how easy it was to deceive men. She was neither simple nor peaceful. "So if Doug Hebert lied about his wife being human, you'd have no way of knowing?"

"You're being ridiculous. Why would he lie?" Hoffman's voice got deeper and his British accent heavier. "If he'd wanted to marry a nymph, no one would have objected. You need to stop concocting lunatic theories and figure out who killed her husband. Forget Melinda Hebert. She's insignificant. She doesn't matter."

Asshat. Everybody matters to somebody.

"One last question. If a prete wants to hide what he is, and has the help of a wizard, what's the best way to do it?"

"You bloody imbecile—you are giving me an oral exam on magic? You work a spell, or charm an item of clothing or jewelry. Now don't call back until you have something to report."

The line went dead. My next report was going to have a lot to say about Adrian Hoffman.

On the rest of the drive home, I tried to come up with a plan. Doug Hebert had married a nymph and kept a charmed peridot around her neck to hide her species. I had no proof, but it would explain the amount of magic active in her house the day we'd questioned her. Why Libby killed both of them, I hadn't figured out. But she'd done it.

I needed to find her, and the best way to do that was to find the Delachaise twins, especially Robert. Did he and Rene know what Libby was up to, or had she fooled them as she claimed it was so easy to do?

Grabbing the mail out of my box, I unlocked the back door and went in the kitchen, noting the slight pressure of my protective wards as I entered.

I sat at the table, watching Sebastian bat the magic-infused eyeglasses off the table and around the floor until he batted them close enough for me to bend over and grab them. "Find your rubber mouse," I told him. "I might need these again."

He jumped on the table and sat a few feet in front of me, giving me the feline stare of death from his crossed blue eyes. I slid the glasses across the table at him. "Fine, have at it." He batted them onto the floor and chased them into the living room.

I dug out my cell and tried to call Alex but got voice mail. I started to call Jake back, but remembered Alex's concerns about sending Jake into the field. What if he wanted to storm off to Plaquemines to find Libby himself?

As much as I wanted this enforcer job to work out for Jake, I wasn't going to be the one to throw him into a trial by fire, or by nymph.

What about the twins? Robert, especially, could be in danger from Libby. He also might not believe me. But Rene might. I scrolled through my phone's contact list for Rene's number, cursing as the low-battery icon began blinking.

Jotting the number on a napkin, I plugged in the cell charger and went to my desk phone. I was surprised to see the message light blinking on the antiquated answering machine I had hooked up to it. The annoying computerized menu said I had two new messages.

The first was from the Tour Blood office, inviting me to sample the company's new vampire-led French Quarter ghost tour.

I erased it and moved to the next message, freezing at the sound of Libby's dusky voice. "Drusilla Jaco, are you there? This is Libby. I would like to meet you at Pointe a la Hache this afternoon to discuss some things that might help your investigation." I just bet she did.

"Hello? Libby?" I stared at the machine, my pulse thumping in fear as Alex intercepted Libby's message. "DJ's not home, but I can meet you if it's important."

She practically purred. "That would be a lovely diversion, Alexander." She gave him instructions on where to go.

"I'll meet you at three."

The call ended. I stood frozen to the spot, ignoring Sebastian as he methodically untied my shoelaces with his teeth. The clock on the wall over the range hood said three thirty.

I grabbed the receiver and punched in Rene's number.

"Yo, wizard. Where y'at?"

Any other time, I'd have laughed at Rene's mix of Urban-Cajun greetings, but I could barely breathe. "Have you talked to Alex? He was supposed to be coming out your way."

"Yeah, babe. He left here and was heading over to Tidewater to talk to those asshole Villeres."

"Have you seen Libby today?"

"Ain't you full of questions? She was here till about two, but ain't here now. Why you wantin' Libby?"

I told him my theory. That Libby might be related to Melinda Hebert, that she'd been the one to kill the professors. And she'd killed Tish, trying to get to me. I didn't know why yet, but I knew in my gut I was right about all of it.

There was a long silence on the other end. "You sure about this? I mean, Libby's been out here with me and Robert a lot these last two weeks, and I ain't seen nothing to make me think she'd kill anybody." He paused. "She don't like wizards much, babe, but lots of us don't, especially the ones who were around in seventy-six."

I was tired of hearing about old grudges. "I'm going out to find Alex. If Libby comes back to Orchard, call me, okay? Don't tell her. And be careful."

"We can handle ourselves, wizard." He hung up.

So he was annoyed. He'd have to get over it.

Before I left, I went upstairs to my library. I had to see where, exactly, Alex was. I pulled a black glass bowl from a shelf and a bottle of purified water I kept in the little refrigerator in the corner. I also grabbed one of Alex's protein bars he kept stashed in the fridge.

Taking my loot to the bathroom and closing the door behind me, I lit candles and sandalwood incense, then doused the lights. Outside under a full moon would have been better, but this would do. Water in bowl, right finger in water, protein bar belonging to Alex in left hand. Time for a little hydromancy. I leaned over the bowl, closed my eyes, and willed a bit of magic into the water as I visualized him.

Hydromancy came in handy for finding missing things— or, in this case, people. Libby had told Alex to meet her in Pointe a la Hache, a tiny riverside community in Plaquemines Parish that spanned the east and west sides of the Mississippi. It was near the last breach site and had about thirty residents before Katrina, most of whom reached the rest of the parish by ferry. I wasn't sure how much the population had rebounded, but Libby had said she'd be at an abandoned building just downriver from the ferry landing.

I opened my eyes and watched the water cloud, then clear. I should have been able to see Alex, no matter where he was. I closed my eyes and fought the panic trying to claw its way into my head. It didn't mean he was dead. It could just mean . . . I shook my head to erase a similar conversation I'd had with myself while trying to scry Gerry after Katrina. He hadn't been dead either, but he'd been in a lot of trouble.

I cleared my mind and visualized Gandalf instead, sending more power into the bowl. This time, an image appeared in the water—the big golden dog on the ground, not moving. I fought back tears as I watched the image, desperate to see movement.

Think, DJ. Alex couldn't be dead—he'd have shifted back to his human form. If he was injured, he could be staying in canine form to heal faster. I moved my fingers around in the water gently, trying to shift the image to see where he was. The river ran to his left, a lot of generic trees and grass around him, some kind of white square building behind him. I'd just have to go to Pointe a la Hache and work from there.

31

I grabbed my keys, cranked the Pathfinder, and drove east. Traffic clogged all the lanes of the Crescent City Connection bridge crossing the river onto the Westbank, and crawled all the way to Belle Chasse. Finally, I was able to get out of traffic and head down Highway 23 into Plaquemines. Banks of clouds gathered overhead, and rain looked inevitable. Our first really cool weather of the year was due overnight.

The rendezvous spot Libby had chosen was easy enough to find. The big ferry terminal came first, crossing the river to Point a la Hache, and then a quarter-mile later a small cinderblock building with a missing roof sat surrounded by piles of rotted hurricane debris. Alex's black Mercedes sat in front.

I jumped out of the truck, reached in for my backpack, and gave a startled yelp. The elven staff lay on the front seat. It had been a while since the damned thing had followed me outside the house. I stared at it for a few heartbeats, then grabbed it and approached the building, scanning the area as I slipped around the side. The last thing I needed was Libby to see me before I saw her.

I flattened myself against the building and peered around the corner to the back. I saw Gandalf on the ground, but no sign of Libby.

Oh, thank God. Gandalf raised his head, and sat up. He moved slowly and didn't make any attempt to stand, but looked toward where I was hidden and whined.

I walked toward him him, looking around me and keeping the staff ready. Finally, I dropped to my knees beside him and took one more look around for Libby.

"What happened?" I asked Gandalf. No, wait. He couldn't talk. But he could understand me.

"Are you hurt?"

Panting heavily, he grunted as he got to his feet, holding his right front paw off the ground. I moved around him and took it in my hand. The paw, sticky and wet with blood, took up my entire palm. A deep gash creviced the top of the paw almost to the elbow joint. Libby and her famous knife. Dried blood was already flaking off of it, though, so he was healing. An hour, and he'd be good as new.

"Can't you shift back?"

He whined and flopped back to the ground, giving me a look of pure misery.

I'd take that as a no. "Stay here, I'm getting the car."

I pulled my Pathfinder behind the cinderblock building, hidden from the road, and tucked the keys inside above the wheel—somebody would have to come and get it later. It was seven years old, driven to death, and got suckalicious gas mileage. If it got stolen, I'd buy something tiny and eco-friendly.

Alex's clothes and gun were on the ground near Gandalf, and I rifled through his pockets for his car keys. I drove the Mercedes around the building and parked it beside him.

"Do you think you can climb in? I can't pick you up." Maybe me and a forklift.

He huffed to his feet and limped on three legs to where I held the passenger door open for him. He stopped and whined.

"You can jump up there, it's—" What was I thinking? This was Alex. It wasn't that he couldn't jump in the car. He didn't want to get blood on his upholstery. We had a murderous nymph on the loose, Alex was stuck in Gandalf mode for some reason, and he was worried about his car interior. "Oh, good grief. Wait a minute."

I got his clothes, pulled out his wallet and cell and put them in my pocket, then spread his pants and shirt over the car seat. He turned and looked at me, and stuck his nose at the edge of the passenger floorboard.

I shook my head. "Fine." I pulled off my light jacket and spread it over the floorboard. Satisfied, he used his three good legs to hop in the car and climb onto the seat.

Once we were settled and I'd started back toward Orleans Parish, I decided to see how far my dog-whispering skills could get me. "Okay, I'm going to ask you questions. Bark once for yes and twice for no. Got it?"

He gave me a withering look, then yipped once.

"Good. Can you shift back?"

Two barks.

"Did you meet Libby here?"

One bark and a curled upper lip.

My sentiments exactly. "Did she do something to keep you from shifting back?"

One bark, a deep growl, and hackles that visibly rose across his shoulders.

I wondered what kind of magic nymphs had. "Was it a potion?"

Two yips.

"A spell?"

He cocked his head and looked at me. Okay, something like a spell but he wasn't sure . . .

"A curse?"

Yip.

Okay, a curse. So Libby had put some kind of curse on Alex to keep him from shifting back. I looked at his paw. The bleeding had slowed, so whatever she had done to him hadn't impacted his shapeshifter healing. "Do you need to see a doctor or . . . a vet?"

I swear he narrowed his eyes before giving me two snippy yaps.

"Okay, in that case, I'm calling the Elders." Again. Twice in one day—or was this the third time? They were probably making bets on how long it would be before I called with another crisis. Hope Adrian Hoffman lost his shirt on that wager. I needed to get Zrakovi's number on speed dial.

Hoffman sounded as snippy as Alex. "Who do you suspect is not human now, Ms. Jaco?"

Asswipe. "Alex—he's stuck in dog mode after being cursed by the nymph you claim there's no reason to distrust because she's so simple and sweet."

He didn't have anything to say? Well, I had plenty to fill in his silence. "Libby called my house while I was out, wanting to meet with me. Alex intercepted the call and met her out in Plaquemines Parish. She used some kind of hex on him after he'd shifted into a dog and now he can't shift back." Or she made him shift into a dog. Same result.

"Bloody hell." That was as close as Hoffman would get to admitting he was wrong, so I got a smug sense of satisfaction from it. "Where is he?"

"Sitting beside me in the car, looking like a big unhappy dog." Gandalf's tail thumped slowly against the door. "I should be able to do a general counter-hex on him and change him back, but it will take a while. If you know a faster way, I wouldn't mind hearing it."

"Hold please." I heard him talking sharply to someone in the background, then he returned to the phone. "Without knowing exactly what she did to him, the counter-hex is probably the only thing we can do," he said, sounding resigned. "Anything more drastic might backfire and make the curse permanent. Elder Zrakovi will inform Mr. Jacob Warin of the situation and he can pursue the murder suspect. Your job is to get Mr. Alexander Warin back to normal."

"I also need someone to get my SUV from behind an old closed convenience store in West Pointe a la Hache." I gave him directions and the location of the key. "I'll let you know what happens."

"You do that."

Jake was going to be sent to hunt down Libby after all—by himself, on his first field assignment as an enforcer? What a freakin' mess.

Gandalf walked despondently beside me as I unlocked the back door and entered the kitchen. Inside, he stilled as Sebastian came galloping out of the parlor to greet him and laid the rubber mouse at his feet. Sweet. The cat always did like him better.

I'd asked Alex once how much his human sentience stayed in place when he shifted into canine form. Most, he'd told me. He could understand conversation and situations, but higher reasoning could spin away if he didn't really concentrate. He'd be trying to figure out what to do about the bad guy coming his way when suddenly he'd be thinking: *Hey, that lady has a hamburger!*

He and Sebastian now sat in tandem, staring at me as I flipped through my mail.

"What?" They were ganging up on me. "Are you hungry?"

I dumped some cat food into Sebastian's bowl, and pulled out a big Pyrex bowl for Gandalf, filling it with cat food as well. I didn't have any dog food.

While Sebastian inhaled his own dinner, then moved over to the big bowl for part deux, Gandalf stared at me.

"It's all I have," I told him. "You know I don't keep much food in the house. You want a protein bar and some Cheetos?"

He curled his upper lip and showed me a row of shiny white, very large teeth.

I sighed. "Fine. I'll order a pizza. You want your usual vegetarian?"

Two barks.

"Pepperoni?"

One.

Good. As Gandalf, he was much less worried about his sodium and fat intake.

I called in the pizza order, then got a warm washcloth from the bathroom and washed off his leg and paw. "Most of this blood is dried—it's already healing. Want me to use a potion on it to speed it up?"

Two barks.

"Okay then, shifter. Heal thyself." I went upstairs to change into pants and a sweater that didn't have blood on it.

When the doorbell rang a half hour later, Jake Warin stood on the porch with the pizza, which he'd intercepted and paid for, a couple of oyster po'boys, a six-pack of Abita, and the keys to the Pathfinder, which he and Ken had picked up. I wondered what he'd told Ken.

He grinned as he took in the sight of Gandalf sitting on the sofa. "Where'd you get the big ugly dog?" he asked, coming inside the front parlor and piling the food on the coffee table. He flashed dimples at Gandalf, who flashed big white teeth in return. Jake kissed me on the cheek, earning a low, rumbling growl from Gandalf. I almost growled myself.

"Don't piss him off more. He's had a hard day." And besides that, buddy boy, you haven't called me on non-business since our disastrous date, so don't use me to tick off your cousin.

Jake chuckled his way to the kitchen to fetch plates, a bottle opener for the beer, and a diet soda for me.

I put pizza slices on the plate and set it on the floor. Gandalf turned his head and stared in the opposite direction.

"You are totally dependent on me right now, so it would behoove you to stop being such a pain in the ass," I said, picking up the plate of pizza, setting it on the coffee table, and dragging the whole thing in front of him so he could eat from his perch on the sofa.

"You forget who you're talking to," Jake said, stealing a slice of pepperoni and sitting on the sofa next to Gandalf. "He specializes in pain-in-the-ass behavior."

Gandalf ignored him, holding the crust of the pizza

between his paws and eating it almost daintily like an ice cream cone.

I settled into one of the armchairs with a po'boy. "Did Zrakovi call you about Libby?"

"He did. My job tonight is to keep an eye on you in case she shows up." He took a sip of beer and smiled at me. "That's an assignment I didn't mind at all."

I wanted to hug him, and then slap the shit out of him. Talk about running hot and cold. I didn't know whether he was still interested in me, or if I was just an assignment and he was a born flirt, or if this was all a show to get a jab at Alex while he couldn't defend himself. Probably a little of all three.

Worse than not knowing how Jake felt, I wasn't sure how I felt. Even if I could do a little empathic mojo and figure out Jake's motives, it wouldn't help with mine.

After dinner, we put on some music and went upstairs to the library. I filled Jake in on the case while I pulled out books and notes on hex reversals. "Since you have to babysit, want to help me bring Alex back?" I wished I hadn't said the word babysit; it reminded me of what happened to the last person who stayed with me to make sure I was safe. It hadn't worked out well for Tish. I couldn't live with one more person being hurt or killed on my account, and Jake had already had his turn.

"I don't know, short stuff. I kind of like Alex better this way."

I expected Gandalf to bite Jake, but he held his furry head high as he sniffed past us and went next door to my bedroom.

I heard a thump as he jumped on my bed, thus ensuring no one else would be using it anytime soon. Sebastian followed him.

My life was an utter zoo.

I sorted the papers on my worktable, and began reading while Jake listened to music and did a close inspection of my shelves. "Don't touch anything," I warned him. "Some of it bites."

He stepped farther back but kept looking. He'd known I was a wizard since Katrina and had been to the house quite a few times before and after, but he'd never been here, in my workspace.

Each glass container on the floor-to-ceiling shelves held magical herbs, stones, or metal shavings. A small refrigerator kept perishable materials usable. Candles stood like colorful sentinels guarding several shelves, different colors for different types of spells. Then there were the oddities I'd occasionally need: alligator skin, a rooster's claw, a jar of cat's-eye marbles, old iron containers.

There were also the books, of course. Jake pulled out a pamphlet on the historical undead, and settled into a chair while I worked.

I finally found three hex-reversal potions I thought might do the job. Two were fairly simple; the third not so simple but guaranteed to work. I made sure none of the ingredients would hurt Alex if the reversal didn't take, and picked the first of the easier ones.

"Want to help?" I asked Jake.

"Sure." He put the pamphlet aside and returned to the worktable, which I'd cleared of everything except the big wrought-iron cross permanently affixed to the center.

Jake fingered it absently. "All this craziness I never knew existed. You have to believe in God to stay sane, don't you?"

I nodded. "You have to believe there's a reason behind it all, that at least in the end, the good guys win."

"Just wish I knew why things happen."

I thought of what Jake had been through between Afghanistan and werewolves, and the fact that he was still standing here, willing to find his place in a new world. I thought of Katrina. I thought of Tish. "I'm not sure we ever really understand the reason. We just have to believe there is one."

I made a list of ingredients for the first potion and had him gather them from the shelves while I pulled out the bowls and pans I'd need. While he finished, I went into the bedroom. Gandalf was stretched across the bed horizontally, head on his paws, looking morose. Sebastian snored softly on top of the dresser.

I stretched out on the bed next to Gandalf and scratched his head. "I found three things to try. If they don't work, they won't hurt you. I want to try the simplest ones first because if they work, they're faster. Are you willing to experiment?"

He rolled over in a dead cockroach pose, and I rubbed his tummy.

"Sorry to interrupt such an intimate moment, but the stuff's ready." Jake stood in the doorway, a half smile on his face I couldn't interpret. I sent out a few emotional feelers, but got very little. On top of his new garou nature, his enforcer training was showing; he'd learned how to shield his mind. Interesting that he thought to do it around me.

I got to my feet and headed for the library, Gandalf padding behind me and Jake bringing up the rear.

The first potion was four simple ingredients: a piece of string for memory, a bit of a broken mirror for self, some ground horehound for reversing sorcery, and something of Alex's. I clipped a small corner from his wallet and added the leather bit to the other items in a small box of onyx, used for breaking bonds. I sat on a floor cushion in the corner, where I did my grounding rituals in the mornings, and shut my eyes, gathering my magic and channeling it into the box. I might have to use the staff later tonight, but I'd put it off as long as I could.

Once the box grew hot enough to begin burning my hand, I set it carefully on the floor and opened the lid. A clear liquid floated inside, a puff of steam rising from it.

Gandalf walked over to look at it, sniffed, then cocked his head at me.

"If it works, it will work within a few minutes," I said. "It might not be strong enough, but if it doesn't work it won't hurt you." It might have some short-term side effects but I didn't want to freak him out.

His tail lowered, he lapped up the potion. When it was gone, he looked up and growled at me.

"I didn't promise it would taste good," I said. "Now, we wait."

And waited and waited. After twenty minutes, Gandalf sneezed four times. Jake and I sat up from where we'd slouched in the armchairs by the window, watching him. He watched us back, and sneezed again.

"What's with the sneezing?" Jake asked.

"Side effect. It didn't work. He'll quit in a few minutes." I whispered, but Alex had canine ears now. He barked at me, then sneezed again.

"Okay, let's try the second one." I took a small iron ring and placed it in a pan, then covered it with a mixture of ground meteorite, some poke greens, and holy water. It had to cook over low heat for an hour, during which time I stretched out on the loveseat by the fireplace with a book on nymphs, and Jake read a biography of Jean Lafitte. Gandalf sneezed and stared at us. It was about as romantic as a bingo game at the assisted-living center.

After an hour, I poured the mixture into a clean glass bowl, let it cool off, and again put it down for Gandalf to drink. He sneezed twice and lapped it up.

The changes began within seconds, only they weren't the changes I'd hoped for. It started with one ear, which began to change from gold, first to gray, then white, then palest pink, then darker. Within ten minutes, Gandalf's body looked like it had been dipped in bubblegum.

Jake and I couldn't look at each other. If we did, we'd laugh and Alex would never forgive us. He didn't realize what had happened until he noticed a pink paw and began trying to look at himself. He ran to the full-length mirror in my bedroom, then raced back, barking furiously at me and bouncing up and down so hard all four pink paws left the ground at once. I was glad I didn't speak dog. Foam dripped from his jaws and his white teeth flashed, but it just wasn't scary coming from a giant pink fluffball.

I tried to keep a straight face, to let Alex know I appreciated the depth of his humiliation, but Jake finally lost it. He practically brayed, and I bit my lip so hard I tasted blood.

"I'm sorry, I'm sorry, I'm sorry." I closed my eyes. The only way I could keep from laughing was not to look at him. "I'll do the third spell. It's a guarantee, but it takes a long time. I thought it was worth it to try the easy ones first."

Gandalf bit Jake soundly on the leg, hard enough to rip his jeans, and huffed back to the bedroom.

"Damn, I'm bleeding." Jake wiped tears of laughter away as he examined his dog bite. "Don't think he has rabies, do you?"

I had already begun pulling out the final hex-reversal ingredients. "I doubt you could catch rabies."

He sobered as that idea sank in. "Yeah, guess I'm pretty much immune to everything now except self-control." His self-hatred had finally shown up to the party, and I wasn't happy to see it.

The third potion differed from the other two in that it

needed something from the person who created the hex—in this case, Libby. I opened a drawer built into one of the shelves and pulled out a tiny vial: remains of the drops of brackish water Alex had collected from my porch the night Tish was murdered. I added a teaspoon of purified water to it and swished it around the vial to blend in what I hoped would be at least a wee bit of Libby DNA. In the remote chance I was wrong and Libby wasn't Tish's killer, the potion simply wouldn't work.

"Why did you want to do this one last?" Jake asked, watching me mix the ingredients.

"This form of reversal takes several hours. He'll probably shift back a piece at a time, a limb or digit or organ at a time. The bones will reform slowly. It's going to hurt."

He winced. "Before I shifted the first time, my enforcer sponsor warned me it was going to hurt but, God, you can't imagine. It's like every bone is breaking and then repairing itself in a span of minutes. After the first few times, you just endure it knowing that once the shift is over, you'll feel amazing."

I nodded. I'd heard weres describe their shifts like that, and I'd shared a taste of it with Rene.

"Alex isn't a were, so his shifts are different. He says they're painless and instantaneous. It's all fueled by magic. So he's never been through what you have, with that kind of pain, and the potion says it can take more than twelve hours to reverse the hex once it starts working."

Jake winced. "Now I'm sorry I made fun of him."

I pulled a locked box from a bottom shelf and dug a tiny key from inside a jar of iron filings. In the box was a bottle of wizard's bane (one sip and any wizard's a goner in seconds) and a bottle of painkillers—the kind people get hooked on and sell their souls to a demon for. In the Beyond, that could be done literally, with a wide variety of demons to choose from.

I ordered a bottle from the Elders each year and kept it on hand in case of an injury. I counted it a good year when I could dispose of the pills and replace them with fresh ones. Wizards didn't heal like shifters.

I held the bottle up and showed the label to Jake, a question on my face. He looked worried, but nodded. I shook out a couple of pills, then added a third after some thought. Alex was a big guy, and he was in for a rough night. Better if he slept through it.

Finally, I gathered my mortar and pestle from a lower cabinet. The pestle made a squeaky noise as it ground the pills into a fine, white powder that I stirred into the potion. I added the drops of Libby juice last, shook the whole mixture well, and poured it into another bowl. Finally, I closed my eyes and infused it with magic using the staff. I wouldn't risk this one on my unenhanced magic.

"Alex, come here—it's ready." I heard a thump as he jumped off the bed and came padding into the room, Sebastian at his heels. He looked at the bowl, then sat and looked at me with doubt written all over his pink face. Sebastian sniffed at the bowl till Jake jerked him up and held him.

"Here's the deal," I told Alex. "I'm certain this will work, at least, as long as I'm right about Libby. If I'm wrong it won't do anything. I saved it for last because it takes a long time. It will make you sleepy, and it will take all night to completely reverse the curse. You sleep and heal, and I'll be here when you wake up. Okay?"

His bark was laced with a low, threatening rumble (still not very scary coming from a bubblegum-pink face), but he slunk to the bowl and lapped up the potion without hesitating.

"You can go back in my room and sleep on my bed," I said. "It's going to knock you out. You need to stay here tonight."

Alex gave Jake a poisonous glare and made his pink way back to the bedroom.

Jake gave me a faint smile. "You look worried. You think this isn't going to work?"

"No, I'm sure it will," I said. "I just hate that he has to go through the pain of it. He never really trusted Libby. I didn't take her seriously enough, and I should have thought about the damned necklace Melinda Hebert was wearing."

Most wizards I knew were so arrogant they'd never dream of disguising what they were or helping anyone else do so. But it wasn't like I'd never heard of bespelling a gemstone.

Jake pulled me to the loveseat and held on to my hand as we sat. "Listen, I'm sorry I've been such a chickenshit. I should have called you." He laced his fingers through mine. "I wanted to, especially after I heard about the thing with the elf. But after what happened on our date and then at

Aunt Norma's . . ." He shrugged. "I figured you were better off without me."

All of a sudden I was tired, just bone tired. "I don't know where things could go between us," I said. "But I don't think you get to make the decision about what is or isn't good for me. You scared me that night, yes. But I still don't think you'd hurt me. Thing is"—I shifted on the sofa to face him—"I don't want to make things harder for you. If it's easier to not be around me, just say so. I hope we can at least be friends."

"What's easier isn't always what a person wants." He leaned in and kissed me, then rested his forehead against mine. I wasn't sure if he was saying hello or good-bye, and wasn't sure what I wanted. Except that at this particular moment I needed simple, and Jake would never be simple.

"While we're being honest here, I have to ask you some-thing," he said.

"Okay." We shifted till we sat side by side again, his arm around me and my head resting on his shoulder. "What's between you and Alex? And don't give me the 'We're just partners' stuff or the 'We're friends' stuff. I want you to think about it and give me an answer."

So I thought about it. And in the end all I could come up with was an answer that didn't help anybody. "I don't know anymore. I honestly don't know."

He nodded. "Good. Because if you'd told me nothing, I wouldn't believe you. And if you'd told me you loved him, I'd have been really, really"—he kissed my cheek—"really disappointed. Now, I figure we're both in the game."

I sighed. "It's not a game, Jake. I'm not part of your rivalry. Or at least I shouldn't be. I don't want to be."

He ran a hand through his hair. "I have a confession to make, since we're laying it all on the table tonight."

Much more honesty and I was going to have to hurt something. "Yeah, what's that?"

"I showed up tonight because I knew Alex would be here."

I turned to look at him. "Of course you did—you knew he'd been cursed. So?"

Pain haunted his gaze. "So, I knew I'd have a chaperone, even if it was a furry one."

Understanding didn't sink in for a few seconds. "You don't want to be alone with me without a chaperone? What are we, thirteen?"

"Thirteen-year-olds don't have to worry about being killed by their dates."

I couldn't answer that. I was tired of talking and wasn't sure how much longer I could argue something I no longer felt certain was true. I didn't think he'd ever hurt me. But I didn't know it.

He smoothed my hair away from my face and kissed my forehead. "You still got that magic stick of yours in case Libby shows up tonight?"

I pointed to the worktable, where the staff had moved itself. "You need me to take you back to the Gator?"

"I'm sleeping here. Loup-Garou Security, at your service. I'll crash downstairs; you stay up here in case Alex needs you."

I nodded, thinking about Tish, the last person to stay in the guest room. "There are fresh sheets on the bed downstairs. Help yourself to whatever you want."

He squeezed my shoulder and got to his feet. "Not whatever I want, DJ."

32

Jake's call woke me at noon, and I wrestled to find the phone in my pocket. My arm didn't want to work. I'd fallen asleep, fully dressed, on the chair next to my bed about five a.m. after spending hours poring through some of Gerry's black grimoires and sending Jake home in a cab. I wasn't sure if Libby was immortal—some nymphs were and some weren't—but, just in case, I wanted to know how to kill her.

Finally, I'd tried to stretch out on the bed, but when Alex's shifting began, he'd thrashed so violently I was afraid I'd end up with a black eye. But I didn't want to leave him alone, which brought back Jake's unsettling question about my relationship with Alex. I'd want to stay with anyone in this situation I considered a friend, right? My concern for him didn't mean anything more or less than that.

Except for a bit of pink fur on one foot, he looked like his old self. He was still zonked, but his flushed, feverish skin testified to the trauma his body had gone through over the past nine hours. I straightened the sheet I'd pulled over him and took the phone to the library.

"Any sign of Libby?" I asked Jake, after giving him the update on Alex.

"No, but I'm on my way to Plaquemines to talk to Rene and Robert—see if she's with them. That's where she'll show up, sooner or later." He sounded pissed off. Anger would make his control even worse.

Leftover pizza melted into a sticky goo in the microwave and that, along with a diet soda, made for a quease-inducing breakfast. One of these days I'd concede adulthood and actually start cooking. Or not.

By the time my cell rang, just before two, I was in a bored stupor reading *The Compleat History of Elves*' chapter on their political structure, trying to figure out what Synod leader Mace Banyan had done to me when we shook hands. The phone's caller ID read 504-MER-TWIN, and I answered the phone with a "Yo, mer," expecting Rene. But it was Robert.

"Yo yourself, darlin'."

I regrouped. Laid-back twin, not serious twin. "Hey, Robert, what's up? Did Rene talk to you last night about Libby? Has Jake been out there today?"

"Yeah and yeah." He laughed. "Jake was here earlier but he'd done gone by the time Libby called—think Rene said he was headed to the Villeres' place. Thought I'd give you a heads-up. I'm meetin' Libby at three thirty at Pointe a la Hache. Thought you and the shifters might wanna be there."

Holy crap. Alex was out of commission. I could probably wake him up now, but he'd be groggy for a few hours and sore as hell. He wasn't ready to face off with Libby. I should be able to catch Jake, though.

My watch said three twenty. "It's almost that time now," I said. "Are you already on your way?"

"Yeah, just getting here, darlin'."

I groaned. He hadn't called me till he'd almost gotten there? The idiot. "Stay out of this, Robert. Just tell me exactly where she is, then you hang back and wait for us."

He made an impatient snort into the phone. "Rene's boat is tied up behind a white cinderblock building just past the ferry on Highway 23."

Yeah, I knew exactly where it was.

"Robert—"

He cut me off. "She won't hurt me none, darlin'. I'll keep her busy till you get here. Might be my last chance." He laughed again and hung up.

Damn it, Robert wasn't taking this seriously. Big surprise. I wondered if Rene knew what he was up to. I raced upstairs, almost tripping over Sebastian, and flew around the library. I might not be able to keep up with my back-pack, so I picked out a few helpful potions and charms already made up, small things that would fit in the pockets of my jeans. On the way out, I grabbed a couple of other items from the kitchen.

Mahout stood propped against the back door, blocking my path. "Good idea," I said, grabbing the staff and the thigh holster Alex had rigged for it. "But you're the last resort."

Although if Mace Banyan wanted to pop over from Elfheim and take down the nymph, that would be okay.

I went into the darkened bedroom and sat on the edge of the bed, debating whether or not to wake Alex. He looked like a big kid with his hair tousled, dark lashes brushing his cheeks, and not a weapon in sight. I swept his hair aside and put my palm to his forehead. He felt less feverish, but I decided to let him sleep. I'd pumped enough painkillers in that potion last night to keep him groggy for a while.

"Wish me luck," I whispered.

On the way to the car, I called Jake and got voice mail. I left a message. I tried again en route to Pointe a la Hache. He's probably just in a reception dead zone, I told myself. Doesn't mean he's in trouble.

Next I called Rene at the MERTWIN number, hoping he'd pick up rather than Robert, and finally got lucky.

"Yo, wizard."

"You talked to Robert this afternoon?"

Rene grumbled something I couldn't understand, but I'd bet it was some kind of Cajun curse. "No, I tried talking to the SOB 'bout Libby last night but he don't listen so good. What's he done?"

I told him, at least as much as I knew. Our biggest piece of evidence was asleep in my bed. "I'm headed to Pointe a la Hache," I said, and described the location. "Do you know where it is?"

"I'm over in Harahan, but I'll go that way now, babe. Don't be runnin' in there all commando, wizard. Libby won't hurt Robert but if you're right about all this she'd hurt you plenty. Nothin' against your magic, but she'll be one tough broad to kill."

Tough broad, my ass. "I'll see what things look like when I get there. Just come as soon as you can."

If Rene was in Harahan, a western suburb of New Orleans, he was a good forty-five minutes behind me, depending on traffic. I wasn't as confident Libby wouldn't hurt Robert, especially if he let it slip that we were looking for her. If nothing else, she might hex him into permanent fishhood.

I fidgeted through Westbank traffic again, and finally made my way back to Highway 23 into Plaquemines. I'd been in the parish more these past few weeks than in my previous twenty-eight years combined. I found it charming, as all of rural Southeast Louisiana was, with its dark marsh and swamp, its remains of old cypress, the exotic tang of its air, its sheer otherness.

Lately, it had been a bit too *other*.

I passed the ferry landing and looked for Robert's white pickup, the light twin to Rene's black extended cab. It was parked in front of the crumbling cinderblock shrine to Katrina.

I parked next to it and tried Jake again, without luck. I left messages telling him where I was and what was happening. I thought about it a few seconds and left a message on Alex's phone as well. It was still on my downstairs coffee table. He wouldn't find it unless he was awake and lucid enough to get down the stairwell.

I took a few deep breaths, climbed out of the truck, and slipped the elven staff into the holster. Most pretes have sharpened senses, and Libby and Robert could have heard me coming before I pulled off the road. I hoped Robert hadn't exaggerated his ability to distract the nymph, not that I really wanted to watch his distraction technique.

I headed up the steep river levee, looking for the *Dieu de la Mer*. I planned to see where things stood, then wait for Rene or Jake to arrive.

The boat had been tied to the short, half-rotted pier that jutted out from a stand of scrubby bush, near where I'd found Alex yesterday. We'd need to check the river in this area for another breach—Libby seemed to be hanging out here a lot.

Squatting behind the foliage, I watched the boat for any movement and heard a male voice. Talk, then soft laughter. Robert chased Libby around the wheelhouse and onto the raised forward deck. She wore a short, white halter dress, and Robert was in jeans, so at least I wasn't going to have to deal with naked pretes. They were both laughing, which meant Robert hadn't given us away.

Libby stood with her back to me. Robert looked at the bank, then slowly scanned until he spotted me. I hoped he'd side with me against Libby, but I wasn't sure.

He returned his focus to Libby. What an Amazon. I'd forgotten how tall she was. Robert was a good two or three inches shorter, and he was several inches taller than me. She'd also be strong, like any other prete. My days of underestimating Libby were behind me. But Robert was prete-strong too. I just wished I knew which side he was on.

Libby walked behind the wheelhouse again, and Robert paused behind her long enough to look back at me. He held a finger to his lips in a quieting motion, then waved me toward the boat.

I looked back toward the highway, straining my ears for any hint that Jake or Rene—or somebody—was coming. All I heard were gulls. If Robert was backing Libby, he'd have already told her I was here. If I left, she'd either lie in wait till she could kill me or someone else I cared about, or she'd escape back into the Beyond.

If Robert was backing me, he could help me bring her down as well as Rene could. Maybe better—he'd spent more time with her.

I duckwalked to the pier, crossed it as quietly as I could, and climbed aboard the boat on the narrow side by the wheelhouse, opposite where Robert and Libby had gone. Creeping to the edge of the wheelhouse, I peered around the corner. The rear deck was empty.

"Looking for us?" Robert slipped an arm around my waist from behind and jerked me around to face Libby. She stretched her lips in a broad smile. "Finally, wizard. I tried to kill you once before, but your wards kept me out. Did you like what I did to your friend?"

"Go back to hell." I can be eloquent when I'm mad. I struggled against Robert, but he held me tightly against him, my arms pinned to my sides. "Robert, what the hell are you doing?" I grunted, trying to squirm out of his grip. "Don't you understand what she's done? Rene would not want you to do this."

"Rene's been loyal to the wrong people—you blinded him. Libby killed some wizards, right. Her sister was an accident—just wouldn't cooperate when she tried to take her back home. I got no problem with offing wizards after what they done to our people. I figure me and Libby make a good team."

"Rene is going to kill you." I kicked backward, jamming my heel into his kneecap, but all he did was grunt and tighten his grip. Hoping that wisp of our mind-meld was still active, I sent a mental SOS to Rene and got a mental ping in return. He was on his way.

"Hold her still," Libby said, stepping closer, and Robert changed his grasp so that he held me in place with his left arm. I still couldn't break loose. With his right hand, he grabbed my hair and pulled my head back against his shoulder. I couldn't move above the waist but I kicked at Libby as she approached. Panic threatened to paralyze me, but I knew I'd find a way to get a hand free to reach the tiny vials in my pockets or the staff. I just had to stay focused.

My foot caught Libby just above her ankle, but I might as well have kicked a tree. She didn't react, just stopped in front of me and put a hand on either side of my face, advancing till we stood nose-to-nose. She really had to bend down to get on my level. She caught my gaze and tried to hold it. Guess she didn't get the memo that enthrallment doesn't work on me because of the elven genes.

But I could pretend. I didn't have to act well enough to earn an Oscar, just convince one crazy nymph I was enthralled enough for Robert to let me go. Damned mer. If we lived through this, Rene was going to kick his fins all the way to Pass a Loutre and back.

I willed my muscles to grow slack even though they wanted to fight and scream. I stopped kicking at Libby and gazed in her green eyes, letting my focus grow soft after a few seconds.

"I think she's under," Robert said, loosening his grip on me. I let my legs go rubbery so I'd waver a little as he released me.

"Excellent," Libby murmured. Her hands were still on either side of my face. "I thought you said she was a strong wizard, Robert. She's just another stupid Green Congress bitch."

I slipped my right hand slowly onto Libby's arm and she tensed. My left hand I lowered to the staff, an excruciating inch at a time. I stroked her arm, keeping a blank look on my face and my eyes on hers.

She relaxed and chuckled. "I think she likes me."

I willed every ounce of physical magic I could muster into her arm, pulled the staff, and caught her on the thigh.

She shrieked and threw me away from Robert, cursing in an incomprehensible gibber.

The wheelhouse and the wooden deck blurred past as I flew headfirst across the width of the broad aft deck, bounced off the rails, and landed with a thud against the corner of an old wooden box full of hooks and tackle. The shoulder of my sweater ripped as I fell hard across the storage box's rough corner, splinters digging into my skin. Blood began soaking through the tears in the sweater, but I didn't think it was serious.

In movies, when the bad guy gets the jump on the hero and hurls him across an alley or barroom like a sack of trash, the hero shakes his head and comes out swinging, stronger than ever. Not that I was any hero in this scene except by default, but it doesn't happen that way. In fact, it hurts like hell.

I looked around for the staff, but it had fallen mid-flight. I finally spotted it lying on the opposite side of the deck by Libby's feet, unnoticed.

If Libby had been less emotional, she'd have followed me across the deck and finished me off. She had plenty of time while I shook the colorful shooting stars out of my head and located the staff. But she had to scream at Robert first for letting me go, sending a fiery blaze of anger at the mer, who looked crestfallen and not a little tense.

Ironic, I thought, struggling to sit. Here I am, an empath, and the one time I'd like to feed off someone else's anger I'm with a preternatural water creature whose emotions I can't absorb and a mer who'd either been enthralled by her or wasn't feeling much of anything. Too bad mers weren't immune to her enthrallment like a true shapeshifter. Otherwise, Robert might be thinking more clearly.

I needed to neutralize him so I could focus on Libby. I felt in my pockets, thankful for unbreakable vials, and identified the camouflage potion by the raised dot on its cap. Time for the magic to begin.

33

I flipped off the top of the vial and guzzled the potion. Libby continued screaming at Robert, wanting to know why she couldn't enthrall me.

"Why don't you ask me, Libby?" I pulled myself to my feet, holding on to the rail, and she whirled to face me. I think in her rage she'd forgotten I was there. Libby wasn't stupid, but Adrian Hoffman had been right in calling nymphs unstable. Good to know. Unfortunately, I'd just reminded her I was here.

"Redeem yourself, mer," she said. "Bring her to the back deck."

Robert looked around wildly, and I didn't move. A true invisibility potion doesn't exist. Magic can take solid matter like a person, break it down, and move it—but it can't make something solid disappear. Camouflage potions soften the edges, and make the thing or person blend with their surroundings. If I moved while Robert and Libby looked straight at me, they might be able to figure it out. So I stayed where I was.

Libby pointed at me. "She's right there, you fool."

Oops. Guess the potion didn't work with Libby. Luckily, she didn't want to do her own dirty work.

"I can't see the bitch," Robert yammered, looking around wildly. "She ain't there."

Libby hissed and backhanded him hard enough to knock him over the rails. He hit the water with a splash, but I wasn't concerned. He was a freaking mer. Not to mention a fool, and I've heard God always looks out for fools. Since I probably qualified as one myself, it was a good thing.

"So, here we are, Libby," I said. Maybe she'd go for a little girl talk while I figured out how to get closer to my staff. "What's your real name, anyway?"

She limped toward me, not walking too well courtesy of my little zap with Mahout. She should have been hurt worse than that. A glint of silver flashed in the sunlight; she held a knife, probably the one she'd used to kill Tish. My own anger fired up and burned off some of the pain from my shoulder.

"Libetta is my name," she said softly. "Mellind was my sister."

I edged along the rear of the aft deck. If I could lure her to circle me, I might get within reach of the staff. So far, it was working.

"So, Mellind married Doug Hebert after the war, and you didn't like it?"

"She gave up everything and he gave up nothing," she said. "As soon as the borders came down, I decided to find her. Our father wanted her home."

I tried to turn, but Libby was too fast. She had preternatural speed. I wasn't all that fast on a good day, and this wasn't shaping up to be a good day. I'd stayed up all night with a pink shapeshifter and a loup-garou who needed a chaperone.

I twisted as she launched at me with the knife, and was able to get enough leverage to throw her off balance. I felt the blade grind into my calf, but there were worse places it could have gone.

Still, if I didn't get a break soon, I'd be spouting blood like a sieve. Libby rolled me and reached down to pull the knife free. It gave me a split second to pull another vial from my pocket and flick off the top. I tried to get it toward her face but she pulled up with the knife and I caught her in the stomach instead.

I groaned as the knife went into my upper arm. She released it and rolled away when my acid charm finally ate through her dress and hit skin.

I scrambled behind the large winch near the rear of the deck. The shiny white contraption glinted in the sun. It wasn't wide, but it offered some cover.

When she finally stopped screaming, Libby sat on the deck and stared at me. "You are just a young wizard. You should not be able to hurt me this way."

"Surprise." That was about all the witty repartee I could

muster with splinters poking out of my shoulder and my left leg and right arm bleeding freely from stab wounds. There was some cold comfort in knowing that as much as I'd underestimated Libby, she'd also underestimated me. Stupid Green Congress bitch, my ass. I had Red Congress warriors and elves in my family tree.

My right shoulder screamed in protest as I dug in my pocket for a small plastic jar of honey shaped like a bear. It was just a silly honey bear from the Winn-Dixie next to my office, only my bear had swallowed a bunch of sweet belladonna berries left over from my power-share with Rene that had been ground to a fine powder. Ten of them would kill a human adult. I'd crushed thirty, my whole supply, figuring I'd need that much to take down an Amazon-sized nymph.

I unscrewed the lid, waved the honey bear around to distribute the scent, and hoped to God the information in the black grimoire was true. Nymphs couldn't resist honey. They considered it a food of offering for the gods, and Libby had been hanging around the mertwins so much she was probably missing it.

Her nostrils flared, and I said a silent thanks to the rogue streak in my late father that spurred his interest in the arcane and the illegal.

Libby scrambled to her feet, revealing burnt skin through her torn dress where my acid spell had seared her and limping from my shot with the staff. I hoped she hurt as badly as I did.

Where the hell was Rene? And Jake? Exactly who was supposed to be the fighter here? Last time I checked, it sure wasn't me.

Libby slowly walked toward me as I held the jar of honey out to my left. Her eyes fixed on the plastic bear like nectar-seeking missiles.

"What was the purpose of all this, Libby?" I asked. "Your sister made her choice."

She spoke in a monotone, focused on the honey. "I visited her after the borders opened up, and she was unhappy. The foolish wizard had made her unhappy and my people do not tolerate a slight from an inferior. So I lured him out and killed him using our sacrificial ritual." Such mutilation gave rituals a bad name.

She'd slowed to a stop as she talked, so I waved the honey around to get her started again. "What about Jeffrey Klein? For that matter, what about Melinda—why kill your sister?"

Libby's face hardened. "I tried to take Mellind back to our home but she wouldn't go. She wanted to tell the wizards everything, and I could not allow that. As for Jeffrey Klein, I do not know that person."

"The other man you killed."

She shrugged. "He was there."

Wrong place, wrong time. Just like Tish. I'd read the Stygian nymphs were nuts. Libby was a whole fruitcake.

Libby's halting steps brought her within a foot of the honey, and she reached for it with both hands.

A solid, wet mass barreled into me from behind, knocking the honey loose and sending it rolling across the deck.

Robert was back, the camouflage spell had worn off, and he was really starting to piss me off.

I elbowed him in the head and managed to scramble behind the winch again. I wished for Red Congress skills. If Gerry had been here, he could have pointed a finger and summoned enough physical magic to zap Robert and Libby off the deck and out of sight. I had only a small, sharp knife that I'd pulled out of my arm, but I ran at Robert with it and buried it as deep in his stomach as it would go.

All I managed to do was surprise him and knock him off his feet for a few seconds while the nymph tried to scoop honey off the deck. Happy dining, Libs.

I jerked a piece of chalk from my pocket and drew a circle on the deck around my hiding spot behind the winch, with me in the center. I touched my finger to it and willed in as much energy as I could pull together in three seconds. I let some blood drip on it for extra oomph, seeing as how I was bleeding from multiple locations and had plenty to spare.

I wasn't sure how long I could hold my circle, but enough to give me a couple of minutes to think. I collapsed to the deck with a thump, making sure not even a hair broke the plane of my protective cylinder.

Robert charged at me, and if I hadn't been getting dizzy from blood loss and scared for my life his expression when he bounced off my invisible shield would have been comical. He fell on his ass and shouted at Libby to stop licking the deck. She finished the honey with one final sweep of her tongue, and finally focused on him. I could see the awareness creeping through her honey stupor as she turned glittering eyes toward me.

"You fool, break through it," she shouted, then began coughing. Just a single cough at first, and then a strangled series of them. She held on to the rail, one hand on her burned stomach, and looked at the honey jar on the deck, then back at me as suspicion dawned. "What have you done, wizard?"

I smiled as Robert beat on the protective shield that surrounded me. Thank God she looked to be one of the mortal nymphs, or at least susceptible to poison. "Just a little belladonna cocktail, Libs. Did you like it?"

She charged at me, knife raised. It didn't pierce the shield, but every blow made it harder for me to maintain. I fed more blood into the circle and prayed for the belladonna to work faster. Robert would fold like a pleated fan if Libby went down.

The nymph panicked. When she couldn't break the plane of my circle, she screamed for Robert to do it. When he couldn't, she went after him.

The focus of her rage centered on him. I reached out to stop her, but some spark of self-preservation made me jerk my arm back before I broke my own circle. She grabbed the knife I'd left next to Robert and arced it straight across his neck, sending a spray of blood running down my shield, onto Libby herself, and across the deck.

Robert fell, wide-eyed, and his shock and dismay flowed out of him and washed over my empathic senses as the enthrallment broke and he felt the hard slap of reality. He really hadn't believed Libby would hurt him. I couldn't find it in me to feel sorry for Robert, at least not yet. But knowing what Rene would see when he got here broke my heart. I could feel his presence in my head, frantic and getting closer.

Libby dropped to her knees, panting. The belladonna was working. Her hands and fingers spasmed, and her pulsating pupils dilated. Which would all be well and good except my magic was failing and I wasn't sure how long I could stay conscious. I needed my freaking staff.

I let my circle drop, hoping Libby would be too far gone to notice, and scanned the deck again. It remained on the far side, near the wheelhouse. The damn thing had been following me around since I found it. Mahout had picked a fine time to abandon me.

Glancing to make sure Libby was still sitting near the wheelhouse, I pulled the chalk from my pocket again and drew a small summoning circle in front of me, quickly sending a ragged spike of magic into it and concentrating on the staff. I wasn't sure it would work with an elven object; summoning enchanted objects is dicey. Still, the staff had claimed me. It might work.

My movement caught Libby's attention, and she began crawling toward me.

The staff reached me first, sliding across the deck. Breaking the circle, I grabbed the staff, whipping it toward her and willing my few remaining shreds of energy into it.

Strong red ropes of flame flew out of the staff and wrapped around Libby's arm as she reached for me. She screamed, or tried. Her voice was failing and the sound was little more than a hoarse whisper. She didn't retreat. Even with her arm burning under the fiery threads, she grabbed the end of the staff and jerked it toward her. We each held an end of it, pulling in a weak tug-of-war that propelled us against the rail.

Even dying, Libby was physically stronger than me, and she knew it. She laughed and gave the staff one hard jerk that sent us both tumbling over the rails and into the cool, muddy water of the Mississippi.

I tried to hold on to the staff as I hit the water, but Libby was too strong and I'd spent too much of my energy. She dragged me with her as she dove toward the riverbed, until finally the currents from a passing barge swept us away from each other. The staff was gone, Libby was gone, and I was alone.

I struggled toward the surface, adrenaline propelling my arms and legs, panic causing me to want to gulp water in a bid for air. My lungs screamed for release, but there wasn't any. Light shimmered through the water's surface and I reached for it, but then I took a watery breath and everything began to fade.

I've heard a person's life flashes through his mind when

he dies, that he sees his loved one's faces and a fast reel of special memories, both good and bad. I've heard a shining light beckons you to let go and be at peace.

I only felt cold, and saw nothing.

34

Burning. Pain. Choking.

Somehow, I was alive. My lungs burned as they rasped air in and out, an elephant sat on my chest and crushed it with pain, and I choked and coughed out water. Then, to make sure I was as miserable as possible, someone slapped me hard enough to jar my teeth.

I have teeth. I'd barely had time to register the presence of molars before someone rolled me roughly to my side and pounded on my back. I coughed out more water, gasping to fill my lungs with oxygen minus the two parts hydrogen. *I'm breathing.*

I opened my eyes and saw the world tilt as I was rolled on my back again, and the image of Libby's face came back in full Technicolor. I tried to pull away but my arms and legs were heavy and I couldn't move.

"Be still, DJ. You hear me?"

I frowned, and focused on the face. Not Libby. Rene. He

knelt over me, water dripping off his skin. He nodded, and I couldn't tell if the water trailing down his face was from the river or his own tears. I opened my mouth but my voice was gone.

"You'll be okay, babe, just keep suckin' in air. Saw you go over the side with that bitch Libby, but you got swept in a ship's current." He smoothed the hair away from my face, and pried one of my eyes open. "Stay awake on me. You want I should call an ambulance? I found the staff and put it here by you."

I mouthed the word no, but couldn't get any words out.

"Where's Robert? Did he shift?"

Oh, God. Robert. I thought Rene knew from our mental exchanges that Robert was dead. Maybe he wasn't, though. Maybe there was a chance he was still alive. "Boat."

"He's on the *la Mer* and didn't go in after you? I'll kill the sonofabitch."

I managed to shake my head, or at least I think I did. "Hurt. He's . . . hurt."

Rene disappeared. I tried to turn my head to see where he'd gone but couldn't. I didn't have the strength.

I don't know how long I lay there, concentrating on pulling air in and pushing air out. I heard cicadas behind and around me, and a ship's horn passing on the river. The sun seemed low, and then it was dusk, and I couldn't stop shivering. I thought I heard someone crying.

Time passed, and I managed to roll to my side again. I opened my eyes to see a man standing among the trees at the edge of the clearing beyond the cinderblock building. Long blond hair, good cheekbones. What the hell was Eugenie's boyfriend doing here? I closed my eyes as a spasm brought on another coughing jag. When I opened them again, he was gone. Great. I was hallucinating a hippie landscaper.

I sensed someone on the pier behind me and tried to sit up. I couldn't do it, not yet. A sharp pain in my belly took my breath away as I rolled onto my back again. When I looked up, I tried to scream.

A huge wolf, red fur thick and bristly, stood over me. His eyes were a bright yellow-gold, and I knew them.

"Jake?" I coughed again, my voice no more than a whisper.

The wolf looked at me again and bared its teeth. This wasn't like Alex when he was Gandalf. I wasn't sure how much of Jake was reachable in there. Maybe it would help to touch him. I lifted my left hand as slowly as I could; it shook from the effort. The wolf growled and snapped at it, a sharp *click* as his jaws clamped shut. I snatched it back, which sent another sharp pain into my gut.

"Jake!" Alex's voice boomed from somewhere behind my head. Oh, God. Jake would kill him. "Jacob Warin. I know you can hear me. Move away from her. This doesn't have to go south, man. Back off." The sound of his chambering a bullet seemed impossibly loud. I knew the bullet was silver.

The wolf's upper lip curved away from the sharpest,

whitest teeth I'd ever seen, and he took a step toward my head, toward Alex's voice.

"Jake, it's okay," I whispered. "Run. Let Alex take me home."

The wolf turned his head and looked down at me. The high-pitched whine seemed absurdly small coming from such a large animal.

"I'm okay." I tried to breathe without coughing and startling him. "You go home now."

He lifted his head at the sound of approaching sirens and ran toward the woods.

Footsteps crunched behind my head and Alex leaned over me. "Sounds like an ambulance—I don't know who called them. You going to come out weird on blood tests or anything?"

Crap. "Yeah, call Zrakovi," I whispered. The Elders would have to send a Blue Congress team to fuzz up hospital tests and falsify medical records. "Help me sit up first."

He slipped an arm behind my back and lifted me to a seated position. Pain shot through me in sharp waves, and I cried out before I could stop myself. He lowered me again. Cool air hit my skin as he jerked up the bottom of my sweater. "Shit, you're bruised to hell and back. Wouldn't be surprised if you have broken ribs." He pressed on my abdomen and I jolted from the agony. "Did someone do CPR?"

I tried to think. Rand was in the woods . . . no, I'd imagined that. "Rene," I rasped. "On the boat. He needs to get out of here before—"

The ambulance siren died and vehicle doors slammed. "Just keep your mouth shut and let me do the talking," Alex said. "Your assault is now part of an ongoing FBI investigation."

35

I was debriefed in a freakin' ass-out hospital gown, pumped full of painkillers that made me want to giggle at everything. The Elders brought in extra chairs and put a silencing charm on the room so no one could hear from the outside. A ward on the door convinced doctors and nurses not to enter. We were sealed up like a prete-filled Fort Knox.

Alex had shown up first, in full enforcer regalia.

"Is that a gun in your shoulder holster or are you happy to see me?" I grinned at him.

He stopped in the door and crossed his arms. "You drugged out?"

"Yup, big-time."

"Good. You deserve it." He came in and pulled a chair next to my bed. "Sexy lingerie."

I looked down at the blue and white dotted cotton gown that tied at the neck. "Yeah, and it's air-conditioned in the back."

He laughed. "So, what's the verdict?"

I tried to remember the numbers. "Thirty stitches left leg, forty-five right arm, sixteen class-A contusions—that's bruises—and a hyperextended knee. I don't know how I got that. Oh, and two cracked ribs from merman CPR that hurt worse than the rest combined."

"Impressive." Alex nodded. "I guess you'll be earning that new salary."

"Yeah, you're right." I closed my eyes, frowned as his words sunk in, opened them again. "Huh?"

He smiled. "I wanted to get here first to tell you, but pretend you're surprised when Zrakovi breaks the news. You're the new sole sentinel of Southeast Louisiana."

I felt the drugged-out high drain from me. This was what I wanted, right? Why did I feel like crying all of a sudden? "You're being transferred?"

He took my hand and squeezed it. "Nope, I'll be your number-one security consultant—and neighbor, of course. The Elders are setting up a new prete security division and I'll be running it. Jake will work for me so I can ease him into field work. And we're talking about bringing someone from NOPD in—probably Ken Hachette."

His eyes were bright and he'd smiled more in the last few minutes than in the last year. "I can tell you're happy about it."

"Yeah and—"

The sound of raised voices preceded Elder Zrakovi and Adrian Hoffman into the room. They stopped speaking abruptly at the sight of Alex and me. "DJ, Alex." Zrakovi, dressed in a spiffy black suit and striped tie, greeted us, then looked around the room. The navy-suited Hoffman ignored us, and we returned the non-salutation. That man deserved to be horsewhipped, in my opinion, and I might have just enough drugs in me to share that opinion, should he look at me wrong.

"We'll be debriefing here, since you won't be going home until tomorrow and business calls us to Edinburgh," Zrakovi told me. "Ah, here are the others."

Jake had stuck his head in the door, and Zrakovi motioned him in. Behind him, looking like he'd rather be just about anywhere else, walked Rene Delachaise. I almost didn't recognize him in dark jeans, a white shirt, and a black sports coat.

You okay, babe?

I smiled at him and nodded.

We admittin' we still got some of the brain thing goin'?

"Hell no." I wasn't aware I'd spoken aloud until everyone except Rene turned to stare at me. I coughed a little, holding on to my ribcage. "Sorry. Painkillers."

During this time, Hoffman had been sealing the room and people had been finding seats. Alex shifted his chair closer to the bed. I felt like a half-dressed, waifish queen surrounded by her factotums.

Rene cleared his throat and shook his head. *Act right, you.*

"We'll keep this short," Zrakovi said. "Drusilla, tell us what led you to suspect the nymph Libetta? Mostly, I'm looking for clues we should have picked up on earlier so that we'll not make the same mistakes."

I tried to sort through the events of the last two weeks. "I didn't take her seriously, for one thing. Since she answered the phone at the River Nymphs' office—did you know they had brought in satyrs as male escorts, by the way?"

Zrakovi frowned.

"Painkillers," I said. "Well, since she answered the phone, I assumed she was one of them. I didn't follow up to see if she was legit till I'd already figured out it was her."

"How could you have figured it out faster?" Zrakovi asked, and I shifted a reptilian gaze to Adrian Hoffman. I had a bus I wanted to throw him under, but you couldn't tank a guy in public just for being an asshole. I'd be writing a report full of buses, though.

"I honestly don't know who knew what, and when. The thing that tied it together was linking Libby with Melinda Hebert, and unless the wizards change the marriage rules so non-wizard spouses submit to blood tests—there's no way to know. Doug Hebert lied about what his wife was, probably out of fear of reprisals from her family, and he charmed her necklace to help her hide it."

Zrakovi made some marks in his notebook, and I wondered if he had to write reports for the Congress of Elders like we had to write them for him. I bet he did. Poor guy.

"Mr. Warin"—he realized both Alex and Jake had

snapped to attention—"Mr. Alexander Warin. What happened when you met Libetta after intercepting Ms. Jaco's phone call?"

Alex shifted in his chair. "She tried to enthrall me, got piss . . . uh, got angry when it didn't work, came after me with a knife. I shifted, thinking I could chase her down better, but she hexed me. Not really sure what she did, but I couldn't shift back. DJ found me an hour later and reversed the hex."

"He turned pink," I said. Alex kicked the bed, jarring my ribs. "Painkillers," I gasped.

Zrakovi stared at me a moment, then went back to his notebook. "Ms. Jaco, why did you decide to go without backup to confront Libetta?"

"Uh." Now things were getting dicey. "Alex was still out from his hex reversal, Jake had gotten tied up at the Villeres', Rene was on his way. I didn't realize"—I mentally apologized to Rene—"that Robert Delachaise had been enthralled and would help her."

Zrakovi looked at Rene, who sat next to him. "My condolences on the loss of your brother, but I have to ask—did you know what the nymph had done, or that your brother was helping her?"

Rene's anger rose fast, like a tidal wave. "No. Robert was a victim here, just like the wizard. Wasn't like Denis Villere, who knew what was goin' on and kept his trap shut. If you gonna hold my brother accountable, you gotta hold them accountable too."

I frowned as Zrakovi put a conciliatory hand on Rene's arm. I hadn't known that Denis was involved. "You are right, Mr. Delachaise. We have issued an explanation and apology to your father, although I know that will be of little comfort, and we also have given the Villeres the choice of relocating back to their former homestead in the Atchafalaya Basin or going into the Beyond. Their business dealings have been curtailed, and they will no longer be allowed in Plaquemines or St. Bernard parishes, near you or any of your family."

I felt Rene's anger morph into deep pain, and I knew he was trying not to cry in front of a roomful of wizards.

"Does Rene have to stay for the rest of this?" I asked. "He's been through enough, and he's been a big help in repairing the river breaches."

"I told you, Willem," Hoffman said. "I suspect she has done elven magic with a non-wizard. It can't be tolerated."

Zrakovi gave Hoffman a look that would curdle cream. I laughed, at least until Alex kicked the side of the bed again.

"Yes, Mr. Delachaise. You can go. We all appreciate the work you've done with Ms. Jaco to restore the river water. I heard this morning that two elderly humans had died in Plaquemines, but that number would have been much higher if you hadn't been willing to assist."

I smiled at Rene as he eased around Adrian Hoffman and headed for the door.

We still on for another power-transfer, babe? Still got that last rift to repair.

Give me a week to get my strength back—use the temporary charms till then, I told him. We were having to really concentrate to communicate now, so I felt pretty sure it would eventually wear off.

Gotcha. Outta here.

I relaxed back on my pillow as the door closed behind him.

Jake's report was short. He'd gone to talk to Denis Villere, and had been told the senior mer was in the shed. When Jake went to look for him, *Grandmère* had locked him in. He'd shifted to loup-garou, broken his way out, and ran home.

He didn't mention stopping in Pointe a la Hache, and neither did Alex. Even in my drugged state, neither did I.

Zrakovi closed his notebook with a snap. "That should about do it. I have to file a report about Libetta's death—she passed away shortly after re-entering the Styx. I assume, Mr. Warin, that the missing-persons cases will be suitably wrapped up?"

"Yes, sir," Alex said. "They'll both be declared cold cases and I heard this morning that Melinda Hebert's body mysteriously disappeared from the CDC."

"Imagine that," Zrakovi said drily. He stood and everyone else stood with him, as if on cue. Except me. I giggled again, wondering what they'd think of my gown if I stood with them.

"I'm glad you're feeling better," Zrakovi told me with a grim smile. "We'll talk soon about the plans we're making for the future."

"Oh, it's okay. Alex told me," I said, smiling, then gasped as Alex kicked the bed on his way out.

36

Does this dress look stupid with my leg bandaged?" I asked Eugenie, frowning at myself in the full-length mirror that hung inside my bedroom door. Sebastian sat beside me, probably trying to figure out the worst possible time for him to jump up and latch his teeth and claws onto my short billowy skirt.

The dress in question was red and white checked, had a fitted waist, short capped sleeves, and the ridiculous poufy skirt. Eugenie had rented it from a costume shop in Metairie. I was still barefoot, not because it was warm enough to go without shoes but because I couldn't find any that didn't look ridiculous with this outfit. It also hurt to bend over far enough to reach my feet.

"Honey, that dress looks stupid no matter what you do to it, but live with it. You're the one that wanted to dress up like Little Red Riding Hood. I was pushing for Britney—you know, the whole sexy schoolgirl thing."

"Yeah, well, you're one to talk, hippie chick."

We were getting ready for Alex's housewarming/ Halloween party—costumes required. I'd been home from the hospital two days after a lot of fabricated bloodwork, memory erasures, and malfunctioning monitors.

"This must have been a bad case," Eugenie said, adjusting her tie-dyed bandana. "What I don't understand is why you thought you saw Quince—why in the world would he be there?"

"I told you I was hallucinating." Although there was still something fishy about that guy, and thanks to the fast-fading mind-meld with Rene, I knew all about fishy.

"Well, keep your hands off my man, DJ. He's taken."

"Yeah, he's something, that's for sure," I muttered, looking for the red hooded cape that fit over my gingham dress.

Going to the party as Red Riding Hood and the Big Bad Wolf had been Jake's idea, and nothing I said would talk him out of it. Rand and Eugenie were going as Deadheads. Eugenie had been forcing me to listen to Grateful Dead music all week.

The doorbell sent Sebastian trotting down the stairs with his rubber rat dangling from his mouth, followed by Eugenie. I thumped along much more slowly with my stiff leg and sore ribcage.

A situation brewed by the time I got to the front parlor. Eugenie was having the pants charmed off her, possibly quite literally, by Jean Lafitte. He was dressed in his usual garb.

Like a pirate, in other words. Indigo shirt half-buttoned, tight black pants, boots, curved knife gleaming from its spot under a wide belt. His dark blue eyes had fairly twinkled Eugenie into a swoon.

I hated to break the mood, but I couldn't walk into the room quietly. Just call me Peg-leg. Maybe that could be my pirate wench name.

"Honey, you didn't tell me you had a new man friend." Eugenie turned on me, practically quivering with excitement. Maybe she wasn't as serious about weird Quince/Rand as I feared. Not that Jean would be an improvement.

He looked at me over her head with a smug smile. "*Oui, Jolie*, I cannot believe you have not shared our relationship with your friend Eugenie. Such a pretty name for such a pretty friend."

Oh brother. He was spreading on the French charm like butter on a croissant, and Eugenie had lined up for second helpings.

"Yes, I'm sure he's introduced himself." What name he gave her was anybody's guess.

Eugenie tittered. "He insists he's Jean Lafitte, so I told him he could get away with that today since we're having the costume party."

Egads. Jean wasn't invited to the party. "Well, then, Jean Lafitte he is," I said. As soon as it was vaguely polite, I shuffled Eugenie out the back door.

Before she'd gotten to the driveway, Jean had reached me in two long strides, frowning, no doubt ready to have his turn yelling at me for putting myself in danger. These guys were just going to have to get a life. I was a lone sentinel now.

He gripped my upper arms in his big hands.

"Ow!" I yelped, slapping him away. "Stitches. Hurts."

He frowned and tugged the neck of my ugly red gingham dress aside to bare my right shoulder and upper arm, and his expression softened. "My apologies, *Jolie*. Where are you injured?"

I wasn't expecting Jake for another half hour and Alex was busy with party preparations (with the able and willing assistance of the lovely Leyla, not that I was paying attention). So I'd sop up some sympathy where I could get it. I ran through my list of injuries, head to toe. I'm sure Jean had seen much worse. He'd probably inflicted much worse.

After that, he wanted a blow-by-blow of the events, so we sat in a couple of armchairs in the front parlor. I told him about Rene fishing me out of the river and giving me CPR, although admittedly most of that story came from Rene because I didn't remember much. Then I finished with a colorful recounting of my experience with Jake's wolf and Alex's smooth mouthful of lies with the EMTs on the ride to the hospital.

I could feel Jean's anger rising the more I talked about the fight, and fingered my mojo bag. I'd left off my grounding ritual since I'd been hurt, letting my psychic reserves regenerate. I didn't want his anger, though. Not this soon.

He let loose a torrent of French. I couldn't understand

the words, but finally decided it had something to do with Denis Villere.

"This entire *désastre* could have been avoided but for his treachery." Jean stormed back and forth across the parlor. "I will travel to Atchafalaya. It is time I visited those waters again. He has damaged my friend Rene and my . . ." He looked at me, and I waited for him to finish the sentence. Exactly what was I to Jean? "And he has damaged you," he finished.

Uh-huh. He didn't know, either.

I levered myself out of my chair with a complete lack of grace. "Jean, it's not your place to get vengeance for me or for Rene. Let the Elders handle it. The Villeres are on house arrest in Iberia Parish."

"Bah." He sat in one of the armchairs, reached out, and pulled me to sit beside him on the low arm, facing him. He reached across my lap and slid his right arm around my waist to hold me in place. It put us on even eye-level.

"Are you certain, *Jolie*? Such a man in my day would not be allowed to live."

Damn. He was going to kill Denis Villere, and then T-Jacques and his murderous *Grandmère* would be back, blaming the whole thing on the Delachaises, and we'd start all over again.

Still, it was kind of nice having a man who was willing to risk temporary death just to defend your honor. He couldn't be killed, but he could suffer. I reached out and ran my fingers along his jawline. "I don't want you to hurt him.

Let the wizards handle it. But thanks for being willing to avenge me."

"Very well, *Jolie*. If that is what you wish."

I smiled at this unexpected turn into a kinder, gentler Jean Lafitte.

"So you will stay away from the Villeres?"

"Ah, sadly, no. I still must go to Atchafalaya. Denis will interfere with my business interests there, and of course I must not allow that to happen. However, if it pleases you, I shall allow him to live. And then you will owe me another debt." His mouth curved at the edges.

So much for the kinder, gentler Jean. "Fine, don't kill him and I'll owe you."

"*Très bien.*" Jean cleared his throat. "I do not mean to be rude, *Jolie*, but I do not like that dress. I hope you will not wear it on our next dinner date."

Had I agreed to a dinner date? I guess it was the price of Denis Villere's life.

I scowled at him. "It's a costume party. This is a costume." I didn't want to explain who Little Red Riding Hood was.

He chuckled. "So I am not invited to your party, even as Jean Lafitte the famous privateer?"

"It's not my party. It's Alex's party."

"Bah, *Monsieur Chien*. I do not wish to attend his affair."

I didn't volunteer the information that Alex had bought the house next door, though he'd probably find out soon enough. Jean had struck a deal with the Elders to provide navigation services within the Beyond. He was going to be around, at least when he wasn't terrorizing the mers of the Atchafalaya Basin.

His cab arrived to take him back to the Quarter just as Jake pulled his truck in the driveway. I watched out the back window as the two met, and was surprised to see them shake hands. They talked for a long minute and seemed almost cordial. That bore some thinking about.

I opened the door as the cab pulled away, and Jake headed toward me in his rust-brown sweater and black pants. He grinned, dimples deep enough to drown in, and pulled a brown furry thing from behind his back.

"What the—"

He pulled the big wolf head over his own, and I could barely see his amber eyes shining through the wolf's open mouth.

I laughed, which made my ribs send stabbing pains through my chest. "Grandmother, what big teeth you have."

"Well, I would say better to eat you with," said a soft Southern drawl echoing out of the wolf's neck. "But that is one ugly dress, sunshine."

I clomped into the guest room to get Alex's housewarming gift—a large, framed painting of Gandalf raising his staff above the Balrog at the Bridge of Khazad-dûm. We walked next door, climbed the front steps, and entered Chez Alex.

I liked it. He'd had the walls painted in varying shades of brown, from pale café au lait to a rich milk chocolate, which helped break up the long narrow spaces. I spotted the perfect place for Gandalf to hang and propped the frame against the wall.

Jake stopped to talk to Leyla and I searched the faces around me. Ken was there with a date, looking relaxed and even smiling.

Eugenie and Rand cuddled in a corner, and I smiled and waved at them. The light glinted on his earring, and my smile faded as I realized what it was. A peridot, not unlike the one Melinda Hebert wore around her neck to hide her species. I raised my eyes to meet the gaze of Quince Randolph, who was looking over the head of his besotted date and watching me. Holy shit. What *was* he?

"Why are you in an eyelock with Eugenie's boyfriend?" Alex slipped up on me from behind, and I wrenched my gaze away from Rand. That man was next on my agenda, though. He was up to something.

I turned to Alex. "I love your house."

"Good. I hope you'll spend some time here." He'd dressed as a ninja, or so he said. His costume looked like normal enforcer-wear to me. He leaned against the wall, sipping a beer, watching me with a look I couldn't interpret. I'd give half of Jean Lafitte's treasure to know what he was thinking.

"Where's Leyla?" I asked.

"Don't know. Did Zrakovi officially tell you about the new working arrangement?"

I nodded. "He came by the first day I got home from the hospital."

He leaned over and whispered, "You remember we agreed we couldn't play ball because we were on the same team?"

I swallowed hard, the air suddenly close and warm as I

pondered the sports metaphors he trotted out when he couldn't bring himself to actually discuss relationship stuff. Did play ball mean what I think it did? "I remember."

His breath was hot against my ear. "We aren't on the same team anymore." He kissed my cheek and walked toward the kitchen.

Holy crap. He'd just changed the rules.

ACKNOWLEDGMENTS

A big Jean Lafitte *merci beaucoup* to uber-editor Stacy Hill and all the other talented folks at Tor Books; super-agent Marlene Stringer; alpha reader Dianne, the only one who gets to read craptastic first drafts; Debbie and Susan, who continue to talk me off ledges; my friends in the Auburn Writers' Circle, who graciously heard this book more than once; New Orleans author Dawn Chartier, who not only provided moral support but photos from Venice and Pilottown; and Lora, Jami, Kat, and Amber, for love and crits.

C